THE CASEBOOK OF

Victor Frankenstein

ALSO BY PETER ACKROYD

FICTION

The Great Fire of London

The Last Testament of Oscar Wilde

Hawksmoor

Chatterton

First Light

English Music

The House of Doctor Dee

Dan Leno and the Limehouse Golem

Milton in America

The Plato Papers

The Clerkenwell Tales

The Lambs of London

The Fall of Troy

NONFICTION

Dressing Up: Transvestism and Drag: The History of an Obsession

London: The Biography

Albion: The Origins of the English Imagination

Thames: The Biography

THE CASEBOOK OF

𝕼𝖎𝖈𝖙𝖔𝖗 𝕱𝖗𝖆𝖓𝖐𝖊𝖓𝖘𝖙𝖊𝖎𝖓

A NOVEL

PETER ACKROYD

NAN A. TALESE | DOUBLEDAY

NEW YORK LONDON TORONTO SYDNEY AUCKLAND

Copyright © 2008 by Peter Ackroyd

All rights reserved. Published in the United States by Nan A. Talese/Doubleday, a division of Random House, Inc., New York. www.nanatalese.com

Originally published in Great Britain by Chatto & Windus, The Random House Group Limited, London, in 2008.

DOUBLEDAY is a registered trademark of Random House, Inc. Nan A. Talese and the colophon are trademarks of Random House, Inc.

Frontispiece image © Hulton-Deutsch Collection/CORBIS

LIBRARY OF CONGRESS CATALOGING-IN-PUBLICATION DATA
Ackroyd, Peter, 1949-
The casebook of Victor Frankenstein / Peter Ackroyd. — 1st U.S. ed.
p. cm.
1. Frankenstein (Fictitious character)—Fiction. 2. Shelley, Percy Bysshe, 1792-1822—Fiction. 3. Shelley, Mary Wollstonecraft, 1797-1851—Fiction. 4. Byron, George Gordon Byron, Baron, 1788-1824—Fiction. 5. Polidori, John William, 1795-1821—Fiction. 6. Scientists—Fiction. 7. Monsters—Fiction. 8. England—Social life and customs—19th century—Fiction. 9. Psychological fiction. I. Title.
PR6051.C64C37 2009
823'.914—dc22
2008055196

ISBN 978-0-385-53084-2

PRINTED IN THE UNITED STATES OF AMERICA

1 3 5 7 9 10 8 6 4 2

FIRST U.S. EDITION

THE CASEBOOK OF

Victor Frankenstein

One

I WAS BORN IN THE ALPINE REGION of Switzerland, my father owning much territory between Geneva and the village of Chamonix where my family resided. My earliest memories are of those glistening peaks, and I believe that my spirit of daring and ambition was bred directly from the vision of altitudes. I felt the power and grandeur of nature there. The ravines and the precipices, the smoking waterfalls and the raging torrents, had always the effect of sanctifying my life until one white and shining morning I felt compelled to cry out to the Maker of the Universe, "God of the mountains and the glaciers, preserve me! I see, and feel, the solitude of your spirit among the ice and snow!" As if in response to my voice I heard the cracking of the ice and thunder of an avalanche, on a distant peak, louder than the bells of the cathedral St.-Pierre in the narrow streets of old Geneva.

I exulted in storms. Nothing entranced me more than the roaring of the wind among the upright masses of rock, the crags and caverns of my native region; when the wind swept away the smoking mists, the woods of pine and oak were filled with its music. The clouds there seemed to haunt the upper air, wishing to touch the source of such beauty. In these moments my individual nature ebbed away. I felt as if I were dissolved into the surrounding universe, or as if that universe were absorbed into my being. Like the infant in the womb I was conscious of no distinction. It is the state that the poets wish to achieve, when all the manifestations of the world become "blossoms upon one tree." Yet I had been blessed by the poetry of nature itself.

So in my earliest years my soul overflowed with ardent affections, and my wild and enthusiastic imagination was chastened only by my inclination towards study and mental industry. How I loved to learn! I imbibed knowledge as a sapling takes in water, never ceasing to grow upwards. The worst of my faults even then was ambition. I wished to know everything about the world and the great universe. Why was I born if not to learn? I dreamed of distant stars. In my imagination (and even then I believe that I understood the true meaning of that word) I saw beneath the crust the glowing core which caused the mountains all around me. I, Victor Frankenstein, would solve its mysteries! I would examine the beetle and the butterfly in my earnest wish to learn the secrets of nature. Desire and delight—as those secrets were unfolded to me—are among the earliest sensations I can remember. My father purchased for me a microscope through which I observed with indescribable interest the hidden existence of the world. Who does not wish to study the unseen and the unknown? The force instilled within the most minute organisms, making them move and meet, filled me with wonder.

⇒ ⇐

AFTER MY SCHOOLING IN GENEVA, on the Calvinist pattern of industrious and patient study, my father sent me to the renowned university of Ingolstadt where I began my first enquiries into natural philosophy. Even then, I believe, I knew that I would carve my passage to greatness. Yet I had always wished to visit England, where the latest experiments in natural science were being performed by galvanists and biologists. It was a place of practical learning. My father did not believe that country to be favourable to the education of my morals, however, but after many earnest entreaties and urgent letters from Ingolstadt he finally relented. He gave me permission to enter the university of Oxford, in my eighteenth year, after many warnings on the laxity of English youth. I promised him that neither my virtue nor my character would be tainted in any respect. I spoke too soon.

It was at Oxford that I first met Bysshe. We both arrived at our college on the same day; confusing to a mere foreigner, it is called University College. My rooms were in the south-west corner of the courtyard known as the quad, and those of Bysshe were on the next staircase. I had seen him from my window and had been much struck by his long auburn locks, at a time when the style of hair was short. I am referring now to the very early years of this century. He had a rapid manner of walking, with long strides, but this was combined with a curious hesitancy as if he were not entirely sure of the destination he was pursuing with such ardour; he would sway slightly, guided by the wind. I saw him each morning in chapel, but we did not speak until we sat together during one of the lamentable dinners in hall. My impression of English cooking was much like my father's view of English morals.

Bysshe was beside me, and I heard him speak approvingly to a companion about a Gothic tale written some years previously, *The Fatal Ring* by Isaac Crookenden.

"Oh, no," I said. "You must read the novels of Eisner for pure sensation."

Of course he noticed my accent at once. "You admire the German tales of terror?"

"I do. But I am not a German. I am by birth a Genevese."

"The nurse of liberty! Of Rousseau and Voltaire! Why, sir, have you come here to the home of tyranny and oppression?" I had not heard such sentiments before, having been accustomed to think of England as the source of political freedoms, and Bysshe laughed at my expression of surprise. "You have not lived among us for long, I take it?"

"I arrived last week. But I believed that the liberties of the people—"

He put his hands up to his ears. "I did not hear that. Take care. You will be accused of sedition. Of blasphemy. How much do you think that fine body of yours is worth?"

"I beg your pardon?"

"According to government, it is worth nothing. It can be removed with no apology and no explanation. We have repealed habeas corpus, you see." I was quite at a loss to understand him, but then immediately he changed the subject of conversation. "Have you read *The Buried Monk* by Canaris? Now there is a tale of diablerie!" I had read the book a month previously and, to my astonishment, Bysshe began to quote extempore the entire first paragraph beginning, "*There was never a peaceful hour in the monastery that, to the simple inhabitants of the region, was known as the place of echoes.*" He would have continued but his companion at dinner, whom I afterwards ascertained to be Thomas Hogg, begged him to stop.

"Why do you call it government?" Hogg asked him.

"Why ever not?"

"Should it not be 'the government'?"

"No. Government is more powerful and more insidious. Government is some abstract and overwhelming force. Government is absolute. Do you not agree, minister from Geneva?"

Bysshe looked at me, keenly and curiously, and I replied as best I could. "If I were a minister, I would tell you that God differs from the god."

He laughed out loud. "Bravo! We will be friends. Permit me to introduce you to Shelley." He placed his hands upon his chest, and bowed. "And Hogg."

"My name is Victor Frankenstein."

"A fine name. Victor is Roman, is it not? *Victor ludorum* and such like."

"It is an old name in my family."

"Frankenstein is more perplexing. You are not an Israelite, since you attend chapel." I had not expected him to notice me there. "A *stein* is a jar for holding beer, I believe. Perhaps your ancestors were connected with the Frankish court in the honourable occupation of potters. You come from a family of makers, my dear Frankenstein. Your name is worthy of acclaim." By this time we had got up from the long table, and were walking back through the quad. "I have wine," Bysshe said. "Come and join us."

As soon as I entered his rooms, I knew that I was in the abode of an ardent spirit: on the floor, on the carpet, on the desk, on every available surface, lay a scattered profusion of objects of every description. There were papers, books, prints, and boxes innumerable with stockings, boots, shirts and other linen crammed among them. I observed that the carpet had already been stained and scorched in several places, which instinctively I ascribed to scientific experiment. He noticed my glance, and laughed. He had an immoderate laugh. "Sal ammoniac," he said. "Come and see my laboratory."

I followed him into the next room, where a narrow bed was lodged in a corner. He had set up a bench, upon which he had placed an electrical machine that I took to be a voltaic battery. Beside it was a solar microscope as well as several large glass jars and phials. "You are an experimenter," I said.

"Of course. And so should be every inquirer after knowledge. We do not need to read Aristotle. We need to look into the world."

"I also have a solar microscope."

"Do you? Did you hear that, Hogg?"

"I have been studying the corpuscles of life."

"And where have you found them?"

"In the water of the glaciers. In my own blood. The world is full of energy."

"Bravo!" He had become very eager, and he took my shoulders in a tight grasp. "There is another place where you will find life. In the storm!" I thought that he was about to embrace me, but he released me from his grip. I recognised later that he was curiously, almost unnaturally, sensitive to the very thoughts that passed through my mind. With some people there is no need whatsoever for words. Seeing a slight tremor in my eyes, he would always look away.

"Have you noticed the voltaic battery?" he asked me now. "It recreates the lightning flash. I have been like Isaac Newton. Staring into the light."

Bysshe was openly contemptuous of the regimen of the

university, and attended no lectures. I was unsure, in fact, what studies he was meant to be pursuing. To him they did not matter in the slightest. There was one task that we were assigned by rote, that of translating each week an essay from the *Spectator* into Latin. This he accomplished with the greatest ease, and indeed he could write Latin with as much facility and fluency as he wrote English. He told me that the secret was to imagine himself a Roman orator in the first years of the Republic. This inspired him with such fervour that the words came naturally to him in their proper order. I did not doubt it. His imagination was like the voltaic battery from which lightning issued forth.

We would take long walks in the country outside Oxford, often following the Thames upward past Binsey and Godstow, or downstream to Iffley and its curious twelfth-century church. Bysshe loved the river with a passion I have seldom seen equalled, and would extol its merits over the languid Nile and the turbid Rhine. I had thought him all fire, but there were other elements in his constitution—fluent, pliant, fertile, like the water around us. On these expeditions he would often declaim to me the poetry of Coleridge on the powers of the imagination. "The poet dreams of that which the scientist deems to be impossible," he told me. "Once it is envisaged, then it is made true." He knelt down to examine a small flower, the name of which I did not know. "It is magnificent to aspire beyond the common reach of man."

"In what endeavour?"

"Who knows? Who can tell? The great poets of the past were philosophers or alchemists. Or magicians. They cast off the vesture of the body, and in their pursuits, became pure spirit.

Do you know of Paracelsus and Albertus Magnus?" I noted them as worthy of study. "We must make a pilgrimage, you and I, to Folly Bridge and worship at the shrine of Roger Bacon. There is a house there said to be his laboratory. Do you know the legend? If a man wiser than Friar Bacon ever walks beside it, then it will collapse and fall. In this city of dunces, it has already stood for six hundred years. Shall we test it? We will walk over the bridge in turn, and see which one of us performs the miracle."

"It was Bacon who created the talking head, was it not?"

"Yes. The head that spoke and said, 'Time is.' Except that it spoke in Latin. It had studied the classical authors. That may account for the spirit of animation."

"But how did the lips move?"

I would put questions to Bysshe, simply to delight in the extravagance of his answers. I am quite convinced that he invented as he talked, but that did not dispel the enchantment. Indeed it contributed to it. I followed his meaning as if it were a firefly glowing in the darkness.

He would often talk to himself, in a low muttered voice. It seemed to be some form of communication with his inward being, but there were some of course who questioned his sanity. "Mad Shelley" was the epithet often used against him. I never saw any sign of madness, unless it be insanity to possess a highly charged and sensitive spirit alert to every delicate change in the atmosphere around him. His eyes would often fill with tears, when his feelings were touched by some generous gesture or by the story of another's misfortune. In that respect, at least, he did not have a common sensibility. He had the temperament of a Rousseau or of a Werther.

IN THOSE DAYS I was more than ever intent upon exploring the secrets of nature, and I gave myself up to the study of the source where life began. Bysshe and I would argue into the night over the respective merits of the Italians Galvani and Volta. He favoured the animal electricity of Signor Galvani, while I was deeply excited by the success of the voltaic plates.

"Do you not see," I told him one winter evening, "that the electrical battery is a new engine of immense promise?"

"My dear Victor, Galvani has proved that there is electricity in the world around us. Nature is electricity itself. By the simple expedient of a metallic thread, he has brought life back into a frog. Why could he not achieve the same with the human frame?"

"I have not thought of it." I went over to the window, and looked out at the snow falling onto the quad.

Bysshe was lying on the sofa, and I heard him murmuring to himself some lines of poetry:

"Happy is he who lives to understand
Not human nature only, but explores
All natures, to the end that he may find
The law that governs each."

"Do you know who wrote that, Victor?"

"I have no idea."

"Wordsworth."

"He is one of your new poets."

"He is *the* poet. Consider the lightning flash," he continued.

"Of all the powers in nature, it is the most tremendous. In its light you can see the fiery breath of the universe!"

"And how can you harness the lightning?"

"If you were to send into the atmosphere some electrical kite, it would draw down from the sky an immense volume of electricity. Think of it. The whole ammunition of a mighty thunderstorm directed at a certain point. Can you imagine the stupendous results?"

"We have come a long way from the humble frog."

"Don't you see? The smallest thing has life and energy."

"Why not call it spiritual force?"

"What is the difference between body and spirit? In the lightning flash they are the same. Incandescent!"

I must admit that his words had a tremendous effect upon me. But Bysshe began to speculate upon balloon trips over the continent of Africa. His mind could not remain on one course for very long. When I returned to my rooms, however, I brooded over our conversation. What if it were possible to endow the human form with life by means of the immortal spark? Would it be deemed unholy? This claim I dismissed. No. All progress in electrical science will be condemned as irreligious by those who have no faith in human progress. If I could harness the ethereal flame to practical and benign use, I would consider myself to be a benefactor of the human race. More than that. I would be considered a hero. To bring life to dead or dormant matter—to invest mere clay with the fire of life—this would be an admirable and wonderful triumph!

Thus I rushed on to my destruction.

⇒ Two ⇐

SO I PURSUED MY STUDIES with great and, I believe, unexampled fervour; no Zealot or Essene could have more eagerly hunted after truth. Yet my evening discussions with Bysshe continued, and were no less animated. He longed passionately for the dissolution of Christianity and had sworn revenge on the one he called "the pale Galilean," but his fury was reserved for the omniscient God of the prophets. I had been educated in the Reformed Church of Geneva, but the religion of my father and my family had left little impression on my mind. I had affirmed the god of Nature itself, but my early faith in some maker of the universe was now shaken by Bysshe's denial of an eternal and omnipotent being. This deity was venerated as the creator of life, but what if others of less exalted nature were able to perform that miracle? What then?

Bysshe argued from the precepts of reason that there was no God. He affirmed that truth was the only means to promote the best interests of mankind. Once he had discovered a truth, then it was incumbent upon him to declare it as forcefully as possible. He also stated that, since belief is a passion of the mind, no degree of criminality can be attached to disbelief. In this, as he realised soon enough, he ignored the general prejudices of English society. He wrote a short essay, entitled "On the Necessity of Atheism," which was then printed and put on sale at the bookseller across the high street from the college. It had been on the shelves for no more than twenty minutes when one of the fellows of the college, Mr. Gibson, read it and berated the owner of the shop for putting such incendiary literature on display. The copies were immediately withdrawn and, I believe, burned in a stove at the rear of the premises.

The authorship of the anonymous pamphlet was soon detected, on the information of the bookseller himself, and Bysshe was summoned to a meeting of the Master and fellows. A copy of "On the Necessity of Atheism" lay before them, as he told me later. But he refused to answer their questions on the grounds that the pamphlet had been published anonymously. It would be an act of tyranny and injustice, he said, to press him when they had no legal cause. His was a nature that turned into fire at any hint of oppression. Of course he was judged to be guilty. He hammered upon my door immediately after leaving this gathering.

"I am sent down," he said as soon as he entered my rooms. "Not merely rusticated, Victor. Expelled! Can you believe it?"

"Expelled? From what date?"

"From now. This moment. I am no longer a member of the university." He sat down, trembling. "I have no notion what my father will say." He always spoke of his father in terms of the greatest disquiet.

"Where will you go, Bysshe?"

"I cannot go home. That would be too hard to bear." He looked up at me. "And I would not wish to be deprived of your company for very long, Victor."

"There is only one place for you."

"I know it. London." He jumped up from the chair, and

walked over to the window. "I have been in correspondence with Leigh Hunt for some weeks. He knows all the revolutionaries in the city. I will live in their society." Already he seemed to be recovering his spirit. "I will grow towards the sun of liberty! I will find lodgings. And you must accompany me, Victor. Will you come?"

⇒ ⇐

I WAITED UNTIL THE END OF TERM before following Bysshe to London. He had rented lodgings in Poland Street, in the district of Soho, and I had found rooms close by in Berners Street. I had been in London once before, on my arrival from my homeland, but of course I was still amazed by the immensity of its life. No Alpine storm, no torrent among the glaciers, no avalanche among the peaks, can give the least idea of the roar of the city. I had never seen so many people, and I wandered through the streets in a constant state of excitation. What power human lives have in the aggregate! To me the city resembled some vast electrical machine, galvanising rich and poor alike, sending its current down every alley and lane and thoroughfare in the course of its pulsating life. London seemed ungovernable, obeying laws mysterious to itself, like some dim phantasm stalking through the world.

Bysshe meanwhile had sought out and found the men of liberty. Together we attended a meeting of the Popular Reform League above a perfume shop in Store Street, where to our delight we heard epithets hurled against the members of the administration that would have marked them and burned them like firebrands! I was intoxicated by the language of liberty, convinced as I was that the old order of oppression and corruption must surely pass away. It was time to breach the foundations of tyranny, and to abrogate the laws by which humanity had been enslaved. There was a new world waiting to be brought to life and light!

We were cordially welcomed by the members of the League, having satisfied themselves very quickly that we were not government spies but friends of freedom or *Citizens* as they called us. When I confessed that I came from Geneva there was an "hoorah" for "the home of liberty." Bread and beer were ordered, and all became very merry. This was followed by a general debate in which the demands for annual parliaments and universal suffrage were loudly proclaimed. One young man by the name of Pearce rose to his feet and proclaimed that, "Truth and Liberty, in an age so enlightened as the present, must be invincible and omnipotent." I could not help but interpret his words in the light of my own researches where truth, if pursued in a scientific manner, might also prove invincible. There was no possible limit to the power of the human mind if it were properly and justly harnessed.

Pearce's words were greeted with acclamation, in which Bysshe and I joined, and I could not help but compare these enthusiastic *Citizens* with the supine youth of the university. I was about to whisper this to Bysshe when, his eyes shining, he rose to his feet and declared to the gathering that "we have no occasion for kings." This was loudly huzzahed, and several men got up and shook hands with him. "What have we to fear?" he asked them. "If we stay fast to our principles of truth and freedom, then all will be well. Follow the lightning flash!" The members of the League, roused by his rhetoric, then began a song of great fervour:

"Come you sons of true liberty, let us agree
To form an alliance firm honest and free
Let's join hand in hand as reason upholds
Her bright torch of friendship. Let us be bold!"

I do not know if Bysshe admired the poetry, but he thoroughly approved of the sentiments.

At the end of the meeting one of the *Citizens* came up to Bysshe and introduced himself. "How do you do, sir? I hope your Oxford residency agreed with you?"

Bysshe was taken aback. "How do you know of that?"

"I am a particular friend of Mr. Hunt. He has been in correspondence with you, has he not?"

"I have met him in London."

"Have you? As soon as I saw you and your companion—" he bowed to me, "I knew you to be the men expelled from the university."

"This is Mr Frankenstein. He is not expelled. But he shares my principles."

"My name is Westbrook. I am a shoemaker." He looked around the hall for a moment. "We rarely give our names here, for fear of spies. But you are exceptional, Mr. Shelley. You are the son of a baronet, are you not?"

"I am. But I will use every particle of my birthright in the service of the cause."

"Well said, sir. Now we must make our way into the street. Before the magistrates interrupt us. We have learned to avoid what we call the war whoop of Church and King."

We walked down into Store Street, and stood together on the corner of Tottenham Court Road. Westbrook seemed to me to bear a noble mind. His physiognomy was firm and, with a prominent forehead, inclined to ideality; he was by no means shabbily dressed, despite his trade, and he wore his hair short without powder in the "liberty" fashion. "May I take you," he asked us, "to a place where my sister is employed? It is not far from here. Distress is never far in this city. And there you will see the enemy."

He led us through the neighbourhood of St. Giles, as he called it, which was only a few streets from where we stood. It seemed to me the most wretched and depraved district imaginable on this earth. No low quarter of Geneva, however ruinous, had the least resemblance to this foul and degrading patch of London. The streets were no more than paths of mud, or filth, where the effluent ran in rivulets from the ragged courtyards and alleys. The stench was indescribable. "Are we safe here?" I whispered to Westbrook.

"I am known. But if not—" He took from the interior pocket of his jacket a large knife with a bone handle and long blade. "This is what the French call *couteau secret*," he said. "You cannot open it without being acquainted with the secret spring."

"Have you ever used it?"

"Not yet. I keep it for the bloodhounds after me and my companions."

There was a shriek from an upstairs window, patched with rags, followed by the sound of confused blows and oaths being exchanged. We hurried on. I had not known that such monstrousness, such abject horror, could exist in any Christian country. How had this fetid body grown in the largest city on earth, without anyone so much as noticing its existence? We were only a few moments from the glare of the Oxford Road, as I judged it, but these alleys were like some black shadow forever following its steps. We picked our way around the prone body of a woman, in the last stages of intoxication; her legs were covered with her own filth. If life could become so fearful a thing, then how could it be God's handiwork? I fully believe that this entrance into the underworld of London took from me the last vestiges of Christian faith. Man was not a creature of God's making. I thought that then, and I know it now.

➤ ⬅

WE CAME INTO AN OPEN THOROUGHFARE, gasping for cleaner air.

"Just a little further, gentlemen," Westbrook said.

Bysshe was scarcely able to stand upright, and was bent double in the street. "Are you unwell?" I asked him.

"Not me," he replied. "The world. The world is sick. I am the least part of it." Then he retched in a corner.

We came into a narrow street, of which I did not see the name. There was a circular building of red brick, much like a tabernacle of the sects, and Westbrook went up to a little door set in the side of it. He knocked upon it loudly, and then pushed it open. The air within was filled with the welcome fragrance of spice, such as I imagine might have embalmed the body of a pharaoh. The room itself was circular in shape, like the building, and seemed to be entirely populated by girls and young women. They were sitting upon stools along the sides of two long tables, pouring powders into small earthenware jars. I watched them closely for a moment or two, as long as it took to view their whole operation. They cut out a piece of oil paper from a sheet beside them, placed it over the opening of the jar, and then secured a piece of blue paper over that; then they tied it with string around the neck of the jar. Their speed and dexterity were extraordinary; they seemed to be imitating some mechanism with their nimbleness and efficiency.

"Here is my sister," Westbrook said. "Harriet." He went over to one of the girls, and touched her shoulder. She smiled but she did not look up at him; she was too intent upon her labours. Her hair was pinned and held up in a linen cap, and it was clear that she had great beauty and delicacy of features. She could have been no more than fourteen or fifteen years old. Bysshe quoted some words of Dante, or so he informed me later, and I must say that I was also smitten with some secret wound. I noticed her strange pallor, no doubt from the inhalation of the spices, and saw that her fingers were bruised and torn from their continual operations. "She prepares spices for the households of the rich," Westbrook said. "Twelve hours each day. Six days each week. She works for the sake of our family. Her shillings bring food to the table. Not spices." He spoke with such bitterness that his sister glanced up at him for a moment, concerned, before she resumed her labours. "We will not detain you any longer, Harriet. Your overseer is coming to admonish us."

An elderly female approached us, her hands held out. "Now Mr. Westbrook, you must not divert your sister from her work. She is all eyes for you and not her duties." She seemed to be an amiable, comfortable woman not at all strict with her charges. "Go along now with your friends, and leave us poor females in peace."

We left the building. "You are thirsty now, gentlemen? The

spice gets to the throat. Poor Harriet is often afflicted with a cough." We walked past a row of cottages, and he stopped to look around. "There is a respectable tavern on the other side of this street," he said. He led us across the cobbles. "She is little better than a slave."

"Who placed her there?" Bysshe asked him.

"My father. Here we are."

We walked into the tavern, low and dark in the London fashion, and ordered three measures of stingo. Then we sat down at a table in the corner. "My father believes that the duty of mankind—and of womankind—is to work. He is a Particular Covenanter."

"The worst of the Christian sects," Bysshe said.

"He believes that the female is far inferior to the male. So he gave no thought to Harriet's future welfare. He has decreed that she must work."

"That is abominable." Bysshe clutched his tankard, and began to tap it upon the table. His face had become quite red, quite fiery, and for the first time I noticed the trace of a white scar upon his forehead. "How could she be tamed and enslaved like some animal?"

"I pleaded with my father. I pointed out the benefits to Harriet of attendance at even a dame school. But he had hardened his heart."

"Monstrous. Terrible. Can you not support her?"

"Me? I can hardly support myself."

"Then I will free her!" Bysshe was glowing now with energy and ardour.

"What will you do?" I asked him.

"I will go to her father and offer him the same sum—the same sum as she earns—if he will allow her to enter some school or academy. I will not rest until it is done."

"You must wait until she finishes her work," Westbrook said.

"Every moment is an agony. Forgive me. I must go outside." I accompanied him to the door of the tavern, and gave him a handkerchief with which he wiped the moisture from his face. "Thank you, Victor. I have become quite molten."

"Where will you go?"

"Go? I am going nowhere." Then, to my surprise, he began walking up and down on the cobbles outside the tavern.

When I returned to Westbrook I found that he had already ordered two more measures of stingo. "Bysshe is treading out his fury," I told him. "He has a fervent soul."

"Mr. Shelley is red hot. That is good. We need natures forged in fire."

"I have noticed that here, in England, emotions run freely."

"Ever since the Revolution in Paris. Mr. Shelley is right. There he goes. Do you see his cane swinging by the window? We, too, have been liberated. The events helped to create a new man."

"A new kind of man?"

"You are laughing at me."

"No. Believe me. I am not."

"We cry more freely these days, do we not?"

"I have no standard of comparison. Ah, here is Bysshe."

"I believe," Bysshe said, laughing as he joined us, "that I was becoming an object of attention. There were comments."

"You are an unusual sight in the neighbourhood." Westbrook went over to the counter, and brought back Bysshe another tankard.

"Am I?" He seemed genuinely surprised, and it occurred to me that he was not aware of his own uniqueness. "One young man was eyeing my cane."

"They are all poor, sir. But they mean you no harm. Most of them are honest enough."

Bysshe seemed embarrassed. "Forgive me. I did not mean to impugn their honesty—" He drank quickly from his tankard.

"I am surprised," I said, "that they are not howling with rage."

"What was that, Victor?"

"If I were forced to live in abject horror, while those around me were dripping with riches, I would wish to tear this city down stone by stone. I would wish to destroy the world that imprisoned me. That created me."

"Well said." Westbrook raised his tankard to me. "I have often wondered what keeps these poor men in servitude."

"Religion," Bysshe said.

"No. Not that. They are not impressed by anything of that kind. They are as pagan as the men of Africa."

"I am glad to hear it," Bysshe replied. "Let us drink to the death of Christianity."

"No," Westbrook said. "It is the fear of punishment. The fear of the gallows."

"What do they gain from life?" I asked him. I was becoming drunk on the stingo.

"Life itself," Westbrook replied.

"That is enough, I think." Bysshe had gone over to the

counter, and brought back three more tankards. "Life is its own value. There is nothing more precious."

"Yet," Westbrook said, "it could be led with dignity. And without suffering."

"I wish that were possible in this life." Bysshe raised his tankard. "Health to you all."

"What do you mean?" Westbrook asked him.

"Suffering is intrinsic to human existence. There is no joy without its attendant pain."

"It need not be," I said. "We must create a new standard of value. That is all."

"Oh, you will transform nature, will you, Victor?"

"If necessary. Yes."

"Bravo. Victor Frankenstein will create a new kind of man!"

"You have always told me, Bysshe, that we must find the unfindable. Gain the unattainable."

"I do believe that. We are all agreed upon it, I think. Yet to remove suffering itself—"

"What if there were a new race of beings," Westbrook asked, "who could not feel pain or grief? They would be terrible."

I took his arm. "Is not St. Giles, where we walked, more terrible still? Is it not?"

We continued our drinking and, I believe, aroused some comment from the clerks and tradesmen who were sitting on other benches. It was a more respectable neighbourhood than that of St. Giles adjoining, but the presence of gentlemen was not necessarily welcomed. "We should go now," Westbrook said. He took Bysshe's arm, and helped him from the seat. "I think, Mr. Shelley, you should visit my father another time. He is not a friend to drink."

"What of your sister? What of Harriet?" Bysshe stood uncertainly on his feet.

"Two or three days will make no conceivable difference, I assure you. Come now. And you, too, Mr. Frankenstein. I will find you both a cab in St. Martin's Lane."

⇒ Three ⇐

I HAD AVIDLY READ ACCOUNTS in *Blackwood's Magazine* of Mr. Humphry Davy's work, and had managed at Oxford to obtain a copy of the *Proceedings of the Royal Society* in which he explained the process by which he had galvanised a cat. Quite by chance I opened a copy of the *Gentleman's Magazine*, two or three days after arriving in London, and saw there advertised a course of lectures by Mr. Davy at the Society for the Encouragement of Arts and Manufactures under the title "Electricity Not Mysterious."

When I attended the first lecture, having purchased a ticket for the entire series at the door, I was surprised to find that the hall of the Society was all but full. Mr. Davy was younger than I expected, fresh-faced, keen and quick in all his movements; the young men in the audience held their hats upon their knees, and strained forward to watch him. He was preparing some galvanic batteries on a table while, on the opposite side of the raised stage, there was a cylindrical device that glistened in the light of the oil-lamps.

Mr. Davy seemed to have the temperament of an artist. He spoke of the electrical current as a fulfilment of the Greek philosophers' proposition that there is a fire within all things. He called it the spark of life, the Promethean flame, and the light of the world. "Pray do not be alarmed," he said. "Nothing will touch you or harm you in any way." Then he connected the galvanic equipment and, at the touch of his hand, a great arc of flashing light crossed from one table to the other. Two or three ladies shrieked, only to be rebuked by their companions with laughter, but there was a general fervour and excitement in the hall. I blinked, but there was still an after-image of the flash upon my retina; it seemed that I had looked into the heart of creation.

"It is over," Mr. Davy said in reassurance to the ladies. "It is gone. But it is infinitely repeatable." There was a slight smell of burning, or of singeing, in the air. "We have come to no harm," he continued, "because electricity is the most natural force in the world. In truth it is *the* natural force. To my reckoning, like air and water, it is one of the constituents of life. It may be one of the principal means of begetting life. The electrical fluid itself is infinitely sensitive and subtle. It works with miraculous effect in the aether, yet it also flows through the human frame silently and invisibly. Dr. Darwin, who very sensibly proposed the differentiation between vitreous and resinous electricity according to their seats of operation, preserved a piece of vermicelli in an electrical case until it began to move with voluntary motion. What could then not be achieved with the human organs under like conditions?"

Mr. Davy went on to describe the curious experiments of the Scottish galvanist, James Macpherson, who had been given especial permission by the Company of Surgeons to be present at the dissection of a felon in Surgeons' Hall. The body had been taken fresh from the gallows at Newgate and delivered while it was still warm; the hanged man was young, the murderer of his mother, and there was no popular execration against the use of his body. The corpse was laid flat upon the wooden slab in the middle of the hall. Eager students were sitting around it in what can only be described as the theatre of operations. I began to feel a prickling sensation down my back: I believed that I could see it all before me.

Mr. Macpherson attached electrical wires, altogether slender and pliable, to the extremities of the corpse. When the galvanic equipment was brought into operation the body shuddered and then, with no principle of movement apparent, rolled itself into a tight ball. The head, according to Mr. Davy, was between the legs of the young man and the hands tightly clenched. He compared it to the image of an abortive infant taken from the womb. Like many others in the audience, I am sure, I listened with horror as Mr. Davy explained how the body could not be unravelled and how in this clenched and unnatural posture it was consigned to the lime pit in the grounds of Newgate Prison. Such was the power of the electrical current.

I left while questions were being put to Mr. Davy, and walked out into the street. Whether it was the atmosphere of the place, or whether it was the influence of the electric current in the aether, I felt stifled. I walked quickly, but then broke into a run. I knew that I had to escape the confines of the city. It was the strangest impulse I had ever experienced, so alarming and so urgent that my heart seemed to beat faster with every pace I took. I might have been fleeing from someone, or something, but the nature of my pursuer was not known to me. Was it an episode of madness? I may even have looked over my shoulder on one or two occasions. I do not recall.

I continued my flight past the Oxford Road and continued northwards. There were some who called after me, presuming that I was escaping from the Runners or some other force—they shouted encouragement. By a timber yard some children ran with me for a while, hooting and jeering, but they soon left off. And then, as I passed a public house and turnpike on the edge of fields, I had the most curious notion that someone else was running beside me. I could not see him, or hear him, but I was fully aware of his presence as I ran over a rough track. It could not have been my shadow, because the moon was obscured behind clouds. It was some image, some phantasm I scarcely knew—which insisted on keeping up with my rapid strides. I ran all the faster to shake off this extraordinary sensation, and I skirted a large pond before crossing a field of brick kilns and smoking refuse. I was now on the very edge of the city, where there were a few straggling tenements, fetid ditches and hog pens. Still I did not slacken my pace, and still the other ran close beside me. The ground now began to rise and, as I passed beside some infirm and wasted trees, I stumbled upon a root or branch; I was about to fall upon the ground when, to my astonishment and fear, something seemed to lift me up and save me from falling. It occurred to me even then that I was sick of some nervous fever, and I slowed my pace a little. I made my way towards an oak, its shape outlined in the darkness, and rested against it.

I sat there, recovering my breath; I felt my forehead for evidence of fever, but perceived none.

I do not think I slept, or ever lost my waking consciousness, but the fear left me without any sign of its passing. I had returned to myself, as it were; yet with a sense of resignation that felt almost like weariness. I experienced a curious sense of acceptance—not of relief or of gratitude—when I had no notion of any burden being taken from me. I believed that I had been marked out in a way that I could not then comprehend. Gradually I became aware of a sound, like that of some avalanche or rock-fall; I sat up alarmed, recalling the disasters of my own region, but I quickly realised that it was the noise of London, a confused but not inharmonious muttering as if the city were talking in its sleep. I could see some fitful lights; but the predominant impression was one of brooding darkness, an inchoate roar of vast life momentarily stilled. I got up from the base of the oak tree, and walked down towards it.

＞＜

IT WAS RAINING WHEN I CAME to the threshold of the city, a quiet steady rain that cast a veil over the streets. On such a night there were few people abroad, and my footsteps rang distinctly against the cobbles as I made my way towards the Oxford Road. I did not want to return to Berners Street, not yet. I had the absurd superstition that something might be waiting to greet me there, and instead I decided to walk on to Poland Street where I hoped to find Bysshe still awake. It was his custom to write, or to talk, by candlelight and then to watch the first stirrings of dawn creep beneath his casement window. Sure enough, when I passed his first-floor lodgings, I saw the light burning. I threw some pebbles against the pane, and he unfastened the shutter; seeing me in the narrow street below, he opened the window and threw down the keys. "You have heard the chimes at midnight," he called to me. "Come up!"

"Are you quite well, Victor?" he asked me when he opened his door above the first flight of stair. I must have been breathing heavily. "You seem to be in a cold sweat."

"Rain. Nothing more. It is a bad night."

"Come in and warm yourself." Then he said to someone, over his shoulder, "We have a visitor."

Daniel Westbrook rose to greet me when I entered the room. "We were just discussing you, Mr. Frankenstein," he said.

"Please call me Victor."

"I was curious about your studies."

"Oh, yes?"

"I told him, Victor, that you are a student of galvanism. You are interested in the principles of life."

"I am interested in the springs of life," I said. "That is true."

"Where it comes from?" Westbrook asked me.

"Where it might come from. What else have you two been discussing? I cannot be a topic of absorbing interest."

"We have been discussing, Victor, the future of Daniel's sister."

"Mr. Shelley has seen my father."

"Really? When did this occur?" The conversation in the tavern, when Bysshe pledged himself to educate Harriet Westbrook at his own expense, had taken place three days before.

"I visited the Westbrook family yesterday morning," Bysshe replied. "I believed that Sunday was, for Daniel's father, the only day of consideration."

"Mr. Shelley—" Westbrook began.

"Bysshe," he said. "Merely Bysshe and Victor."

"Bysshe was remorseless. He remonstrated with my father for allowing Harriet to consort with loose females."

"I exaggerated. To make the point. Harriet had already left the room."

"He pleaded with him to allow her the study of improving authors."

"I know that she can read. She told me so."

"And then, in a final moment of passion, he offered my father money."

"That did it. I promised to pay to him the exact amount of Harriet's earnings, with another guinea a week. These religious men love lucre. Stand by the fire, Victor, you are still trembling."

"My father," Westbrook said, "is a poor man as well as a religious one."

"I am not blaming him for his poverty. I am blaming him for his neglect of Harriet."

"Where will you place her?" I asked Bysshe.

"I do not intend to place her anywhere. No. That is not true. I will place her here."

"You mean—" I looked around at the mass of books and papers; his lodgings were in the same degree of confusion as his rooms in Oxford.

"I intend to educate her myself. Daniel and I have been discussing the question of female education as the necessary preliminary to female suffrage. I will introduce Harriet to Plato, Voltaire, the divine Shakespeare."

"That is rich fare for a young girl."

"Daniel assures me that she is eager to learn on her own account. They began to read under the tutelage of their mother."

"She is dead now," Westbrook said.

"And Daniel passes books to her still which she reads on Sunday within the pages of her Bible."

"So she will come here?" I asked.

"What of it?"

"She has no female to accompany her?"

"You are still the solid citizen of Geneva, Victor. There are no such conventions in London. In this part of London. And, if there were, I would be happy to break them!" He looked at Westbrook. "I have Harriet's interests wholly at heart. I will read to her. Look." He went over to a pile of books, half-fallen on the carpet, and picked up one of them. "Volney's *Ruin of Empires.* You know it, Victor?" I nodded. "From this she will learn how unjust power is doomed and how all tyrants decay."

"I trust she enjoys it," I said.

"And what would you have me read to her? The novels of Fanny Burney? They are the fetters that bind young women in their servitude. I am lending *this* book to Daniel." He returned to the pile, and held up Mary Wollstonecraft's *A Vindication of the Rights of Woman.* "When he has thoroughly absorbed it, I will present it to his sister. Do you agree, Daniel?"

"What was the phrase you used to me?" Westbrook asked. "'We must break up the ground.'"

"Precisely. We speak of radical reformation, but radical means root. Root and branch. We must take reform to all spheres of activity. Victor is interested in voltaic activity. I am interested in Harriet's soul. They are precisely comparable." He had excited himself in the course of this conversation, and opened the window to breathe in the cool damp air.

"What a night," he said. "On such a night as this I imagine stray watery phantoms in the streets of London. But can you see ghosts in mists?"

I went over to Westbrook. "Your sister is happy with the new arrangement?"

"She is overjoyed, Mr. Frankenstein. She has a thirst for knowledge."

"So be it." I turned to Shelley. "I had never considered you to be a teacher, Bysshe."

"Every poet is a teacher. Daniel agrees with me in that matter. He worships the Lake poets. He can quote from memory 'Tintern Abbey.'"

"I know the last lines," Westbrook murmured to me. "I have never forgotten them."

"When does Miss Westbrook begin her studies with you?" I asked Bysshe.

"Tomorrow morning. She will be coming here early. I gave her a copy of Mrs. Barbauld's *Moral Tales* to impress her father, but we will discard it. I would like her to read some Aesop to begin. He charms the fancy, and instructs the mind. There will be some hard words, too, which I will interpret."

"I will call for her at six tomorrow evening," Daniel Westbrook said.

"But that means you cannot come to the play."

"The play? What play?"

"*Melmoth the Wanderer.* It is Cunningham's latest. It opens tomorrow night. But wait. If you take her home in a cab, Daniel, you can meet us in front of the theatre."

"I am not accustomed to cabs," Westbrook said.

"Here." Bysshe took from his pocket a sovereign. "You cannot miss the drama."

It was clear to me that Westbrook did not want to accept the coin; he was awkward and abashed. Bysshe understood this immediately, and regretted what had been an instinctive gesture. "Or would you rather enjoy the evening with your sister?"

"I think so. Yes." Westbrook returned the sovereign to Bysshe. "It is generous of you, sir, but I am not really used to generosity. My sister is more worthy of it."

"We are all unworthy," Shelley said. "Of course you must come, Victor. We will sup full of horrors."

I agreed, and I took my leave soon after. I was dreadfully tired by the events of that night. Westbrook accompanied me to Berners Street since, as he said, I needed a native to guide me through Soho. I could hear the sound of revelry close by, and instinctively I shrank from it.

"Are you a lover of London?" he asked me.

"I scarcely know it. I am excited by it."

"In what way?"

"By its energetic life. It is possible to feel here that you are part of the movement of the age. Part of a great enterprise. I come from a secluded region where such things are unknown."

"I heard you say that you came from Geneva."

"In a sense. Yes. But Geneva is a small city. I am really from the Alpine country, where we walk among the mountains. We are by nature solitary."

"I envy you very much."

"Do you? I have never considered it a state to be envied."

"It gives you power, Mr. Frankenstein. It gives you will."

I was surprised by this and stayed silent as we crossed the Oxford Road. "In Geneva, we have no gas lamps."

"These are a novelty. Yet it is surprising how quickly one grows accustomed to the glare. Do you see the intense shadows that it casts? Look how your shadow stretches across the wall! Here is your street."

"Which way do you go, Mr. Westbrook?"

"East. Where else?" He laughed. "That is where my destiny lies. We will see each other soon. Goodnight to you."

I watched him walking briskly down the Oxford Road, and then I turned into Berners Street. I approached the door with some dread, all the more powerful for being indefinable, but then I quickly crossed the threshold and mounted the stairs. My chambers were dark, and I lit with a Lucifer match a small oil-lamp; in its sputtering wick the room seemed to change shape and size before settling to its customary dimensions. I sat down in an old-fashioned elbow chair, by the side of my bed, and sought to reflect upon the experiences of that night. I was aware that I had been brushed by some power, but I did not know how I was supposed to consider it.

In the silence I could hear footsteps coming along Berners Street—the tread of one person, but very pronounced and awkward as if he or she were labouring under some burden. The steps then halted, just outside my window. I sat very still, all my faculties in absolute suspense. Then after a minute or so the footsteps resumed upon the cobbles, but with a lighter tread than before. I went over to the window. But I could see no one.

As I lay in my bed that night, I dreamed that I was being buried, and that my coffin was being slowly lowered into the earth. I seemed to be aware of this without any particular consciousness of dread. But then, as my coffin was settled onto the bed of soil, I became aware that I was not alone. Someone was lying beside me.

⇒ Four ⇐

ON THE EVENING OF THE NEXT DAY I called upon Bysshe in Poland Street. He was in very good humour, and embraced me as I entered the door. "The first lesson has ended," he said.

"Miss Westbrook has gone?"

"Daniel has just escorted her home. On foot." He laughed. "She will be the most wonderful scholar, Victor. I spoke to her today about the poetry of Chaucer and the troubadours, and I recited some lines from Guillaume de Lorris."

"I thought that you were to teach her Aesop."

"I found him too dry. I wish that you had seen her face, Victor, when I read to her from *The Romance of the Rose*. It was shining. As if her soul were peeping out of her eyes!"

I suspected then that Bysshe's interest in Harriet Westbrook was stronger than that of master and pupil. "You read to her from French romance?"

"Of course. I must begin somewhere. Where else but in a medieval garden? And then we will go on to Spenser. Then Shakespeare. I will shower her with delights!"

"It must be strange for her to be freed from work."

"I believe that it terrifies her and delights her equally. Do you know what she said to me? She said that it was like dying and being reborn. Do you see what a soul she has?"

"I see that she has impressed you. Where is the play?"

"Drury Lane. You are not accustomed to our theatres, Victor. Everything begins and ends in Drury Lane. We should go now."

The street was filled with carriages, on our arrival, but we made our way without difficulty into the Theatre Royal where we were accosted by comfit-makers, fruit-sellers, and the women of the town. "We are in the pit," Bysshe said. "A box was not to be had at any price."

I had never before visited a London theatre, and I was immediately struck by the disorder of the assembly. We were obliged to stand, close to the small orchestra beneath the stage, and we might as well have been in a fruit market or a horse fair. "Look over there," Bysshe shouted at me over the general din. "There is Mr. Hunt. Do you see him? With the violet hat? A great man, Victor. A champion of the coming age." When Leigh Hunt caught sight of Bysshe, he smiled broadly and raised his hat. "Do you know why he is here, Victor? Mr. Hunt is a friend of Cunningham. Our author is a son of liberty. It would not surprise me if there were some demonstrations tonight against the government."

Bysshe looked around with satisfaction as the pit filled to its margins, while the seats behind us and the boxes around us were soon fully occupied. I had never before witnessed a London crowd, if I may call it that, and I must say that I was somewhat in fear of it. Despite the laughter, and the general mood of animation, it resembled some restless creature in search of prey. Could many lives make up one life?

The orchestra struck up an air, a melody no doubt composed for the occasion, and the curtains were drawn apart to reveal a landscape of ice and rock and mountain. "Do you recognise it?" Bysshe whispered to me. "We are in Switzerland." Then there came upon the stage a hooded figure, accoutred all in black; he walked forward with a quick step like that of some wild creature, so odd and so menacing that it reduced the audience to silence. "*Immortal Heaven, what is man?*" he exclaimed in an unnaturally loud voice. "*A being with the ignorance, but not the instinct, of the feeblest animal!*"

"This is Nugent," Bysshe murmured. "Very accomplished actor."

The figure then turned to the audience, and removed his hood. There was an involuntary exclamation of surprise, or dismay, at his pale and sunken features—emaciated, ravaged, and tremulous.

"The cosmetic artists have been busy," Bysshe said.

Yet I scarcely heeded him. There was something so woeful, so awful, about this figure that he commanded my attention. "*There is an oak beside the froth-clad pool where in old time, as I have often heard, a woman desperate, a wretch like me, ended her woes. Her woes were not like mine. And mine will never end.*" He seemed to be looking around the auditorium, searching out every face and every eye, and I had a most irrational fear that he would find mine! "*I have committed the great angelic sin—pride and intellectual glorying. Now I am doomed to wander. Melmoth has become Cain, outcast upon the face of the earth!*" I had no notion, then, of why these words so powerfully affected me. "*The secret of my destiny rests with myself. If all that fear has invented, and incredulity believe of me to be true, to what does it amount? That if my crimes have exceeded those of mortality, so will my punishment. I have been on earth a terror—*"

Someone called out "Liverpool!," then prime minister, and the people around me broke into laughter.

Nugent seemed for a moment startled but, with his hand upon his breast and his gaze directed towards the scene of distant mountains, he waited for the uproar to subside. Then he was Melmoth once more. *"I go cursing, and to curse. I go conquering, and to conquer."* I had never before witnessed the art of personation at close quarters, and I was astonished at the apparent ease with which Nugent had assumed the identity of Melmoth; he was the more vivid for being two people, himself and the desperate man. It was as if he had acquired twice the power of any single human being. *"I go condemned by every human heart, yet untouched by one human hand. There is the ruin."* He pointed with trembling hand at the pile of rocks on the side of the stage. *"And there beyond it is the chapel where I will marry my chosen bride."*

I was struck by the acting and the spectacle rather than the plot. I had never before seen so large a stage or so lavish a production, and I had scarcely become habituated to the particular brightness of the gas lamps. The effect of the intense shadows, the richness of the colours, and the symmetry of the composition upon the stage, combined to form an image more real than reality itself. I was reminded of the book of illuminations that was kept in the sacristy of St. Mary the Virgin in Oxford; it could be seen on presenting a letter from a fellow of the college, and I had spent a delightful morning in turning over the pages of blue and gold, decorated with the burnished images of saints and devils. So it was at Drury Lane that evening. This was like no mountainous region in my own country, but a wonderfully heightened vision of barren desolation. There were some real stones and gravel, as far as I could tell, but I noticed that the larger rocks were made out of stretched canvas that had been painted grey and blue. The stream that ran behind was no stream of water, but a long strip of silver paper that was being agitated by unseen hands.

It was the end of the first act. The little orchestra struck up a melody, as Bysshe put his arm around my shoulders. "This is the true thing," he said with great animation. "This is the full sublime!" I said nothing. "The outcast the wanderer over the face of the earth—there we all tread! Only the exile has a tongue of fire! The imagination can form a thousand different men and worlds. It is the creator. It is the seed of new life."

"It can do so much?"

"Of course. The imagination is the divine spark leaping across chaos."

"The stream was made of silver paper."

"Oh, that is nothing. Mortal men make up the scene, but the vision—" He stopped to purchase a bottled beer, and drank it down without a pause. Then he wiped his hand across his mouth.

The musical interlude had stopped, and the second act began in the setting of the ruined chapel. Yet once more I was distracted. There was someone speaking to a companion, immediately behind me, his voice quite audible. "I wonder if the monster lives or dies? I wonder if he feels remorse for what he has done? What is your opinion?" There was silence for a few moments. "Who created him, do you think? What man and woman gave him birth?" He paused again. "I could never forgive the person who created such a being." I could feel the hot breath of the man upon my neck. "I could never condone the making of a blighted life. It would deserve dire and condign punishment. Punishment without end." I turned round but those closest to me seemed to be enthralled in the drama and not to have spoken. The acoustics of the theatre were no doubt peculiar.

The curtains were pulled for a short interval, and then drawn back to reveal a pool or what the Scottish people call a tarn on the summit of a mountain. Melmoth now stood against a fading perspective of mountain tops and crevasses, as he grasped by her wrists the reluctant bride. "The seed of such a creature will be barren." It was the same voice again, speaking distinctly behind me. "By his own account he has aged more than a century. Yet if he has risen above the confines of ordinary life, well, who is to say?" The girl broke away from his restraining hold, and flung herself into the water. I had been expecting a splash, or some movement in the water, but instead she descended slowly with her arms raised above her head. Of course it was part of the mechanics of the stage.

Bysshe clutched my arm, and whispered to me. "I cannot endure this. It is too disturbing. Too tremendous."

"Do you wish to leave?"

"Yes. I am in a fearful fright." I had always believed that Bysshe was too sensitive to endure the buffets of the world, and this sign of his tremulous nature did not wholly surprise me.

"Let us go then," I said. "If we can make our way through this crowd."

When we came out into the vestibule he stopped and, taking my arm again, he laughed. "I am a fool," he said. "Forgive me. I was seized by some panic fear. Now it has passed. You look surprised."

"I am curious."

"When the girl threw herself into the lake, and lifted her arms above her head. That seized me with a frightful rush of terror. I am at a loss to explain why."

"Shall we go back?"

"I have seen enough. Unless you, Victor—"

"Oh, no."

We had reached the street, when all at once we heard someone calling out, "Mr. Shelley! Mr. Shelley!" It was Daniel Westbrook, running towards us. "Thank God I am in time!"

"Whatever is the matter?"

"It is Harriet. She has been taken ill. She is asking for you."

"What? What has happened? What is the matter with her?"

"She collapsed just before we reached home. She was talking wildly."

Bysshe ran out into the road, and hailed a cab that had just turned into Drury Lane. Hurriedly we stepped in, as Daniel called out the destination in Whitechapel High Street, and the sudden jolt of the carriage threw us all into the back seat. "Is this your arm or mine?" Bysshe asked as he extricated himself and sat on the wooden seat opposite to us. "Is she in a fever? We must get ice. The fever will break. Can we go no faster?" All the time he was looking out of the window, which was covered with linen and not glass, as if he were estimating the speed of our journey. "Tell me exactly what happened."

Daniel explained that he and Harriet had left Poland Street, and walked eastwards down the Oxford Road. Daniel had been telling Harriet that we were about to visit Drury Lane for the performance of *Melmoth the Wanderer*, and she had expressed a wish to see the theatre herself. "There are so many things," she said to her brother, "that I would now like to see!" He said that her eyes had filled with tears, but that he had taken her hand; together they had crossed the city by way of St. Paul's and Cannon Street, and had come out in Aldgate High Street. She had stopped him by the pump there, he said, and exclaimed to him, "I am so happy, Daniel! I could die now!"

They had walked down Aldgate High Street and crossed into Whitechapel—into the main street, as he put it. They had come within a hundred yards of their home when, looking around at the shops and tenements, she had cried out to Daniel that, "I feel as if I am suffocating. I am afraid my heart will burst!" Then she collapsed into his arms. In his distress and alarm he managed to carry her back the short distance to their house. She was placed in the parlour where she began a most unusual rambling speech in which she called upon "Mr. Shelley" several times. "If Mr. Shelley will come," she said, "then I will be at rest."

So naturally Daniel had left immediately, and had run all the way to Drury Lane in the hope that the play would still be continuing. By good chance, he had seen us just as we left the theatre.

Bysshe was still impatiently looking out of the window. "This is the east, Victor." He was silent for a while, as the cab clattered and shook over the low cobbles.

"This is where we live." Daniel pointed to a small cul-de-sac off the principal highway, and then called out to the driver, "Here we are!" Bysshe jumped out of the carriage and handed the man a sovereign before we had a chance to disembark; he was, I believe, in a furious and restless eagerness to see Harriet.

I looked back at the main street and one glance was enough to reveal its poverty to me; there must have been a market there an hour or so previously, because the area was now filled with makeshift counters and platforms, with a plentiful assortment of discarded fruit, vegetable leaves, and papers among them. Bysshe had run on to the house, and knocked upon the door, not waiting for Daniel to join him. The door was opened quickly, and Bysshe gained admittance at once.

"I trust him," Daniel said. "He may have more efficacy than any surgeon or apothecary."

"Upon your sister, at least."

"Yes. That is what I mean." We followed Bysshe into the house, small and narrow and imbued with the faint odour of damp straw that I had noticed in other London dwellings. There is an expression in English—no room to swing a cat. Bysshe had gone into a little parlour that overlooked the road, and joined two young women whom I assumed to be Harriet's sisters. Daniel and I made our way into the room, now quite overcrowded, where Bysshe was already kneeling beside the prostrate girl.

"She has been speaking of you, Mr. Shelley," one of the sisters whispered. "But she is quite overcome."

Bysshe leaned over and murmured to her, "Harriet, Harriet, do you hear me?"

His voice seemed to rouse her. "I have been quite happy, Mr. Shelley. Oh, so happy."

"And you will be happy again. Here. Let me place this cushion beneath your head."

"It was the suddenness. I was surprised."

"Sudden?"

"*Surprised by joy*. Is that not Mr. Wordsworth's phrase?"
He bent down and kissed her hand.

I was standing by the door and, at a slight noise, I turned my head. A man of middle age was standing on the stairs. He was wearing an old-fashioned swallow-tail coat of faded black, and his cravat had come untied. I noticed, too, that his hands were clenched into fists. He came down the remaining stairs very slowly, as if unaware of my presence, and stood listening to the sounds within the room. Bysshe was asking for water.

"He will have to go to the pump," the man said. "There is no water here." Then he turned to me. "Your servant, sir. Look what you have brought into the house." I did not understand what he meant, but he looked at me in what I believed to be a threatening manner.

One of the young women came out. "Pa, there is no time to lose. Will you fetch me the pail while I put on my shawl?"

"*Their children also shall be dashed to pieces before their eyes; their houses shall be spoiled, and their wives ravished.*"

"There is no time for this, Pa. Oh, where is my shawl?" She took up a large wooden vessel, beneath the stairs, and ran out into the street.

I followed her, not wishing to linger in the baleful presence of her father. "Let me help you," I said.

"There is no need for help, sir. I am going to the pump for poor Harriet."

"You are one of her sisters?"

"Yes. Emily. She has caused us such a fright, but she is calmer now. Mr. Shelley has spoken to her." It seemed that Bysshe had by general consent become the saviour of the household. "We turn down here." We had come into a courtyard, surrounded on all sides by the dwellings of the poorer sort, patched and peeling, with here and there a stray flowerpot perched upon a windowsill. The pump had its complement of old ladies and children. "Let me through, if you please." Emily was obviously accustomed to the scene. "My sister has been taken ill."

"Don't give her the water then, Em," an ancient woman called out to the vast amusement of her companions. "A sure way to kill her."

"It is just to cool her, Mrs. Sykes."

"It is cold enough, I grant you. But it is ever so dirty. Plenty here have turned queer from it."

"Who's the fancy man, Em?" The question came from a young boy, who had been staring at me in mingled astonishment and hilarity. I tried to dress as an Englishman, but there was some undefinable difference in my costume or manner that always proclaimed me to be a foreigner. "Does his mother know he's out?" This brought further laughter from the assembled ladies, but by now Emily had filled her pail and turned away from the pump.

"I apologise for them, sir," she said as we walked out of the courtyard. "They are not accustomed to strangers. I do not know your name—"

"Victor Frankenstein."

"You came as a friend of Mr. Shelley?"

"Yes, indeed. And of your brother. You say that Harriet is improving?"

"She is calmer. She is not talking such nonsense. No. I did not mean that. She is resting."

I was surprised at Emily's demeanour, much like that of her

sister, in so unpromising a place. She had not been touched by the general filthiness. They were an unusual family. "You have another sister, I think?"

"Yes. Jane is with us. She lives with her husband in Bethnal Green, but she happened to be calling on Pa."

"So you and Harriet live with your father?"

"Jane was wed a few months after Ma died. We look after the house."

"Does your father work still?"

"Oh, no. He was obliged to retire. His nerves are very bad." I admit that I was troubled by desire for Emily, but now all such feelings were a source of distaste to me. The purity of my purpose could not be put to jeopardy by the lusts of the flesh. I held myself apart.

"Your last name confused me," she said.

"It often does. Let me help you with the water."

"I am accustomed to it."

Emily took the pail over the threshold, and went into the parlour where Harriet was now sitting up on the settle. Emily knelt beside her, and began to smooth the water over her forehead and temples with such a sisterly tenderness that I marvelled once more at the presence of this family in so mean and coarse a neighbourhood.

"She is recovered," Bysshe said to me. "It was a fever."

"Then we should not stay." I felt quite ill at ease in this small dwelling. It was as clean and wholesome as it could be, but the quality of the surroundings tainted it like that faint odour of straw; it left me with a feeling of depression, even of weariness, that I could not master. "There is so little room here. We will suffocate Harriet."

"Of course. You are right. She needs air. We will go at once." Bysshe put his hand upon Daniel's shoulder, and told him that we intended to return to Soho.

Daniel insisted on escorting us to a busy crossroads, just beyond Whitechapel, where there were cabs going into the city. "It was very good of you, Mr. Shelley," he said. "And of you, Mr. Frankenstein. You have brought her back to health in less time than I thought possible."

"Not us, Daniel. Her natural strength supported her. She has her own star." We hailed a cab, and Daniel waved us off. Then Bysshe put his head out of the window, and shouted, "Assure her that I will see her tomorrow!" He leaned back in his seat with a sigh. "We have done a good deed," he said.

"Still, I pity her."

"For what reason?"

"Look around you. Do you see the squalor? It would be easy, in such a place, to slip into crime and evil."

"Yes. It is wretched enough." Bysshe seemed very tired.

"Wretched? It is monstrous. And it will create monsters. Have you ever seen such squalor?"

Bysshe had murmured something in reply, but I had not listened. "What was that?"

"I said, did you see the father?"

"He was on the stairs. He is no threat."

"Threat?"

"Forgive me," I replied. "My mind is wandering." Yet I believed that Mr. Westbrook considered me to be his family's enemy.

⇒ ⇐

I ATTENDED LESSONS EVERY MORNING at the dissecting room of St. Thomas's Hospital. I gained admission, as a voluntary student, by paying a trifling fee for a course of lectures I never attended. I wanted only the practical work of cutting. Theory and conjecture were not sufficient for me. The only road to knowledge lay in the examinations of the dead. I was obliged to observe, and to experiment, before I arrived at any reasonable opinion.

The dissecting room was not a place for the fearful or the faint of heart. The corpses were placed on the dissection tables, in the middle of the room, with six or seven students intent upon rummaging about their bones and entrails. Some concentrated on an arm, others on a leg or bowel. Many of the bodies had been laid out several days before burial, and many had been dug out of the ground in a state of partial decay. Yet, if the flesh was infirm, the bones were generally still sound.

There were glass cases ranged along the walls with bodily specimens of every conceivable kind. In a large fireplace, on one side of the room, stood a copper pan that was used for boiling the bodies when the work of the knife became too slow. The bones could then be wrenched from the boiled flesh with ease. I had not yet grown accustomed to the smell of rotten or rotting flesh, but its savour did not offend me. When mixed with the smell of the preservative it had a piquant aroma that lingered on the hands, the arms, and even the clothes of the dissectionists, long after the class was over. There were some who shunned the smell, when they detected it upon our frock-coats. There were some, entering the dissection room for the first time, who fainted dead away. Others retched violently, and left the content of their stomachs on the floor among the entrails and faeces of the dead. The stench of death is equivalent to death itself. It is the darkness of fear, the unknown agency, the dissolution of hope. Yet if I were able to conquer death, what then? The stench of death might then become a wonderful perfume!

Among my fellow dissectionists was a young man of bright eye and ruddy complexion. I gathered from his speech that he was a London boy, but he had given up his trade as an ostler on the City Road to become an apprentice surgeon. "I am used to the stink of horses and of London inns," he told me. "The dead don't bother me." We would drink together in the local public house where the other dissectionists congregated; the bar consequently smelled of the charnel house, and was not patronised by many other visitors. Jack Keat and I would sit at a low wooden table, and converse on the events of the day.

"You were holding in your hand, Victor, a very good cancer."

"Of the bowel. Extraordinary corruption. It was difficult to hold secure."

"You have to use your thumb and forefinger. Like so. You may get something stuck beneath your nail. But it will wash out."

"You were in a very good humour."

"I found a tumour eating its way through a brain. It was oozing. I cleaned it out and kept it." He patted his pocket.

He was short enough, and one or two drinks would send him, as he put it, "up the Monument." He would declaim lectures and speeches he had read. He recited passages from the poetry he most admired. I remember that he had an especial passion for Shakespeare. "This is where the future is being made," he said one evening. "Here. In the dissection room. This is where we will find improvement. Progress. This is where we can alleviate human suffering and disease. You and I, and all our fellows, must work with ardour for the common cause! We must be energetic, Victor. We must be confident." And then he broke down in a fit of coughing.

➤ Five ❦

I RETURNED TO OXFORD two days before the beginning of the Hilary term; Bysshe urged me to stay in London, citing the radical enterprise with which he had become associated and remonstrating with me about my lack of fervour for the cause (as he put it). But in truth I was eager to renew my own studies. I had seen and heard much in London, but nothing had impressed me so profoundly as the electrical demonstrations of Mr. Davy. I burned with impatience to consult all the volumes of physical science, ancient and modern, thereby to discover the secret springs of life; I wished to dedicate myself to this pursuit, to the exclusion of all else, and I believed that no power on earth could divert me from my purpose.

When I entered the college I greeted the porters as old companions, although their welcome for me was slightly subdued; I was still too much associated with Bysshe to be wholly accepted. Yet my college servant seemed genuinely pleased by my return. "Oh, Mr. Frankenlime," she said, "not a moment too soon." She had much difficulty in pronouncing my last name, and would try several different expedients in the course of one conversation. "I had ever so much trouble with your bottles."

"I would hate to put you to any inconvenience, Florence."

"Them bottles were filled, half-filled and not filled at all. I didn't know where to put them in the general clean."

She was referring to the experimental laboratory I had set up in my bedroom. It was a modest affair—some crucibles, tubes, and a portable burner—but she had a nervous dread of anything she called "medicinal." For some reason it reminded her of her husband's untimely death, an event which she took much pleasure in describing to me in all its detail. "I left them where they was," she said. "I did not touch them, Mr. Frankentine."

"That was very good of you."

"I never touch my gentlemen's properties. Oh, no. Did you have a good journey from Old Smokey?" She was a Londoner by birth, as she never ceased to inform me, but she had married the short-lived Oxford man and had never moved away. "I suppose there was a good fog."

"Much rain, Florence, I'm afraid."

"I am sorry to hear that." She seemed delighted that the city continued to suffer from bad weather. "But it clears the fog, you see." She lowered her voice to a whisper. "How is Mr. Shelley?"

"He is very well. He flourishes in London."

"He is often spoken of here." She was still whispering, although there was no one to overhear us. "He is considered wild."

"He is not savage, Florence. He is very thoughtful."

"Is that what you call it? Well." She took my trunk, and hauled it into the bedroom where she began to unpack my shirts and general linen. "Whatever is this?" I heard the question, and knew at once what she meant. I had placed for safekeeping among my linen a small model of vitreous clay; it was a simulacrum of the human brain, perfect in all of its details, that I had purchased from an apothecary in Dean Street. He had told me that it was a copy of the brain of one Davy Morgan, a notorious highwayman who had been hanged a few months before.

"It is nothing, Florence. Leave it on the table."

"I will not touch it, Mr. Frankenline. It is worm-eaten."

I went into the bedroom, and picked up the model. "These are not worms. These are the fibres of the brain. Do you see? They are like the channels and currents of the ocean." How slight was the knowledge of the human organism! There was not one person in a thousand—a hundred thousand—who had stopped to consider the workings of the mind or of the body.

"It isn't natural," she said.

"It is nature itself, Florence. I believe that to be the optic lobe."

"It is no good telling me things like that, sir." She looked at me in horror. "I want nothing to do with it."

"If we could stimulate that area, then we might see for many miles. Would that not be an advantage?"

"It would not. With your eyes popping out of your head? Oh dear, no."

I put the model on the work-table I had set up by the window of the room. "I am afraid that you will remain in ignorance, Florence."

"At least, sir, I will be happy."

It did not occur to me then that Florence's words expressed some instinctive truth; the natural sentiments of mankind, however coarsely expressed, have a justice of their own. But I had already separated myself for ever from the ordinary pursuits of men. My mind was filled with one thought, one conception, one purpose. I wished to achieve more, far more, than those around me and I fully believed that I would pioneer a new way, explore unknown powers, and unfold to the world the deepest mysteries of creation.

I read widely in the libraries of Oxford, straying very far from the directions of my moral tutor who seemed to know nothing beyond Galen and Aristotle. Once a week I climbed the stairs to Professor Saville's rooms, across the quadrangle from my own, where I always found him sitting in a high-backed chair with a tumbler of brandy and cold water by his side. My early education in Geneva had given me a sufficiency of Greek and Latin, so that the weekly requirements of translation caused no difficulties for me. I had already informed him that my interest lay in the growth and development of the human frame, at which he seemed genuinely astonished.

"It is not a pursuit," he said, "that I associate with gentlemen."

"But if gentlemen do not venture upon it, sir, who will?"

"Are there not anatomists in the world?"

"I am concerned with the workings of human life. What subject is of more importance?"

"Surely Galen and Avicenna have informed us on all such matters?" Saville had a habit of rising from his seat, after delivering an opinion, and then walking around the room before resuming his position. Only then would he take a sip from the tumbler.

"I believe, sir, that Galen used the anatomy of a Barbary ape?"

"Quite satisfactory." He took another tour of the room. "You are not suggesting that we defile the human temple?"

"How else can we learn from where the principle of life proceeds?"

"You need only open your Bible, Mr. Frankenstein, to be assured on these matters."

"I know the Bible well, sir—"

"I very much hope so."

"But I confess myself ignorant of the actual mechanism."

"Mechanism? Whatever do you mean?"

"We learn in Genesis, sir, that God formed man out of the dust of the ground and then breathed into his nostrils the breath of life."

"What of it?"

"My question is, of what did that breath consist?"

"You have been too much in the company of Mr. Shelley." He began another perambulation of the room and, on his return to his chair, swallowed a large portion of brandy and water. "You are beginning to doubt Holy Scripture."

"I am simply curious."

"Never be curious. It is the path to perdition. Now, shall we turn to the subject at hand?" He began to examine my translation into Greek of an editorial from *The Times*, on the prospects for Dalmatian independence, and I left his chambers soon after.

⇒ ⇐

SO THERE WAS TO BE NO ENLIGHTENMENT for me at Oxford. I had already determined to study enough to attain my degree, principally for the sake of my father, but like a pilgrim I prepared myself for another journey. The mind that is ambitious makes itself. I found a small barn outside Oxford, in the little village of

Headington; I rented this from a farmer for an inconsiderable sum, on the understanding that I was a student of medicine who was mixing noxious chemicals and combinations that needed to be prepared away from the haunts of men. The barn was surrounded by open fields, but had the advantage of a small track leading towards it. It was, as I told him, ideal for my purposes. And so it proved.

I began my experiments on the animal kingdom without, I hope, inflicting unnecessary or excessive pain. I had learned, from my studies of Priestley and Davy, the effectiveness of nitrous oxide as a means of anaesthesia; and I already knew the sedative effect of henbane when administered in large quantities. Yet I began with the smallest creatures. Even the humble worm, and the water-beetle, are objects of wonder to the student of Nature. Under the microscope the fly became a chamber of delights: the vessels of the eye were lustrous and brimming with life, crystals with manifold gleamings. How complex, and yet how vulnerable! All was held in such delicate poise and balance that the breadth of a hair separated life and brightness from darkness and nonentity.

I purchased turtle doves and other birds in the market off Corn Street and, when I felt the quick breathing warmth beneath my fingers, I sensed the elusive pulse of life. Was it the same warmth that suffused the mechanism of the voltaic batteries? Warmth meant motion and excitation, and movement visible or invisible was the condition of life itself. I believed that I was on the edge of a great discovery. If I could create movement, would it not then reproduce itself in sequence just as the waves beating against the shore rise up in harmonious array? The world followed one dance.

I was suffused with such hope and enthusiasm, in those Oxford days, that I would often run through the fields beside the barn in sheer overabundance of energy. I could look up at the clouds rolling above me and see within them the patterns I discerned in the pearly iridescence of a fly's wing or the shifting colours in the eye of an expiring dove. I considered myself to be a liberator of mankind, freeing the world from the mechanical philosophy of Newton and of Locke. If I could find one single principle from the observation of all types of organism, if in the study of cells and tissues I could detect one presiding element, then I might be able to formulate the general physiology of all living things. There is one life, one way to live, one energetic spirit.

Yet there were periods of my existence when, in the last reaches of the night, I awoke with horror. The first hours of the day provoked in me alarm, and I would rise from my bed and pace through the dark streets as if they were my prison. On the first faint appearance of dawn, however, I became calm. The low and even light, across the water meadows, filled me with a sensation akin to courage. I needed it more than ever. I had begun my anatomy of dogs and cats, purchased at small expense from the poorer people of Oxford. I told them separately that I needed the creature to catch the mice and rats in my lodging, and they parted with it willingly enough. It was easy to sedate the animal with nitrous oxide, and I calculated that the heart would beat for thirty minutes before it relapsed into a painless death. In those few minutes I began the process of dissection, turning the floor of my experimental theatre into a pool of blood. But I persevered in my course. I wished to prove that the organs of the creature were not distinct entities, but depended for their efficacy upon the interdependence of them all. Thus if I hindered the workings of one, then the others would be harmed or damaged in some fashion. And so it proved. I was making such strides in my experimental philosophy that I could see all difficulties falling away.

≫ €

IN THE WEEK BEFORE THE END of that term I received a letter from my father in Geneva, informing me that my sister had become gravely ill. Elizabeth was my twin in all but name. We had grown up in each other's company. We had played together from infancy and, although we had not studied together, I had acquainted her with the import of my schoolbooks. We were said to resemble each other in features, too, and both possessed the same nervous and restless temperament.

I made plans to return home immediately. There was a packet boat leaving for Le Havre from London Bridge on the Monday following, and I travelled to London two nights before to arrange my ticket. I had hoped to see Bysshe, of course. He had not communicated with me since my departure from the city, and I was eager to learn of his adventures in my absence. I walked into Poland Street soon after my arrival, but there was no light at his window. I called up to him, but no answer came.

I had hired a small cabin on the boat to Le Havre, but it smelled so strongly of brandy and camphor that I was happy to spend much of the voyage on the open deck. The journey downriver was uneventful enough, apart from the sight of the great number of vessels that seemed like a forest of masts slowly moving past, but I was much struck by the flat marshes of the estuary near the mouth of the Thames. The isolation and loneliness of this region (which, as a passenger told me, was shunned because of the ague), stirred my spirit. I think that even then I had some faint intimations of my future labours, and of the necessity for secret and silent work far beyond the haunts of men. Had I not begun that course in the fields outside Oxford? Yet as I sailed away from England, I did not foresee that I was destined to become the most wretched of human beings.

My journey took me overland by coach from Le Havre to Paris; from there I travelled on to Dijon, and so to Geneva. I was impatient to see my sister, but was obliged to change horses and rest overnight in Paris. I arrived in the early evening at an inn along the Rue St. Sulpice and, after the recent interdiction of travel between France and England, the proprietor was delighted to receive my English companions. He called together a small number of musicians, who played in the courtyard, while his wife and daughters danced a Polish mazurka before us. Such is the warmth of Gallic hospitality, about which so many libels are spread in neighbouring countries. I was to share my chamber with an Englishman travelling on business, Mr. Armitage. He was selling spectacles, lenses and such like. He was the one who had warned me of the ague upon the estuary, and he had already regaled me with several stories concerning the trade in optical goods before I decided to take the air.

I walked outside where my attention was drawn at once to a line of Parisians standing and shuffling their feet outside a pair of folding gates. Some were obviously poor, some affluent, and some of that mixed nature known to the English as shabby genteel. But their variety interested me. They stood nervously and uncertainly before the gates, speaking not at all and keeping their eyes averted from one another. I asked the proprietor, who was standing in the porch of the inn, what this signified. "Ah, *monsieur*, we do not talk of it." Why did they not speak of it? "It is bad fortune for the inn. *C'est la maison des morts. La Morgue.*"

The house of the dead? I believed I knew to what he was referring. It was an institution well known in the city, where the unidentified bodies of the dead were put on display at certain fixed points of the day so that they might be recognised by friends or relatives. There are no doubt some who consider it to be an unpleasing spectacle, but I was delighted by the good fortune that had put it in my way. I could see nothing to loathe in nature. Just as there are some who love to walk in ruins, savouring the traces and sensations of old time, so I saw no objection to walking among the dead and the decomposed. The human frame is in a continual state of decomposition, day by day; its tissues and its fibres wear away, even as we use them, and I saw nothing to be feared in the close observation of that process. If I were to be practised in the art and method of anatomy, I must also observe the natural corruption of the human body.

So I joined the waiting Parisians and, when the folding gates were unlocked by an official, I moved forward into the Morgue. I became at once aware of a peculiar and not unpleasing odour, much like that of damp umbrellas or of the wet straw generally to be found on the floor of a hansom cab. The air was humid, as if a coal fire had been introduced into the room. It was a long low chamber with small-paned windows, much like the interior of a London coffee-house. Where the seats and boxes might have been there were several shallow partitions, with sloping platforms fixed in them. On these the bodies of the dead had been placed, with their clothes hanging above them as a further means of identification. Each was protected from the inquisitive throng by a sheet of plate glass, just as if they were lying in the window of a shop. There were five on the occasion of my visit, three males and two females, and it was a nice calculation to determine the causes of their deaths. One middle-aged man, thickset with a heavy jaw and shaved head, appeared to have been burned; but the livid red bruising, and the swollen limbs, convinced me that he had been drowned. My guess was confirmed when I noticed the pool of water seeping below the body. The face of an adjacent female was almost unrecognisable, looking like nothing so much as a bunch of bruised and overripe grapes: I could fathom no reason for the savage pulping of her visage, unless it were some frightful accident. Yet she interested me. The rest of her body was quite untouched, apart from some streaks of blood and dirt, and it occurred to me that with a new head she might have been an object of lust. She could be identified now only by a lover, or perhaps by a parent.

I did not approach these sights with any levity, but I did not feel the least repulsion; my principal feeling was one of fascination for the curious stillness of the bodies. Once the principle of life had left them they became vacant rooms, more devoid of animation than any waxwork or mannequin. You could imagine a waxwork to be capable of breath and movement, but no act of sympathetic imagination could grant these cold limbs life. I was looking at objects that would never be able to return my look.

In another partition I found the body of an elderly man who

had no mark upon him at all. I could tell from his curled boots, placed beside him, that he was an artisan or labourer. There was a curious feature about him, however. I noticed a slight wetness about his eyes, and what seemed to be a tear had settled upon his cheek. The residue of emotion, on what was now an empty visage, affected me in the strangest way. I turned to leave, and was caught momentarily in the crowd clustering around. I glanced towards the open door, at the far end of the low room, and for a moment caught sight of an elderly man standing beside it. He seemed to be exactly the man I had just seen behind the glass, as if by some intervention of the black arts he had brushed away the tear and come alive. Then he smiled at me. I knew all this to be a momentary illusion, but it did not lessen my horror. I walked slowly towards the door, where the official of the Morgue held out his hand for a *pourboire*, but the figure of the old man had gone. I was relieved to find myself in the open air of the street, and tried to dismiss the incident from my mind, but it lingered with me even as I climbed the stair to the chamber in the inn.

My fellow traveller, Armitage, was lying on his bed fully clothed. Fresh as I was from the sights of the Morgue, for a moment he startled me. "Now, Mr. Frankenstein," he said. "Will you sup with me? The wine here is very cheap." He had a low, deep voice that for no reason at all irritated me.

"An early night for me, I am afraid. The coach for Dijon leaves at daybreak. It will be a hard journey."

"So you need sustenance." He was older than me, at the age of thirty or thereabouts, but he had an indefinably ancient manner. "You gentlemen of Oxford have been known to starve."

"How do you know that I am from Oxford?"

"It is printed on your luggage. Eyes, you see. Good eyes." I had already become aware that he was a salesman of optical goods. "The eye is a tender organism." He spoke slowly, and with great emphasis. "It swims in a sea of water."

"I beg your pardon. It does not."

"Oh?"

"It has roots and tendrils. It is like a trailing plant connected to the soil of the brain."

"Can we say that it is like a lily? It swims on the surface."

"You may say that, Mr. Armitage."

He smiled broadly, having settled the matter to his satisfaction, and clapped me on the back as if he were congratulating me for agreeing with him. "We must get you bread. And meat. And wine."

Over the rough meal, which the chambermaid brought to us, we exchanged the usual remarks. He lived in Friday Street, off Cheapside, with his father; his father manufactured the lenses and the spectacles, in a workshop on the ground floor of their property, while he acted as a commercial traveller. He had taken advantage of the peace to sail to France, with specimens of his father's latest work. "You will not find lenses more finely ground," he said. "You can pick out a distant spire by moonlight."

"Does he build microscopes?"

"Of course he does. At the moment he has in hand a design that has cylindrical eyes, so to speak, that will make the smallest object clear."

"I would be very interested in that."

"You would? What is your study at Oxford, Mr. Frankenstein?"

"I am concerned with the workings of human life."

"Is that all?" He smiled at me. I could not imagine him breaking into laughter.

"That is how I learned of the nervous fibres of the eye."

"You are an anatomist then?" He suddenly became very grave, as if I had trespassed upon some private pursuit.

"Not exactly. Not essentially. I cannot claim any great proficiency."

"Do you know how long the eye survives when it is released from its casing?"

"I have no idea. Minutes, perhaps—"

"Thirty-four seconds. Before its light is extinguished for ever."

"How do you know this?"

"They dry very quickly, when they have left the socket. Do not ask me how I know."

"But if they were kept in an aqueous solution, what then?"

"Then, Mr. Frankenstein, you would be considered to ask too much." He began to eat, very slowly, the meat and bread upon his plate.

I remembered the phrase from Terence. "Nothing human is alien to me, Mr. Armitage."

He did not answer but continued chewing on his meat. It was veal, as I remember, coated in breadcrumbs in the manner of my compatriots. I had very little appetite for it. Occasionally he would look up at me, with no particular expression in his eye beyond that of calm observation. Eventually he spoke. "My father had an interesting apprenticeship. From the age of fourteen he worked for Dr. John Hunter. Do you know that name?"

"Indeed. Very well." Hunter's reputation as a surgeon and anatomist had reached me even in Geneva, where his *Natural History of Teeth* had been translated into French.

"Dr. Hunter was a great observer of the body, Mr. Frankenstein. He made it his profession."

"So I have read."

"His surgical work was second to none. My father has known him to remove a bladder stone in less than three minutes."

"Truly?"

"And the patient did not die." Armitage concentrated once more upon his plate, where he was now very deliberately mopping up the crumbs with a portion of bread soaked in wine. "My father still has the stone."

"The patient did not want it?"

"No. Dr. Hunter called it treasure-trove."

"But what happened to the eyes?"

"I told you. The patient was still alive. Much to his surprise."

"Not his. The other eyes that were preserved in water. I presume that they were taken from the bodies of the less fortunate."

Armitage stared at me with the same curiously dispassionate gaze. "If the patient has died in the operating theatre, then to whom does he belong?" I said nothing, believing that I had already said too much. "Dr. Hunter took the view that, having been entrusted into his care, the body was his responsibility. It became, in a sense, his property."

"I would not disagree."

"Excellent. I am speaking to you now in the utmost harmony of good companionship. These facts are not widely known beyond the confines of the medical schools." My mouth had become dry, and I swallowed a glassful of the wine. "Dr. Hunter believed that the limbs and organs of the deceased patient were of more value to his students than to the soil in which they would otherwise lie. There was a young man, one of Dr. Hunter's assistants, who had a particular interest in the spleen. So—" Armitage stopped, and surprised me with a broad smile. "As we say in Cheapside, Mr. Frankenstein, it passed under the counter."

"And your father had a particular interest in eyes?"

"He had always possessed perfect eyesight. It was remarked of him at a very early age. He became interested in the subject, as boys do. I do not know if you have in your country the travelling telescope?" I shook my head. "They are set up in the thoroughfare, and for a small sum you can purchase their use for five minutes. There was always one in the Strand. As a boy, my father loved it. So by degrees he became interested in the relationship between the lens and the eye. Do you know that the eye has its own lens, as permeable as a gas bubble?"

"I was aware of it."

"It is covered by an exceedingly thin and fine film of transparent substance that my father has named the orb tissue."

"Your father is an experimentalist, then?"

"I do not know if that is the word, Mr. Frankenstein." Armitage poured us both another glass of wine. "I will tell you another secret. There were occasions when the patient did not die, of course. That was a source of great satisfaction to Dr. Hunter. But it posed another problem."

"Of what nature?"

"Scarcity, sir."

"I believe I understand you. Scarcity of corpses. The readies."

"It is not a subject that normally arises in conversation. But it was a constant topic among Dr. Hunter and his assistants."

"How did it resolve itself?"

"You have heard of the resurrectionists, I suppose?"

"Only by report."

"They are not much mentioned in the public prints these days. But they operate still."

I was acquainted with the activities of these grave-robbers, or "resurrection men" as they were more generally known. There had been occasional reports of their activity even in Oxford, but there had been no sensations. They were more active in London, where they dug up the fresh bodies of the lately dead and sold them for large sums to the medical schools.

"Dr. Hunter was obliged to use their services?"

Armitage nodded. "Reluctantly. He told my father that if these purloined bodies helped to restore life to others, then he could not wholly regret their use."

"Life for death is a good bargain."

"You would be welcome on Cheapside, Mr. Frankenstein. My father agreed with you, and helped to negotiate with the men of the resurrectionist profession. He came to know them very well. He said that not one of them was ever sober."

"You say that they work still?"

"Of course. It is a family trade. They frequent certain inns, where they can be persuaded to—" He raised his hand to his lips, in a gesture of drinking. "Unfortunately there was a trial of one of them, for the theft of a silver crucifix from one of the bodies. He blabbed out the name of Dr. Hunter."

"And then?"

"It passed over quickly enough. But there was a pamphlet with his name linked to the vampire. You have heard of this entity, Mr. Frankenstein?"

"It is a Magyar superstition. Of no interest."

"I am glad to hear it. It concerned Dr. Hunter at the time, but his work carried him forward."

"His work was his life."

"Yes, indeed. You are very perceptive, if I may say so." He took some more wine. "You said that you were studying the workings of human life. May I ask what particular aspect interests you?"

I believe that I hesitated for a moment. "I am concerned with the structure of all animals endued with life."

"To what purpose?"

"I mean to discover the source of that life."

"But this would include the human frame?"

"I am determined to proceed by degrees, Mr. Armitage."

"In such a vast undertaking, that is proper. I believe that only a young man could conceive such a scheme. It is tremendous. I would very much like to introduce you to my father."

"Certainly. I would like to see his eyes."

He laughed aloud at this, and clapped me upon the back again as if I were the best fellow in the world. "And so you shall. But beware. His look is very keen."

⇒ Six ⇐

BY THE TIME I ARRIVED IN GENEVA I was sore and weary; the
journey across France had been a difficult one, made infinitely
more uncomfortable by the heavy rain that started as soon as
the coach had left Paris. Only my eagerness to see my sister kept
up my spirits. My father's house was in the Rue de Purgatoire,
just below the cathedral; he had purchased it many years
previously, for his business dealings in the city, and I knew the
neighbourhood very well. A local boy acted as my porter, and I
hurried ahead through the familiar steep streets above the lake.

I was met by a house of silence. Eventually, after my repeated
knocking, a young maidservant came to the door. I did not
recognise her, and the slow-witted girl did not seem to know
that there was such a thing as the son of the household. By dint
of my long explanations, in her native dialect, reluctantly she
allowed me to enter the house. Perhaps she discerned some
resemblance between myself and Elizabeth. I learned from her
that my sister was staying in a sanatorium in Versoix, a small
town by the shore of the lake, and that my father had taken a
villa there to be near her. It was too late to think of travelling
and, in my exhaustion, I chose a bedchamber almost at random
before sinking into a profound sleep.

The next morning I set out on foot to Versoix. It was no more
than two or three miles along the shore, and I took advantage

of the fine weather to savour my return to my native land. It was pleasant to recall the quietness and good nature of my countrymen, especially after the surliness of the English, and of course the landscape of the mountains was infinitely superior to that of Oxford where the vaporous Thames and Cherwell are the only distinctive features. I was reflecting on these matters when, within the hour, I had reached my destination.

Versoix rests above the lake on a small natural plateau, and the grounds of the sanatorium stretch down to the water; it has always been a health-giving spot, and there have been found here the remains of a Roman shrine to Mercury. The local people believe that the god still lingers, but I ascribe the vital fullness of the air to the electrical discharges from the mountains. The atmosphere of the region is full of spirit.

I made my way to the gates of the sanatorium, where I gained admission on the strength of my name: the honour of the family of Frankenstein is widely known. I had never entered such an institution before, and indeed I believe this to have been one of the first of its kind erected according to enlightened principles of public health. I was taken to my sister's room, which proving empty, I was directed towards the shores of the lake. I was told that it was here that Elizabeth liked to sit and sew.

I hardly recognised her. She had become so gaunt and thin that she seemed too weak to rise and greet me. "I am pleased to see you, Victor. I had hoped you would come." There was such resignation, in her slowness and uncertainty, that I might have wept. Her voice, too, had changed; it had become higher and more plaintive.

"How could I not come? I left as soon as I heard from Papa."

"Papa worries too much."

"He is concerned."

She smiled so serenely that it might have been an expression of defeat. "I often thought of you in England. You seemed so far—"

I went up to her, and kissed her on the forehead. "But now you are home." Once more she tried to rise from her bench.

"Sit, Elizabeth. Do not tire yourself."

"I am always tired. I am accustomed to it. Is this not a beautiful place?" We were beside the lake, on a small peninsula of grass and trees; one of the frequent winds had stirred, and the surface of the water was troubled. I took her shawl, which she had placed beside her on the wicker bench, and covered her shoulders. "I enjoy the wind, Victor. It makes me feel that I am part of the world." Her eyes had grown more prominent, in her sickness; she seemed to look at me with a new quality of intentness.

"What are you sewing?"

"It is for you. A Geneva purse." This was the name given to the small, elaborately tapestried purses that the merchants of the region employed. "I am stitching the image of Papa into it. It will be a keepsake for you during your travels."

"I would prefer to keep an image of you, Elizabeth."

"Oh, I am not as I was." She looked over the lake towards the mountains. "At least I will not grow old."

"Please do not say—"

She looked at me again intently. In her emaciated face I thought I could see some vision of the old age she would not reach. "I am not afraid of the truth, Victor. My sun is low in the sky. I know it."

"You will recover here. They have remedies for your malady."

"It is called consumption of the lungs. It is a good word. I am being consumed." I was about to say some word of consolation, but she put up her hand. "No. I am prepared for it. I count it the greatest good fortune that I can sit here beside our beloved lake. You know it speaks to me?" She had a sudden bout of coughing, anguished and prolonged. I wanted to take her in my arms and comfort her, but I believe that she did not wish for consolation. "It is cheerful enough. It reminds me of all the happiness I have known. It tells me of your great adventures in England."

"What else?"

"It speaks to me of peace."

"Elizabeth." I bowed my head.

"No need for tears, Victor. I am quite happy. Sometimes I sit here at night—"

"Do the doctors permit it?"

"I slip away. They allow us to sleep undisturbed, and I always return before the break of day. So I sit here in the darkness and look over the water. Some of the boats carry oil-lamps, and at night they are like little pieces of glowing fire floating before me. It is very exhilarating. I often think death must be like that—gazing at distant lights. Oh, here comes Papa."

Our father was walking over the lawn towards us. He was formally dressed, with a dark green frock-coat and cravat, but his rapid stride suggested his unease. "Victor, you should have called upon me."

"I arrived in Geneva late last night, Papa. There was no time. Did you not get the letter I sent from Oxford?"

"I have received nothing." I knew that he was greatly

agitated by the sight of Elizabeth: it was clear to me that her condition was declining day by day. "I have not been attending to business in Geneva. Have you eaten today, Elizabeth?"

"Some bread steeped in milk, Papa."

"You must eat." He put his hands upon her head, as if he were trying to bestow some blessing upon her. "You must grow stronger. Did you sleep well?"

"Of course."

"Good. Food and rest. Food and rest." He bent down, and rearranged the shawl around her shoulders. "The wind comes directly from the mountains, Elizabeth. May I suggest that you return to your room?"

"The doctors extol the advantages of the open air, Papa."

"That is all very well. But do you see them sitting by the lake? I feel the chill myself. Victor, help me with your sister."

"I am quite able to walk, Papa."

"Of course you are, Elizabeth. We will walk beside you. Victor, will you take your sister's arm?" When she rose from the wicker bench, I realised that she was very frail; she seemed to sway slightly in the wind, and for a moment I thought that she had lost her balance. She leaned against me and laughed: it was as if she were laughing at her own incapacity.

There was a slight incline towards the sanatorium, and she grasped my arm as we slowly climbed the gravel path that led away from the lake. Our father walked on the grass beside us, his head lowered in contemplation, but when we reached the door of the building he went ahead of us. He told me afterwards that he had wished to speak to one of Elizabeth's doctors, away from her presence; and so I escorted her back to her room.

"Papa is very sad," she said. "I rely upon you to comfort him."

"How should I do that?"

"I am not sure."

"I cannot stay here, Elizabeth. I cannot live in Geneva."

"I know that. This is no place for you. You have always been fired by ambition."

"I cannot apologise for that."

"I expect no such thing. It is laudable. I have always been proud of you, Victor. I have watched you with admiration ever since you were a small boy. Do you remember how you showed me the chicken's life in the hen's egg? You had observed it. You made yourself the master of anything you wished to know." Elizabeth became more animated as she spoke, as if she were reliving the days before her illness. "You pestered people with questions for which they had no answers. Why did clouds change their shape? Why did the cut worm divide into two lives? Why did the leaves change colour in the autumn?" She broke off. "Excel in your studies, Victor. Become a great personage."

Papa came into the room with a young man who greeted Elizabeth in the most informal manner possible. I took him to be one of her doctors, but I did not like him. "Elizabeth," he said, "is the most patient subject. She has been cupped and blistered without the least complaint."

"I am glad to hear it," Papa replied. "And she is eating well?"

"She keeps up her strength. We have nothing but the highest hopes."

This seemed to me to be a little piece of theatre contrived for

Elizabeth's sake, but her expression of weariness convinced me that she had not been impressed by it. "I think we should leave you now," I said. "You are tired."

"Yes," Papa said. "She must rest. Rest is the cure."

"May I admit to being tired?" She glanced at the doctor, who had been observing her keenly.

"Of course. Don't forget there is a recital on the pianoforte before supper. We will be listening to Mozart."

"I do not like to listen to music any more."

My father embraced her before we left, once more urging her to eat well and to sleep. I doubted that she would obey his instructions. She was too far out of the world to care for such things. As soon as we had left her, his eyes filled with tears. I had never seen him cry before. "She cannot live," he said. "The doctor knows it."

"Surely there is some hope?"

"None whatever. The doctors have said that there can be no remission. The consumption has taken over her lungs."

"But doctors can be mistaken."

"Did you hear her breathing? The doctor told me that last night her mouth was filled with arterial blood."

"What shall we do?"

"We shall wait. What else is there to do?"

"The sun will no longer warm her."

"What was that?" I had spoken too softly for him to hear me. "This is a hard time, Papa."

"It will become harder. We must cherish your sister."

⇒ ⇐

ELIZABETH'S DEATH OCCURRED two days later. She was found in the morning, sitting in a chair by her bed. It was said that she had suffered no pain, but how that was determined I do not know. My father insisted that she be buried in the little graveyard at Chamonix, the village where the family house was situated. So Elizabeth was placed in a lead coffin, and together with her we travelled on the winding road out of Geneva towards the mountains. I do not need to state that this was a melancholy journey. All I recall of it now was the scent of sweet logs burning that accompanied us for part of the way.

When we reached our old home, I longed to see once more the pure whiteness of the snow, which no one on earth had touched. From the window of my room I could see Mont Blanc, and the summit known to us as l'Aguille du Midi; the snow upon the upper reaches was brilliantly illuminated by the sun, while the rest of the mountain was still caught in shadow with the grey snow and the slopes of the trees cascading into the valley. There was nothing there to limit the range of the gaze. I could see pockets of stone which no light had ever reached, the paths of rivers that would never flow, the rocks hewn into strange shapes by forces I could not fathom, all draped in eternal quiet. It was the quiet that Elizabeth had now entered. But then loud birdsong called me back to earth.

In the evening before the funeral the storm came. Thick clouds covered the mountains, and obscured their summits with lowering grey mist. Small patches of sunlight touched the ground and, when the wind stirred, the leaves of the trees quivered like violins. When the lightning hit the mountainside, it was like a rod beating the ground. The fire came from various regions of the sky; the thunder changed direction, too, and seemed to be travelling beneath the mountains. Then no mountains were visible. The air was heavy with expectation, with the perfume of the lightning upon it. But I saw, on the grass commons, a young girl playing with two small dogs. I wished Elizabeth back again then, to see this with me. If I could bring her alive again, I would! My unspoken thought chimed with the lightning flash in a moment of identity.

❧

WHEN THE BELLS OF THE LITTLE CHURCH at Chamonix rang, as she was laid within the soil, they seemed to reverberate among the rocks and snow. I was once more filled with a sensation of childhood—that, somehow, the bells were inside the mountain pealing through its depths.

After the funeral, which was attended by most of the villagers of Chamonix, I could not rest. I could not stay still. And so I returned to the mountains. I began climbing upwards through the forests of fir trees that flanked the lower reaches, struggling to keep my foothold among the rocks and roots that continually impeded my ascent; there were small streams here, too, falling precipitately from the glaciers on the upper reaches, but eventually I found the winding track used by the peasants of the region. I wanted to climb higher and still higher, to stand upon l'Aiguille du Midi. I could hear the cry of a marmotte somewhere close by, and in its piercing call I realised the loneliness of my position. If I fell here, and died, my body would soon be covered in ice and snow; it might endure for many generations as a relic of my time, as the modern experiments in freezing suggest that it would not decompose.

The air was thinner here, and I could sense the blood

pulsing through my body. It was a glorious sensation, to feel the force of life, but in this vast solitude with the currents of the world circling about me it also induced a feeling akin to terror— to be aware of the power of existence, and at the same time to understand its frailty. I lay down on the frozen earth but I had no sensation of cold. I called out to the marmotte with an imitation of its cry. The creature responded with a more plaintive note, as if he were unsure of the greeting. I called again, with the utmost certainty that all life is one, and the marmotte replied with a thrilling sound of recognition.

⇒ ⇐

AFTER THE DEATH OF ELIZABETH my father seemed to weary of his own life; he grew old very rapidly, and took no more interest in the export business he had created over many years. He refused to go back to Geneva, and locked himself away in his study at Chamonix where he sat from dawn to twilight looking out of the window at the mountains. He joined me at dinner in the evenings, but there was little conversation. There were times, however, when he spoke from a full and overburdened heart. "You are a student of the sciences," he said to me one evening. "Can you tell me why the meanest creature possesses life, and Elizabeth has no life at all?"

"It is not a perpetual gift, Father."

"This moth," he said, "is filled with life. Do you see how it circles around the candle flame? Do you believe that it enjoys its existence?"

"It seems to dance, Father. All living creatures must exert their energy."

"Yet this life, this enjoyment, cannot last."

"The moth does not know of death."

"So it believes itself to be immortal?"

"The concept of immortality does not occur. It is. That is enough. It does not live in time."

"This power of existence that it possesses—could it be found?"

"What do you mean?"

"Is there some essence, some vital spark?"

"That is not a question I can answer, Father. It has been the subject of much debate, but with no very satisfactory conclusion."

"So we do not know what life is."

"It cannot be defined. No."

"What is the use of all your sciences and studies if the essential thing is not understood?"

"We can only proceed from the known to the unknown."

"But when the unknown is so great—"

"It excites my efforts even more, Father." The moth was still fluttering around the candle, and I caught it in my cupped hands; I could feel its pale wings beating against the skin of my palms, and I experienced a sensation of sudden elation. "I am in pursuit of that spirit of life."

"And what do your professors at Oxford think of it?"

"Oh, they do not know of it." Instantly I regretted my quick reply.

"It is a secret pursuit, then?"

"Not secret. Many other men are engaged upon it. We work independently towards the same goal."

"This is a good century in which to live, is it?"

"Of course." I opened my hands, and the moth fluttered

uncertainly into the dusky air. "There will be great discoveries. We will uncover the secrets of the electrical fluid. We will build great cathedrals of voltaic batteries so that we can re-create the lightning."

"And create life?"

"Who knows? Who can tell? It may come too late for me."

"You have always been very determined, Victor. I believe that you will always succeed in whatever task you set for yourself. What do you wish for?"

"I wish to bring Elizabeth back into life."

He bowed his head, but he was alerted suddenly by a faint rumble in the mountains behind us. "Avalanche," he said. "Now if you could master those, Victor, you would be celebrated." And then he sighed.

≫ ≪

A FEW WEEKS AFTER THE FUNERAL he contracted influenza, and weakened daily. It was a lesson to me in the governance of the body by the mind. The life force was mental and spiritual as well as physical, and as soon as my father despaired of life his vital powers began to fail. He would not take to his bed but remained in the armchair in his study. He had such an affection for his books that I believe he did not want to leave them. He never spoke of the business that he had entrusted to his confidential clerk, M. Fabre. Indeed, he never spoke of anything coherently or for very long. "Use the money to advantage," he said to me one evening, at a time when I believed him to be asleep. "Use it for good." I was his sole heir, and quite aware of the financial responsibilities that would devolve upon me.

"Whatever is human, you can accomplish." Then he lapsed back into silence.

I was sitting beside him when he died. I had been reading to him from Goethe's *The Sorrows of Young Werther*, a novel which I had always intended to study with all the more enthusiasm since it had been extolled to me by Bysshe. My father had an excellent knowledge of German, but I am not sure that he understood or was even listening to my words; I simply wished to reassure him of my presence. Suddenly he opened his eyes. "It is not that Werther loved too much," he said. "He lived too long." And then he slipped away.

I had expected some change at the moment of death, some sense of departure, but not of the kind I witnessed. It was as if his life had never been; it was as if he had reverted to some previous state, before life had infused him. He had gone back. I felt his pulse, and the side of his neck, but all had gone.

⟶ ⟵

SO ANOTHER FRANKENSTEIN WAS BURIED in the hill behind the little church at Chamonix; I was the only mourner of my immediate family, but I was followed to the grave by the servants of the household as well as the employees of my father's business and by the same villagers who had attended Elizabeth's funeral. I wept freely—but perhaps I was weeping for myself.

I remained in Switzerland for two months, during which period I put my affairs in order and relinquished the administration of the company to M. Fabre who had always been trusted by my father. I had written to the Master of my college in Oxford, explaining the reasons for my delay and asking him for leave of absence until the following term; this was permitted, under the statutes, and I looked forward to returning to my studies with redoubled zeal and ambition. I was now the heir to a large fortune, which I could employ without check or scrutiny, and I had already determined to devote it to my pursuits in the science of life.

I was happy to return for other reasons. I had heard nothing of Bysshe for several months, and I was eager to learn of all his exploits in London. Now I contemplated the notion of renting a commodious house in the city, where he and I could live in close intercourse. I had other schemes, drawn up in my mind's eye with as much fidelity as if I sat with an architect beside me. I planned to create a great laboratory, where I could engage in experiments on the largest possible scale. I wished to build a "gallery of life" where all the emerging forms of primitive existence could be displayed. In truth, I wished to become a benefactor of mankind. So, in the early autumn of that eventful year, I returned with enthusiasm and anticipation to England. I believed that in London a man with sovereigns in his pocket is master of his destiny. In this, however, I was to be proved mistaken.

⇒ Seven ⇐

WHEN I ARRIVED IN LONDON I rented rooms in Jermyn Street, but took the precaution of having my heavy luggage sent before me to Oxford. I had scarcely swallowed down a plate of beef, in the chop-house next to St. James's church, when I made my way to Poland Street. The windows of Bysshe's old lodging were closed, and so I mounted the stairs and rapped upon the door with the ivory cane I had brought with me from Switzerland. A young woman came to the door, nursing a small infant. I was at a loss for words in that instant, and simply stared at her.

"Yes, sir?"

"Mr. Shelley?"

"I beg your pardon?"

"Is Mr. Shelley here?"

"No one of that name."

"Percy Bysshe Shelley?"

"No, sir. John Donaldson. His wife, Amelia, which is me. And this is Arthur." She patted the baby with her free hand.

I must say that I experienced a moment of relief. "Forgive me, Mrs. Donaldson. May I ask if you have lived here long?"

"We came early in the summer, sir. We are from Devon."

"There was a young man here before you, I believe. He is a friend of mine—"

"Oh. The young party. I did hear something of him from

Mr. Lawson above us. A strange party. Very volatile. Is that so?" I nodded. "He vanished, sir. He left one morning. Never seen again. Now you are here—" She retreated into the rooms which I knew so well, and presently returned with a small volume. "If you were to find him, would you give him this?" She handed me the book that I recognised as a copy of *Lyrical Ballads*. He had often read from it, during our evening conversations. "I found it beneath the settle. It must have fallen. Mr. Donaldson and I have no use for it, sir."

I gave her a sovereign, which she accepted with many expressions of delight. I considered calling upon Daniel Westbrook in Whitechapel for news of Bysshe. Yet the memory of that neighbourhood, dark and dim, dissuaded me. Instead I determined to return to Oxford, where Bysshe might find me if he so wished. I retained my chambers in Jermyn Street, however, as a refuge from the quiet life of the university.

➤✦

FLORENCE, MY COLLEGE SERVANT, greeted me at the top of the staircase with an expression of surprise. "Well, Mr. Frankenlime, we was despairing of you."

"Never despair, Florence."

"Then the head porter tells us you was coming back. So I gave them a good clean." She motioned towards my rooms. "You will find them in a state of perfection."

"I am pleased to hear it." I walked past her and, on opening the door, was relieved to see my luggage piled high in a corner.

So I entered once more the diurnal round of divine service, college meals, and college friendships. Such was the nature of the place that, as soon as I had settled myself in my rooms, I felt a resurgence of my old life. I sought out the company of Horace Lang, who had known Bysshe before my own arrival at Oxford; together we walked by the Thames towards Binsey, or towards Godstow, and speculated about our poet. Lang had heard nothing from him since Bysshe's forced departure from the college, and so I enlightened him about the radical meetings in London. It was with a feeling of some excitement, then, that we learned of the imminent arrival of Mr. Coleridge as a lecturer in the Welsh Hall in Cornmarket Street. His poetry was already known to me, of course, partly through *Lyrical Ballads* and partly through my own earnest enquiries into the political and economic science of the day. Ever since I had begun reading his essays in the *Friend*, I had entertained a vast respect for his intellectual powers no less than for his mental agility that seemed to surmount every challenge.

The series of lectures he was about to undertake was entitled "The Course of English Poetry," and on the evening of the first lecture the Welsh Hall was packed to suffocation with the young men of the university. When Mr. Coleridge walked upon the platform he seemed unwell; he had a hectic flush upon his cheeks but otherwise his complexion was pale. He appeared older than I had imagined, unless his hair were preternaturally white, and his hands shook as he approached the rostrum. He was by no means ill favoured, having the open visage of a child, but there was an indefinable languor about him that suggested sloth or lack of will.

"Gentlemen," he said, taking some papers from the pocket of his jacket, "you must forgive my frailty. I have recently returned from a long journey, during which my health has suffered. But I pray and hope that the mind is untouched by the tortures of the body." At this the audience hurrahed and, given the generosity of the reception, Coleridge seemed to be eased. He began talking from his notes on the roots of English poetry in the Anglo-Saxon bards, but it was laboured stuff. He had no real enthusiasm for these subjects. Sensing the restlessness of his audience, I think, he laid aside his papers and began to speak warmly and spontaneously about the genius of the language itself. He had an inspired eye, if I may put it that way, and seemed able to catch sight of phrases and sentences before he uttered them. He spoke of language possessing an organic rather than a mechanical form; he extolled its active agency, as an instrument of the imagination, and declared that "man creates the world in which he lives." I noted down one sentiment in particular that interested me immensely. "Newton," he said, "claimed that his theories were created by experiment and observation. Not so. They were created by his mind and imagination." Coleridge no longer seemed weary, and in the fire of his utterance his countenance had become ennobled; he spoke very freely, with a sibilance that was strangely appealing, and he used his gestures to great effect. "Under the impress of the imagination," he went on, "nature is instinct with passion and with change. It is altered—it is moved—by human perception." In what sense did he mean "moved"? Did it simply denote change, or could it be construed as the sensation of pity or of joy?

I believe that these sentiments were quite novel to the audience assembled in the Welsh Hall, and they listened with keen anticipation. Coleridge seemed to be exalted by their attention, and I noticed that the hectic flush upon his cheeks had been succeeded by a radiance of—I know not what—of belief, of self-belief. "All knowledge," he said, "rests on the coincidence of a subject with an object in living unity. We must discover the in-dwelling and living ground of all things. In that procedure, we may render the mind intuitive of the spiritual."

I was greatly encouraged by his words, since I pursued my own researches with the firm conviction that all life was one and that the same spirit of existence breathed through all created forms. These were almost the very words that Coleridge himself then used, when he stepped towards us from behind the rostrum, and declared that "everything has a life of its own, and we are all *one life*." There was some scattered applause at this, although his sentiments were so far from the usual that many could not follow their path or, rather, their ascent. I had never seen a man so transformed by the power of utterance, so that it would not have seemed to me at all surprising if he had ascended to the ceiling in an act of apotheosis. He spoke eloquently of Shakespeare, and of the dramatist's words bringing the whole soul of man into activity, and then proceeded with an improvised celebration of the imagination itself. I wished that Bysshe had been with me at this hour. "The primary imagination," Coleridge said, "I hold to be the living power and prime agent of all human perception, and as a representation in the finite mind of the eternal act of creation." So men could become like gods. Was that his meaning? What can be imagined, can be formed into the image of truth. The vision could be created.

I walked back to my rooms in a state of great excitement, while explaining to Lang the importance of Coleridge's lecture.

"Do you mean to say," he asked me, "that you are willing to test your wildest fantasies?"

"The imagination is the strongest possible power. Do you not recall that Adam dreamed, and that when he awoke he found it truth?"

"In the same narrative, Victor, there is a warning against the fruit of the Tree of Knowledge."

"Are we to be prevented from reaching up to the branch? Surely not."

"I am a mere student of theology."

"Where there is nothing more to learn?"

"The ways of God are infinite. But I do not share your—"

"Ambition?"

"Craving. Your fierce desire to explore unknown ways. You have spoken to me of the forbidden knowledge of the adepts. Of the ancient conjurors."

"Not conjurors. Philosophers. Men of science."

"Of the *secreta secretorum* of their arts. And I must say that I have been alarmed."

"My dear Lang, there are people alarmed by Faraday and by Mesmer. All new forms of thought and practice provoke disquiet. What did Coleridge just say to us? Under the force of the imagination, nature itself is changed. Faraday has awakened dead limbs with his electrical fluid. Mesmer has relieved suffering invalids of all pain. Is that not an alteration in nature's laws?"

"It cannot lead to good."

"Is the passage from death to life not good? Is the alleviation of pain not good? Come now. You must think like a man, Horace, not like a theologian."

We fell into silence, my companion uttering a subdued farewell as we parted from each other in the quad, but I climbed my staircase with a light heart. Coleridge's valedictory words, on the shaping role of the imagination, had aroused my enthusiasm to such a pitch that I could think of nothing else. I mixed myself a hot collation of rum and milk, a legacy from my days in Chamonix, and then retired to bed with a fixed determination to rise early and to pitch myself into my studies.

When I placed my head on the pillow, however, I did not sleep; nor could I be said to think of anything in particular. My mind was like a canvas on which a succession of images passed. Once, when I had been ill of a fever in Chamonix, the same sensation had possessed me; it was as if my imagination had become my guide, leading me forward in a direction over which I had no possible control. As I lay in my bed in Oxford I saw Elizabeth, as she would have been had she still been in life; there were pictures of my father climbing steadily, along the side of a vast glacier that threatened to overwhelm him; there were pictures of Bysshe, fleeing across an open plain with a girl in his arms. And then, most tremendous of all, I saw myself kneeling by the bed of some gigantic shadowy form. This bed was my bed, and the shape was stretched out upon it. Yet I could not be sure of its nature. Then it began to show signs of life, and to stir with an uneasy, half-vital motion.

I must have lapsed into sleep, for I can then only recall a sequence of sounds like some roll of drums in the prelude to an opera. I heard a gate creaking upon its hinges and then swinging back, a number of heavy steps, a key turning and then a door opening. I opened my eyes in terror, to find Florence entering the room. "You will miss the service, Mr. Frankenstone," she was saying. "You must rouse yourself."

Never had I washed and dressed myself with such relief, to

find the phantasms of the night quite dispersed. I rushed down into chapel, where I saw Lang blinking and yawning as if he had not slept at all. I was about to join him in hall for breakfast, after the service, when the porter brought over to me a note. "This has been left for you, sir," he said. "Just this morning."

There was a message scrawled in pencil on a small sheet of paper torn from a notebook: *May I see you? I am by the bridge at the end of the street.* It was signed by Daniel Westbrook.

⇒ ⇐

I HURRIED DOWN THE HIGH STREET to Magdalen Bridge. He was waiting for me on the parapet, looking down at the green ooze of the Cherwell. "Thank goodness you are here," he said as soon as he saw me hastening towards him. "Good day to you, Mr. Frankenstein."

"Good morning, Daniel. I hardly expected to see you in Oxford."

"I travelled on the overnight coach. You are the only one I know—"

"What has happened?"

"Harriet has vanished."

"What?"

"We believe that she has eloped with Mr. Shelley. There is no sign of either of them. Mr. Frankenstein, they are not married!"

"Pause a moment. Go back. How do you know that she has gone?"

"All her possessions have been taken away, including her precious books. Of course I went immediately to Mr. Shelley's rooms."

"Where are these rooms?"

"In Aldgate. He moved there to be closer to us. But he had gone. His landlady said that he had entered a carriage with a young woman, and that he had taken his portmanteau with him. Her description was that of Harriet. They have fled, Mr. Frankenstein. My father is in a weakened state. My sisters are dreadfully upset. What shall we do? My first thought was of you."

"We shall stay very calm. No progress will be made in a state of excitement." I took his arm, and we walked back towards my college. "You will have some tea with me, and revive yourself. Look how cold you are."

"I was sitting outside during the journey. The wind was very fresh."

"Come back to my rooms then. We will make our plans."

⇒ ⇐

WHEN WE WERE SETTLED, and the kettle warming by the hearth, Daniel explained the course of events since my departure for Switzerland four months before. Bysshe had continued to tutor Harriet, in his rooms at Poland Street, and within a few weeks there had grown up a friendship between them. That is when he had moved to Aldgate, so that she could have further lessons with him without the inconvenience of travelling across London. Harriet had no chaperone, of course, since her sisters were obliged to work; but there had been no sign of any intimacy. "Harriet would repeat to me what she had learned each day," Daniel said. "Mr. Shelley had introduced her to the Greek poets and philosophers, but he had also acquainted her with what he called the new spirit. He read to her from the Lake poets and, in her words, guided her through wild and magical

91

landscapes. I really do believe, Mr. Frankenstein, that she was a changed person. I had never seen her so animated, so bold."

"And then?"

"I had not the slightest suspicion, as I said, of any connection other than that of teacher and pupil. I would not have dreamed of anything else. The gulf between them was too wide. Mr. Shelley is the son of a baronet whereas Harriet—well—she is merely the daughter of Mr. Westbrook."

"There must have been an occasion—"

"No. Never. Not until she had fled."

I rose, and went over to the window. "He is hardly likely to have come to Oxford. Of all places on earth, this is the one he most detests. He could not have returned to his father. That would be unthinkable. Did you enquire at the principal coach offices?"

"I went to Snow Hill and Aldersgate. They had not been seen. I even walked out to Knightsbridge, in case they had tried to avoid pursuit, but there had been no sign of them."

"They may have gone to some other part of London."

"In which case, we are lost."

"This is what I will do. I will write to him, and address the letter to his father's house. He will not have gone there, but he may have sent a message. It is the only possible means of reaching him. You must return to London, Daniel, in case your sister tries to communicate with you. Try the other coaches."

"There is an office in Bishopsgate. And in the Tottenham Court Road. What was he thinking? Harriet is still young—"

"Be cheerful. I do not believe that Bysshe is guilty of any dishonourable action."

I HAD RETAINED MY FAITH in Bysshe and that evening, after Daniel had gone back to London, I began a letter to him in which I wrote broadly of my own affairs. It was possible that it might be opened and read by his father, for whom he professed the most invincible dislike, and so I refrained from mentioning his removal from Oxford and his attachment to Harriet Westbrook. Instead I told him of my journey to Geneva, of the death of my sister and my father, and ended with an appeal to him for news of his own travels over the past months.

Yet I had no need to send it. The following afternoon a letter was delivered by the London carrier. It was from Bysshe, announcing in the most abrupt fashion that he had taken Harriet from Whitechapel for the simple reason that her father "was persecuting her in the most horrible way" and was about to force her return to the spice factory. She had spoken of suicide, and had clamoured for Bysshe's "protection." That was his word. He had felt obliged to rescue her in her distress, and to take her beyond the reach of her father's anger. In a hurried postscript he asked me for funds. It seems that his detested father had stopped his allowance, and he had scarcely the means to live.

Bysshe had inscribed his address at the end of the letter—a house in Queen's Square—and at once I wrote back, offering him the use of my rooms in Jermyn Street and enclosing a note for the payment of fifty guineas at Coutts. I also urged him to communicate with Daniel Westbrook, and explain the circumstances of his sister's sudden departure. I had no doubt that

Bysshe's intentions were as honourable as he described them. He was, in a sense, my mentor. So I experienced the noble sense of a duty well performed, and secretly congratulated myself on my liberality to my friend.

Imagine my surprise and horror, therefore, when three days later I received a further letter from London. It came from Daniel Westbrook, who had received a note from Bysshe. He was now writing to inform me, as he put it, that Mr. Shelley and Harriet had absconded to Edinburgh, with the help of the money I had given them, where they intended to be married.

My bewilderment was followed by anger. I believed that Bysshe had betrayed my trust, not only in asking money for such a purpose but also in concocting the story of Harriet's despair. He had lied to me under the most shameful circumstances.

I took the letter Bysshe had sent to me, and tore off a small piece of it. I put it in my mouth and swallowed it. Systematically I reduced the paper to shreds, and devoured every one of them.

⇒ Eight ⇐

I HAD ALREADY RETURNED TO MY EXPERIMENTS with renewed enthusiasm after the long absence from my studies. My anger at Bysshe prompted me to work ever more arduously, and to shun all human company so that I could lose myself in my pursuits. I felt myself to be truly alone, having been so signally betrayed by one whom I looked upon as friend and companion. I purchased electrical apparatus from a manufacturer in Mill Street, but I soon realised that the scale of his work was not sufficient. I had made some advances. I had acquainted myself with the coroner of Oxford, a former student of my college. I explained to him that my studies required the use of human specimens, and after some reflection on the matter he agreed to help me in the cause of the advancement of science. He was himself an explorer of natural phenomena, having become interested in geological speculation and the structure of the earth, and so he sympathised with my desire to seek out the sources of life in the human frame. I promised to bring him some Alpine rocks after my next visit to Geneva.

I still used the barn in Headington for my experiments and, in the quiet of the evening, the coroner's two servants would bring me the corpses—or, on occasions, the parts of the corpses—which the coroner had viewed that day. They waited while I worked on them through the night, and then returned them to the coroner's office in Clarendon Street. I paid them liberally—a guinea each—for every visit. I do believe that the English will do anything for money.

I made some startling discoveries in the course of this work. I found a method of passing electricity through the entire human frame so that it seemed to tremble and to quiver. I was also able to transmit an electrical current through the spine of one child that prompted the eyes to open and the mouth to part. I had hoped for some sounds to be manifested by the vocal cords, but in that I was disappointed. Mr. Franklin had already suggested that electricity might be used to revive the heart, in patients just expired, and I had no reason to doubt him. Green shoots can spring from a blasted tree. I remembered the case in Geneva, some years before, when a young girl was pronounced dead after falling from a first-storey window; yet she had been restored to life by the use of the electrical vessel known as the Leyden jar.

The subjects sent to me by the coroner were generally too long gone for any hope of revival, although I nurtured a strange and wild hope when I was presented with an infant lately drowned in the Thames. I had read of drowned men being chafed or pummelled into life, and I believed that the body of an infant still contained the primal fire or the living principle. I drained the excess fluid from a small hole in the abdomen, and then placed the child on tin-foil as a good conductor. I then surrounded her with hermetically sealed jars, making up the Leyden device; there was a crack, as of summer thunder, and to my dismay the infant was dreadfully burned. But there was no life. I believe that I told the coroner that the burns were the discoloration attendant on drowning.

I could not remain in Oxford without arousing suspicion, even though I worked in the remotest corner of Headington. I had bribed the porters to ignore my nocturnal journeys, before the gates of the college were closed, and my return to my rooms after the gates had opened. They believed a woman to be in the case, and I chose not to disabuse them. But they would talk. When the Master called me into his study, for what he called a conversation, I suspected the worst. But I had already come to the conclusion that it was time for my departure. I would not obtain my degree; but with my father dead and an independent fortune bequeathed to me, I really had no need of the initials after my name.

The Master greeted me warmly enough, and we engaged in what the English call "chat."

"Your tutor tells me that you are following the principles of natural science, Mr. Frankenstein."

"That is my aim, sir."

"Do they by chance lead you towards the mystic and the transcendental?"

"I do not understand you."

"Is there a spiritual aspect?"

"I am a student of the brain and body, not of the soul."

"This is a Christian university, Mr. Frankenstein. We must always consider the soul."

He was a tall man, with bald head and pronounced side-whiskers; he offered me a glass of amontillado, which I accepted.

"Have you ever considered, sir, the growth of limbs?" I asked him.

"I beg your pardon?"

"There is some power that forms them in embryo. There is a seed which they contain within their own frame."

"What has this to do with the soul?"

"It is a question I might put to you, sir. What *has* it to do with the soul? If we possess such an entity, then surely it must play its part in the formation of the body. It is often said that the eyes are the windows of the soul. Professor Stokes has proved that the eyes are formed in the womb."

"Our knowledge is finite, Mr. Frankenstein."

"Oh, but I wish to stretch it. I wish to travel further in every sense."

"I do not follow you."

"There is no other way of telling you this, sir. I have determined to leave Oxford. I must thank you for your kindness, and I can say with some certainty that this has been the most formative epoch of my life."

We shook hands. I must say that I had never been more delighted to leave anyone's presence: the Master represented all the weight of the dead learning that I wished to shake off.

Within a week I had packed all my belongings, tipped a tearful Florence, and hired a coach to London. I set off in the highest spirits, convinced that I was about to fashion a new world. In the solitude of the carriage I recited some lines from Lord Byron as we passed through the village of Acton:

> *" 'Tis to create, and in creating live*
> *A being more intense, that we endow*
> *With form and fancy, gaining as we give*
> *The life we image . . ."*

In my search for life, I believed that I was about to re-create myself.

⇒ ⇐

ON ARRIVING IN JERMYN STREET I hired a young day porter, whose stand was in the little path beside the church, to take my parcels and my other belongings to my set of rooms on the third floor. It was the top storey of the building, but he performed the task without the usual complaint and bluster of the English working man. I discovered his name to be Frederick, or Fred, and I was so taken by his eager and enthusiastic manner that I wished to learn more of him. He could have been no more than thirteen or fourteen. "Well, Fred, how is your trade?"

"So-so, sir. It could be worse. It could be better. There is no telling." He had a mournful manner of speaking, but then he smiled as if all were a great comedy.

"How did you come by it?"

"Inheritance, sir. My father was porter here all of his life. He dropped down dead while lifting a donkey out of its traces. Terrible event." Then he smiled again.

"When was this?"

"Three months ago. I stood at his post the very same afternoon. My mother told me it was my station in life. She says it runs in the family."

"Do you have a brother who could take over from you?"

"Several of them, sir. All willing."

"Then I would like to offer you another post."

"In another street, sir?"

"No. I mean to say, I would like to offer you another position. Would you care to be my servant here?" He looked at me, and took off his cap. "Your duties will be light. I am alone in the world."

"Where would I sleep, sir?"

"There is a small room at the end of this passage. It looks over the alley."

"The well-beloved alley." He seemed relieved by my answer. "I would be what they call a general boy, sir?"

"You would prepare my meals. Lay out my clothes. And so forth."

"I would run errands, would I?"

"Naturally." He smiled broadly. "You would be my factotum, Fred."

"I do not know if I could do that."

"You would do everything. A guinea a week."

He smiled, and seemed about to break into laughter. "That would be every week, would it?"

"Every week."

"Under the circumstances, sir, I am happy to accept. I must just run and tell Mother."

The mother returned with him an hour later. She was a weak-legged and somewhat woebegone woman; her shawl had the remains of snuff upon it, and there was a distinct smell of spirits upon her breath. She had difficulty in recovering herself, after climbing the flights of stairs, and I offered her my flask of strong water. She accepted it readily, and gulped down most of its contents before putting her hand upon her son's head. "He is a good boy," she said. "He is worth the guinea."

"Mother—"

"I hear you are a foreign gentleman, sir."

"Yes. From the land of the Swiss."

"Is that so? You are handsome enough to be an Englishman, if I may say so."

"It is very kind of you."

All the while she was scrutinising my apartments. "Fred," she said, "you must take care of that hearth. It is rotten in the corner. And those windows need a clean."

"You are quite right, Mrs.—"

"Shoeberry." When she smiled at me I could distinctly see that some of her teeth were missing. "You have heard of Mr. Shoeberry and the donkey?"

"Indeed."

"It was a blow to the neighbourhood, sir. Yet I still do the laundry. That is my profession."

She seemed to be waiting for me to speak. "It would be very good of you, Mrs. Shoeberry, if you were to take in my laundry."

"A shilling for the linen. Sixpence for the sheets."

"That is very reasonable."

"I hope I am, sir. Do you have laundresses in Swisserland, sir?"

"I do not know. I believe so."

"They will not come cheaper than me, I can assure you of that. Now then, Fred, look sharp and brush the gentleman's coat. He has been travelling."

So it was that Fred Shoeberry and his mother took charge of my life in Jermyn Street. I was happy for them to do so, since I was intent upon nothing except my work. I wished to begin immediately, but of course there was no possibility of undertaking it in such a fashionable district of London; I needed as much secrecy and isolation as I could find, and so I roamed through the less respectable areas of the city in search of suitable premises. The eastern sections, abutting on the river, seemed most promising. I inspected Wapping and Rotherhithe, in the hours of daylight, when in plain dress I walked unnoticed among the throng of nationalities and trades; it was remarkable to see the variety of garbs and faces, from Turk to Chinaman, passing along the narrow thoroughfares beside the Thames. I had never seen such human life congregated together, and it put me in mind of the adage that London is a drink containing the lees of all nations.

Then I found a structure perfectly suited to my purposes. It was an old pottery manufactory in Limehouse, with its own yard or wharf upon the river. The buildings around it were warehouses of various descriptions and, as I imagined, quite deserted at night. I made enquiries in the neighbouring taverns, and I discovered that the employees had left several months before—after the owner had been declared bankrupt. Further enquiries led me to a commercial agent in Baltic Street who had an "interest" in the property. I soon discovered that he was the owner who had broken, and so it was a relatively easy matter to purchase his abandoned manufactory for what I regarded as a relatively modest sum. So I became a Limehouse freeholder.

❧

I HAD WRITTEN to Daniel Westbrook a few days after my arrival, announcing my intention to remain in London and asking for news of his sister. I had heard nothing from him for several days but, on my return to Jermyn Street one evening, after an inspection of my new premises, I found him in earnest conversation with Fred at the door of the house. "My dear Daniel," I said, "come in at once."

"This lad has been barking at me like a Cerberus."

"He says he knows you, sir."

"Of course he knows me, Fred."

"But he has no card, sir."

"He does not need a card. Mr. Westbrook is an old friend. Now that you know his face, you must welcome him."

"Do you hear that, old fellow?" Daniel asked him.

"My bark is worse than my bite, Mr. Westbrook." Fred had an incurably silly look upon his face, which made us both laugh out loud.

"Well, they are safely married," Daniel said to me as soon as we were settled in the apartment. "Harriet has written to me from Edinburgh. She is now Mrs. Shelley."

"Are you not pleased?"

"I would have preferred better circumstances. But, yes, I am pleased for her. Her prospects in life are now immeasurably greater. Even my father sees the advantage of it."

"Has she discussed her plans with you?"

"They are moving to Cumberland for a few months. Mr. Shelley has an interest in the Lake poets, I believe. Do you know of them?"

"I have read them."

"He has already been in correspondence with one of them, according to Harriet, and has been offered the rental of a cottage by a lake. She did not remember which one."

"It sounds delightful."

"I hope it may be. They have invited me to stay with them."

"Excellent. Did Harriet say anything of Bysshe?"

"He spends his time reading books from a circulating library and composing letters to his father."

I suspected that very little profit would emerge from either activity, but I said nothing. I did not wish to injure Daniel's happy expectations for the marriage, although I could see small cause for optimism. If it was a misalliance, as I believed, then little good would come of it. We spoke of other matters. He told me news of the Popular Reform League, and of a recent meeting on Clerkenwell Green when the army had been called; they had been told to quell any disturbances but the meeting passed off peacefully enough. By Daniel's account the army had in any case been singularly reluctant to intervene. "They are working men, too," he said. "They will not spill our blood." Naturally I was pleased, and relieved for his sake, but my own enthusiasm for the cause had diminished. I was so intent upon my own studies that I had little inclination for other pursuits. What can stop the determined heart and resolved will of man? I was as fixed as fate.

⇒ ⇐

NOW THAT I HAD OBTAINED the pottery manufactory in Limehouse, I had to furnish it with all the equipment and apparatus I would need to create and to store the electrical fluid. I enquired in many different workshops until one afternoon I found myself in the laboratory of Mr. Francis Hayman, a civil engineer who was employed by the Convex Lights Company to investigate new methods of illumination. He was situated in Bermondsey, next to a hat company, not far across the water from Limehouse itself. Once he had learned the nature of my mission he was happy to show me around his workshop, as he called it, where there were a variety of engines and coils and jars which immediately excited my interest. "What have you so far accomplished?" he asked me.

I told him that I was eager to revive life in animal tissue by means of electricity. "I have begun to experiment," I said, "by small shocks."

"There is no doubt that the fluid can be a healing compound. So why should it not be employed to excite dormant organs? Did you happen to read, in Wesley's journals, that his lameness was mended when he was electrified morning and evening?"

"I did not know of it," I replied. "But it does not surprise me in the least."

"But you have noted the difference between the two electricities?" He was a tall man who had acquired a stoop, no doubt through the agency of the low English door.

"I know what Franklin has called the vitreous and the resinous—"

"Well, Mr. Frankenstein, I prefer my own terminology. There is frictional electricity and magnetical electricity and thermal electricity. Their derivation is obvious."

"Of course."

"Here is the interesting thing. I believe that electrical fluid is also discharged by means of chemical action. I have called it galvanic electricity. It is a great power of nature, sir."

"You have created it here?"

"I have. Now my task is to make all of these various fluids cohere. Observe the means." He took me over to a small wooden bench upon which were placed four elongated glass tubes, with wires passing between them.

"This resembles the electrical balance of Coulomb, Mr. Hayman."

"You know of that? You are better instructed than I thought." He had a crisp, almost harsh, manner of speaking. "I have also done experiments with the electrical gymnotus."

"I beg your pardon?"

"The eel. And also with some electric rays. It is remarkable how the flat fish emits the fluid."

"Not so remarkable," I said. "I have examined a specimen of that fish in the course of my work. Beneath its wings are columns of discs, tightly bound together, which must act as a form of natural battery. They possess electric organs."

"Precisely my conclusion, sir."

"It is my belief," I said, "that the electric fluid is deposited in a latent state in unlimited quantity in the earth, the water and the atmosphere. It is in the sheet of summer lightning. It is in the raindrop."

"In you. And in me." He shook my hand. "I am pleased to greet an electrical friend. Let me show you something else."

He took me across his laboratory to a small alcove, partitioned off from the main room. Within it was a cylindrical instrument, some six feet in height, with levels of vitreous glass and metal. "This is my invention," he said. "It is constructed of zinc, Dutch leaf and quicksilver. It contains almost a thousand small discs, together with cakes of wax and resin." He stroked the side of the device. "I call it the electrical column."

"What is its power?"

"Immense." He opened his eyes very wide. "When it is used in connection with the electrical battery in the outer room. Do you see all those jars connected together? Well—"

"It is a giant nerve, Mr. Hayman."

"That is a good way of putting it. My employers have fixed ideas in such matters. They wish me to examine new modes of lighting the streets. But with engines such as this, we could see the entire nation in an electric state!"

I knew then that my quest had been successful. I had found the very equipment I would need to transmit the electrical fluid to the human frame. It was not hard for me to persuade Mr. Hayman to build for me an identical machine, with all its various appurtenances; the sum I offered him would more than compensate for his labour, and give him funds for further investigations. It was agreed that various parts of the electrical column would be wrapped in canvas and then transported across the Thames in wherries, from Bermondsey to Limehouse, where he would help to assemble them in my own workshop. I was in a state of intense excitement. To have the means of transmitting life within my power—to be able to create the vital spark—thrilled me beyond measure.

With the assistance of two local workmen I assembled a series of benches and shelves in the workshop, sufficient for the materials I was collecting. I wanted some means of refrigeration, too, and so they constructed for me the type of ice-chamber that is found in the cellars of Billingsgate Market. The wives of the workmen cleaned everything to perfection. I told them that I was studying the slow disappearance of the fish that had once been so plentiful in the Thames, and they applauded me for a labour so useful to the area. I told them that I wished to be left in peace, since my work required long and patient study, and that I was obliged to work at night when the business of the river had diminished. I knew well enough that my words would be widely distributed in the neighbourhood.

Within six or seven weeks Hayman began to deliver the equipment he had manufactured for me. Over several nights two wherrymen brought it over the Thames. They made use of my landing stage on the riverside, just in front of the workshop, and on the final night under cover of darkness they carried the precious electrical column into the building. Once the boatmen had departed, Hayman began the arduous task of assembling his invention.

"I have been thinking," I said to him. "I would like another."

"Another column? It is unnecessary, Frankenstein. The power of this machine is unequalled."

"But what if I—I mean, what if it—were to cease operation for any reason?"

"It will not happen. I give you my word."

"I trust you entirely, Hayman, but what if through some error of my own the column ceased to function? My work would be at an utter stand."

"That is a consideration." He stayed silent for a moment, and I could hear the lapping of the tide against a boat; there was a cry somewhere downriver, and a chain splashed into the water. "You must promise me this. You must never employ the columns at the same time. The effect would be incalculable. We know so little of the nature of the electrical fluid that no one can predict its course. It could be deathly."

"I promise you, Hayman." With that, the deed was done. He agreed to construct another column, on the same principles as the first, and to deliver it within a few weeks. I believe that he was also swayed by the pledge of an equivalent sum. As I have written before, the English will do anything for profit. I was exultant. I would have within my control the energies of a vast power—perhaps more power than any one man had harboured—and through that power I would create a new form of science. By restoring human life I was about to begin an enterprise that might change human consciousness itself! I was determined to prove that nature can be a moral force, an agent for good and for benevolent change. To bring life out of death— to restore the lost spirits and functions of the human frame— what could be more beneficent?

$$\Rightarrow \Leftarrow$$

IT REMAINED FOR ME now to procure the subjects. I still recalled very well the conversation I had held in Paris with Armitage, the oculist, whose father had been acquainted with the resurrection men; the father had worked as an assistant for John Hunter, a surgeon of great gifts who had needed the supply of fresh specimens for the rehearsal of his skills. Armitage had given me his card but, foolishly, I had mislaid it. So I called in Fred.

"Have you heard, Fred, of an oculist?"

"I have not, sir. If I lived to be a hundred, I would never have heard of him."

"An opticist? Optician?"

"Is it the same gentleman?"

"Similar."

"Then he might as well be the man in the moon. I do not know him."

"Tell me this then, Fred. In your extensive travels through the metropolis—"

"Beg your pardon, sir. I am always on foot."

"—have you encountered a shop with a large pair of spectacles hanging outside it?"

"Oh, yes. Many times. I took them to be telescopes, sir. Like the one in the Strand. I know of one in Holborn, next to the cheese shop." Then he slapped his hand on his forehead, and did a small mime of disbelief. "Let me pinch myself, sir. There is one here in Piccadilly. Run by a cove with the name of Wilkinson."

"Can you go to this Wilkinson, Fred, and ask if he knows of a maker of spectacles by the name of Armitage?"

"I will try, sir. I don't know if the old codger will speak to me."

"Why ever not?"

"He is a tartar with us boys."

"If he will not help you, then go to Holborn. Wherever you see the sign of the spectacles, ask for Armitage."

So Fred set off. He returned no more than an hour later, bearing in triumph a small piece of paper. "Weeny, waxy, weedy," he said. I must have looked surprised. "That is Julius Caesar, sir. When he won." He handed to me the paper, upon which was written a name and address: *W.W. Armitage and Son, 14 Friday Street, Cheapside.*

Such was my impatience, and urgency, that I journeyed there on the same afternoon. It was a narrow-fronted property, with a small street-door and a thin window rising up the whole length of the ground floor. When I entered a cracked bell rang above me, and within a few moments I heard the sound of shuffling steps. The tall window seemed designed to catch as much light as possible from Friday Street, and on the shelves around me I could see all possible varieties of spectacles—

green spectacles, blue spectacles, convex spectacles, concave spectacles, spectacles with front glasses, spectacles with side glasses, and the like. An old man came into the shop, leaning upon a cane. The crown of his head was quite bald, and his puckered mouth suggested that he had lost his teeth, but I noticed at once the brightness of his eyes. "May I be of service to you, sir?"

"I am looking for Mr. Armitage."

"You see him."

"I believe, sir, that you have a son."

"I have."

"I had the good fortune of meeting him in Paris, and I promised to pay him a visit on my return to London."

"What is your name, sir?"

"Frankenstein. Victor Frankenstein."

"Something—" He put his hand up to his forehead. "I am reminded." He went into the interior passage of the shop, and called out, "Selwyn!"

There came a hurried step down some uncarpeted stairs, and my acquaintance came into the room. "Good Lord," he said. "I was hoping that I would see you again. This is Mr. Frankenstein, Father, who is studying the workings of human life. I told you of him."

The father looked at me, with his bright eyes, and seemed to be satisfied. "Tell Mother to bring us some green tea," he said. "Do you take green tea, Mr. Frankenstein? It is very good for the ocular nerves."

"I will be happy to try it, sir."

"Selwyn drinks it morning and night. I have tested his eyes, sir. He could see the Monument from Temple Bar, if there were no houses between. From Millbank, sir, he has read a shopfront in Lambeth."

"Astonishing."

Mrs. Armitage entered the shop, carrying a tray with teapot and cups. She looked considerably younger than her husband; she was wearing a green satin gown that scarcely concealed her ample bosom, and had arranged her hair in the fashionable style of ringlets. "Will you partake?" she asked me.

"Gladly."

"It will be hot, sir. The water must be boiling to bring out the beauty of the leaves."

So we drank the tea, and Selwyn Armitage recalled to his father the details of our meeting at the coaching inn in Paris. Then I explained to the company the course of my studies in Oxford, taking care to avoid any reference to human experiment; instead I entertained them with descriptions of the efficacy of the electrical fluid. When I mentioned a dead cat whose fur had bristled, and whose mouth had opened, after a small discharge of the fluid, Mrs. Armitage excused herself and returned to the parlour upstairs. The light had begun to fade, and the evening to approach, when the two men asked me to share a bottle of port wine with them. They seemed reluctant to dispense with my company.

After our first glass I ventured upon the matters that most interested me. "Selwyn," I said, "has mentioned that you worked with Mr. John Hunter."

"Of blessed memory, sir. He was the finest surgeon in Europe. He could unblock a stricture in minutes. There was no one like him for a hernia."

"Tell him about your fistula, Father."

"He condescended to treat me, sir, when I had the complaint. He was in and out before I knew it."

"But you must have suffered pain, Mr. Armitage."

"Pain was nothing to me, Mr. Frankenstein. Not when I was in the hands of the master."

"The whole world has been informed of his experiments," I said.

"They were wonderful to behold, sir."

"Did he not attempt to freeze creatures and then to revivify them?"

"He practised upon dormice, but without success. But I recall once that he froze the comb of a rooster. They fall off, you know, in hard frosts."

"But he believed that he might pursue the same course with humans, did he not?"

"Now that, Mr. Frankenstein, is an interesting question." The old Mr. Armitage went to the inner door and called to his wife, who brought down another bottle of port wine. "He held much the same opinion as you, sir, on some matters. That is why my son mentioned you in the first place. Mr. Hunter put his faith in what he called the vital principle. He was of the opinion that it might linger in the body for an hour or more after death."

"And then could be revived."

"That is so."

"I read a curious account in the *Gentleman's Magazine*," I said, "about the attempt to restore Dr. Dodd."

"That account was not accurate, sir, as far as I remember it. We did not put him in a warm bath. It would have had little effect."

"But Mr. Hunter tried other means of restoring him to life, did he not?"

"After he was cut down from the gallows, he was brought to Mr. Hunter's house in Leicester Square at the gallop. We chafed the body to revive its natural heat, while Mr. Hunter tried to inflate the lungs by means of a bellows. But he had been left swinging at Tyburn for too long. Then, sir, he tried your method. He gave the body a series of sharp shocks from a Leyden jar. But Dodd was quite inert."

"I believe, Mr. Armitage, that your level of electrical power was too low. No jar could effect a restoration of life. You need great force to succeed."

"Do you have that power, sir?"

I grew more wary. "One day," I replied, "I hope to achieve it."

"Ah. A dream. Mr. Hunter used to say that an experimenter without a dream is no experimenter at all."

"And he never gave up his experimenting?"

"He did not. He would take a tooth from a healthy child, and plant it in the gum of one who needed it. He tied it with seaweed."

"That must have been a very remarkable operation."

"Oh, sir, that was nothing to him. He could put the testis of a cockerel into the belly of a hen, and see it grow."

"I have heard," I said, "that his dissecting room was always full of observers."

"Crowded, sir. He was a great draw to the students. He could open up a subject in seconds."

"That must have been very gratifying."

"It was a pleasure to see. He was a lovely man with a knife."

"You must enlighten me on one thing, Mr. Armitage. How many subjects did he—"

"There was a regular supply." He took another glass of the port wine, and looked at his son.

"You can tell him, Father."

"In London, sir, there are always more dying than being born. That is a fact. There is no room for all of them. The churchyards are bursting."

"Yet he must have found a source."

"I tell you this in the strictest confidence, sir. Mr. Hunter was the resident surgeon at St. George's Hospital. Can you bring us another bottle, Selwyn? He had the keys of the dead house there. Have I said enough?"

"But he must have dissected some thousands. Surely not all came from one place?"

"You are entirely correct, sir. Not all of them could have done." I waited impatiently as Selwyn Armitage came into the room with a fresh bottle, and began to pour the wine into his father's glass. I declined the offer. "Have you heard of the Sack 'Em Up Men?"

"I do not believe so. No."

"Resurrectionists. Doomsday Men." I knew precisely what he meant, of course, but I feigned ignorance for the sake of further enlightenment. "These are the men who rob the graves of their dead. Or they enter the charnel houses and filch their victims. It is not a delicate trade, Mr. Frankenstein."

"Yet it is necessary, sir. I have no doubt of that."

"How else are we to progress? Would Mr. Hunter have been able to complete his work on the spermatic cord?"

"I think not."

"They were very expensive." He drained his glass, and held it out to his son. "A guinea, or more, for a body. A child was priced by the inch. Will you oblige me, Selwyn? Yet the best of them were very expert. The subject had to be delivered after rigor mortis had passed, but before wholesale corruption. And they had to escape the attention of the mob."

"The mob," Selwyn said, "was worse then."

"They would have been killed on the spot, Mr. Frankenstein. Torn limb from limb. The mob hated resurrectionists."

"You speak of them in the past tense, sir. But surely they still pursue their trade? The market must be as thriving as ever."

"I do not doubt it. The medical schools have grown to enormous size."

"Do they haunt the same places?"

"The graveyards? Of course. There is a paupers' graveyard in Whitechapel—"

"No. I mean their places of business. Where they meet their clients. Where they are paid."

"They are paid at the back door, sir. Every hospital has one."

"Yet they must meet."

"They meet to drink. Drink is their life. Not one of them could do the work sober. I have seen some of them, sir, sitting in a tavern from dusk until dawn."

"What tavern is that?"

"The most celebrated of them all, Mr. Frankenstein." He slowly drank the full glass, and held it out for more. "It is in Smithfield. Just opposite St. Bartholomew's. Now there *is* a meat market."

➢ Nine ⇐

THE SMITHFIELD TAVERN was not difficult to find. I left Jermyn Street at dusk, and the carriage set me down at Snow Hill soon afterwards; I walked up to St. Bartholomew's just as its clock was striking seven, and on my left hand I could see a low public house with the sign of *The Fortune of War*. It showed the deck of a naval frigate, with an officer dying in the arms of his comrades. I could hear it, too, with the noise of song, laughter and raised voices echoing against the stone wall of the hospital. I steeled myself, making sure that my purse of guineas was well concealed beneath my shirt, and entered the premises.

The smell was very strong. I could not help but associate it with dead things, although I knew that it came from the living; the taint of dirty flesh was in the air, mixed with the odours of the privy and the smell of strong spirits. I was of course accustomed to foul odours, in my work, and I registered no discomfort at all. I made my way to the wooden counter, and ordered a glass of porter. I decided to settle, and make myself as conspicuous as possible; I had no desire to be taken as a government spy, and I did not retreat into a corner. I stayed by the counter and, by remarking loudly upon the weather, made sure that my accent was heard by those around me. But they evinced little interest, being in most cases reduced to the last stages of intoxication, and after a while I was able to look around without drawing any particular attention to my presence. There were solitary drinkers, bent over their bottles and tankards; I observed that one had urinated upon the floor, of plain deal planks, without provoking any comment. In Geneva we have chamber pots in the corners of our taverns. My notice was attracted by a company of men, sitting in one alcove; all of them were smoking from the long, thin pipes that I thought were out of use. They were silent, and contemplative, in the extreme. For a moment I conceived the notion that they were the resurrectionists I sought. I discovered later that they were the pure-finders whose trade was to collect the excrement of dogs, horses and humans from the thoroughfares of the city.

Then a rough-looking fellow came in from the street and, advancing upon the counter, asked in a loud voice for a jug of brandy and seltzer. I noticed that the innkeeper served him with a word of recognition; but the fellow paid no attention to that and, slapping a few coins onto the counter, went over to a corner. There was a window there, overlooking the paved space in front of the hospital, and he seemed to be scrutinising the gates lit by a single oil-lamp. He was watching for someone, or something, very keenly; but, from my position by the counter, I could see nothing. A few minutes later two other fellows, smelling strongly of spirits and other less delectable items, joined him by the window. Another man was standing close to me at the counter. He was staring straight ahead, with a glass of gin in his hand, when he said to me, "You do not want to fall into the hands of them dogs, living or dead."

"I have no notion," I replied, "of who or what they are."

"No need to know." He was still staring straight ahead. "Stay clear of them. Otherwise you might end up in there." He jerked his head in the general direction of the hospital.

The innkeeper looked at him angrily. "Are you talking out of turn, Josh?"

"Only saying what we all know. This young man is a new one. He may heed a warning."

I steadied myself by drinking down the porter and ordering another. Then I went over to the table where the three men were sitting, and placed three silver guineas in front of them. They looked at the coins, and then looked up at me.

"You are free with the bunce," one of them said.

"One for each of you."

"Oh?" He picked up a guinea and tried it with his teeth. "What's your game?"

"I need something."

"Speak to them." He pointed towards the group of men with the old fashion of pipes. "They pick up the filth."

"You are a foreign chicken," another said. "Are you a Frenchy?"

"No, sir. I am from Geneva."

"'Tis all one."

He seemed impressed by my calling him "sir," however, and I took advantage of the moment. "I am a student of medicine, gentlemen." They laughed loudly—too loudly, I suspected, but no one else in the tavern so much as glanced in their direction. "May I offer you another jug?" They nodded and, when I returned from the counter, the coins had gone. The bait had been accepted.

Their names, as I discovered later, were Miller, Boothroyd and Lane. Such a trio of villains I had never before encountered.

They were dissolute and depraved to the highest degree, but I trusted that they were expert in their trade. I explained to them that, as a student of anatomy, I wished for a continuous supply of new bodies. As a foreigner, I said, I was obliged to work outside the hospital schools.

"How did you find us?" Lane asked me.

"He smelled you out," Boothroyd replied.

"I will pay you twice as much as any hospital."

"What about smalls?"

"Forgive me?"

"Babes and young 'uns."

"No. No children. I can use only adults. Only males. That is the nature of my work. And they must be good specimens. I want no growths. No deformities. Payment on delivery."

"He wants them handsome so he can fuck them," Miller said.

Boothroyd silenced him with a glance. "You are asking a lot."

"I am paying a lot."

"No questions asked?"

"No answers required. Bring the subjects to me, and you will have your money." I told them how they could find me; as it happened they were used to working by boat, since they had a steady trade with the convict hulks on the estuary where they could pick up three or four items at a time. They told me that they had to drag the bodies through the river in order to cleanse them of the filth that had accrued to them in the holds of the ships. So I described in detail the location of my workshop, and of the small wharf in front of it; they knew the neighbourhood well. I promised I would be ready for them on the Friday night, giving them two nights for their work. They each spat in their hand before shaking mine, a custom that I did not wholly appreciate.

⇒ ⇐

FRED WAS WAITING UP FOR ME. "There is a funny smell in the room," he said as soon as I entered.

"Smell?"

"Of drink, and tobacco, and something else, and something else, all mixed."

"I have been in a tavern," I said. I took off my coat and jacket, and put them on a chair in the hallway.

"Mr. Frankenstein in a tavern. Whatever next?"

"Mr. Frankenstein in bed."

"I was warned against taverns," he said, "when I was a boy. They are too low. You were not robbed, sir, were you?"

"No, Fred, I was not robbed. I was cheated. Porter is threepence a pint. But I was not robbed."

"Porter was the ruin of my father, sir. It was not the donkey that killed him. It was the drink. He never was sober after the dustcart came by."

"What had the dustcart to do with it?"

"He shared a drink with the dustman. He was a regular toper, he was. Never knew which side of the street he was on."

"I have come to the conclusion, Fred, that all Londoners drink."

"They can be very cheerful, sir." He sighed. "They like the flowing bowl."

"You are a poet, Fred."

He laughed and was about to leave the room, when he spun

around and very deftly kicked himself. "I almost forgot, sir. There is a letter for you. It came on the northern coach, so I gave the messenger sixpence."

"He did not carry it all the way, Fred. Never mind. Pass it to me, if you please."

He retreated into the hall and came back with a packet that, as I saw, had been franked by an official in Lancaster. It was from Daniel Westbrook. I hoped that it might have come from Bysshe who, despite my anger at his behaviour, was still often in my thoughts. But the clumsy writing of the address told me otherwise. The letter itself was superscribed *Chestnut Cottage, Keswick.*

My dear Frankenstein,

Forgive me for not writing to you sooner but I have had a deal of business to sort. Neither Mr. Shelley (or, should I say, my brother-in-law) nor Harriet have any head for such matters, so I was obliged to negotiate their lease of the cottage from a Cumberland farmer who was more hard-headed than a London stock jobber. He insisted on counting the flowers in the garden, in the event that we might uproot one of them! Harriet seems very happy, and sparkles with delight whenever we go for one of our walks by the lake or by the mountainside. She is obviously suited to married life, and looks after her husband with the utmost delicacy and attention: she makes sure that he is always neat and clean in his appearance (sometimes to his annoyance, I must admit) and tries to bargain with the villagers for our simple necessities. Mr. Shelley shuts himself away for some of the day, in the upstairs bedroom, where Harriet says that he is composing; I can sometimes hear him reciting verses, which I imagine to be his own. Then he goes on long rambles through the local country, when he prefers to be alone. I am sure that he loves and cherishes Harriet, but the ways of aristocrats are new to me! We sit together in the evenings, and he reads to us from the volume that has most lately taken his fancy. He has been studying Mr. Godwin's treatise on Necessity, and yesterday evening he recited to us the philosopher's belief that in the life of every being there is a chain of events which began in the distant ages that preceded his birth and continued in regular procession through the whole period of his existence. It is called necessitarianism, a long word for a difficult matter. I am sure I have not spelled it properly. In consequence of which, according to Mr. Godwin, it is impossible for us to act in any instance otherwise than we have acted. That is too fatalistic for my taste, but Mr. Shelley believes it to be the case. Harriet agrees with him.

Last week we visited Mr. Southey, who has a grand house in the neighbourhood known as Greta Hall. You must know of Mr. Southey through his connection with the Intelligencer. Quite by chance one of the Lake poets, whom Mr. Shelley reveres, was also there. Mr. Wordsworth's name was known even to me—who am, as you know, no great judge of poetry—and he received a proper amount of veneration and respect from us all. I believe that he relished the opportunity of conversing with his young admirer. Mr. Shelley recited some of his own verses and Mr. Wordsworth deemed them to be, as he put it, "very acceptable." They talked on the subject of poetry and morality, as Harriet and I listened enthralled. Never have I seen such a large measure of genius crammed into one room! Mr. Wordsworth begged to differ when Mr. Shelley grew warm on the subject of kings and oppression, in which I would very willingly have joined, but the older man

preserved his demeanour. I believe that he is a native of this area,
but he seems a good deal more cultivated than anyone else I have
encountered here. His accent is not at all rough. He has a long
sloping nose, and a delicate firmness of expression about the
mouth; his eyes are luminous in the extreme, and he evinced a
great gentility of manner towards Harriet and Mrs. Southey.

I believe that even Mr. Wordsworth was impressed by Mr.
Shelley's ardour, and saw in his excitement some reflection of his
own younger self. He confessed to us that the years had buried him
in a "mound of cares," as he put it, but that as a young man he
had dreamed dreams and seen visions. "I wish you well," he said
to Mr. Shelley as he took his leave. "I am not insensible to the
cravings of youthful ambition."

So ended our meeting with the Lake poet. There is much more
to tell you, but it will be best delivered to you on my return to
London. Harriet sends her greetings to you. Mr. Shelley has just
shouted down the stairs and asked if you remember the Ancient
Druids of Poland Street? I confess I have no idea what he means.
I must sign my name now, or I will write on indefinitely.

Faithfully yours, Daniel Westbrook.

I folded the letter and placed it on the side-table beside my
chair. For some reason I felt close to tears. Perhaps it was a
reminder to me of the life I used to lead, before my immersion
in dangerous experiment; perhaps it represented to me the
pleasures of married life and of human intercourse. I realised,
too, that I still missed the presence of Bysshe. His was the one
true companionship I had ever formed—my one friend and ally
in this world, where there is so much harm and darkness.

Fred came into the room, bearing a smoking dish. "I have a cure for the porter," he said.

"I am not to be cured."

"Saloop, sir. The steam would wake a corpse."

"High praise." I took the bowl of liquid from him; it was milky grey in colour, and had a rough texture. "Is this one of your London dishes?"

"As cockney as a chimney-sweep, sir. Milk and sugar and sassyfrass."

"I have no idea what you are talking about, Fred."

"Uncle Bill sells it on the Haymarket. He owns an urn."

"I am pleased to hear it. I take it that I drink it?" He nodded, with immense satisfaction. I tasted the brew, which had the aroma and the flavour of vanilla. It was curiously soothing. "Your Uncle Bill must be a popular man."

"He is tolerably well liked, sir. The urchins follow him for the smell alone."

The drink must also have been a great soporific, since I retired to bed as soon as I had finished it and slept soundly until dawn. When I woke it was with a sense of impending and urgent duty. I knew what I had to do. I sat upright in my bed, and stared straight ahead. I have an unfortunate habit of gnawing at my fingernails, when I contemplate a problem, and this I proceeded to do. My converse with the resurrection men on the previous night, and my bargain with them, had effectively begun a new phase of my existence. There were still a few hours in which I could turn back from the consequences of my actions—a few brief hours in which I might make my peace with men and God—but I was so blinded by the prospect of success and glory that I used them for quite other purposes.

I took a cab to Limehouse, and began to prepare my workshop for its visitors. Within two nights I would have in my possession two bodies, freshly expired, and I could begin to charge them with life. I inspected the electrical columns that Hayman had constructed for me, and could see no flaw in their design. The pure flow of the power would advance unimpeded into my subjects. I did not yet know what results to expect, since I had never before had in my possession such resources. I knew only that I was upon the threshold of a new world of science. One way or another, it would happen. Did I still yearn for my old life of pure contemplation and study, of youthful visions in the Alpine air? I was not sure of this.

⇒ ⇐

ON THAT FRIDAY EVENING I waited eagerly for the arrival of the resurrection men. I stood outside upon the wharf, and watched the water as the tide came in; it was early autumn now and a mild breeze ruffled the surface. The declining sun lit up the banks of cloud moving from the west, and the radiance spread outwards like a halo. I went back inside, and busied myself about the final preparations of the electrical columns. I had placed them in the space between two low wooden tables lying side by side; there was a plentiful supply of voltaic batteries upon the floor, at the head and foot of each of the tables. I had calculated that the power would be enough to animate two corpses, and so I had devised an elaborate procedure of moving quickly from one subject to the other. I would in any case prepare them both at the same time, with the metal straps and coils attached to their anatomies. Of course I had no conception of what might occur in the course of the electrical charging: I had taken the precaution of having a blunderbuss, primed and loaded, in a corner of the workshop.

As night fell I took a lamp, and walked onto the landing stage. I could hear the lapping of the water against the wooden posts, and there was a splash somewhere in the middle of the river. A thin mist was creeping in from the east, and I prayed that it might deepen so that my visitors would be shrouded from the sight of anyone lingering upon the bank. I put the lamp up to my face. After a few moments I heard the sound of oars, and the steady progress of a boat low in the water; I held out the lamp, and moved it from side to side as a signal. The oars came closer, and in the dim fitful light I saw the dark outline of a boat coming towards the stage. Two men were rowing, and a third sat at the stern on watch.

They made no sound or gesture of recognition, but stayed fixed to their tasks. In less than a minute they had come up by the landing. I called out to them but they motioned me to stay silent. The man at the stern, whom I recognised to be Miller, threw me a rope; I tied the boat to a mooring post beside me. Miller then jumped out, and put his hand across my mouth. "Mum," he whispered. I could smell the drink upon his breath. The two others clambered out from the side of the boat, and then began to unload two hempen sacks. They dragged them across the planking, and I followed them within.

I closed the door, and put the oil-lamp on the table. "I must see them before I pay you."

"Don't you trust us, Mr. Frankenstein?" Boothroyd took out a flask from the pocket of his coat, and swigged from it.

"A proper tradesman surveys his goods," I said.

He laughed at that, but then in the glimmering light he noticed the electrical machines. "What infernal thing is this?"

"It is an engine. The engine of my work."

"The devil's work, is it?"

"It is nothing to do with the devil. I can assure you of that."

"Well, it is all one to me."

Then Miller took out a knife, and cut the cords that bound the tops of the sacks. An arm fell from one of them and, taking hold of it, he pulled out the rest. It was an adult male, as I had requested, but one who had suffered some injury to his chest. It had caved in, and the ribs were broken. "This one is damaged," I said.

"Perfect specimens are hard to find. But look at this one." Boothroyd then took the body from the second sack. It was of a young male in a very good state of repair and preservation; he looked as if he had died quite suddenly, and there was an expression of ghastly terror upon his face.

"This is good," I said. "Excellent. Where did you find him?"

"We found him where he fell."

I did not wish to know more. "Would you be so kind as to place one of them here. And one here." I gestured towards the two long wooden tables. "Be careful with the frame of this one. His ribs are loose."

"He is a genuine rattle-bag," Miller said.

I paid them at once, eager to begin work, and arranged that they would return with a similar cargo one week later. They departed willingly enough, and I suspect that the terrible expression on the young man's face had subdued even their spirits. "Will you be needing them sacks?" Boothroyd asked me.

"I have no further use for them. But you will be needing them again, I think."

So they returned to their boat, and I waited on the landing stage until they had drifted out into the dark water. I noticed on my return that there was a curious smell in the room, similar to that of damp umbrellas or burned rags, and I was concerned lest a state of putrefaction would soon set in. I decided to begin work upon the damaged specimen, in case of some early blunder on my part. So I proceeded quickly to prepare it, washing it first with a solution of chloride of lime. It smelled fresher then. Then I took the precaution of fastening the subject to the table by means of a long leather strap. I had already decided to attach the metal clasps to the neck, the wrists, and the ankles, where the vital motions of the body are most exercised; the voltaic current was to be transmitted by means of thin metal wires that would not impede movement. The engines were ready, with their great strips of zinc and brass separated by pasteboard soaked in salt water. I had primed the batteries, and placed the conductor at both ends. All was in readiness for the creation of the spark that might light a new world.

The apparatus hummed with its own internal motion, and I noticed a slight quivering in the wires; it seemed to me then that the electrical machines had become living things. Their power increased, as each galvanic pile was affected, and I was aware of Hayman's injunction not to test their power to excess. But I was exhilarated beyond measure at the spectacle of such energy unleashed before me. The body began to tremble violently. In the fitful light of the oil-lamp it cast a strange shadow upon the floor. I stepped over to it, and with a certain reluctance touched the arm. It seemed to be increasing in warmth. The head began to toss from side to side, as if the corpse were fighting to find its breath, but then the struggle subsided. The body relapsed into deathly stillness. It was once more quite cold.

I walked away for one moment, to examine the machines, when I heard a sudden movement behind me. My first thought was for the blunderbuss. I turned quickly, and let out an involuntary cry of surprise—the dead man's hands had moved over the deep rift in his chest. By some strange instinct he had wished to touch the source of his extinction. This was a moment of revelation, suggesting to me that there was some power of will or instinct that could survive the death of the body. I had been touched by the lightning flash. I had triumphed. But even then I tried to restrain my overwhelming sense of excitement. Could it perhaps have been some involuntary motion of the muscles that the man had been prevented from performing at the time? Had this been the gesture he had been unable to make?

I was wary of approaching the body, in case of some new and unexpected motion, but I knew that my work depended upon expedition and iron will. I unstrapped the wires from the first subject, and applied them to the second. The discharge of electrical energy seemed to have done no injury to the frame, and I was quite sanguine about the effects on the second and more perfectly preserved corpse. I inwardly delighted, too, that no harm had come to the physical specimen, thus allowing me the opportunity for more experiment.

I charged up the batteries once more, and produced the spark with very little pressure upon the conductors. There was a jolt in the second body as if, so to speak, it had sprung to attention. Then again all was quiet. I attempted a second discharge, and the body stirred again—on this occasion with a more active and anxious motion. I detected some secondary movement in the fingers of his hands that seemed to tremble with the force of the excitation: I admit that my own hands were trembling, too. I charged the wires for a third time, but there was no consequent disturbance of the body. I was about to investigate further, and approached the specimen, when a most desolate and horrible shriek emerged from the mouth. It was the sound of some cursed demon, lost in the pit of hell, and I froze with the noise echoing around me. It was enough to wake the dead—except that the dead had already been awoken.

When I looked down at the body, fearful of what I might see, I observed that the expression of horror had disappeared and that the young man's visage seemed entirely at peace.

Had that terrible cry released his suffering? If it were possible that the agony and horror of his last moments had somehow been confined within his body, then it was also possible that the shock of the electrical fluid had expelled the suffering spirit—or soul—I know not the word for such a momentous change. Could the corpse have been literally suffering its last agony until it was released by my agency? And then I was struck by a further revelation. The vocal cords had survived death.

I embarked upon other electrical experiments with the two subjects, and there were at first no further arousals. It appeared to me that the bodies, having performed their final delayed actions, had relapsed into stillness. Yet I could be certain of nothing. I took a large surgical knife and proceeded to remove the frontal bone of the cranium from the head of the second subject; then, with a compact saw, I cut away the uppermost portion of the dome until I could observe the anterior and posterior lobes of the cranium. The most absurd image then occurred to me—that of slicing the pie-crust from the pie—but I was so intent upon my work that I scarcely had time for any reflections. I then prepared an experiment that I had previously sketched out in my written notes. I placed strips of zinc and brass over the exposed skull, so that they touched the lobes. Then I applied the charge. The effect upon the brain was immediate; of the four lobes, only one seemed able to receive the delicate impress of the electrical current, and I have since named it the electric lobe. It had an immediate effect on the muscles of the body that, if it had not been strapped down, might have been tempted to rise up and walk. The whole frame was invaded by a violent trembling that, as I was astonished to discover, continued for several minutes after I had turned off the current.

To my utmost surprise and horror I then began to observe some contortions of the face. The eyes rolled, and the lips parted; the nostrils flared, and the entire expression seemed to be one of enmity mixed with despair. These were of course the accidents of physiognomy, but at that moment I could have sworn that the corpse strapped to the table was displaying to me all the viciousness of hatred and all the burden of melancholy desolation. Eventually the movements ceased and the face resumed its lifeless shape. But I was so shaken by the phenomenon that I was obliged to walk out beside the river in order to calm myself.

So many impressions crowded in upon me that the night

seemed to stretch into infinity. I had never anticipated that the effects of the electrical fluid would take so profound and terrifying a form. I had proved beyond doubt that the fluid could reanimate a human corpse, but in so unexpected and awful a fashion that I had become afraid of my own handiwork. I had become afraid of myself, so to speak, afraid of what I might accomplish and afraid of what I might witness. What other secrets might be revealed to me, as I pursued my strange experiment?

A little reflection, however, brought me to my senses. The murmur of the Thames soothed me. The mist had lifted, and the outlines of the city became apparent. It was close to dawn. I had worked all night. The round of existence would soon begin anew and, with the feeling of the immensity of London coming to life, my own strength was resumed and confirmed. There was much for me to do.

⇒ Ten ⇐

I WAS DOZING BY THE FIRESIDE, in my apartments at Jermyn Street, when I was roused by a sudden rapping at the street door. I scarcely had time to prepare myself when Fred came into the room. "Ever so much beg your pardon, sir, but there is a Fish to see you."

"Whatever are you saying, Fred?"

"That's what I asked him, sir. But he kept on saying, 'Fish, Fish.' I told him we had a fishmonger just down the street."

At that moment Bysshe rushed into the room, bursting past Fred and embracing me with all the fervour and animation I remembered.

"My dear fellow," I said, "I thought you were living in the North."

"I have returned to warmer climes, Victor. To my friends." He stepped back and looked at me. "Are you angry with me?"

"I was. Yes. I admit. Very. But now that I see you, I cannot be angry."

"I am glad of it. You know, Victor, I can return the fifty guineas. My dreaded father has paid my allowance."

"No need. No need at all."

He resumed his gaze at me for a moment. "Why did you not write to me that you were ill?"

"Ill? I have never felt better in my life. I am in perfect health."
He seemed perplexed. "I am sorry to disappoint you, Bysshe."

"There is a change in your countenance, Victor. I cannot be
deceived in that."

"Well. Youth turns to age. Think no more of it." I tried
to remain cheerful and composed. "Where are you staying in
London?"

"Harriet and I have found rooms in Soho. Back to our old
haunts, Victor."

"And how is Harriet?"

"She is well. She is thriving." He laughed. "She is swelling in
the most peculiar manner."

"Do you mean—?" He nodded. "Very well done, Bysshe!"

"I am not the one to be congratulated. It is the woman who
carries the burden. But I must confess to some pride in creating
life."

"It must be an exhilarating sensation."

"I am reciting poetry to the unborn babe, Victor, so that
in the womb it will become accustomed to sweet sounds. And
Harriet sings lullabies. She swears that it soothes the child."

Fred knocked upon the door, and entered the room with a
flask of brandy spirit. "It has struck five," he said.

Bysshe looked at the liquor in surprise. "You drink brandy
now, Victor?"

"It soothes the child. Will you join me? We will raise a glass
to companionship."

Bysshe was eager to explain his schemes of future happiness.
He wished to start a little community in Wales devoted to the
principles of equality and justice; he was intent upon writing an

epic poem on the subject of the legendary Arthur; he wished to travel to Ireland to assist in the project for freedom. I understood that he had found a new favourite in Mr. Godwin, the philosopher. He had sought him out, and had already visited him in a charming house in Somers Town. Then once more he gave me a quick, watchful glance. "And you, Victor, what is your news?"

"I am experimenting still. I am testing the capacity of the electrical fluid. I am measuring its strength."

"Wonderful! You are going to its limits, as we used to discuss?"

"I remember that we used to speak of electrical kites and balloons. I am not so much in the air now, Bysshe. I am in the earth." I had no desire to explain my work, until it had reached a successful conclusion, and so I discussed with him the generalities of electrical science. He was as impetuous, and as eager to learn, as he had always been. I had never encountered anyone who was so filled with animated and spirited life.

"You will come and visit us then?" he asked me as he was about to take his leave. "Harriet will be overjoyed to see you."

"Of course. Whenever you wish."

He embraced me, and a few moments later I heard his light rapid steps upon the stairs. I heard him speaking to Fred, but could not understand what he said. I went to the window and looked down into Jermyn Street; he was walking quickly through the throng, but then he glanced up at my window. For some reason I stepped back.

Fred came in to clear away the glasses. "That friend of yours," he said, "is curious enough. He asked me if you were in good health. I say yes. He asked if you were eating well. I say yes.

He asked if you was drinking. I say yes and no. Then he opens the door for himself, although I was right behind him, and then he rushes out like a squib."

"What do you mean, Fred, yes and no?"

"Yes, he drinks. And no, he don't drink in that way." He pretended to stagger and fall.

"It is good of you to say so."

"Thank you, sir. I do my best."

⇒ ⇐

I HAD NO INTENTION of visiting Bysshe and Harriet while my work continued. I could no more prepare myself for society than if I had spent the past months in the frozen wastes of the Arctic. Ever since the resurrectionists had first visited me at Limehouse they had plied a busy trade. I had more need than ever of their services since I was intent upon testing every fibre and muscle of the human frame for its electrical potential. I had learned that the muscles of the leg were at first most resistant to the power, but that a slight repositioning of the metal strip above the tarsal bone worked wonders with movement and flexibility. The bones and ligaments of the human hand were highly responsive to the electrical fluid, and I discovered that a slight contact with the various carpal bones set off a frenzy of fluttering and trembling. The carotidal and vertebral arteries were also a source of much satisfaction to me, being highly delicate and flexible when charged. So by degrees I devised an electrical map of the human body.

I had more success than I expected on the transplantation of limbs. I believed that all the emanations of the human body possessed an innate living principle, seeking as well as manifesting life, taking energy and animation from whatever source was available. The late John Hunter had excelled at what he called the transplanting of teeth, from the mouth of a healthy young sweep to the decaying jaw of a London merchant, and I saw no reason to deny the principle to the arm or to the leg. In the Limehouse workshop I removed two arms from the body of a young man by means of surgical amputation, and then quickly stitched them onto the torso of an elderly specimen who, as Boothroyd informed me, had expired of the dropsy. When I applied the electrical charge the hands and forearms worked as if they were in perfect order, with no sign of dropsical trembling; he continued to clench his fists, and raise his palms outward, for the duration of the experiment. When I repeated the procedure, I observed the same movements executed with a slight increase of motion. I was curious to see the extent of the change if I altered the rate and rapidity of the charge, and to my surprise the hands began to communicate with each other—so to speak—by the touching of the fingertips. There was a defined pattern of movement, so much like sign language that I had the strangest sensation of being signalled by the cadaver in front of me. Was it possible that the young man, whose hands and arms had been severed, was skilled in the gestures of the dumb?

My principal concern was with the cerebrum, and with the excitation of sight, hearing and speech. I had isolated the electrical lobe, and in a series of trials I endeavoured to trace the paths of its influence. Much to my delight I soon discovered that it affected the visual and aural nerves equally, and that the vocal cords were stimulated by the charging of the arytenoid cartilages. I had assumed the larynx to be the responsible agent, but I was wrong. The experiments with hearing were most rewarding. Once the lobe was in an alert state I fired my blunderbuss beside the right ear of the subject; the head jerked to one side, away from the noise. On another occasion I began to whisper, and the head moved forward a fraction towards me. With sight the effects were less distinct. The eyes always opened in a state of electrical excitation, but sometimes they were so dull of hue that I could detect no evidence of a visual ray. In what I deemed to be the more intelligent subjects, however, there was a definite reaction to various stimuli. When I lit a candle in front of the eyes of one cadaver, there was a detectable movement of the pupil; when I blew out the light the pupil dilated. In one experiment I held before the eyes of one young specimen, scarcely more than a boy, a little struggling mouse; his eyes became fixed upon the creature, in the same manner as those of some cadaverous animal intent upon its prey.

In the course of these trials I noticed that, in the corpses of the younger specimens, the phallus became erect at the slightest excitation and remained in a state of alertness for the duration of the electrical charge. In the older bodies this did not occur. My work on the phallus was at first confined to an examination of the three columns of erectile tissue, but I then advanced to an attempt at the measurement of the spermal fluid. By means of the firm pressure of my fingers I brought one body to a state of ejaculation, at which point there came a groan; but no spermatozoa appeared. There was no fluid, but there was instead a sprinkling of material with the appearance and consistency of dust. It may have been a principle of nature that the dead could not bring forth new life. I was not sure, but I was determined to continue the experiment.

As the weeks passed, and the London autumn turned to bitter winter, I was still more ardent in execution and more impatient of difficulties. I was exhausting bodies at a great rate; I kept some of them in the ice-house which I had fashioned in the basement space of the old manufactory, while I discharged others into the Thames with the knowledge that the full tide would carry them downstream where they would join the score of other corpses taken up by the sheriffs of Blackwall or Woolwich; there was a promontory at North Woolwich known as Deadman's Point, to which many of the bodies of the drowned used to drift. Many more would find their way by stages to the open sea, where all prospect of discovery was of course abandoned. There were a few specimens that I placed in a pit of lime I had created, between the foreshore and my workshop, where the action of the dissolvent soon removed all traces of their existence.

If you ask me if I had any qualms about the nature of my profession, I would answer you with a solemn denial. I did not rank myself with the herd of common projectors, nor did I consider myself to be in the least tainted by my association with the bodies of the dead. There were occasions when I experienced the pains of solitude, of course, and there came upon my mind a sense of loneliness all the more acute from my presence in the teeming city. Solitude is like despair: it has no remedy. The death of Elizabeth had only confirmed what I believed to be my fate in the world. One afternoon I picked up by chance in a coffee-house a copy of the *Monthly Magazine* and came upon a poem by Bysshe. My attention was immediately arrested by its opening lines:

Youth of tumultuous soul, and haggard eye!
Thy wasted form, thy hurried steps I view
On thy wan forehead starts the lethal dew
And oh! the anguish of that shuddering sigh!

Beside it was a commentary, in smaller type: *His countenance told in a strange and terrible language of agonies that had been, and were, and were still to continue to be.* I could not help but recall Bysshe's look of concern when he came to my apartments, but of course I could not credit him with any prophetic skills.

It was in this period that I began my night walks. I pursued the loneliest and most silent ways, but there were moments when I believed that I could hear footsteps behind me echoing on the cobbles. I would start and look over my shoulder, expecting to see a form or the shadow of a form; but I saw nothing at all. The nights of London are gloomy enough, with all of its miserable lives pent up close together, but for a melancholy man they are an emanation or reflection of his own fearfulness. That was at least how I considered them. In the rain I saw strange shapes moving through the streets, obscure and dark, as if they were carrying burdens. On moonlit nights every sound seemed to be magnified, and a sudden cry or laugh would make me shudder. On such nights, too, the shadows were longer and more intense. Sometimes I stopped on the threshold of a courtyard, or an alley, and peered into the darkness; then a figure would suddenly appear, or pass quickly from one corner to another, and I would step back.

Yet, curiously enough, the night became my home. In the light of day I found myself to be dazed and weary; looking up at the faces of strangers, I sensed hostility and resentment and a thinly veiled contempt. Was this because I possessed a foreign manner? I cannot say. I know only that at night I felt more free. I wandered abroad, through streets of sinister aspect, without the slightest danger of being questioned; I sensed the power of the night, too, when the wildness of the city was manifest.

One dark night I found myself in Wellclose Square, looking down at the emaciated figure of a young man clad in nothing but the filthiest rags. I did not think to touch him, but I leaned over him as he lay upon the uneven stones. He was not sleeping. He opened his eyes. "You have found me," he said. "You know me by the signs."

"Signs?"

"Look at me." He parted the rags across his chest, and I could see that his body was covered with welts and blisters of blood; the stench from the wounds was insupportable, and I turned away. "I am the chosen one," he said, "and you are my disciple."

I walked out of Wellclose Square, and with a shudder returned to my rooms in Jermyn Street.

⇒ ⇐

I HAD NOW THE SETTLED DETERMINATION to create the form of a man. Could we say that a new kind of being might thereby be created, free from the imperfections of the living? My imagination was vivid enough, yet my powers of analysis and application were intense; by the union of their qualities I conceived the idea and began the execution of the task. I was concentrating on the method of creating a sentient human being unencumbered by class or society or faith: it was to be

Bysshe's dream-child, so to speak, free from all the petty tyrannies of prejudice that are to be found in human society.

Where did such a person exist? Of course he existed nowhere. That was the reason, and necessity, for my creation. I believed that the component parts of an excellent human being might be found, brought together, and endued with vital warmth. I had already tested the procedure to my satisfaction, and I had succeeded in discovering the cause of generation and of life. I had achieved much, beyond my most fervent expectations, when I became myself capable of bestowing animation upon lifeless matter. The principle of union or coherency, so that all the organs and fibres of the body might work in unison, was the only one that remained to be explored. This I managed, after much weary labour and experiment, by means of a certain operation in the cerebellum.

Where was I to find the perfect frame upon which to build? There were some in the street who, when I observed them, showed signs of worth. Yet they were still in life, and thus beyond my reach. Then one evening that winter, when he arrived with his cargo, Boothroyd announced that he had a "prize" for me. "This is a good 'un," he said. "He will be as fresh as a peach."

"You have it here?"

"No. He ain't dead yet." With that he burst out laughing.

Then, with prompting from Lane and Miller, he told me the story. There was a student of St. Thomas's Hospital in very poor circumstances; this unfortunate young man had discovered in himself the signs of pulmonary consumption. He had coughed arterial blood into his handkerchief, and had all the signs of lassitude and debility that accompany the disorder.

He knew it to be fatal, since his training with the doctors of Thomas's and his practice among the poorer people of the area had taught him to recognise the progress of the disease. He had also nursed his brother through the stages of the phthisis. Since this young man had worked as a dresser to the surgeons Encliffe and Cato, he knew by sight the resurrectionist men; it was to him, indeed, that they consigned their load at the back steps of the hospital. He knew where they gathered, too, and two weeks previously he had approached them in the Fortune of War.

"So he comes up to us," Boothroyd said, "as pale as a cloth. Ah, I says, there's—"

"I do not wish to know the name," I said.

"I ask him what he is doing in this corner of the world, and he sits down among us. 'I have some business for you,' he says. 'Not perilous business.'"

He then proposed a scheme to them. The young man knew that he was dying, and that he might only have a short time to live. He appealed to the professional instincts of Boothroyd and the two others: if they paid him twenty guineas, he would allow them to take his body at the very instant of death. He required the money for his young sister, a toy-maker who would soon be alone in the world. As for him, he had no fear of being anatomised; he had witnessed the procedure too often in the surgical theatre at Guy's Hospital to shrink from such a fate. He believed his carcass to be worth twenty guineas because it was young, sturdy and well-knit despite the ravages of the disease. He had already ventured upon the subject with his sister herself, who had agreed that the resurrectionists might occupy the little parlour beside the room where he would die.

At the moment of death she would allow them to enter and take away the body of her brother. Neither of the young people had any illusions about the Christian pieties, having seen their parents and two other siblings carried off by epidemic distemper in the most painful circumstances. We are not aware of God, the young man had said.

"What age is he?"

"Tolerably young. Nineteen."

"And you say that he is a fine specimen?"

"None finer. He is like a boxer, Mr Frankenstein. And with a full set of teeth."

Naturally I was excited by the prospect of obtaining such a prize—to retrieve the body moments after its death would be of incalculable benefit, and would certainly expedite the action of the electrical fluid. They told me that the young man lived with his sister near the hospital in a tenement in Carmelite Street, which was no more than yards from Broken Dock and the river; it would take them twenty minutes, with a favourable tide, to bring him to Limehouse.

"I would like to see him," I said. "At the time you have arranged to pass him the money, I wish to be in the vicinity. Then, on my agreement, I will give you the guineas." They consented to this, not without bargaining for a "cut" of ten further guineas for managing the transaction.

≫ ≪

I WAITED BY THE FORTUNE OF WAR. It was a night of fierce rain, such as only London can produce. It rose like smoke all around me, and I sheltered underneath the cabmen's stand just beyond the gate of St. Bartholomew. Boothroyd, Lane and Miller had placed themselves upon a bench by the window overlooking the gate; they had also taken the precaution of placing an oil-lamp on the table in front of them, so that despite the rain I could clearly see their features and gestures. Then I noticed a young man crossing the square, holding his cloak against the driving rain; he walked quickly and purposefully, with no sign of any weakness, but paused for a moment before entering the inn. I saw him for a moment in the flickering light outside the tavern. He had dark curling hair, and in that moment when I saw his bright eyes and full mouth I recognised that this was Jack Keat. He had worked with me in the dissection room of St. Thomas's Hospital. Then he entered the Fortune of War. I crept closer to the window, and watched with dismay as he came up to the resurrectionists and joined them. He seemed uneasy in their company—a circumstance that did not in the least surprise me—but he smiled and said something to Lane. At that moment Boothroyd looked at me through the window. I had told him to expect me there. I nodded, and put up my right hand. That was the signal arranged between us. He came outside and, without saying a word, I passed him the purse of guineas. What else could I have done? The imminent death of Jack troubled and saddened me but, as he had told me himself, we must take courage in the pursuit of our researches. The enlightenment and improvement of the world depended upon human valour. That was what he had said. Was I now to abandon his, and my, beliefs for the sake of my conscience? Yet there was still the possibility—the likelihood—that my electrical treatment would restore him to life. Would he live to smile and to laugh, to walk again with the same quick step? This was not known to me, or to any other being in the world.

I went back to Jermyn Street, where Fred prepared for me the mixture of saloop that always had a curiously soothing effect upon me. I asked him about the business of the day, and he informed me that three brides had married three brothers in the church of St. James across the street, and that the old man who sold the birds on the corner had dropped dead. The birds had not escaped, but had stayed quiet within their little wicker cages. "Nothing else," he said, "has happened in London." I was pleased to hear it, and prepared myself for bed in equable spirits—fully aware, naturally, of the great experiment that lay ahead of me. I could not calculate how long Jack Keat might live, but his pale features were a token of his gathering sickness.

⇒ ⇐

I TRAVELLED DOWN TO LIMEHOUSE that morning in a carriage. I took care to hire a different cab each day, so far as this was possible, in order to avoid any easy recognition. The people of Limehouse I never saw. I always alighted by an empty brick warehouse, built between the river and a lonely path that went across the marshes of the neighbourhood. From there it was a swift journey to my workshop across the debris of the foreshore, where only the gulls observed me with suspicious eyes. There was a path that led from my workshop into the settlement at Limehouse itself, but over the months I had rendered it intractable and even dangerous. I had placed broken glass, and wooden posts, and various pieces of river wreckage, across the track so that no horse or carriage would wish to venture there. The bargees of Limehouse had their own jetty further downstream, and had no reason to cross this land. I had also placed notices saying *Private* on its boundaries. The only true means of access to my workshop, therefore, was by water.

Despite the winter chill I stood upon my wooden quay, wrapped in my greatcoat. I had taken to smoking a pipe, in the manner of the Londoners, and I waited expectantly for any sight or sound of the resurrectionists. Of course I had no hope that their work would be so summarily executed—the young man had walked before me only the evening before—but I was so eager to begin my operation that I could think of nothing else. I had prepared the electrical columns with all the diligence that Hayman had demanded, and according to his strict injunctions, but then in my enforced idleness of waiting I conceived the idea of experimenting upon myself.

A moment's thought would have convinced me of the rashness of my plan; but I was seized with a sudden desire to feel the electrical fluid in as intimate a manner as possible. What was the sensation when it coursed through the fibres and muscles of the body, illuminating and energising every pathway? I was not so lunatic as to test the whole of my body, but instead I placed a metallic band upon my wrist and a small cap or thimble of brass upon each of my fingertips; I chose a relatively low level of current but, even so, when I turned on the column I was at once surrounded by what I can only call a flash of lightning. I had never witnessed this as an observer, so I surmised that the lightning could only be seen by the subject. It lasted no more than two or three seconds, but it seemed to me to have a wave-like pattern. It resembled a curtain of light being shaken.

As the sensation passed I became aware that my hand was trembling violently with some voluntary impulse: it wished to do something and quite by instinct I took up the pen and paper which I always kept by my equipment. My hand seized the pen and immediately began to write in a large and florid manner that I did not recognise as my own. It was the strangest communication I had ever received. *I cannot think of external things as having an external existence,* it wrote, *and I commune with everything I see as something not apart from but inherent in my own nature. To feel is to exist.* Then my hand rested, only to begin again with the same florid and energetic motion. *I am suspended among uncertainties, mysteries, doubts, without any recourse to fact or reason.* At this point I decided to remove, with my free hand, the metal band and the thimbles of brass.

I was perfectly astonished at the outcome of the experiment, and for the next few minutes I wandered around the workshop in a feverish state of excitation. From whom, or where, had these words sprung? Clearly they derived from me in some occluded way. But I had never represented them to myself or, as far as I was aware, ever dreamed of conceiving them. What secret voice was manifesting itself within the power of the electrical fluid? I banged my fist against the wooden side-table by my chair, and at once it splintered into fragments. I seemed to have acquired some fresh access of strength. I went over to the wooden door that separated two of the rooms of the workshop, and with immense ease I struck and shattered one of its panels. I examined my hand with interest, and saw that it was perfectly unharmed by its exertions. I tested it upon the cast-iron stairway leading down into the basement, and realised at once that it was of immense power. The electrical fluid had strengthened it immeasurably, so that I was now capable of curling in my fist a portion of the iron fabric. My other hand retained its normal strength. "I must make sure," I said aloud, "that I do not shake hands with anyone." This was a new power of unutterable consequence. If I had electrified the whole of my body, I would have been resurrected as a being of vast strength. And what of Jack Keat who would soon be entering the workshop? Would he also be endowed with supernatural might?

It was with some relief, I admit, that I felt my hand gradually revert to its state of normal strength; but not without a sensation of painful cramp that lasted for several minutes and caused me agonies of suffering. I could neither flex nor extend it, but laid it down upon the table while it passed through its transition. Eventually the pain abated. I tested my fingers and palm, and found them receptive to ordinary stimuli with no great increase of strength. I did not wish to inflict any pain upon my subject, of course, but I solaced myself with the knowledge that it would not be of any long duration. And surely the dead would react differently from the living?

A week after the experiment I had gone out onto the jetty to witness the effects of a London storm; it was a winter's tale indeed, with great peals of thunder echoing down the chasms and the caverns of the streets while the lightning flash lit up the steeples of the churches and the dome of St. Paul's. The spectacle of the awful and majestic in nature has always the effect of solemnising my mind, especially when it was here so mixed with the haunts of men. All then becomes one life. My reverie was broken by the sight of a small boat making its way to the jetty; the heavy swell and the departing tide seemed to make it ride across the water, and I feared for the safety of its solitary occupant. But he seemed to be a skilful boatman and, when he came closer to the foreshore, I saw that it was Lane. "You have come on a foul night," I said to him as I helped him to secure the rope around the landing post.

"I have never known such a night as this. Boothroyd sent me." I gained the impression that Boothroyd's commands were to be respected.

"What is the matter?"

"Nothing the matter. The boy is going fast. It will be tomorrow or tomorrow night. Be prepared for your body." He asked me for a flask of brandy spirit, which I willingly gave him, and he drank half of it down before venturing once more upon the Thames. The lightning flash seemed to accompany him onto the water, and his shape was soon lost to sight in the veil of rain.

I was deeply interested by the news of Jack's decline. He would come to me within an hour of death, as fresh as if he had fallen asleep, and I would be able to restore his natural warmth and motion. I would awaken him. I had no thought beyond that first moment of resurrection, but now my imagination began to conjure visions of his wonder and gratitude at being restored to life. I busied myself in the workshop, preparing everything for the solemn moment of the electrical charge. I must have gone out to the jetty a thousand times, braving the wind and the rain, in order to look for the resurrectionists and their cargo. I waited throughout that night—sleep was not a consideration for me—and, when dawn came, the rain ceased. All was calm and quiet. Once more I could hear the Thames lapping against the wooden posts of my jetty. Then I heard another sound—the sound of oars splashing in the water. I jumped up from my chair and ran outside to see Boothroyd and

Miller rowing quickly towards the shore. Lane stood at the prow with the landing rope in his hands, and there was another person lying at the back of the boat. It was him. They had not put him in a sack but had lain him carefully in the stern: one arm was hanging over the side, its hand trailing in the water.

I could not keep my eyes from the body as Lane secured the boat. Boothroyd and Miller leapt out, and then knelt down to take it onto the jetty. "Be careful," I murmured. "For his sake."

"Dead only an hour ago," Boothroyd said. "He is served up nice and fresh."

They carried the body into the workshop, and laid it down upon the long wooden table that I had set up. Boothroyd looked upon it with a certain satisfaction, as if he had despatched him himself. "It is the neatest job I have ever done," he said.

I paid them ten guineas, as they had requested, and they returned to their boat. I could hear them laughing as they rowed away across the water.

⇒ Eleven ⇐

HIS WAS THE MOST BEAUTIFUL CORPSE I had ever seen. It seemed
that the flush had not left the cheeks, and that the mouth was
curved in the semblance of a smile. There was no expression
of sadness or of horror upon the face but, rather, one of
sublime resignation. The body itself was muscular and firmly
knit; the phthisis had removed any trace of superfluous fat, and
the chest, abdomen and thighs were perfectly formed. The legs
were fine and muscular, the arms most elegantly proportioned.
The hair was full and thick, curling at the back and sides, and I
noticed that there was a small scar above the left eyebrow. That
was the only defect I could find.

There was no time to lose: perhaps I might still catch the
fluttering spirit, too dazed or bruised to have yet left the body. I
placed the metal bands across the head, and a strip across the
forehead, before I began the procedure of covering the major
nerves and organs with the electrical points. The wrists, the
ankles and the neck were also bound with bracelets of brass
since I believed that the electrical fluid at these points would
bolster the circulation of the blood. The body was soft to
the touch, and I hastened my work to ensure that the stiffness
of death would not intervene. I even took a certain pleasure
in arranging him upon the table, as if I were a sculptor or
painter completing my composition. I intended to employ both

electrical columns, to ensure that the greatest possible charge was available to me, but I had taken the precaution of firing them from several batteries so that I could lower the strength at a moment of danger.

With trembling hands I engaged the power of both and watched in fascination and excitement as the electrical fluid surged through the young body. There was the slightest agitation and then, to my alarm, dark red blood seeped out of his nose and ears; yet I reassured myself that this was an excellent sign of arterial movement. If the blood was circulating through his body, then a first stage had been accomplished. His heart then began to beat very quickly and, when I placed my hand upon his chest, there was a definite sensation of warmth. To my horror I sensed a smell of burning. There was smoke coming from his lower limbs, and I saw at once that the soles of his feet were becoming horribly blistered. I was tempted to lower the charge at once but then the crisis passed; the smoke disappeared, together with the smell of burning. I believed this sudden heat to be the effect of the lightning which I had observed around myself, in the earlier experiment, which had departed after a few seconds. His teeth then began to chatter, with such violence that I feared he might bite off his tongue; I placed a wooden spatula between his open lips. At this point I noticed that his penis had become erect, with a small bead of seminal fluid at its tip; then, *mirabile dictu*, tears began to roll down his face. I could not believe that he wept. I could only surmise that it was some organic or instinctive reaction to the changes wrought in his body. The tear ducts are notoriously weak.

What occurred in the next few minutes has left so deep and

frightful a hold upon my imagination that I can never forget it, night or day; it haunts my sleeping as well as my waking hours, with a horror that is hardly capable of being endured. I noticed first the alteration to his hair: from lustrous black it changed by degrees to a ghastly yellow, and from its curled state it became lank and lifeless.

There is a fear of the dead coming alive, but this was more frightful: in a moment the body in front of me had gone through all the stages of decomposition before being reclaimed and restored to life. His skin seemed to quiver, with a motion like that of waves. But then he grew still. Now his appearance resembled nothing so much as wickerwork. His eyes had opened, but where before they had been of a blue-green hue they were now grey. The body itself had not been deformed in any way: it was as compact and as muscular as before, but it was of a different texture. It looked as if it had been baked. The face still had the remnants of beauty but was now utterly changed in hue, with the curious pattern of wickerwork I had already observed. All this was the work of an instant.

I stepped back in horror, and his eyes followed my movement.

I could not resist the strangeness of his gaze, and we stared at one another. I was observing someone who had gone beyond death and had returned, but what did he imagine that I was? I could see nothing in his eyes except the darkness from which he had come. His lips parted, and then there issued from him the strangest sequence of sounds I had ever heard: it was like a rolling cascade of tones and pitches, but utterly discordant and repulsive. They were the sounds from the depths, sounds which should have been muffled or stifled, but to my astonishment I realised that he was attempting to sing. He was singing to me, while he continued to gaze upon me, and I stood in such awe of him that I could not move. This was no longer Jack. This was something else.

I do not know how long I stood there, but he was at length overcome by some kind of convulsion of restlessness. He began to rise from the table. With no more effort than would suffice for the breaking of a twig he snapped the bands which held down his neck, wrists and ankles; then he sat upright.

He looked around the workshop, as an animal might survey his cage, and then once more turned to me. He smiled, if it may be called a smile; his blackened lips opened, and there was a frightful rictus running from ear to ear. I could see a set of brilliantly white teeth, all the more startling in his discoloured mouth.

I backed away, taking a few paces, and found myself against the wall of the workshop where I kept my glass vessels and retorts for experimental use. For a moment he seemed to lose interest in me. He noticed his penis, still erect, and with a groan he began to stimulate himself in front of me. I looked on in absolute astonishment as he laboured to produce the seminal fluid. What monstrous issue might emerge from one who had died and had been reborn? His most devoted efforts were unavailing, however, and he turned to me with a curiously submissive or perhaps embarrassed look. Did he consider me to be his keeper, or his guardian, or his creator? Had he sinned like Adam in the Garden?

He walked a few steps, and I noticed that his movements were light and vigorous. I saw that he was about to walk towards me and, in my alarm, I put out both of my hands in supplication. "No!" I shouted to him. "Come no closer, if you please!" He hesitated. I was not sure whether he still understood human speech, or whether my strident voice and gestures had deterred him.

He stood uncertainly in the middle of the room, and moved his head from side to side as if testing the muscles of his neck. He put his hands up to his face, and seemed perplexed by the mottled texture of his flesh; he examined his hands very carefully, and seemed not to recognise them as his own. Again he looked at me, craftily and almost cunningly; again I put out my hands to prevent him.

To my utter relief he turned away from me and began walking towards the door that led to the jetty. He raised his face as if he had sensed the river close by. He did not open the door; he pushed himself past it, overthrowing it with one blow of his right arm. He seemed to relish the scents of the night and the river, the tar and the smoke and the filth that accrue to the foreshore. He surveyed the scene of both of the banks, and then seemed to look keenly downstream towards the sea. He raised his arms above his head, in a gesture of celebration or supplication, and plunged into the water. He was able to swim at an extraordinary speed, and within a very few moments he was out of my sight.

My first sensation was one of relief, that my odious handiwork had left me, but that was quickly followed by a fear and horror so intense that I could scarcely stand. I could not bring myself to remain in my workshop, the site of that terrible rebirth, and I staggered along the foreshore until I reached

Limehouse Stairs. It was not an area to be visited by night, but I had lost all sense of physical danger. I was beset by a horror more frightful than any with which a human being could threaten me. I sat upon the damp steps, with bowed head, seeing nothing ahead of me but darkness. I hoped that the foul being might disappear for ever—might even be lost in the sea, if that was indeed his destination. It was possible that he might have no memory of his origin, and never return to Limehouse or to London in search of the mystery of his existence. Nevertheless I had created a being that might become a terror to the world, unhewn and endowed with unnatural strength. A rat scuttled past me and dropped into the water. Or perhaps he might quickly lose his strength, as my hand had done, and revert to a position of incapacity or weakness? In that case he would be a wretched being indeed, but not one to instil panic fear. Yet what kind of being was he? Was he aware that he possessed human existence? Did he even possess a consciousness?

I stood up, and walked from the stairs to the church of St. Lawrence by the Causeway. Never had I felt so strong a need for comfort and consolation, from whatever source it might come, and I mounted the worn steps towards the great door. I could not bring myself to cross the threshold. I was an accursed thing. I had taken my stand outside the range of God's creation. I had usurped the Creator himself. This was no place for me. It was then, I believe, that the fever fell upon me. I do not remember where I wandered, but I was in a mist of fears and delusions. I recall entering a public house, and being served gin and other spirits until I dropped unconscious. I must have been robbed, and left in the street, because I woke up in a stinking alley. Still

I wandered. For a few moments I must have believed that I had returned to my native Geneva, for I spoke a few words in French and German; then I was buffeted by the crowds along the highway, and I recall that my body was soaking with sweat and ague. It began to rain, and I crept down a side street where the overhanging roofs were able to shield me. I had never been more wretched—I, who had dreamed of renown, was no more than a wanderer in the streets of men. I heard a sudden sound behind me, at the other end of the street, and a cat screeched. I turned around in horror. I was struck by the terror that *he* might be pursuing me; I fled back into the highway and, joining without choice or thought the steady stream of people, I made my way eventually into the central neighbourhoods of London. I had been weeping—for how long, I do not know—and a gingerbread seller passed me a red cloth as I leaned against the wall beside her stall.

"Do you know what you are doing?" she asked me.

"I must go on." I wanted to ask her the direction in which I lived, but for that moment I could not remember the name of the street. I could not remember anything. She gave me one of her cakes; my mouth was too dry and inflamed to swallow it, and I spat it out before moving on. Some instinct, common to all life, led me home. I found myself in Piccadilly. I staggered and fell against a horse post, but then who helped me to my feet but Fred?

"Whatever has happened to you, Mr. Frankenstein?"

"I don't know. I don't know what has happened to me."

"You have had a mauling, you have."

"Have I?"

"Do you know who did it?"

"I did it."

He led me down Piccadilly and around the corner into Jermyn Street. I recognised the neighbourhood but then I became delirious again, and Fred explained to me later that I had been muttering words and phrases to myself that he could not understand. He washed me, put me in my bed, and called his mother. Mrs. Shoeberry ministered to me during the whole period of my fever. I discovered later that she piled the sheets and blankets on me "to force it out," as she put it; all the windows and doors to my room were closed, and a fire was left perpetually burning in the grate. I wondered that she did not stifle me to death. The first thing I recall is her sitting by me, with a piece of needlework on her lap.

"Oh, there you are again, Mr. Frankenstein. I am ever so glad to see you."

"Thank you."

"I suppose you would like some small beer, would you?"

"My throat."

"It will be dry, sir. It has been torrid in here. It has been something fierce. Fred, bring some beer."

"Saloop," I said weakly. I scarcely recognised where I was, and was dimly aware of the old woman as someone I had met in the past. "Fred will brew it rich," she said. "He is a good boy."

Then I saw Fred standing at the foot of the bed, grinning at me and hopping from one foot to the next in his excitement. All at once the memory of my situation came back to me. "I knew you was coming round," he said, "when you took some water from me." I had no memory of this. "Before that, you was raving."

"Raving? What was I saying?"

"Don't you worry a bit about it," Mrs. Shoeberry replied for him. "It was a lot of nonsense, Mr. Frankenstein. Fred, get on with that saloop."

"But what kind of nonsense?"

"Devils and fiends and such stuff. I paid no attention to it." I hoped that I had not said too much, and made a note to question Fred later on the subject. He brought me in a dish of saloop, and I drank it down greedily.

"How long have I lain here?"

"A little over a week," she said. "The children have been doing the laundry. Would you be requiring some dry toast, Mr. Frankenstein?" I shook my head. I felt too weak to eat. Yet slowly, during that day and over the next week, I recovered my strength. When Mrs. Shoeberry had departed, quite satisfied with her payment of seven guineas, I questioned Fred about my ravings.

"There was a song you sung," he said.

"A mountain song?"

"I would not know about that, sir. But there was no mountains in it." Then he stood quite still, his arms hanging down against his sides, and recited:

Like one, that on a lonesome road
Doth walk in fear and dread,
And having once turned round, walks on
And turns no more his head:
Because he knows, a frightful fiend
Doth close behind him tread.

It was all the more horrible coming from the mouth of an innocent boy. I knew the lines at once, since they came from one of Mr. Coleridge's poems, but I do not remember being particularly impressed by them at the time of reading them. They must have been in the air around me, as I lay in a fever.

I was able to bathe, and dress, myself on the following morning. The one subject of course oppressed and haunted me like some giant despair. My enforced retirement had also left me restless and fretful: I could not keep still. I hailed a cab in Jermyn Street, and was taken to Limehouse where I leapt out and all but ran along the path towards my workshop. As soon as I came close to it I knew that he had returned: the door facing the river had been smashed by the giant blow he had delivered on first gaining his freedom; but now part of the brick wall beside it had been dislodged, and there were pieces of broken glass on the muddy ground that led to the jetty. I slowed my pace, and my immediate impulse was to flee or at least to conceal myself. But some graver sense—of responsibility, or of submission, I do not know which—overcame me. I walked towards the workshop, and entered through the gaping hole which he had left. The place was in ruinous disorder: the great electrical columns had been overturned and lay smashed upon the floor, and my experimental apparatus had been systematically destroyed. My notes and papers, as well as some bills of lading for the electrical equipment, had been removed from my desk; the cloak and hat that I had left behind, on that dreadful night, were also gone. He had taken some kind of revenge, and had then left the scene of his rebirth.

I was placed in a state of fearful indecision. The records of all my experiments had been taken by him, and the equipment had been destroyed by his hand, but what possible use could any of it now possess? My work had come to an end—or, rather, it had been usurped by the emergence of a living being. There was no more to be done. I decided then to leave the workshop, never to return. I was happy to imagine it falling into ruin, the home of scavengers and of seabirds, rather than to see any new dwellings built upon its accursed ground. It would be for me a place of mournful and never-ending remembrance.

I walked back through streets, familiar and unfamiliar, with a general apprehension that he did indeed "somewhere behind me tread"; there were moments when my own shadow alarmed me, and I looked back with dread on several occasions. There was often the echo of a footfall in the alleys and along the quieter streets, and again I would glance around in fear. Eventually I found myself in Jermyn Street, and the expression on Fred's face was enough to tell me that I had sustained a great anxiety. "You look like you was touched by Old Nick," he said.

"No. Not touched."

"The gentleman came to see you."

"Gentleman? What gentleman?" For a moment I believed him to be referring to the creature.

Fred seemed genuinely alarmed by my response. "No need to disturb yourself, sir. It was only him."

He handed me a card on which Bysshe had scrawled a note to the effect that he and Harriet were intending to visit me early that evening: *We have something, or someone, to show you.*

I prepared myself for their arrival as best I could. I took a spoonful of laudanum to calm myself, having become acquainted with the merits of that preparation by Mrs. Shoeberry who seems to have dosed me liberally during my confinement. "There is nothing like it," she had said just before leaving me. "It is safer than the drink, and more soothing to the soul." I had indeed found it a palliative for wounded nerves, and had regained a measure of composure when Fred announced the arrival of Bysshe and Harriet. I had not seen Harriet since the days before the elopement to the Lakes, and she seemed to be much improved by marriage. She had more vitality and assurance than I remembered, assisted no doubt by the infant she was carrying in her arms. "This is Eliza," she said. "Eliza Ianthe."

"Not the first of my productions, Victor, but the finest." There was so wide a difference, between Bysshe's creation and my own, that I felt like weeping. A young woman followed them up the stairs, to whom I was not introduced; I took her to be the wet-nurse, and indeed Harriet gave her the baby after a moment's petting.

"You look changed," Harriet said to me as I took them into the drawing room. "You have become more serious. You are no longer a young man."

"I have experienced much since I last saw you."

"Oh?"

"But nothing of any consequence. Tell me, Bysshe, what is the news?"

"The usual record of crimes and miseries. You do not read the public prints?" I shook my head. "Then you know nothing of the outrages."

"I lead a retired existence."

"We are advertising a subscription for the families of the frame-makers." I must have looked puzzled. "You should begin to live in the world, Victor. Fourteen frame-makers were executed at York last week. For the crime of wishing employment." He then went on to inveigh against the undue respect that men paid to property, and began to enlist the history of Greece for the sake of his argument. Harriet and the wet-nurse sat exchanging remarks about the infant. His soliloquy reminded me of our evenings in Oxford, and I was curiously reassured by it. "So Harriet is not my property," he began to inform me. "Eliza is not my property. Love is free. Its very essence is liberty, Victor, not compatible with obedience or jealousy or fear."

"I am sure your wife will be pleased to hear it."

"Harriet understands me perfectly well. We are in unity. No. We are a trinity now. The infant child is our saviour." He continued in the same fanciful vein for a little longer, but the events of the day soon began to render me weary. With his quick sympathy he realised that I was no longer in a suitable frame of mind to enjoy his society, and he rose to leave with good grace. "Victor must rest," he told Harriet. "His spirits need restoring."

"Will you not stay for supper?"

"No. Your need is greater. You look as if all the cares of the world had fallen upon you."

"I have not slept. That is all."

"Then sleep. Sleep is the balm for woe."

They took their leave, with many professions of friendship, and I watched them as they made their way out of Jermyn Street in search of a carriage. The crowd surrounded them instantly and I felt a curious anxiety or fear on their behalf. It was a momentary sensation, but it left me more wretched than before. For the rest of the evening, I walked through the city. I do not know how I passed the succeeding days.

⇒ Twelve ⇐

IT WAS A MORNING in November. The light of dawn filtered through an opening in the shutters, and I could discern the outlines of my shirt and jacket that Fred had folded; in the half-light they looked curiously alive, as if they had been waiting expectantly for me to awake. I slumbered again for a few minutes, in a blissful state of non-consciousness, before being aroused by the sound of horses in the street outside. I rose from my bed, and threw open the shutters. That is when I saw him, standing on the corner and looking fixedly up at my window. Yet at first I did not see him. He seemed to be part of a wooden porch there, wood upon wood, until he stepped forward. He was wearing my cloak, and my broad-brimmed hat, but I could not mistake him for a moment; the face was white, seemingly curved and crumpled like a sheet of paper, with the same blank eyes that had stared at me from the table in my workshop. He must have taken my address from the bills of exchange he had purloined, and now he had tracked me down. He stood quite still, and made no attempt to claim my attention. He simply looked up without expression. And then, very suddenly, he turned and walked away.

I was in a state of astonishment and fearfulness not to be expressed. I ran into the kitchen, where Fred was frying a veal chop for my breakfast. "Stop what you are doing," I said, "and leave."

He looked at me in disbelief.

"You have done nothing wrong, Fred. Here is money to keep you. I must go. I must go at once."

"You are still dreaming, Mr. Frankenstein."

"This is no dream, Fred. This is reality. I must leave the house as soon as possible. A terrible fate hangs over it."

My impatience and anxiety seemed then to infect him. He ran into the bedroom, and began to pack my portmanteau, even though I did not have the slightest notion of my destination.

Within a very short time I was ready to depart. I gave Fred a set of the keys, with strict instructions to lock every door and window. "If I am not the guard-dog here I will be with my mother," he said. "In Short's Rents."

"I have given you enough money to support yourself?"

"You have been very generous, sir. When will you be back?"

"I am not sure. I do not know."

When I came out into the street I looked fearfully from side to side, in case he had returned; but there was no sign. I still had no notion of where I might travel, but then Bysshe's recent journey came into my head. He had told me that the coach for the north left from the Angel at Islington, and on a sudden and peremptory instinct it was there I travelled. By great good fortune the coach had been delayed by a collision blocking the Essex Road, and I managed to purchase a ticket that would take me—if I wished—as far as Carlisle. I was delighted to put as many miles as possible between myself and London.

I must have seemed a strange fellow traveller, for I remained in silence and in a kind of stupor throughout the whole journey; we rested and changed horses at Matlock, and I tried to sleep in a box-seat in the parlour of the inn there. But I could find no rest. In my mind was always his image, wrapped in my dark cloak, his blank eyes staring up at my window. I alighted at Kendal and caught a local post-chaise to Keswick, to which Bysshe had once referred; during my ride the landscape did indeed seem delightful, although I was scarcely in a frame of mind to entertain its beauties. The great lake reminded me of Lake Geneva, and the mountains around it were like a smaller relic of the mountains around my native city. I was half-expecting the bell of the great cathedral to sound across the waters. I took in all this at a glance, while my anxious thoughts remained elsewhere. How could I ever be able to shake off this demon, this incubus, that haunted me?

I was directed to a small inn that lodged travellers, where I lay that night. I slept only fitfully, woken by a storm that had rolled down over the mountains and by the stirrings of my own unquiet mind, but I spent my first day attempting to tire myself by walking over the steepest ground. To be free—to live among the mountains—now seemed to me the height of my endeavours. I contemplated removing myself to my native land, and there leading a life of blissful withdrawal from the world.

I returned to the inn that evening weary and in need of sleep. I ate the meal that the landlord's wife put in front of me, and drank copious quantities of Cumberland ale seasoned with port and pepper. But still I could not rest. I slumbered only fitfully, my rest interrupted as it were by flashes of lightning in which I glimpsed the form and figure of the creature. I rose at dawn, and walked to the side of the lake; the garden of the inn sloped downward until it reached the bank, where I stood and surveyed a scene of stillness and silence. There was an island near the middle of the lake, already partly illuminated by the rays of the rising sun, while the landscape of hills and mountains behind it was still in shadow. There was a mist coming off the water that swirled across its surface; curiously, too, there were congregations of wispy vapours that seemed to hover above the water in the pattern of a vortex or whirlpool.

A small boat emerged from the other side of the island, a speck in the mist around me, but steadily it grew larger. The fishermen rose early here. As the craft came nearer to the shore I could discern a man standing upright at the prow, a dark figure silhouetted against the water and the vapour. As he came closer still I could see that his arms were raised above his head, and that he seemed to be waving at me. It was possible that he was in distress, and I waved back in reassurance. Then to my utter horror and amazement I realised who it was that stood in the boat and hailed me. The creature came steadily closer, and I could see the lurid yellow hair and the blank grey eyes. Now he held out his arms: his hands were covered in blood.

I turned back and ran towards the inn, in my haste stumbling over the root of a tree; as I rose from the ground I looked back fearfully over my shoulder. The boat, and its occupant, had gone. They must have been swallowed up in the mist which now crept over the further shore. Still I hastened back to the inn and, although I knew that nothing could hold him at bay, instinctively I locked the door of my chamber. This visitation was evidence of some terrible event. I was sure of it. His bloody hands were the token of some crime perpetrated in vengeance. I went to my window, overlooking the garden and the lake, but he was no more to be seen. My first impulse was to flee, but then I checked myself. I could not spend the rest of my life in headlong flight from my persecutor; even the fate of Cain was less terrible than that.

I decided to return to London, and there verify any deeds he might have committed. I was in a sense curious about the nature of his exploits, since he may thus have displayed something of his debased temperament. I might discover at first hand the nature of that which I had created. But these were fugitive thoughts, not to be expressed even to myself in a definite form. I was still too much in a whirlwind of fearfulness and foreboding.

I discovered that the next carriage to London left from Kendal on the following morning; so for the rest of that day I stayed in my room, looking steadfastly at the lake for any further sight of him. There was none. I suspected—I knew—that he would follow me back to London, just as he had traced me to this secluded place. How he travelled I had not the faintest idea, but I believed that he was still possessed of some preternatural strength. My apprehension rose as, on the following morning, I boarded the coach and began the journey southwards.

WHEN EVENTUALLY I BEGAN to smell London, among the fields and market gardens of its periphery, my fear increased to an alarming degree. It was as if I had smelled *him*. We came by way of Highgate, and from the hill I could see the great immensity boiling and smoking ahead of me. If I went down once more into its streets, its entrails, would I ever be free again? The encroaching sound was like that of a vast herd of beasts; among them, too, I knew that he would soon be dwelling.

From the Angel I took a carriage to Jermyn Street. I approached the house with some trepidation, since in my imagination I had seen him putting it to the torch or inflicting some harm upon it. But it stood as chastely as before, shuttered and locked in the quiet street. I took my keys, and entered. As I climbed the stairs, I heard a faint sound. Then, as I climbed higher, I realised that there was someone talking in a low voice in my rooms above. I could hear a voice, quiet, thoughtful. There was then a sudden movement, alarming me for that instant, and then at the head of the stairs appeared Bysshe and Fred.

"Thank God you are here, Victor!" Bysshe's troubled voice aroused all my own fears.

"What is it? Whatever is the matter?"

"Harriet has been killed."

I swayed upon the stairs, and clutched the banister for support. "I don't . . ."

"She was found in the Serpentine. Foully strangled."

"I met him in the street, sir," Fred was telling me. "He begged a place of privacy."

I was scarcely listening to him. "When did this thing happen?"

"Four nights ago." So I had seen the creature, standing by the corner, on the morning after his crime. "And there is worse."

"What could be worse?"

"Her necklace, the instrument that killed her, was found in Daniel Westbrook's pocket."

"Her brother Daniel? No, that is not possible. That is beyond reckoning. He adored her. He protected her." I climbed the stairs slowly, my hand over my eyes; at that moment, I did not wish to see anything of the world.

"He has been locked away in Clerkenwell," Fred said.

"It cannot be so." I had a sudden vision of the creature, waving at me from the lake with bloodstained hands; I ran up the stairs, and rushed over to the basin in my bedroom where I retched violently.

Bysshe followed me in. "Ianthe has gone to Harriet's sisters. It is her best possible home. After the funeral, I do not know."

"And you?"

"Fred kindly agreed that I might stay here. Until your return, of course."

"No. It is not safe for you here, Bysshe."

"Not safe?"

"I think, Bysshe, that you must leave London. Until your grief is allayed. There are too many memories for you here. What have you done with Harriet's clothes?"

"Her clothes? They are hanging still in our lodgings."

"Fred will collect them. He will give them away on the streets. It is the only course, Bysshe."

I must have been talking wildly, because he laid his hand upon my arm. "That will not lessen my grief, Victor. How could it? She is absent from me every waking moment. I saw her body on the bank by the water."

"It is a beginning. I will accompany you now to the coaching office. I will purchase a ticket. I have heard you speak of Marlow, by the Thames. Did you not stay there for a boating holiday?"

"Yes. In my school days."

"There you must go. Do you have money for your journey?"

He shook his head. "I have exhausted my allowance."

I took out my purse of sovereigns, and gave it to him. "That will suffice."

Before he had time for reflection or for argument, I accompanied him to the office on Snow Hill and persuaded him to board a post-chaise. I knew that he must leave the city. As my friend and companion, he was not safe from the vengeance that had been wreaked upon Harriet.

⇒ ⇐

I DID NOT WISH TO RETURN to Jermyn Street. Not yet. Instead I made my way to the Serpentine in Hyde Park; it is a modest stretch of water, longer than it is broad, populated by wildfowl of every description. I walked along its length, hoping to locate that spot where Harriet had been strangled and thrown into the water; I wished to see if I could find any traces of the creature. I had no doubt that he had followed Harriet and had murdered her: I knew it as soberly and as exactly as if I had witnessed the deed. He was the murderer. I could not doubt it. Yet in that sense I was also the murderer. I had fashioned the instrument that had killed Harriet, just as surely as if I had put my own hands around her neck. What was I to do? I could proclaim my guilt, but I would be deemed a madman in thrall to all the ravings of insanity. I would not save Daniel Westbrook.

There was a dark stretch of the bank, beneath a foot-tunnel, to which I made my way. There was a slight movement among the trees and bushes that bordered the water here, and a barely perceptible sweeping sound suggested that something was walking there with slow and steady step. Something was keeping pace with me. Then I glimpsed him, in hat and cloak, his white furrowed face turned towards me for a moment before he bounded away. No other proof was required. He wished to see my tears, and perhaps to exult over them. Yet he also had some facility to anticipate my thoughts. Why else had he waited for me to come to the scene of his crime?

Once more the utter impossibility of revealing this to any living being left me feeling bewildered and abased. I would be locked away in Bedlam, where in the end I might even seek for madness as a relief from my sufferings. In my wretchedness, however, I began to sense within myself an unexpected purpose and a fresh courage. I would return to the workshop along the river, and wait for his appearance. I would question him. I might even implore him to leave for ever the scene of his desperate crime. I did not for one moment think him capable of argument, but he might be open to command. If I were his creator, he might learn obedience.

⇒ ⇐

YET IT WAS MY DUTY first to visit Daniel Westbrook in his prison cell, and offer him what comfort I might provide. On the next morning I made my way to the New Prison at Clerkenwell, furnished with payment for his gaolers as well as books and wholesome food for Daniel himself. He had been placed in a cell below ground, and I was led down a gloomy passageway; it was lit by torches, and smelled of urine and fetid air. "More fierce than Newgate," the gaoler whispered to me.

Daniel was in a small cell at the end of the row; he jumped up from his plank-bed when I entered, and embraced me. "It is so good of you, Victor, so good of you."

"It is not good. I am not good." I scarcely knew what I was saying, faced as I was with the unwitting and innocent victim of my own crime.

"You know what I am accused of?"

"Take your time. I fervently believe in your innocence, and will essay every means in my power to free you."

"They say that I murdered Harriet, Victor!"

"Tell me what occurred."

"I had gone to the Serpentine to meet her. We often walked there together in the evening. She was not at our usual meeting place. I was fatigued after my day's work; I slept beneath a tree— lulled to rest by the sound of the water—but then I was roughly shaken awake. It was a party of the watch. To my horror I saw that my hands were smeared with blood. When they searched me at their office, they found a necklace in my pocket. It was her necklace, Victor. How could it have been in my pocket? At first they considered me no more than a thief or footpad. But then her body was found in the water. She had been strangled with the necklace, and had bled copiously from the nose. Who could think it, Victor? Who could accuse me of murdering her?"

"There has been some terrible miscarriage here, Daniel. Some wilful perversion of facts. Do you have a solicitor?"

"I have no funds—"

"Leave that to me. What are your circumstances here?"

"Look around. My only comfort is that the gaol is used for democrats and revolutionaries. But they have no fellow feeling for me. They look upon me with horror. As the murderer of my sister."

As I stood in the wretched cell, with its floor of beaten earth, I resolved to use any and every means to save Daniel from the executioner. I believed that I understood the sequence of events. The creature, having committed the crime, had decided in his malevolence to throw the suspicion upon someone else. Or perhaps in some primitive sense he believed that he might avoid the guilt by placing it upon someone other. Who could fathom his reasons? Had he known that Daniel was Harriet's brother, or had he come by chance upon his sleeping form?

When I took my leave of Daniel I glanced back at his dimly lit cell, where he seemed to be the most isolated and wretched being on the earth. And I had placed him there! It was my crime for which he was to be judged, and my doom to which he had been assigned. If I could have changed places with him, I would have done so without hesitation.

⋙⋘

AS SOON AS I HAD LEFT Clerkenwell I made my way to Bartholomew Close, where my lawyer kept his chambers. Mr. Garnett had assisted me over the purchase of the workshop in Lambeth, but I knew from his own account that he also dealt in criminal matters. He was a man of sanguine complexion, full of pleasantries, and he listened attentively as I laid out the facts of the matter.

"Your friend," he said, "is in a deal of trouble. I have read of the case, Mr. Frankenstein, in the *Chronicle*."

"Is opinion against him?"

"Decidedly. But that is no bar to justice."

He possessed a reassuring manner, which I caught at eagerly. "Can Daniel be saved then?"

"If it is within the bounds of possibility, then it will be done. Where are the husband and child of the unfortunate lady?"

"The child is with her sisters in Whitechapel. The husband—has retired to the country for some rest."

"He is the son of a baronet, is he not? According to the *Chronicle*."

"That is so."

"Your friend's position is all the more difficult. Will you join me in a glass of sherry? Cold weather, is it not?" He rose from his desk and, after pouring out two glasses, he went over to the window. "I get a very good view of the churchyard, Mr. Frankenstein. It is an interesting speculation how many lie buried there. Over the centuries, it amounts to a fair number. If they were all to rise again, I feel sure that the neighbourhood would be crowded."

It was not a speculation that I cared to pursue. "Is there any chance that Daniel might be released before his trial?"

He laughed, in the politest manner. "Not the slightest possibility, I am afraid. Unthinkable. If he is innocent, of course, then the murderer is still walking on the streets of London. It is to be hoped that he kills again, in exactly the same circumstances."

"So Daniel might then be cleared?"

"A case could be made. Do you have any doubts about your friend's innocence?"

"No. None whatever."

"What makes you so certain?"

I hesitated for a moment. "I know him very well. Violence is utterly foreign to his nature. Especially against his beloved sister."

"But people are not always what they seem, Mr. Frankenstein. They harbour secrets. They work in the dark."

"Not Daniel."

"Very well. I will visit the police office this afternoon, and acquaint myself with the evidence in this case. Do not attempt to see the prisoner, if you please. You should not be implicated in this matter. I will be your messenger. The authorities know me well enough. In the meantime I suggest that you leave London for the cleaner air. The fogs are almost upon us."

"But Daniel—"

"Nothing can be done before the trial. Leave me an address where I can find you."

⇒ ⇐

MY EXPERIENCES OF THAT DAY, and my encounter with Daniel in his prison cell, had left me exhausted. I returned to Jermyn Street where Fred had prepared me a dish of eggs and butter. "Have you seen the fiend in human form?" he asked me.

"What? What are you saying to me?"

I must have looked fiercely at him, because he recoiled from my glance. "The brother, sir."

"The brother?" I paused for a moment to collect my thoughts. "Yes. I have seen him. He is not a fiend. He is as innocent of this crime as you are, Fred." At this moment, I sank my head and wept.

Fred became agitated, hopping from one leg to the other. "Would you care for more butter, sir?" He rushed out of the room, and came back with a handkerchief that he placed delicately beside my chair. I cried for myself—I cried for Daniel—I cried for Harriet—the whole storm of tears all the darker for the absence of any possible relief. Mr. Garnett had advised me to leave London, and for an instant I thought of travelling to Marlow to be with Bysshe, but a moment's consideration dissuaded me. I still wished to encounter the creature: if I could not placate him, or persuade him to retire to some solitary place, I would somehow have to end the life that I had created. There was no other course. He had overturned my electrical machines in the Limehouse workshop, but might there be some way of harnessing the batteries and of destroying him?

∌∈

IN MY EAGERNESS to hear news of Daniel I went back to Bartholomew Close the next day, where Mr. Garnett welcomed me with a grave countenance. "I can offer you very little hope," he said. "The evidence is very powerful. It seems that your friend—that Mr. Westbrook—has almost confessed to the crime."

"How could he confess to that which he did not commit?"

"When he was apprehended at the Serpentine, he was confused and scarcely intelligible."

"He had just been rudely awaken from sleep."

"He muttered that something dreadful had happened to his sister."

"A premonition. A vision."

"The law places no trust in visions, Mr. Frankenstein." He went over to the window, and once more looked over the churchyard of St. Bartholomew's. "Will you be staying in London, after all?"

"I must remain for a few days."

"Of course. The funeral of Mrs. Shelley is to be conducted on Friday. Would you wish me to accompany you?"

"No. That is kind of you. But I will go with Bysshe."

"At the church of St. Barnabas. In Whitechapel." He wrote down the locality, and the time, upon a card. "Please pay my compliments to Mr. Shelley."

AS SOON AS I RETURNED to Jermyn Street I summoned Fred, and asked him to travel with all possible speed to Marlow. "Change coaches if you must," I told him. "Fly like the wind. Take this note with you." I scribbled a message begging him to abandon his isolation and return for Harriet's funeral. "Do not rest," I said as I pressed the note into his hand.

"I am here," he said. "But I am gone already."

"Mr. Shelley will not be difficult to find."

"Odd cove, I shall say. Dressed in blue. Cravat untied."

I awaited their return with eagerness. Mr. Garnett was a good prognosticator: the fogs did arrive, early that afternoon, and I could see nothing from my window but the curling grey and green vapours stirred by a fitful wind. I could make out the figures in the street only vaguely, just as dark shapes against the shifting miasma. There were occasions when a figure taller, or faster, than others arrested my attention. Could it be the creature pacing up and down beside my door? In my restless state of mind I could almost have welcomed the confrontation—I was resolute in my intention to tame him.

On the following afternoon I heard the step of Fred upon the stairs. He came into the room alone. "Where is Mr. Shelley?" "He sends his regrets, sir. He was ever so tearful."

Fred then handed me a letter, addressed to me in Bysshe's characteristic large and sprawling hand. He apologised for remaining in Marlow, but blamed his wretched and enfeebled state; he did not have the strength to attend Harriet's funeral, which would only add another burden of woe to the sorrow he now felt. Although he bitterly remonstrated with himself for his incapacity, he knew that it would be a blow to shatter him:

I cannot as yet comprehend Harriet's death, and to see her lowered in a few feet of churchyard earth, and to hear the nonsense of the parson, would diminish the significance of her loss to me.

He then went on to inform me that the Godwins had taken a house at Marlow to be near him:

I have spoken before of Mr. Godwin, the social philosopher. He is a great exponent of Progress, and offers me much comfort. He is accompanied by his daughter, Mary, who is the child of the revered Mary Wollstonecraft. Mr. Godwin tells me that she has all of her mother's fire and intelligence. I can quite believe it. Pray kiss the Westbrook sisters for me. I will be writing to them.
Your ever devoted Bysshe.

I was surprised by the brevity of the letter, and by Bysshe's reluctance to be present at the funeral, but I ascribed both to his overwhelming grief.

I ATTENDED THE FUNERAL on that Friday morning, in the little church of St. Barnabas just beyond the Whitechapel High Road. Harriet's sisters were blank with grief. Emily was carrying the infant, Ianthe, who remained quite silent throughout the ceremony. Once I had looked upon Emily with affection, but the faint stirrings of that emotion had long since left me. Their father seemed more robust and, if I may say it, more cheerful than on the occasion when I had last encountered him. It was snowing thickly when we stepped into the churchyard, and the open grave was already fringed with white when poor Harriet's coffin was laid into the soil. Just as it reached the level earth there was a sudden rustling in the bank of trees behind us, as if someone or something was thrashing in the branches. I am convinced that all of us at that moment experienced a sudden horror—for me it was evidence of the creature, as I thought, but for the others the object of some unknown fear.

"A fox," Mr. Westbrook said in a loud voice. "The little foxes that spoil the vines."

Emily came up to me afterwards, still holding Ianthe in her arms. "Daniel's trial is set for Monday morning," she said. "Will you come?"

"Of course."

"Is there hope?"

"I cannot pretend to you, Emily, that I harbour any."

"I thought not. But you will be there?" I promised once more to attend. "Mr. Shelley has written to us about Ianthe."

"He told me so."

"He strongly desires that we should continue to be her guardians. It is what we wish to do."

"She could have no better care."

"We will teach her to respect her father and to venerate the memory of her mother." I was struck, as I had been on first meeting her, by Emily's strength of purpose.

⇒ ⇐

I WENT TO THE COURT OF JUSTICE at the Old Bailey on that Monday morning; the Sessions House, where the trial was to be held, looked to me more like a cardboard puppet theatre than a place of justice. The judge was adorned with scarlet and white, and he held a linen handkerchief up to his nose to ward off the lingering putrescence of gaol fever. The jurors sat on two rows of benches on the left-hand side of the court; they were London rate-payers, of course, with all the smugness and self-sufficiency of their type. There was a large crowd in the body of the courtroom itself, made up of shopmen and apprentices, of vagrant boys and ballad singers, of anyone who had no other pastime or occupation that afternoon. There were reporters and sketch-makers there, too, all of them causing an incessant bustle and noise. It was very like watching the activity of a London street. On the right-hand side of the court was a small wooden witness box into which, much to the excitement of the spectators, Daniel was now led. His wrists were bound with manacles, and he was wearing the same clothes that I had seen on him in the cell at Clerkenwell. The judge then called all those present to be silent, as a prayer was intoned by the clerk of the court to the Divine Judge who—it must be presumed— would watch over these proceedings. Daniel did not join in the prayer, but stood calmly looking down at his manacled hands. Then, in a round and portentous voice, one of the attorneys sitting at a table immediately beneath the judge began to read out the charges. Daniel stood almost at attention, without any perceptible movement; he was intent upon every word, as if it were a story of someone else's crime. When the attorney had finished his account, Daniel looked around at the court with an expression of impatience.

He was asked if he wished to enter any plea, and he replied with an earnest "Not guilty!" The officers of the watch were then called to a witness box, directly opposite that in which Daniel stood. The first of them, Stephen Martin, explained the circumstances of finding "the accused" sleeping beneath a tree by the Serpentine. "That is a lake," the judge told the jurors, "to be found in the Hyde Park." The jurors, who must have known this very well already, received the information with great seriousness. Martin then went on to explain how the hands and cheeks of the accused were bloodied. When the accused was thereupon taken into custody, at the watch-house on the corner of Queen's Gate, a necklace was found in the pocket of his breeches. Martin spoke rapidly, much to the dismay of the penny-a-liners, and in a high voice that caused amusement among the more vulgar spectators.

It seems that in English law the accused is able to question and to challenge witnesses, in a way that would seem unfitting on the Continent, and Daniel at once asked Martin if he, Daniel, had seemed surprised by the discovery of the necklace.

"Yes. Oh, yes," he replied in his rapid way. "You seemed to be much taken aback. But that was because you was play-acting. Lawks."

"You found me sleeping beneath a tree?"

"Of course I did."

"Why should a murderer and a thief fall asleep at the scene of his own crime?"

"For why? For the reason that the person accused, being yourself, is touched." Martin tapped his forehead, much to the delight of the spectators.

"Well, Mr. Martin, am I a lunatic or an actor? I really do not think I can be both."

"Whatever you wish, Mr. Westbrook. I am not particular." Martin laughed quite gaily.

The second and third members of the watch described, in identical terms, the discovery of Harriet's body. She had been found by two children, in the shadow of a bridge that crossed over the middle point of the Serpentine. Daniel listened to the testimony of the witnesses with great attention, his manacled hands stretched out before him, and at the end he merely bowed his head. He did not wish to question them. The account of the discovery of his sister seemed to have left him momentarily without the power of speech.

But then, when asked by the judge if he wished to make any final statement, he raised his head and looked steadily at the jurors. "I do not expect justice in this place," he said. "I have long since concluded that the judicial system of our country is a tissue of corruption."

At which point the judge interrupted him. "You are here to defend yourself, sir. You are not here to deliver your opinion of English law."

"But that is the point, is it not? That justice is not to be found in the well of an English court?"

"That is not the point. You have no point." The judge was growing angry. "The point is worthless. I throw it out."

"I defend myself then with a simple phrase. I am innocent. I had no part in my sister's death. I abhor the notion of violence. But to direct it against a member of my own family—it is unthinkable to me. Surely you cannot accuse a brother of such a crime? A loving brother who helped to raise her from her infant days? No, no. Never can it be." He paused, to regain control of his feelings. "I have no conception of how she met her end. I do not know how my face and hands were bloody. I do not know how her necklace was found in my pocket. I can only guess at some malign conspiracy. At some infernal evil. Yet I know this. I am not the man." His words of evident sincerity received the murmured approval of many spectators, who were then quickly silenced by the judge. Daniel was led away, and the jurors retired to another room.

I stayed in the court, not trusting myself to be alone. I knew Daniel to be entirely blameless, and yet here he was obliged to defend his life while I sat idly watching him. I knew, too, what the verdict would be. The law is a net, a snare, which binds its victims even as they struggle to be free. After no more than an hour the jurors returned, and Daniel was again led out in manacles. His face was flushed red, and he stumbled as he mounted the stairs of the witness box. Someone shouted out, "Not guilty," and there was scattered applause in the court-room. Daniel shook his head, frowning slightly, and strained forward to listen to the jurors' verdict. It came without cere-mony. Guilty of unlawful killing. There was silence after that, a silence in which the darkness of his fate was absorbed.

Then with a barely perceptible expression of disquiet Daniel turned towards the judge, who made a great ceremony out of placing the black cloth upon his wig. He recited the circumstances of Daniel's supposed murder of his sister, dwelling with evident relish on the details of the discovery of the body, before pronouncing sentence on what he called "the heinous slaughter" and the "barely conceivable evil" of the crime. I agreed with him upon that point, although I knew that the perpetrator was elsewhere. Daniel no doubt received the sentence of death with remarkable calm; I could not see him, since his back was turned to the court while he faced the judge. He carried himself erect, as he left the courtroom, and did not look in my direction.

⇒ Thirteen ⇐

ON THE MORNING OF THE EXECUTION, I rose before dawn. How could I sleep? Mr. Garnett had informed me that Daniel would be taken to Newgate, where the ceremony was performed outside the wall, and I had spent the night imagining all the tortures of the condemned man. I dressed and went out into the street, in order to clear my head, but then some involuntary and peremptory impulse sent me walking towards Newgate itself. I was like some man of the crowd, hastening towards a spectacle. If it were possible to be two people, then this was my condition: I wished to be hidden away, lamenting the fate of Daniel in the secrecy of some locked chamber, but at the same time I walked with fiery eyes towards the prison to see him despatched. I seemed to be possessed by some spirit that broods over London on a hanging day, some craving for blood and punishment that is beyond rational calculation. A further consideration occurred to me later. I had given life to the creature, but could the presence of the creature be changing me?

I arrived at Newgate very early, but such was the press of people that I could only reach as far as the churchyard of St. Sepulchre. A mob of children were already assembled in the most prominent places, setting up a cacophony of cries and howls that would have shamed a tribe of monkeys in the jungles of the Niger. Their catcalls were taken up by others in the crowd, some of whom began dancing and singing obscenities. Such grotesque merriment in the face of death was for me unexampled. The English mob, screeching and laughing and yelling, is a thing of horror in what we deign to call the civilised world. The open space in front of the prison was taken up by men and women who had all the appearance of thieves and prostitutes, as well as other rogues and ruffians of every description. Their smell was insupportable. They whistled and imitated Mr. Punch; they drank from bottles, and fought among themselves. Some of them urinated freely against the walls of the prison itself calling out, according to the London tradition, "In pain!"

There was a lull when Daniel was brought out from a little door that opened onto Newgate Street; then, after the instant of recognition, there was a great roar of execration and triumph. It was as if the whole foul ceremony represented some ritual of human sacrifice by which the community would be healed. The sun had come out from behind clouds as Daniel mounted the steps to the scaffold, greeted with such a chorus of abuse and obscenity that I am surprised he could endure it. But he seemed to hear none of the execration. In the face of the general disorder he was quite calm; if anything, his bearing expressed resolution and, even, resignation. Yet that did not stop the baying of the mob. I looked at the upturned faces of the crowd, so delighted and excited by the coming scene that they seemed to be images of evil itself. Who can believe that humankind is created in God's image, when observing that desperate and dissolute assembly? The human form is not divine.

The noose was fastened around Daniel's neck, and a coarse

sack pulled over his head; whether this was some courtesy to his own feelings, I am not sure. Who could bear to see the rictus of death upon his face? The crowd could. The executioner then positioned him carefully above the trap. The cries and yells grew stronger, as the executioner was urged to pull the lever. Then with a sudden movement the platform opened under Daniel. He plunged down as if he had been a stone descending through the air. The crowd then bayed for his death as his body heaved and struggled in the last palpitations of life. The executioner took hold of his legs and jerked them down. Then Daniel was still. The life had gone from him.

I had seen the moment when new life was instilled; now I had seen the instant of departure, when the fire and energy vanished as swiftly as once they had come.

There was a general rush towards the body, for tokens or mementoes, but the line of constables somehow managed to keep the crowd back. Again there was such a roar of abuse and filthy words and ribald songs that I felt quite sickened and shamed by my fellow creatures. The body was cut down from the rope by the executioner, and placed upon a wooden board. According to custom Daniel would now be given to the anatomists, who would begin their ministrations immediately in their hall nearby. I knew enough of that work. So I did not linger at Newgate.

With difficulty I freed myself from the crowd, and walked quickly down towards Fleet Street and the river. I caught a wherry there to Limehouse and, as my boatman rowed against the freezing wind, I exulted in the cold. It tamed my blood. It steadied my excited nerves. I disembarked from the wherry a little upriver from the workshop, and made my way slowly along the deserted foreshore. It was a forlorn enough scene, with the small wooden jetties and the narrow stone stairs descending into the water.

I came up to the workshop, where I discerned no trace of life. It was as I had left it three months before, wrecked and empty, with the broken glass and detritus covering the floor. There must have been tides higher than usual because there were pools and puddles of river water among the confusion. Any hope of restoring or renovating the broken equipment was clearly misplaced: my whole venture would be left to rack and ruin. I picked up a chair, lying on the ground, and, placing it in the middle of the workshop, sat down. From here I could see the river, through an opening in the broken door, and I waited. My resolution was so intense, and my attention so alert, that I hardly felt the cold. I knew that he would come to this place— that he would wish to encounter me and, if he had the use of language, to converse with me. He had done everything with the simple object of taking vengeance upon me, and he would not miss the opportunity of confronting his creator in the place where he had risen from the dead.

I waited throughout that day. I was shielded from the rain and the wind, and with a phosphorous match I managed to make a fire from the broken wooden shelves that lay upon the floor. Just before dusk I ventured onto the jetty. There was a smell of oil and tar coming from the water, and I could hear the low murmur of the tide against the wooden walls of the embankment. I could see a log, perhaps fallen from a merchant-man, coming up with the current—yet it was no log. It was a swimmer, quite straight in the water; I saw his arms moving with almost mechanical force, and he left no wake behind him.

The figure approached, and raised his head from the water; an oil-lamp from an alley on the north bank illuminated him for a moment. It was the creature, swimming steadily towards the workshop. He must have seen me, but he gave no sign of greeting or recognition. He plunged once more into the water, and I lost sight of him.

I walked back into the workshop, and sat down. I was quite composed.

I heard the sound of something raising itself onto the jetty, with a laboured and heavy motion, and then two footsteps. All at once he stood before me, his clothes steaming; I noticed that, curiously enough, they were drying quickly before my eyes. He was possessed of some extraordinary inward heat.

I suppressed a sudden and overwhelming desire to flee his presence, and remained seated. "You have sought me out," I said.

He looked at me with an expression of the utmost curiosity. His eyes were gleaming, as if a candle or a lamp had been lit behind them. I knew them, then, to be eyes of the keenest intelligence. Then he bowed his head. "There is no substance," he replied, "without a shadow."

I was astonished—no, lost in amazement—at the purity and refinement of his diction. I might have been talking to an angel rather than a devil. "What have you done?" I asked him.

"I? I have done nothing. What have you done? Can you look at me and not weep?" As if under the impress of overwhelming feeling he turned and walked out onto the jetty; yet after a moment he returned, and once more stood before me. I now observed him carefully. Somehow or other he had acquired breeches and linen, and strong leather boots that came up to his calves; he still possessed the black cloak he had taken from me, on the night of his creation, but he had lost or forgotten the hat. His long yellow hair, parted at the crown, reached down to his shoulders and somehow gave him a preternatural image of age; and his skin still had the frightful appearance of being furrowed and folded.

"Why did you kill her?" I asked him.

"I wished you to notice me."

"What?"

"I wished you to think of me. To consider my plight."

"By killing Harriet?"

"I knew then that you would not be able to throw me off. To disdain me."

"Have you no conscience?"

"I have heard the word." He smiled, or what I took to be a smile passed across his face. "I have heard many words for which I do not feel the sentiment here." He tapped his breast. "But you understand that, do you not, sir?"

"I cannot understand anything so devoid of principle, so utterly malicious."

"Oh, surely you have some inkling? I am hardly unknown to you." I realised then that his was the voice of youth—of the youth he had once been—and that a cause of horror lay in the disparity between the mellifluous expression and the distorted appearance of the creature. "You have not lost your memory, I trust?"

"I wish to God I had."

"God? That is another word I have heard. Are you my God?"

I must have given an expression of disdain, or disgust, because he gave out a howl of anguish in a manner very different from the way he had conversed. With one sudden movement he picked up the great oaken table, lying damaged upon the floor, and set it upright. "You will remember this. This was my cradle, was it not? Here was I rocked. Or will you pretend that the river gave me birth?" He took a step towards me. "You were the first thing that I saw upon this earth. Is it any wonder that your form is more real to me than that of any other living creature?"

I turned away, in disgust at myself for having created this being. But he misunderstood my movement. He sprang in front of me, with a celerity unparalleled. "You cannot leave me. You cannot shut out my words, however distasteful they may be to you. Were you covered by oceans, or buried in mountains, you would still hear me." He paused. "I am not devoid of intelligence. Perhaps you made sure of that?"

"I had hoped," I said in utter sorrow and weariness of spirit, "that you would be a natural man."

"There now. I have you. You have confirmed what I have long since discovered. You are indeed responsible for my being." I inclined my head, but my silence was for him assurance enough. "Did I ask you to mould me? Did I solicit you to take me from the darkness?" I could not bring myself to look at him. "Do you hear the blast of the cold wind? To me it is a sweet whisper that lulls me to sleep." When I looked up at him, he was kneeling upon the floor in a state of abject desolation; if ever I might have felt pity for him, it was at that moment. Once again he exhibited some preternatural awareness of my own thoughts, for he turned and stared at me for a time. "So you have pity on me," he said, "as I will have pity on you."

"I do not need your pity."

"Not need pity? You are the guilty agent of my misfortunes. I did not seek for life, nor did I make myself. Thou art the man!" With that phrase he pointed at me, and his quivering finger seemed to be aimed at my heart. Under the powerful force of his gaze I bowed my head once more and wept. "You may weep now," he said. "You will weep again."

I do not know how long we sat in silence together, with only the sound of the wind and the chaffing of the river as companions. Eventually he roused himself and walked towards the door overlooking the Thames. "Look," he said, "even the rats fly from my approach. The fear I inspire in these creatures was the first evidence of my existence when I left this place, on the cold and howling night of my birth. I will tell you the story, sir. You should know what you yourself have made."

⇝ Fourteen ⇜

"I HAD THE SENSATION that I had come out of darkness, but I did not understand the nature of that darkness. Then there was light and warmth, an infinite comfort and delight as if I lay suspended in some voluptuous medium. I believe then that I uttered my first sounds."

"You sang."

"Was that singing? The sounds emerged from within my form, as if all the fibres of my being were coming out in harmony for the first time. I was in a state of the utmost excitement. Here." He touched his genitals without any sense of shame or embarrassment. "And then I saw you. I believe that I knew at once that you were my author, that you had transmitted life into my own frame. I did not experience any sensation of gratitude, however, but one of curiosity. What was this breath and motion with which I was endowed? At that moment the world could show me no greater marvel than my own existence: yet I did not know what it was to exist! I believe that you said something to me—some imprecation, some refusal—yet to me your strange voice seemed to issue from the darkness that I had lately escaped. It was as dark and hollow as an echo. I turned from you. It was not fear. Believe me, I hardly know what fear is. It was wonder. I saw beyond the confines of this place a great river, and a world. I sensed the ocean beyond. I sensed life.

"I recall then plunging into the water, in which I moved as if it were my natural element. I knew—by what means, I cannot say—that I was going in the direction of the open sea, and I exulted in my speed and agility. I did not feel the cold; or rather I did not know the meaning of the cold. The water seemed to be alive, too, and to welcome my presence; it flowed across my limbs, and lifted me onwards. So within a short time I had reached the sea. Then I ducked and dived within its waves in the sheer joy of my nature. But a sailing boat approached me. When I came above the water the men on the vessel showed such signs of terror and of horror that one of them threw himself overboard in an effort to escape me, and from the others issued screams and oaths that persuaded me I was not of their kind. You may ask how I was aware of such things, being only recently thrust into the world; I believe now that the mind is a creative power that gives as much as it receives. Like the power of speech, it came to me unbidden.

"I grew weary of the dim expanse of the ocean, and eventually I made my journey back towards the land. On some instinct I made my way here, returning to the place of my origin. You had gone, I discovered, but all the instruments of your art were around me. You may believe that I destroyed them out of fury and resentment at my making. Not so. I threw them down, and scattered them, from the fear that through their agency I might be sent back—that I might be returned to that state of non-being from which I had come. I took your hat and coat then, to shield my nakedness and desolation from the eyes of others, and tried to find a place apart from human habitation. I came upon a lonely path by the shoreline of the river and I met no one for some miles until, just before dawn, I saw a solitary traveller walking ahead of me. I was moving very rapidly along the path, endowed as I seem to be with great strength and nimbleness, and it was only a few moments before he sensed my presence. I stopped and went down to the water's edge, so that I might not alarm him further. In your hat and cloak I managed to escape detection, but with quickened step he wandered off the path into a neighbouring field. Some instinct had moved him I walked on until I came to an area I now know to be the estuary, a place of marsh and pasture that seemed to be a wilderness. But there in the distance, beyond some trees and a deep brook, I glimpsed a light. I approached slowly and saw that it came from a solitary dwelling. There was a thatched barn beside it, a rough stone building with one opening; as I came over to it, having easily overstepped the brook, I felt the need for shelter and repose. Yes, even I must rest. I had grown weary after my journey, and to my relief I found the place empty. There was a ladder that afforded access to a small loft or alcove in which straw had been placed; here I lay down and slept.

"I was awoken by the sound of voices. But you wish me to tell you of my dreams before I continue my story? That is easily performed. I did not dream. I have never dreamed since I came to life in this room. When I heard the voices, outside the barn, I instantly arose. I can still recall the words. 'There is a hare in the field, Father. See him scudding past the horses there.' These are the first words I remember comprehending—comprehending not as sounds merely but as stirrings and tokens of the mind. I knew these words somewhere within me. I recognised them, and at once a whole host of analogies and associations flooded through me. The world before me was quite changed. The labourer and his daughter, as I discovered them to be, were monarchs and angels in my eyes: they had led me into a kingdom of light, where the words opened the very portals of reality. I stayed in that resting place for most of the day, listening to their quiet conversations. They did not enter it— they never did enter it—and by degrees I came to consider it as my habitation. You wish to ask me how I live? My wants are simpler than yours. I can survive upon a harsher diet than men who subsist in luxury; I found that I could eat the leaves upon the trees, and drink from the waters of the brook, without the least discomfort. But there was better food. The labourer and his daughter had a store of turnips in a small shed behind their cottage and, in the deep night, I would take them and feast on them as if they were the most dainty fare in the world. I heard soon enough how puzzled they were by the disappearance of their crop, but they blamed it on the rats or on the foxes. I have told you of the power of their words, opening up the world to me little by little. I found that, on listening to them, new words came unbidden to my lips—forming chains and associations that became sentences. The power of language must be deeply innate so that, after my awakening, all the details of its fabric and structure rose up somewhere within me.

"I can bear the intensity of heat and the extremity of cold without the least discomfort or danger, but nevertheless I felt the want of clothing. I had wrapped myself in your black cloak when I lay down to sleep, yet I knew that to make my way among strangers I must be more fully and decently clad. One evening, therefore, I ventured onto the marshes of the estuary in search of a village or small town where such items might be found. By good fortune, and by keeping to the shoreline, I came upon the town of Gravesend. The streets were quite silent and deserted, at that hour of the night, and down one narrow thoroughfare I saw the sign of a tailor and gentleman's outfitter. I forced the door with no difficulty and there, in the darkness, I equipped myself with all the garments I would need including the fine linen stock with which you see me now endowed. I am a gentleman, am I not?

"I went back to my barn, and lay me down to sleep. I had come to anticipate and enjoy the early rising of the labourer and his daughter; her childish prattle was my music, and I listened eagerly to the slightest and most inconsequential discourse between them. I felt emboldened by my new garments, too, and when I saw them working in the distant fields I entered their little cottage and surveyed the setting of their lives. It was humble enough, with a plain table and chairs, and two easy-chairs beside a stone fireplace; but it was neat and clean, with an indescribable air of comfort. I envisaged what it might mean to share their life with them; but that was as yet out of my power. Then I noticed the shelf of books. Out of curiosity I took one of them down from the shelf, and left the cottage.

"I had come upon a treasure in *Robinson Crusoe*. I saw words at first through a veil; they were all familiar to me, but they seemed to be written in an unknown language. Yet, as with sound and speech, I felt a world forming itself around me; the power of the words seemed to rise up within my own being, so that I recognised myself in the same moment as I recognised phrases and sentences. I spoke the words out loud, and one seemed to follow another in the utmost harmony; each one seemed complementary to the next, and all joined in the great music of meaning. In my previous state I believe that I must have been an ardent reader, because I took so eagerly to the perusal of the pages before me. I became so enthralled by the adventures of the castaway on the desert island that I did not note the declension of the sun or the emergence of the moon. I read as if for life. And life it was for me—to enter the state of another existence, to look with newly awakened eyes on an unfamiliar landscape, was a form of bliss. I chanted the words of the book again, and I noticed that there had grown a melody in my voice. I was being nurtured by words. I have told you that the mind is a creative power, and I believed in my innocence that I could now learn the instinctive expression of human passion. If I were a natural man, then I must be naturally benevolent.

"From the remarks that the labourer and his daughter passed to one another when they were engaged in their work, I learned that the girl's mother had died from the ague, a common sickness in this region, and that she was buried in a little churchyard two miles away across the flats, as they called the fields. They worked hard for their bare subsistence, but I learned how to help them. In the deep of the night I would uproot turnips and other bulbs for them, leaving them in the shed from which I had once taken their food. With my great strength, too, I was able to provide them with firewood and dry logs that I left beyond their little garden. They were astonished by these gifts, but I heard the father extol the 'good spirits' and 'sprites' of the neighbourhood as the possible cause of the bounty.

"The girl of course could receive no proper schooling, but her father tried to instruct her in the basic materials of knowledge. In the evening he must have taught her to read and to write, because in the morning she would recite to him in her clear voice the passages she had learned. Through her agency, indeed, I first became aware of the power of poetry to assuage the troubled spirit and to lift the mind towards thoughts of eternity:

". . . that blessed mood
In which the burthen of the mystery,
In which the heavy and the weary weight
Of this unintelligible world
Is lightened—that serene and blessed mood—

"I confess that I remember no more. Her father used to instruct her, too, in the history of their country—of all the great events that had passed over this estuarial land without disturbing its quietness. I learned then of battles long ago, of the ruins of ancient civilisations, of the Romans and the Saxons and the Normans who sailed along the great river. I shared the girl's wonder, too, at the stories of Creation, of Adam and Eve, of the angel with the flaming sword. It was her father's intention to read to her the chapters in the Bible so that she might be fully acquainted with what he described to her as the holiest book in the world. I admit that I held it in the same reverence, after listening to the first sentences he recited to her, and I looked forward eagerly to the next day's lesson.

"I would have been content, I think, to have spent my time thus; I wandered at night among the flat lands of the estuary, singing to the wind and holding communion with the earth. I lay upon the ground and whispered the words, and perceptions, I had learned. I was as free as the sun, and as lonely as the sun. Where rose the tide and the billowing waters of the river, there was my home; where dwelled the owls and the foxes, there were my friends and roamers of the night. There is a pleasure in the pathless and solitary fields; there is a rapture in the lonely shore. I sat quite still and observed the heavens revolving above my head, and wondered if they were the origin of my being. Or had I come from the creeping waters of the river? Or from the mild earth that nurtured all the plants and flowers of the world? When at first light a wood pigeon came before me, I took part in its existence and pecked upon the ground; when a gull flew above my head I shared its soaring form; when I watched an otter upon the bank, I could feel the sleekness of its limbs. In all creatures now I felt the force of one life, a life I shared, of which the principles were energy and joy.

"I might have continued in this blessed state, if I had not become aware of my true being. You look away, do you? I had no memory of what I was, and yet my instinct for speech and my understanding of words assured me that I had existed here before in some altered shape. Then I recalled the papers that I had taken from your desk, and put at random in the capacious pockets of your cloak. I had had no use for them before. But now that I had discovered within myself the gift of understanding, I could look upon them with different eyes. You know well enough that I found your journal of the weeks that had preceded my creation, and of the odious circumstances in which I was found and delivered to you. Here they are, the proof of your handiwork. You saved me from the blank of death without my knowing that I had died; you lifted me out of the grave and led me once more into the light and the air where new springs of thought and feeling have emerged in me. Do you believe me to be grateful? I now know that I was a young man with the marks of consumption upon me: I believe that you mention me to have been a student of medicine in a London hospital. I had a sister, had I not, who cared for me until I died? Oh, if only my death had endured for ever! For I soon learned that to live again is to be frightful to all those who beheld me My renewed form is a more odious type of yours, more loathsome even from the resemblance. I soon learned, too, that I would have to hide myself and cover my face from every living eye—to start if I heard a human step, and seek out some dark and silent corner. How do you think I learned these lessons?

"I was taught them in the most searing and shameful manner. I had grown so accustomed to the voices of father and daughter that I almost believed myself to be a part of their little society; I fully imagined a time when I would be accepted by them, and might even be welcomed into their cottage as a friend and guest. Then, one morning, I heard her father discoursing upon the effect of the moon on the tides—and of the high tide some years before that had completely covered the fields of the vicinity.

"'Oh,' I said aloud, 'the moon is a great enchanter.'

"I scarcely knew that I had spoken so openly, and I was greeted with silence. 'Who is in there?' the father called out, with something like fear in his voice. 'Come out!'

"'He has a pretty voice,' the daughter said. 'Please come out, sir.'

"'I fear,' I replied, 'that my person may not be pleasing to you.'

"'We do not see many strangers,' she said. 'But we are not afraid.'

"I heard her step closer to the barn, and instinctively I shrank back into a corner. Then I saw her shape outlined against the opening.

"It took a moment for her eyes to become accustomed to the gloom—but then she saw me. I have never seen such a look of horror and fear upon any other face. She uttered a confused sound, and then fell upon the floor of the barn. Her father called out her name—it was Jane—and rushed towards her. He caught sight of me at once. 'Great God! What are you?' The look of anguish and terror upon his face is one that I shall never forget.

"He took his daughter up in his arms and, with the strength born out of fear, he ran quickly from me across the fields. They had fled from me as from an abhorred thing. I, who had deemed myself worthy of human companionship, was for them a creature of horror and nightmare. I went over to the place where she had fallen, and violently stamped upon the earth; then I fell upon my knees, and beat the ground with my fists. I may have howled, or shrieked, I do not remember. But my thoughts were of rage and revenge—against the father and daughter, against the human species, and against you my creator!

"I do not know how long I remained in my condition of blank despair. I understood then I could never hope for human sympathy, but I had not harmed the smallest creature on the earth. Where had I offended? I sat in my desolation, until I was

roused by the sound of horses and of voices. I have a preternatural sense of hearing—you must know that—and they
were still far off. But they were coming closer.

"I sensed that the horses were restless as they approached
me, and I fled from the barn as if I had committed some great
and heinous crime. I took flight across the land, behind the
cottage, so that they could not see me on their approach; and I
hid myself within a small watercourse that had become dry. At
that moment I despised all things that lived—all things that
died—but I stayed trembling in my cover. I could have con-
fronted them all, men and horses, but I could not put to the
test once more the sensations of horror that I excited in others. I
saw them approach the cottage; there were eight of them, three
of them with muskets, together with the farmer. He pointed
towards the barn where I had sheltered. One of them shouted
something, in warning or defiance, and they very slowly came up
to it with their guns primed. Of course I was nowhere to be
found. Then they turned back and went towards the cottage;
they encircled it, and the farmer entered only to emerge a few
moments later. It was clear that they debated amongst each
other, and after a few minutes they moved out in pairs over the
surrounding countryside. I lowered myself into the dry course,
so that I had fallen below the level of the flat landscape. Two of
them came close to me. I heard them talking. One of them
exclaimed about a 'fiend' or 'monster.' There was some reference
to ancient legends of the locality, and to the presence of a thing
known to them as Moldwark. But it was clear that their
knowledge was slight and imprecise. They passed by my hiding
place and rejoined the others beside the cottage. There was a
discussion between them, and then they all departed.

"I waited until darkness fell, and then I went back. My shame and dismay had once more given way to anger. How could I be described as 'fiend' or 'monster'? I move, I exist, I stir within my prison.

"I took logs and branches, piling them high within the interior of the little cottage; a fierce wind came up from the sea, and drove away the clouds that had obscured the stars. It filled me with purpose, and I lighted the dry branches of a tree; in my unappeasable rage I began to dance around the cottage, watching all the time the great orb of the moon on the western horizon. Then with a loud shout of triumph I fired the dwelling. The flames were soon lifted by the wind until they had taken hold of the whole, and within a short time the cottage was reduced to a smoking ruin. I had achieved my purpose.

"I went back inside the shell, lay down upon the blackened floor, and fell asleep. I awoke with a fresh access of energy—yes, this is the sensation I must put to you. The effect of heat, in any form, is to restore and revivify me. I have learned now to anticipate storm and lightning. I know them to be near, from the scent in my nostrils, and my whole being is excited by their approach. I am made strong by the lightning flash and, when I studied your own notes on the process of my rebirth, I understood the reason. You had divined the electric principles of the human body, and I can testify to their power. I courted the lightning and the thunder, and exulted in the storms that blew over the estuary. Some vast principle of power animates infinity.

"As I read your notes, too, I became wholly absorbed in the narrative of my own discovery. There was some mention of the men who brought me to you, and who exchanged me for money. I had become interested in them. You referred to a public house called the Fortune of War in Smithfield, which I believed that I would be able to find in the great labyrinth of this city. I realised now that before I ventured from the estuary I had to muffle myself as completely as I was able. So I clothed myself. By covering my form with your great cloak, and then by unwinding my stock and fastening it across my face, I was assured that only my eyes and forehead could be seen. In this guise I hoped to avoid detection. By great good fortune this was a time of freezing fog, and the majority of the citizens had covered their mouths and nostrils with scarves or hand-kerchiefs to protect themselves from the vapour. So I could wander unnoticed through the crowd, except for the delicate apprehension of those closest to me that I was not quite how can I put it—of the customary sort.

"In this guise I made my way one evening towards Smith-field, and asked for directions to the hospital there. You know the area well, do you not? The public house was a few yards from the entrance and as I approached it I could hear the mayhem of voices and of oaths coming from the interior. So I waited on the corner, just beyond the entrance. I was waiting for three men. It was raining that night but the cool drops hardly reached me. I am a powerful source of heat, and the water is dispersed. There were many who hurried past me, but not one of them looked up at me. A dark stranger, on a dark night, is to be avoided.

"Many people came and went from the inn, but they came out singly or in pairs; some of them reeled out into the night, some of them slouched in the rain, some of them ran across the cobbled stones of Smithfield. I was so intent upon my purpose that I did not grow tired of waiting. Eventually three men came out into the night. One of them gave a violent kick to his companion, as if he had been his dog. I knew then that these were the three men whom I sought. I followed them down a small thoroughfare, keeping my distance from them; they turned a corner, where they stopped and fell into a fierce argument concerning the division of some money. No doubt this would be the proceeds from one of their graveyard robberies. I stood against the wall, on the other side, and then spoke very softly.

"'Gentlemen, where is my sister?'

"'Who is that?'

"'One of your friends. I will ask you again. Where is my sister?'

"Then I turned the corner and stood in front of them.

"I think one of them may have had a glimmer of recognition. 'What in the buggery are you?'

"'You know very well.' I unwrapped the stock, and showed them my face.

"One of them yelled, and made to run down the alley. Before he could move I took him by the arm and held him firm.

"'You see,' I said, 'the dead can move very quickly. Now where is my sister?'

"One of them, the oldest, was in a state of fear so excessive that he could not speak. The other stared at me with an expression of exquisite alarm. I shook him roughly, and I suppose that I fractured a bone in his arm; he gave out a yell.

"'That is not the least injury I will inflict upon you,' I said, 'if you do not give me the location of my sister. You must remember it. You took my body from there and conveyed it over the water to Mr. Frankenstein. You bartered me for guineas. Where is she?'

"'By Broken Dock. In Bermondsey.' He seemed too confused, or alarmed, to continue; so I shook him again. 'She lives in the last tenement on the left as you approach the river. On the third floor. A toy-maker.'

"'What is her name?'

"'Annie. Annie Keat.'

"I squeezed his arm tighter, so that once more he yelled in pain. 'And mine?'

"'Jack.'

"I released him from my grasp. Once his companions realised that they were free, they turned and ran down the alley. I stood there for a moment, watching them flee, and then I fastened the stock across my face and returned to Smithfield.

"Like some distant echo I recalled the name of Jack Keat; it might have been revealed to me in the low rolling of the thunder, or the instant of the lightning flash, so subdued and sudden that I scarcely grasped it.

"It was too late now to call upon my sister. So I returned to the estuary, by means of the river, and laid myself down in the blackened ruin of the cottage. No one had come back to that place, and I believe that no one ever will. It has been marked down in the vicinity as a spot of darkness.

"I endured a few days of repose and silent thought. Sometimes I sat with my eyes fixed to the ground; on these occasions I had rather have been a stone than what I am. Is it not better to die than to live and not be loved? I yearned for extinction. Can any being die twice? So I encountered tempests without the hope of their blasting me. The light revived me. The sun revived me. I longed and prayed for utter oblivion, but my despair was stronger than my prayers. I cannot die. I must endure. That is my destiny. That which I am, I am. I am no longer Jack Keat, but something deeper and darker than any individual doom.

"After some days and nights had passed I resolved to visit my sister. I again took the precaution of wrapping myself well, and swam one evening from the estuary to Bermondsey and Broken Dock; I could escape detection only by travelling at night, when a dark shape in the river provokes no interest whatever. As I climbed the stairs, the water fell from me; I took the hat—your hat—from the pocket of the cloak and placed it on my head. Then once more I wound the stock about my face. The villain had told me the location of the tenement: it was a ruinous building close to the side of the wooden dock, and sharing its general air of dilapidation. There were some stubs of candle-light in one or two of the rooms, and some shreds of linen or cloth had been draped across the windows. I stared up at the window on the third floor on which there glimmered some fitful illumination, as if an oil-lamp had been placed in a far corner. That room had been the scene of my death. I glimpsed my sister's figure, and watched her as she moved back and forth across the room; she seemed restless, as if my presence had unnerved her. When she came over to the window and looked out, I moved into the shadows. I could see her only dimly in the half-light, but she seemed to me then the most beautiful creature in the world; there was something indefinably familiar in her bearing, as if I could recall her bowing over me in my last sickness. I have no real memory of that time, but it is *as if I have*.

After a few moments apparently lost in thought she moved away, and the light was extinguished.

"I crossed the threshold, and entered a dim hallway that seemed like the phantom of something half-remembered. To the dead, does the real world appear to be wraith-like, populated by ghosts? There were two doors on the third landing, and as a matter of instinct I turned towards the left one. It seemed that my physical body had some memory of the past buried within it. I hesitated before the door; how could I present myself to my sister, without terrifying her perhaps beyond reason? I had an earnest desire to talk to her, but she could hardly view the appearance of her dead brother with equanimity. I put my ear to the door, and could hear sounds of movement. On a sudden instinct I tapped and whispered, 'Annie!'

"'Who is there?'

"'Annie!'

"'I know that voice. Who are you?'

"My fear of frightening her now returned, and I hurried down the stairs into the street. I concealed myself when the window was opened, and she leaned out. 'Annie!' I called again.

"She closed the window. Then, a few moments later, she came out into the street with a shawl but no bonnet; her long hair fell across her shoulders, and she seemed to be in a state of some excitement or distress. Still she could not see me, as I had retreated at once into a doorway which hid me from view; when I peeped out from my vantage I saw her hurrying down to the riverside, looking about her. I followed her, at a distance, but I could no longer curb my desire to talk to her; so I advanced slowly towards her. 'Annie, do not be afraid. You can come to no possible harm. No. Do not look around.'

"'That voice—'

"'Do you know me?'

"'If I were dreaming, I would know you.'

"'This is not a dream. Do you remember your brother?'

"'Oh, God. What are you?' She turned and, on seeing me, screamed out. 'My God! Out of the grave!'

"In a frenzy of fear she ran towards the bank of the river; she did not stop or even hesitate, but in her terror she threw herself into the water. I stood for a moment, utterly horrified and helpless at her reaction to me. Then I flung myself into the river and swam towards her. The Thames is deep at this point, and the current of the ebbing tide had already carried her a little way. In a moment I was beside her and I lifted her out of the water; but she gave no sign of movement. I took her back to the shore, and laid her down upon the cobbles. There was no life in her. She had died—of panic fear, of immersion, I did not know the cause. I knew only that I was responsible for her death. I, who had sought her out as a companion or as a friend, was her murderer. I howled upon the bank, prostrated over her body in a state of abject grief. But then I heard the sound of running footsteps, and of shouts. In my extremity I still possessed the instinct of self-preservation, and I dived into the water.

"I believed that I had not been seen, under the cover of darkness, and I made my way back to the estuary.

"I have read somewhere that suffering shares the nature of infinity; that it is permanent, obscure and dark. Such has been my experience. I was a being so repugnant that my own sister cast away her life in an effort to escape me. I had hoped that, pardoning my outward form, she would come to cherish me for the excellent qualities that I was capable of unfolding. This was a fond hope. She had run from me screaming in terror. I cannot cry. Do you have an explanation for that? I have no tears. I presume that the heat of my birth has blasted me. Yet if I could not weep, I could still lament. I cursed the day when I regained life, and I cursed you with a bitterness for which there is no expression. Yet I expressed it in a different fashion. I sought you out. I found your lodging. At first I considered myself to be your executioner, but there is a bond between us which no human force may break; I stayed my hand. I watched instead for those dearest to you, and chose one who like my sister was young and innocent of any wrong. You know the rest."

⇒ Fifteen ⇐

HE HAD FINISHED SPEAKING, and turned back towards the Thames. I could see that he was in thrall to some powerful emotion, and I could almost feel pity for his miserable state. He was doomed to wander across the earth, in search of nothing that the world could give to him—love, friendship, compassion were all denied to him. If it were true that he could not die, that the fearful terms of his existence were ever renewed, he would endure in his wilderness. "What would you have me do?" I asked him.

"Do? Once you create life, you must take responsibility for it. You *are* responsible!"

"I will create no more life. I pledge that to you."

"A weak answer, sir. Do you not realise the bond between us? There is a pact of fire that can never be abrogated. I am wedded to you so closely that we might be the same person. I was conceived and shaped in your hands." He turned around at that moment, and faced me. "I have no one except you. Will you abandon me? You are my last hope. My last refuge." I bowed down and wept. "You weep for yourself, and not for me."

"I pity you."

"Spare your pity for yourself."

"I would give everything I have to release you from your

suffering. If I could reduce you once more to inanimate matter, I would gladly do so. Do you wish for that?"

We both remained in silence for a long time. I was still seated, while he paced up and down the workshop in an agony of thought. Finally he stopped beside my chair. "I can be your child. Or your servant. I can watch over you, and protect you from harm."

"That cannot be."

"Cannot? I know no such word. We have an adamantine bond. What is 'cannot'?"

"That bond is a frightful one. You have become the dark agent of desolation."

"Through your will."

"My purpose was benign. I had hoped to create a being of infinite benevolence. One in whom the forces of nature would have worked together to awaken a new spiritual being. I believed in the perfectibility of mankind—"

"Oh, don't speak of that. Since you awakened me, as you put it, I have witnessed nothing but fear and woe and violence."

"You have caused them."

"But you are the ultimate cause."

"Listen to me. I shared with my friends a new creed of liberty and unselfishness. I had hoped to advance it."

"Your new creed has proved to be an illusion then. Mankind is not to be improved."

"You are mistaken in that. There will be, there must be, progress in the sciences."

"Behold your progress. Here I stand."

When I saw him exulting over me, my pity for him turned to

anger. "I abjure you. I beg you to remove yourself to some distant place and trouble men no more."

"You wish me to travel to some vast desert or distant island. Or perhaps to some ice precipice among the loftiest mountains?"

"Anywhere out of this world."

"So my suffering is less important than your repose."

"The repose of all."

"It is an interesting proposition. In this instance, then, I would ask you to form for me a companion in this secluded life."

"What?"

"Create me another being who can become my bride, of the same nature and the same characteristics as myself."

"Insanity."

"Wherefore insane? We will be estranged from all the world, but we will never be separated from one another. I do not say that we will enjoy bliss, but we will at least be free from suffering. Who can I speak to? There is no one. I am alone in the world. Do you know this affliction? I think not. You have not experienced the feeling of being utterly cast away, of being adrift on the margin of life unseen and unheard. If I cry out, there is no one to care for me. If I am in agony of spirit, there is no one to console me. It is in your power to mend my loneliness. Do not deny me this request."

"How can I proceed with such a monstrous task? My instruments have all been destroyed—by you."

"It is a matter of expense. That is all. You know how to conjure forth the electrical power. You can construct the machines."

"You seriously intend me to take a female from the grave and animate her?"

"If you consent, neither you nor any other man will look upon this face again. My companion and I will lead a harmless life of simple toil. We shall find our rest on the kind earth, and content ourselves with the seclusion of a hidden island; we shall drink the waters of the brook, and eat the acorns. We shall be sufficient one to another."

I sat in a daze of wonder and apprehension. I envisaged all the scenes of this process: the assembly of the electrical machines, the body or the parts of a woman taken from the tomb and brought down to Limehouse, the light and heat of the terrible creation. And then yet one more being to arise from the table, with all the powers I knew she would possess! Might they then not couple, and have offspring? No. The dead could not breed new life. Of that I was certain.

"She must be young and beautiful," he said.

"I cannot consent."

"We will leave the world to those who are happy in it. Freed from the hatred of my fellow creatures, I shall express all the benevolence that you once hoped to find in me. I will no longer curse and rage against you. I swear by the light of the sun. I swear that I will leave you for ever."

I entertained his argument for a moment only, since I remained firm in my detestation and rejection of a proposal that might have intolerable consequences. "It is not to be contemplated."

"You would destroy my one chance of happiness? Of salvation?"

"I would deny you the chance of wreaking more havoc and

misery upon the world, with a companion your equal in strength and purpose."

"Very well, sir. I am fearless, and therefore powerful. I say this clearly to you now, even though I am wrapped in anger and in the contemplation of revenge. Your days will pass in dread and horror, and soon enough you will repent of all the injuries you have inflicted on me. One day you will curse the sun that gazes on your misery."

"I charge you this. Do not follow me!"

"Oh, is that the sum of your fears? Let me tell you now that you can never escape me. If you will not create for me a companion, then I choose you to be my spouse. We shall be inseparable, two living things joined together. Do you delight in the prospect as much as I do?"

"I can travel to the outermost reaches of the world—"

"Do not think of fleeing to the wilderness. The wilderness in me is greater. I will find you out."

"Can I not reason with you?"

"Reason? What has reason to do with this? The pact between us is of fire and blood."

"So you will shadow me, will you? Then you will be a subordinate creature, a slave to my wishes."

"No. I will not be with you always. I will not be with you often. But when you are least ready, then I will be there. What if I were to appear on your wedding night?"

"How can there be such a thing, when I know that you are somewhere around me?"

"Precisely. I am no slave. I am your master. And remember this, sir. You are sure to be visited by me." He went over to the door, and seemed to exult in the power of the night and the river. "Now for the estuary," he said. "I pledge myself to eternal pain!"

$$\Rightarrow \Leftarrow$$

I SAT, OR RATHER CROUCHED, in my chair, amid the rubble which was all that remained of my work, as the hours passed. It has been said that evils come to an end, but that fear endures for ever. I had entered a state of being which could only be curtailed with my death. And how, how, in these first hours, did I long for death to come! I sat in the workshop until dawn but then, through some brute or animal instinct, I returned home through the streets of London. There was a heavy rain to which I paid very little regard; it seemed to be no more than the accompaniment of my dread, throwing up vistas of mist and mud along every street.

When eventually I came up to my door in Jermyn Street, Fred greeted me with a most perplexed expression. "You are all water, sir. You will rush into the gutter."

"Take me inside, Fred. I can hardly stand."

He helped me across the threshold, and at once began to take off my boots. "There is enough water here," he said, "to fill the Fleet." He began wringing out my coarse woollen socks. Then he went into my private closet, and brought me several towels; with these I retreated into my bedroom where I undressed myself and lay down upon the bed.

How many hours I slept, I do not know. I was awoken by the entrance of Fred, bearing a plate of chops and tomatoes. He placed it carefully beside me on the bed, and from a pocket withdrew a letter sealed with a wafer. "This has come from a gentleman," he said. "You know who."

It was a letter from Bysshe, entreating me to travel up to Marlow and join him in what he called *my riparian paradise*. I realised, in the instant of reflection upon this proposal, that I had contracted a most curious weakness. I had lost all of my energy of mind, my animation in the affairs of life. I had in effect lost all will and sense of volition. It was the most singular sensation in the world. Out of dread, and horror, had come meekness and submission. The fear had not left me. Far from it. But it had become my perpetual partner, my double, my shadow, without which I would not exist. So I was left singularly unable or unwilling to make any decision for myself, in any matter concerning my fate. I ate the chops and tomatoes that Fred had prepared for me, and told him to pack my valise for Marlow. He asked if he could accompany me on the journey—as my "jolly" as he put it in the language of the street—and I assented without giving the matter any thought.

⇒ ⇐

WE LEFT JERMYN STREET SOON AFTER, and hired a post-chaise from Catherine Street to Marlow; Fred kept up a continuous line of chatter all the while, which pleased me greatly. It relieved me of any need to talk, or to think, as we made our way out of the capital into the fields and hedgerows of Buckinghamshire. He pointed out the milestones on the way, the number of gravel pits in Kensington, the geese in Chiswick, and the bad roads of Brentford. He told me that he and his brother used to bathe in the Thames, until the filth in the river became insupportable. He told me that twelve thousand people passed over London Bridge each day, and that there were elves in the Highgate woods. He reckoned Marlow to be a "comfortable" town, and explained to me in some detail how he had found Bysshe's house by dint of earnest enquiries among the tradesmen. After a short silence he volunteered the information that he also had witnessed Daniel Westbrook's execution.

"What?" I said. "You walked to Newgate after I had left the house?"

"Yes, sir. I hope I did no wrong in that. There was nothing to mind in the house, you see. It was all neat and perfect."

"You rogue. You led me to believe that you stood guard perpetually."

"Nobody can be perpetual, Mr. Frankenstein. I needed the air."

"A foul air by Newgate."

"This it is, sir. I had never been to a hanging before. I wished to see the thing."

"And you did." I leaned over to him. "So did I."

Suddenly I began to weep. I bent forward in the carriage and sobbed, the tears unbidden and unexpected. Fred passed me a handkerchief, and looked steadfastly out of the window until I had composed myself. Eventually I sat back, and put my head against the leather rest. We were travelling along a stretch of road beside the Thames, and I noticed that the current of the river was turbid and irregular. There was something lying in the water, impeding its progress. "There is the boundary stone," Fred said. "We will be there shortly."

We arrived at dusk. The air by the river was chill and laden with moisture, but Fred led me briskly down the principal street of the town. It was wide enough for two carriages, and muddy after recent rain, but we crossed it without any difficulty. We turned left down a smaller thoroughfare, lined with superior shops and houses. "Here we are, sir. This is the house."

It was a two-storey villa of recent construction with a plain lattice-work porch and large windows on the ground floor. "Will you knock, Fred?" I had not the slightest energy.

The door was opened by Bysshe himself, who seemed astonished to see me so soon after he had despatched his invitation. "My dear Frankenstein," he said, "you are like an apparition. I was just speaking of you! And here is the boy, looking as fresh scrubbed as a Tenterden apple. Come in." We entered a narrow hallway, where there was a plentiful supply of boots and umbrellas. I had forgotten that Bysshe had a strange partiality for umbrellas, of whatever description, and an equally strong propensity for losing them. He led us into the drawing room, a brilliantly lit room with long damask curtains and comfortable furniture of the provincial style. Sitting by the fireside were a gentleman of middle age and a young lady, evidently deep in talk.

"Here is the man," Bysshe said, "whom I was describing. It is the oddest and most singular coincidence. This is Mr. Godwin, Victor, and his daughter Mary."

The man rose from his chair, and greeted me with great cordiality; his daughter took my hand, and welcomed me to Albion House as if she were the mistress of it. "We have been considering the name of Albion, Mr. Frankenstein," her father said. "Bysshe believes it is derived from Alba, the Celtic word for Britain. But I believe it to be more classical. I take it to spring from *albus*, meaning white. Thus from the white cliffs. What is your opinion?" He was wearing a pair of pebble spectacles that seemed to emphasise his pale and almost rimless eyes. His manner was cordial, as I have said, but somewhat too intense and magisterial; it seemed to be a forced cordiality.

"I have not the least idea, sir. I am sorry—"

Bysshe brought a chair for me, and offered me a glass of Madeira wine that I willingly accepted. "You are tired after your journey, Victor." He had noticed my listlessness and weariness. "This will revive you."

The father and daughter looked at me with placid interest, and waited for me to speak.

"It has been a hard time," I said.

"Of course. William and Mary know all the sad facts of the matter. You can speak freely."

"I do not know if I can speak at all."

"You attended Harriet's funeral?"

"Yes."

"And were you present at Daniel's execution?"

I looked round for Fred, but he had silently left the room, no doubt in search of the company of Bysshe's servants.

"Yes. He died bravely. He was an innocent man."

"How do you know that, sir?" Mr. Godwin put the question to me in a challenging manner.

"I know it. I know—I knew—Daniel Westbrook. I saw him in his prison cell. There was no gentler being on the earth. He had nothing to do with this crime. Nothing whatever."

"No one else was suspected," Mr. Godwin said. "We read the public prints, even in Marlow."

"The murderer walks free."

"Do you have private information, Mr. Frankenstein?" Miss Godwin asked me this with the faintest impression of a smile.

"No. I have no information on the subject except that which

instinct and intuition give me. I am sure that, as a lady, you will grant me that right."

She gave me a keen glance then. "Instinct is very right and just. My father adopts more rational principles, but I have always believed in the divining powers of the imagination."

"She has read Coleridge," her father said. "She is an enthusiast for the divine afflatus."

"Without the imagination, Father, the human frame is dust and ashes."

"You cannot go so far, Mary."

"I may trespass into the world of the ideal, may I not?"

Bysshe had been listening in silence to their conversation, and I could not help but notice the profound admiration that he evinced for Mary. It seemed to me strange that, after the recent death of Harriet, he should be so struck by another woman. Yet I was not wholly surprised by his interest. I had heard of Mary's mother, Mary Wollstonecraft Godwin. She was the author of *A Vindication of the Rights of Woman* that, as a student in Switzerland, I had read with great fervour. Yes. Fervour is the word. She had instilled in me a love of liberty in all its forms, and I believed that human happiness should be the prerogative of all regardless of sex. I hoped to see in Miss Godwin some sign or token of her mother's genius. I soon gathered that she had quieter but no less interesting virtues.

Bysshe seemed to divine my interest because, a moment later, he led me to the other end of the room on the excuse that he wished for a "private symposium." "I could not have endured the funeral, Victor," he said. "The horror of it. The senselessness of it. I still think of her as a dear, good girl. I will never lose that memory."

"What of your child?"

"Ianthe is better with the Westbrooks. I have made arrangements that an annual income be paid to them through my banker." He looked at me in appeal, as if seeking my approval.

"You have done what is necessary, Bysshe."

"And what is right?"

"Of course." I was silent for a moment. "You have mentioned Mr. Godwin to me before."

"Did I tell you that I visited him in Somers Town? I have always admired him, ever since I read his *Enquiry Concerning Political Justice*. I share his belief that Man can be improved and even perfected."

"Indeed? How does he reach that conclusion?"

"You never used to be so sceptical, Victor."

"I merely ask the question."

"Mr. Godwin is animated by a keen sense of the natural man. The first men were not savage or cruel. In their natural state they were peaceful and benevolent. It is only the tyranny of law and custom that has made us what we are. But man is perfectible. Once we have removed his shackles, he will be capable of perpetual improvement."

"And you also believe this?"

"It is an article of faith. There was a time, Victor, when you would also have subscribed to it."

"I do not have all of my old enthusiasm, Bysshe."

"Are you sure you are quite well? You seem to have lost your spring."

"It has turned to winter, I am afraid." I longed to unburden myself to him, to explain all that had occurred in the most exact and methodical manner, but I knew well enough that even Bysshe would deem me to be a madman.

"The deaths of Harriet and of Daniel," he replied, "have been a monstrous blow to us. You have fallen, dear Victor, into a melancholy from which I vow to save you. You will stay with us here in Marlow until you are quite recovered. We will spend long quiet days at our ease. We will journey along the Thames. You see. Already you are returning to life. Come. Let us join the Godwins."

It transpired, in the course of conversation, that the father and daughter had decided to settle themselves in Marlow in order to console Bysshe after the death of Harriet. They had rented a house close by but, at Bysshe's urgent entreaty, they had agreed to take up quarters in Albion House itself. There was room for all, he said, in Albion. I gained the impression that Mr. Godwin was in straitened circumstances and, as a consequence, had welcomed the offer. I wondered, too, if he was also accepting contributions from Bysshe's purse. Bysshe had not the slightest regard for money.

"I wonder, Mr. Shelley," Miss Godwin said, "that you keep a boat in this dreadful weather."

"I have asked you to call me Bysshe."

"I know. I must learn to forget my manners."

She was a striking young woman, with a mass of black hair descending in curls and ringlets; she had a fine forehead, suggesting a highly developed ideality, and dark expressive eyes. She always looked as if she had just awoken from sleep, and in repose had a dreamy and even passive expression. She looked intently at me as she spoke to me, but would then drift back into some world of private reflection. "Will you join me, Mary, on the water?" Bysshe asked her. "I will show you the delights of the river even in dreadful weather, as you call it. There is an inexpressible comfort in seeing the rain dissolving into the water, and we can shelter beneath the branches of a willow. There is often a mist where the rain and the river are reunited."

"Will it not be cold?" she asked him.

"Not if you have shawl and bonnet."

"The hydrologic cycle," Mr. Godwin said. "There is not one drop of water, more or less, than there was at the creation of the world."

"Is that not an enchanting thought, Victor?" Bysshe had handed me another glass of Madeira wine. "As it was in the beginning, is now, and ever shall be."

"You are quoting an old prayer," I said, "for deliverance."

"A prayer of celebration, I think."

"Eternity fills me with dread," I replied. "It is not to be imagined."

"Now there, sir," Mr. Godwin said, "you have touched upon a great truth. Eternity is incomprehensible. Literally so. Even the angels, if such beings exist, cannot envisage it. Every creature that is made is imbued with a sense of ending."

The conversation continued in this vein for a little longer, until I pleaded tiredness and was taken by a maidservant to my room. She told me that her name was Martha. "Where is Fred?" I asked her.

"He is in the kitchen, sir, tucking into some ham."

"Not to be disturbed then."

"Do you need him, sir?"

"No. Not at all. Leave him to his ham. I will see to myself."

I undressed and lay down upon the bed. It was a stormy night, and the rain lashed the windows; I found a certain comfort in the sound, and very quickly fell asleep.

⤞⤝

I WAS STARTLED INTO WAKEFULNESS by a prolonged scream coming from some part of the house close to me. It was a shriek of the utmost terror. I took my gown and hastened into the hallway, with many dark thoughts descending upon me. Suddenly Bysshe appeared in his nightshirt, at the other end of the hallway, and beckoned me to come forward. "Did you hear that?" he asked me.

"Who could not?"

"I believe it came from Mary's room. Here." He tapped lightly upon the door, whispering her name.

It was opened a few moments later. "I am sorry," she said. "There is nothing to fear." She was wearing a white muslin nightgown, but it was not as luminously pale as her face or her trembling hands. She stood uncertainly, and the door remained half-opened. "I dreamed that I saw a phantom by the window. It was a dream. I am certain of it. There was a face."

"Of course it was a dream, Mary. But dreams may take on the appearance of a terrible reality. You were right to scream."

"I am sorry to have awoken you. I awoke myself."

"Think nothing of it. Now try and sleep."

She closed the door. Bysshe and I returned to our chambers. I had said nothing during this exchange, but it was a long time before I managed to find rest.

ON THE FOLLOWING MORNING Mr. Godwin was in fine spirits. He had slept peacefully through the night, he told us at breakfast, and was feeling "very sound." Miss Godwin looked pale still; she could not eat, and said very little. "I have been extolling to Martha the virtues of Baxter's beetroots," her father was saying. He helped himself to a large portion of kedgeree. "They are sweet. They are tender. They are delicious. They surpass all others in the kingdom. You must remind Martha of them."

"I have not seen Martha this morning," Bysshe replied. "She will be at the market."

"I will speak to her when she returns."

We did not mention the incident in the night, but I noticed that Miss Godwin and Bysshe exchanged glances of a private kind: I could not help but think that my friend was growing greatly attached to her. After the meal was over Bysshe repeated his proposal for an expedition on the river. The storm had passed, and the sky was clear. What better morning for a jaunt upon the Thames? Mr. Godwin was enthusiastic at the prospect, and so his daughter dutifully assented. I merely followed the general wish.

We sauntered from the house down the main street towards the river. The Godwins walked ahead, and Bysshe took the opportunity of discussing with me the events of the previous night. "Mary has seen phantoms before," he said.

"Do you mean ghosts? Spirits?"

"No. Creatures that seem to be of flesh and blood. But they are not truly alive. She dreams of them often."

"She has not seen one in reality?"

"Of course not. Whatever are you thinking?"

"Thinking of nothing."

"She knows that they exist only in her sleeping mind. But they scare her. Ah, the river beckons."

Bysshe had hired a skiff for the duration of his stay, and he kept the vessel by Marlow Bridge. It was large enough for us all, and he took the oars with some aplomb, guiding us from the bank into the main current of the river. In his enthusiasm he began to recite a poem that I did not recognise, but that seemed to be of his own composition:

"O stream,
Whose source is inaccessibly profound,
Whither do thy mysterious waters tend?
Thou imagest my life!"

"That is very fine," Miss Godwin said. She trailed the fingers of her left hand in the water. "Where *is* the source?"

"Some say that it is Thames Head. Others insist that it lies at Seven Springs. There is great debate about the matter."

"Which do you favour?" she asked him.

"I do not understand why a river cannot have two sources. A living being requires two parents, does it not?"

"It is believed," Mr. Godwin said, "that some molluscs are auto-generative."

"Too painful to contemplate," Bysshe replied. We passed a small island in the middle of the river, where two swans were resting. "Faithful until death," he said.

Miss Godwin looked at him for a moment, and then resumed her contemplation of the water. "It used to be said that the swans greeted the ships sailing home with song," she said to no one in particular. "But how can that be so?"

"Precisely," Mr. Godwin said. "They are mute swan."

"I hope to have a swan-like end, fading in music," Bysshe replied.

"I would rather prefer swan pie."

So we continued downriver, following the current. Miss Godwin seemed to be lulled to sleep by the movement of the water, and for a moment closed her eyes. I hoped that she was not dreaming of phantoms. "What was that?" Bysshe asked suddenly.

Miss Godwin opened her eyes very wide. "What?"

"Over there. By the bank. I thought something reared its head and then went under the water."

"An otter," Mr. Godwin said. "I understand that they are common here."

"It did not seem to be an otter. It was too big. Too awkward." I looked in the direction Bysshe was pointing, and I did indeed notice some perturbation on the surface of the river; it was as if something had gone down to the bottom leaving its wake behind. Mary took her hand out of the water.

Bysshe eased the boat forward with a barely perceptible movement of the oars; the river was muddied, and I could see where the bank had been eroded by more than usual motion. And then I felt the first drops of rain. The sky, so clear before, had suddenly become overcast. The water turned from a lucent green to slate grey, and a cold breeze brushed across us. Bysshe looked up at the sky and laughed. "You see, Mary, you are especially favoured. The river wishes you to see all of its moods."

"It is only a light rain," she said.

"We will recline beneath the willow boughs. Here is the spot."

He manoeuvred the skiff beneath the trailing branches of a willow leaning over the water; it was a natural shelter, of a kind I would once have relished, and my companions seemed happy to remain secluded amid the gentle pattering of the rain around us. Then Miss Godwin spoke in a low voice. "What is that? Oh God, what is it?"

Her eyes were fixed upon a stretch of water just beyond the tree. There was a hand among the trailing weeds, apparently clutching at them; and then on a motion of the current a face broke the surface of the water. A few moments later the whole body emerged, with a white linen nightgown billowing around it. "God, God, God." Miss Godwin chanted the word.

"What is this frightful thing?"

I do not know who spoke. The words might have come from my own mouth.

Bysshe leapt from the bench and quickly steered the skiff towards the body; then with the oars he managed to push it against the bank, where it was caught amid the roots and weeds. He jumped from the boat onto the bank, and managed to haul the corpse on shore before it floated further downstream. "It cannot be," he said. "This is Martha." He stepped back, and stood at a short distance from the body without saying anything further. Miss Godwin clung to her father, and pressed her head against his jacket.

"Whatever has happened?" Godwin seemed genuinely puzzled, as if he had come upon a calculation he could not settle. I clambered out of the boat onto the shore, and surveyed

Martha. Her body had been pinched and bruised in death, no doubt by immersion in the water, but there were also livid marks around her neck and upper thorax. I had no doubt that she had been strangled before being consigned to the river; Harriet Westbrook had met approximately the same fate in the Serpentine.

"I saw her last night," Bysshe said. "She was eating ham in the kitchen."

"With Fred."

"She was brimful of laughter, as usual. What is to be done, Victor? What are we to make of this fearful thing?"

"We will be steady, Bysshe. We will take the body back to Marlow, and alert the parish constables. We must leave the matter in their hands."

"Why would she have wished to drown herself?"

"I do not know that she did."

"Could she have fallen into the river in some terrible accident?"

"Do you see the marks upon her neck and body? She was held in a powerful grip."

He looked at me in horror. "Is that possible? That she was destroyed by someone?"

"I believe so. Now is not the time to debate, Bysshe. We must act with urgency. Come. Help me with the body."

"I cannot touch her, Victor. I cannot."

Miss Godwin would not stay in the skiff with the corpse of Martha. But with the help of her father I managed to place the body in the boat. It was agreed that Bysshe and Mr. Godwin would take it back to Marlow, while Miss Godwin and I would walk back along the bank to the town. We watched as the skiff slowly made its way upstream with its unhappy burden. She was silent as we began our walk beside the bank. "I know it is wrong of me," she said eventually, "but I cannot help thinking of Ophelia. *There is a willow grows aslant a brook.* You know it, Mr. Frankenstein?"

"Please call me Victor."

"We have gone beyond ceremony, I think. You shall call me Mary."

"Ophelia drowned herself, did she not?"

"*Her garments, heavy with their drink, pulled the poor wretch from her melodious lay to muddy death.* Those are the words of the queen. Not mine."

"I am afraid that Martha may not have been a suicide."

She stopped, and was seized with a fit of coughing. It was as if she were trying to expel something from her body. After a few moments she recovered.

"You mean that someone has killed her?"

"I believe so. Yes."

"I knew it. I knew it when I saw her in the weeds."

"What made you suspect it?" I was eager to hear her account, touching, as it might, upon my own secret.

"The face at the window," she replied. "It was no dream. No phantasm. I am sure of that now. I had tried to comfort myself, and you, with my explanation last night. But it was not a face I had ever seen before in my dreams."

"Can you describe it, Mary?"

"It seemed crumpled, creased rather, like a sheet of paper hastily thrown away. The eyes were of such malevolence that even now I shudder."

It was clear enough to me that she had seen the creature. He had come to the house at Marlow in pursuit of me and my friends, with the object of performing another act of vengeance. "You must tell the constables everything you saw," I said. "There will be a search for this demon." I had conceived the hope, only half-formed, that the creature might be taken and killed by the mob—or that in some other way he might be destroyed by the forces of the law.

"Demon? No. He was a man, I believe, but one of terrible appearance."

"We must speak to the constables as quickly as possible. They may be able to capture this man before he can flee."

"It is possible, Victor, that he wished to murder me. Only my scream prevented him. But then poor Martha—" She said no more. We walked the rest of the way in silence.

⇒ Sixteen ⇐

WHEN MARY AND I CAME BACK into Marlow, we saw the commotion by the side of the bridge. A small crowd had gathered on the path sloping down to the river. I could see Bysshe in animated conversation with an elderly gentleman in rusty black who, as I discovered later, was the watchman of the high street. As we came up to them I realised that the crowd had formed a circle around the body of Martha. Mr. Godwin and one of the parish constables, in tall hat and blue surtout, were standing beside the corpse and looking down upon it with scarcely concealed relish.

"Look into her eyes, Mr. Wilby," one of the women in the crowd called out to the constable. "You will see the face of the murderer there."

"You do it, Sarah," he replied. "You are the wise woman. Not me."

"These superstitions," Mary whispered to me, "are very strong."

Sarah had obliged the constable by coming forward and kneeling down beside the body. She peered into Martha's open eyes, and then suddenly jerked her head back. "I see a fiend," she said.

Mr. Godwin laughed. "If it is a fiend, Mr. Wilby, you will not be able to catch him."

"We will have difficulty, sir. That is sure enough. Be good, Sarah. Stand up now." The crowd were murmuring, unsure whether to accept or to ridicule the woman's verdict. I decided now to act. I walked up to Mr. Godwin and the constable. "Miss Godwin," I said, "has something very important to tell you. She saw the murderer last night. Outside her bedroom window."

"What?" Mr. Godwin seemed offended. "Why did Mary not tell me of this?"

"Before we found Martha's body, sir, there was no possible reason to alarm you. She thought it might have been a dream."

"Where is this lady?" Mr. Wilby was very solemn.

"She is conversing with Mr. Shelley. There." The constable walked over to her, and they stood together in earnest conversation. Bysshe seemed strangely excited; his eyes were bright and, as he approached me, I saw that his face had the faintest flush. "I should have searched the garden," he said. "I should have caught this madman before he came upon Martha."

"We had not the slightest notion that he was real, Bysshe."

"I should have trusted Mary."

"She did not even trust herself. She considered it to be a vision. A dream."

"But she sees into the heart of things. She knew that some dreadful event was about to take place."

"It is too late for this, Bysshe. All our efforts must now be bent on finding the killer."

"He will have fled. I am sure of it."

"But we may find traces of his presence. He may be hunted down."

"Hunted down. That is a good phrase." He glanced at Mary, still standing with the constable. "I will keep her safe. I will protect her."

Mr. Wilby began to organise a party of men for the search of the immediate neighbourhood; it was composed of shopkeepers, boatmen, and other workmen of the town. In addition three men were sent out to inform the inhabitants of the outlying villages. The constable hoped that there might have been sightings of the killer in the locality, even if the villain himself was not found. Inwardly I exulted. The creature was no longer the embodiment of my private despair; he had to some extent become a public agent, an object of concerted horror and suspicion. I joined the band of Marlow townsmen, and explained to them that they should begin their search along the stretch of the Thames where we had found the body of Martha. For a moment they were suspicious of my Swiss accent, but Bysshe reassured them that I was a good friend of him and of England. So they willingly followed me along the towing path until we reached that spot where Martha had risen among the weeds. There was no sign of disturbance in the vicinity. The recent fall of rain had left a film or haze of moisture over the trees and bushes around us, and all was still. We advanced further along the path and, following a slight bend in the river, came upon a water meadow where the grass had grown tall. "Something has been here," I said. "Do you see the dark line in the grass? Something has left a track."

"A cow," one of the men suggested.

"I see no cattle. And there are no horses in the fields." When we approached the track I noticed that it was discontinuous.

"Do you see," I said to them, "how the grass has been trampled down in sequence, with gaps between each mark? It is as if someone has proceeded in leaps and bounds."

"Hopping. Like a hare." It was the same man who had spoken before; he wore the garb of a market trader, with a red scarf tied loosely around his neck. "Who could leap such a distance?"

"It would take great strength and energy, I grant you."

"No man on earth could do it, sir."

"I am not so sure," I replied. "It has been said that murderers, after committing the deed, are possessed of enormous energy."

"So we follow the trail, do we?"

"Most certainly. Make sure that your guns are primed. He may be ferocious." I had the faintest hope that, if the creature could be injured or in some way rendered insensible, I might be able to act upon him. Could I remove his cerebral hemispheres, taking away all his powers of speech and motion? We walked in his track to the edge of the meadow, where our advance was checked by a broad channel of water running between the fields. "The bank has been disturbed here," I said. "Do you see the loose stones and earth? There is a depression, where he has sat down."

"Finding his breath, I imagine," one of the men replied.

"Or reflecting upon his next move. Where did he go?" I could see nothing in the field ahead, but then I noticed that the waters of the channel were muddied. "He has gone in," I said. "He has followed the channel. It was deep enough for him to remain hidden."

"Why would a man wish to take to water rather than land?" the man with the red scarf asked me.

"He may be no ordinary man."

"A water demon then?" He was smiling at me.

"I cannot tell."

Then we heard laughter—it was the most serene and melodious laugh that I had ever heard. And then came his voice. "I have been waiting for you, gentlemen. Do you wish to see me now?"

"Prepare your guns," I said.

One of the men then shot wildly into the field. On the sound of the report I saw a movement in a copse some distance away—he had projected his voice by some physical means unknown to me—and then a dark shape bounded off. "He is gone," I said. "You must alert the villagers in the neighbourhood. We do not have the means to overtake him."

The men were disturbed by the manner of the creature's flight—so sudden and so swift—and were subdued as they returned to Marlow. Some of them wondered out loud how any man could run at such a speed. "He must be possessed," I said. "I have heard of such cases."

I walked back slowly to Albion House, where Bysshe and the Godwins were sitting in the drawing room. "Mary wishes to return to London," Bysshe said as soon as I came into the room. "She has become nervous of this place."

"I do not believe the creature—the man—will come back," I replied. "We saw him fleeing across the fields."

"You saw him?" Mary was looking at me with the intentness I had noticed before. "What was he? What did he wear?"

"We saw only his running form. I believe that he was wrapped in a dark cloak. But I cannot be sure."

"Did he speak?"

"Yes. He said something like, 'I have been waiting for you, gentlemen.' Then one of my party fired. He ran. That is all I can tell you."

"Does that satisfy you, Mary?" her father asked.

"I will feel safe only in London, Pa. Here we are too—too vulnerable."

"You and Fred can stay on," Bysshe said to me. "You have only just arrived. And I doubt that the villain will come for you."

"His actions are not predictable."

"You think not?"

"That is my assumption. I am afraid, Bysshe, that I share Mary's anxiety. Where is Fred?"

"In the kitchen."

"Excuse me for a moment." I went down into the kitchen where Fred was sitting at the table, stirring a bowl of milk pudding. "Are you composed, Fred?"

"She was a good girl. I liked Martha, Mr. Frankenstein. She was a cheerful one."

"Did you hear anything in the night?"

"Not so much as a bed bug. The ham makes me sleep. The first thing I know of it is when the constable comes to the house. He was all in a sweat. When he told me, I could have fainted away. But I steadied myself. Was she bloated, sir? I've seen a few from the Thames."

"She was bruised."

"Where, sir?"

"Around the neck."

He continued stirring the milk pudding. "That was not nice."

"Not nice at all. The others are going back to London, Fred. Mr. Shelley has suggested that we can remain at Albion House."

"Nothing here, sir. Just fields."

"So you would like to return with them?" He looked at me. "Very well. We will go back."

In truth I had no desire to be left in Marlow. I knew well enough that there was no safety from the creature, in any place on earth. But in London, at least, there was comfort in the massed ranks of people. Here, in the open, I felt afraid.

We could not, as it transpired, return at once. The parish constable came to inform us that, two days hence, we would be obliged to attend the coroner's inquest; it would take place in an upper room of a public house along the high street.

"This is very unfortunate, Mr. Wilby." Mr. Godwin had decided to remonstrate with him. "My daughter is in very low spirits as a consequence of this affair. She wishes to return to London."

"It cannot be helped, sir. All Marlow is in a fever over this case. Justice must be seen to be done, sir."

"Where is poor Martha?" Mary asked him.

"The deceased is lying in an ice-house. Behind the butcher's shop in Lady Place. She will be a little damaged, but she will last."

We spent the next two days in a state of some gloom; the rain continued, more intensely than before, and on one afternoon Bysshe read to us some stanzas from the poem he was then composing. Certain lines struck me very forcibly:

"I curse thee! Let a sufferer's curse
Clasp thee, his torturer, like remorse,
Till thine Infinity shall be
A robe of envenomed agony;
And thine Omnipotence a crown of pain,
To cling like burning gold round thy dissolving brain."

"Very good," Mr. Godwin remarked. "Very strong."

"It is a powerful curse," Mary said. "It issues from a broken heart."

"I see the curse," I said, "like a smoking plain, filled with fires and fissures from which billows of livid smoke erupt." They looked at me in surprise, and then Bysshe continued reading.

⇒ ⇐

ON THE MORNING of the coroner's inquest, there was great excitement in the town. A crowd had gathered outside the public house, the Cat and Currant, where the proceedings were to be held; but, as soon as the beadle saw us, we were led with great ceremony through the townspeople and in single file mounted the staircase to the first-floor room. It smelled strongly of sawdust and spirits, with the aroma of beer and tobacco somewhere in the mixture; some tables had been pushed together in the middle of the room which, the beadle informed us, were reserved for the gentlemen of the jury. The coroner then walked in. He was dressed in clerical garb, and Bysshe whispered to me that he was indeed the rector of the parish church; he had seen him in the garden of his vicarage, pruning his vines. That gentleman was followed by the jurors;

they entered the room with an air of solemn distinction, although I had seen one or two of them drinking ale in the parlour when we had first arrived. Then the people of Marlow crowded in, taking up every particle of space until the air became almost insupportable. Bysshe pointed out to me two or three gentlemen sitting at a table evidently reserved for them. "Penny-a-liners," he said. "You can tell them from their cuffs. They will be reporting this for the public prints. The news has reached London."

"Gentlemen—" The coroner began to speak.

"Silence!" called the beadle.

"Gentlemen. You have viewed the unfortunate young woman known as Martha Delaney."

"I never knew her last name," Mary whispered to me.

"You are impanelled here to ascertain the causes of her lamentable death. Evidence will be given before you, as to the circumstances attending that death, and you will give your verdict according to that evidence and not anything else. Anything else must be disregarded and blotted from the copybook." Bysshe gave me an odd look of merriment. "A young lady is present here." Bysshe assumed an expression of intense seriousness. "A young lady who may have seen the perpetrator of this foul crime. May I ask you to rise, Miss Godwin, and take the oath?" There was a general murmur of approval, from the people of Marlow, as Mary stood beside the jurors and recited the oath. But there was absolute silence when she recounted the events of that night. She had glimpsed a face at the window—"a leering countenance," as she put it. When her scream woke the others in the house (she refrained from saying who they were) the intruder was gone. Mary had great skill in narrative, and added little touches of description to the simple story. Then she nodded to the coroner and resumed her seat, while the penny-a-liners were still busy with their pens. "Thank you, Miss Godwin, for that affecting testimony. Now I will call an eminent gentleman who, I am informed, was accidentally present when discovery of the death was made. I will call Mr. Percy Bysshe Shelley." There was a murmur of interest among those assembled, and evidence of the keenest attention among the penny-a-liners; they were no doubt aware, or had been informed, of the fate of Harriet. Bysshe stood beside the table of jurors but, when asked to take the oath, replied in a calm clear voice. "I will say to you, sir, that I swear to tell the truth before the eyes of my fellow men."

"This is very irregular, Mr. Shelley."

"I hope and trust that I will follow the principles of the utmost honesty in anything I may say."

"Mr. Shelley is the son of a baronet, gentlemen," the coroner informed the men of the jury. "Are you content to accept his unsupported word?" They were content. So Bysshe narrated the story of our recent journey down the Thames, and the discovery of Martha's body among the weeds; he particularly noted the marks of bruising about her neck and upper torso. Then one of the party tracking the path of the creature was called—it was he who had fired the shot into the field—and he described the pursuit and flight of the supposed killer. He described him as "monstrous big" with a "wonderful celerity." In his opinion we were dealing with an escaped convict, or a lunatic, hiding in the woods beside the river. The session was quickly concluded, with a verdict from the jury that the young lady, Martha Delaney, had been killed unlawfully by person unknown. She could now be buried in the churchyard.

Bysshe hired a carriage for our return to London. He intended to lodge with the Godwins, at their house in Somers Town, until he could find accommodation of his own. I suspected, however, that he would wish to remain in the closest possible proximity to Mary Godwin. Fred and I disembarked at Jermyn Street, to the great delight of the crossing sweeper's dog that had formed an attachment to Fred over the last few months. The dog jumped against him, and left traces of mud and mire on his serge breeches. "That reminds me, sir," he said as we climbed the stairs. "I have left your laundry with Ma."

"Then you must fetch it, Fred. I need clean linen after Marlow."

"The country is a dirty place, sir. It abounds in soil."

"We are fortunate, then, to live in a clean city?"

"Oh, yes. The mud in London don't stick. Look. I can brush it off." After he had unpacked, and taken up the linen in a great bundle, he made his way to Mrs. Shoeberry.

There had been a marked change in my constitution, I discovered, after the journey to Marlow. I was no longer so listless, so devoid of energy. The murder of Martha served to inflame my desire for vengeance and, in the carriage, I had consulted with myself over all possible means of fulfilling it. It was then I decided upon a course of action. I would return to Limehouse, where I would reconstruct my shattered equipment in the hope of reversing my experiment and reducing the creature once more to lifeless matter. The more I contemplated the venture, the more fervently I embraced it. Would it be possible to build an engine that by means of magnetic force might extract the electricity from the body of the creature? Or was there some way of discharging a negative energy that might balance the power of the electrical fluid already within him? I determined to begin my studies anew, with the single purpose of destroying that which I had created. I also conceived a scheme with which I might trick and deceive the creature. If he visited me in Limehouse, I would welcome him. I would tell him that his frightful acts had forced me to revise my judgement, and that I was willing to create for him a bride as long as he swore a solemn oath to depart these shores for ever. I might even be able to persuade him to endure certain experiments; I would assure him that these would have to be undertaken before I could start work on his female double. He would then be within my power. Such were my enthusiasm and optimism that I considered travelling down to the estuary, and there confronting him in his hidden retreat with the news of my intentions. I had no compunction about deceiving him. Had he not already betrayed me in as deadly a fashion as I could envisage?

I heard the voice of Mrs. Shoeberry. She was trailing her son up the staircase, all the while complaining of her "poor knees" that could hardly stand the strain of climbing. "Well, here you are, sir," she said when she came onto the landing. She seemed surprised to see me in my own lodging. "I have laboured long and hard over your linen, sir. Fred, give Mr. Frankenstein the parcel. All crisp and white like a snow field."

"I am glad to hear it, Mrs. Shoeberry."

"The sheets are perfection. You will sleep as cleanly as a nun."

"I hope so." I took her into the drawing room and paid her a florin, which she accepted with alacrity.

"I hear, sir, that you have been in strange parts."

"Ma!"

"It is my way to converse with my gentlemen, Fred. I am not a post."

"We have been to Marlow, if that is what you mean."

"I don't exactly know where that is, sir."

"Along the Thames."

"Oh, the Thames, is it? Quite a long river, sir." It was clear to me that Fred had not informed his mother of Martha's death; it was no doubt too explosive a topic. "There is an awful lot of water in the Thames, sir. Mark my words."

"Undoubtedly, Mrs. Shoeberry."

"And to be plain, sir, we don't quite know where it all comes from. There is a deal of dirt in it. It is ever such a hindrance to us laundry women. I never go down to the stairs no more. I would come back more dead than alive. Filthy smell, sir. Pah!" She mimed all the symptoms of disgust, much to Fred's annoyance.

"You must get back, Ma," he urged her. "Little Tom will be missing his tea."

"Stop your pushing and your pulling, boy. Mr. Frankenstein and I are enjoying a quiet chat." Her eyes roamed about the room. "I shall look after them shirts as if they were my own, sir. Do you happen to have an ounce of spirits about you? This rain has upset my constitution. Women are frail, sir, in wet weather." I went over to my cabinet and poured her a glass of gin, which she swallowed in a moment—taking care afterwards to lick her lips, in case any of the precious fluid had escaped her. "The water gets into our bones."

"Ma, I have to prepare Mr. Frankenstein's supper."

"Oh? What are you having, sir?"

"What am I having, Fred?"

"Pork chops in onion gravy. With a good head of crackling."

"That's sumptuous, that is. Make sure the crackling is moist, Fred. It draws up the richness."

"We must not detain you any longer, Mrs. Shoeberry. I know you are a very busy woman."

"Busy? I am like a cartwheel, sir. Always turning." Fred left the room and began to descend the stairs, with the clear understanding that his mother should follow. "Yes, boy," she said. "Don't fluster me. You will make me all of a quiver." She went out of the door, and then stopped. "I will starch your cuffs, sir. They will be so stiff that you will not know them."

"I am obliged, Mrs. Shoeberry."

≫ ≪

ON THE FOLLOWING MORNING I took once more the familiar way to Limehouse, but fired now by a new eagerness to embark upon the means of destroying the creature. The workshop was still in disarray, of course, but there was no evidence of further incursions by him. All lay in disorder. The pieces of the electrical columns, constructed for me by Francis Hayman, lay upon the floor. They had some marks of the elements, where the rain had blown upon them, but I observed that each part was still intact: the discs, the cakes of wax and resin, the vitreous glass and metal lay in separate pieces. There was rust upon the metal, but it would be easily removed. If I could enlist the aid of Hayman once again, I could re-create the conditions of my original experiment. But first I needed to restore the workshop itself. Over the next few days, with the help of the workmen who had rebuilt the interior so many months before, I repaired the walls and replaced the shelves and cabinets. I told them that a gang of scuffle-hunters, the local name for the river thieves, had broken in and searched for money. They warned me of the dangers of working by the Thames, and placed a great padlock upon the newly fitted door.

I called upon Hayman at the offices of the Convex Light Company in Abchurch Lane. Here I explained to him the injury to the equipment he had constructed for me—blaming once more the activities of the scuffle-hunters—and asked his help in restoring it. Then I asked him the question that most concerned me. "Have you debated, sir, on the possibilities of a negative fluid?"

"You will have to be more precise, Mr. Frankenstein."

"What I mean is this. We believe the electrical fluid to be transmitted in wave form, do we not?"

"That is the theory. Although some deem it to be comprised of particles."

"Let us assume it to be waves. Would I be right in conceiving of these waves, in effect, as a series of curves?"

"You are close. I am convinced that there are innumerable magnetic curves, packed so closely together that they seem to form an indivisible line."

"But each curve could in theory be traced and measured?"

"In theory."

"It would have a high point and a low point?"

"There will be parabolic and hyperbolic arcs."

"Precisely my meaning. And what, Mr. Hayman, if they were reversed?"

"You astonish me, Mr. Frankenstein. It would entirely change the nature of the electrical fluid. But it could not be done. The laws of physical science stand in the way."

"I am used to defying such laws."

"Truly?"

"I mean only that like you I wish to make advances in our knowledge of the world. All physical laws are provisional, are they not?"

"How far have you proceeded, sir, with your original research?"

I had told him, in the course of our earlier conversations, that by means of the electrical fluid I wished to restore life and energy to animal tissue. "I have made some small steps," I replied. "I have found it possible to restore animation to certain fish. But for a short time only."

"Carry on with the work, Mr. Frankenstein. It is of the utmost interest and importance to the rest of us. Be assured of that."

He agreed to visit the Limehouse workshop on the following Sunday, and to assist me in the restoration of the broken equipment. On his arrival, as I had hoped, he concluded that the damage could be repaired without undue effort; in fact, he began the task at once. "Sunday," he said, "is my day for private working. I gain strength from it. Work is my church."

"I am glad to hear it, Mr. Hayman. There is much to be done." He worked tirelessly throughout the day, carefully testing and retesting every constituent of the electrical columns.

"It is fortunate," he said, "the original elements are so sturdy. Their assembly is helped immensely by their durability."

"That is your genius, sir. You were the artificer."

"Genius has nothing to do with it. Just common sense, sir. And practice. It resolves all knots." I knew that to be the English way. Yet I believed also that passion, and imagination, had their place in the investigation of science. What is a natural philosopher without vision? "I have been considering, Mr. Frankenstein, your questions on the electrical fluid. You recall that you asked me the effects of the waves being reversed, as it were?"

"I do indeed."

"I have done the mathematics. And in theory there should be no discernible difference in the nature of the fluid. But its direction would be utterly changed. It would flow inward rather than outward."

"How is that possible?"

"This is the puzzle. What, in this case, is inward? Does it mean that it would return into itself? But, since we do not understand its nature, the concept is meaningless to us. Does it mean that it would harbour its powers in some infinitely small space? Then it might pose an extreme hazard. Or would it change its nature and become some wholly new and unknown force? Here I will leave common sense behind, Mr. Frankenstein. I thank God it will never be accomplished. It might wreak unexampled havoc on the world."

"And you believe that it cannot be done?"

"Undoubtedly. Faraday himself could not accomplish it."

He had not completed the work, by the end of that day, and he pledged to return on the following Sunday. I spent the intervening days in intense study of the electrical phenomena; I visited the library of the Royal Society, where I was shown the latest treatises of Hans Oersted and Joseph Henry; I studied the details of the Wimshurst Machine and the Electric Rocking Machine. In the last few months Oersted had in fact published his experiments on what he called the "magneto-electrical field," having created trials in which a magnetic needle had moved at right angles to a current of the electrical fluid. Could the power and direction of the current thus be measured and, if measured, changed? The mighty Newton had observed that to every action there is an equal and opposite reaction—could not the power of magnetism therefore change the direction of the fluid?

On the following Sunday Hayman completed the work. He had added further refinements, too, in the capacity of the voltaic batteries and in the substitution of bitumen for some of the wax and resin. "I hope you can continue your work in peace," he said. "There are many who fear the electrical fluid. They deem it to be monstrous. An attempt to distort God's laws."

"I have no intention of creating a monster, Mr. Hayman. Quite the opposite."

After he had gone I sat down upon the long wooden table restored by the workmen. Here the creature had risen from death. It was here that he would be once more returned to silence and darkness. I heard the sound of the Thames as the tide came up, lapping against the wooden piles of the landing stage, and for the first time it afforded me the sensation of expectancy and hope.

⤜ Seventeen ⤛

THE PENNY-A-LINERS had not been idle. Two days after our return from Marlow there had been reports in the London newspapers of the "unexampled tragedy" and "terrible misadventure" that had befallen Bysshe. The details of Martha's death were recounted in some detail, with particular attention to the "foul creature" and "fiendish villain" seen at Mary's window; but this news was swiftly followed by further and more sensational reports of Harriet's death at the Serpentine. The coincidence of these deaths in water led some public prints to question the competence of the constabulary in London and the adjacent counties; but others, such as the *Mercury* and the *Advertiser*, had somehow acquired the information that Bysshe had been sent down from Oxford on the charge of atheism. The writers of these journals suggested, though they did not state, that the two murders might be construed as a terrible warning to the unbeliever Shelley. "How a merciful God," Bysshe said to me on his first visit to Jermyn Street after Marlow, "could arrange the death of two young women for my benefit—is quite beyond me. It would be as good a reason for atheism as any I have proposed myself."

"Pay no attention. These papers are forgotten in an hour."

"I have absolutely no regard for them, Victor. I read them as comedy. I recite them to Mary, with all the actions and attitudes of the zany."

"How is Mary?"

"How is she? She is sweet. She is lovely. She is witty. She is wise beyond her sex. Anything else you wish me to add?"

"So life in Somers Town is pure Eden?"

"Mr. Godwin is sometimes an obstacle to bliss. But we walk together in the churchyard of St. Pancras. Do you know it? Where the graves and the roots of the oaks are entangled?"

"No."

"There is the grave of Mary's mother. We visit it."

"You make love in graveyards, Bysshe?"

"Make love is not the just phrase, Victor. We are friends deep in accord and in mutual harmony. We are devoted to one another's interests."

"Well, this is love by another name."

"Do you think so? By the way, there is something we must attend. It will afford endless delight." He took from his pocket a sheet of paper which, when he had unfolded it, turned out to be a playbill announcing the imminent performance of *The Atheist's Curse*. It was subtitled "Two Deaths Too Many." "Isn't it delicious, Victor? Isn't it rich?"

It was clearly designed to be a drama on Bysshe and the events of the previous few months. I must say that I was surprised by his good humour. But he had a remarkable ability to rise above circumstances, if I may put it like that, and to see himself in a wholly impersonal light. "We will not tell Mary," he said. "It will disturb her. But we must go, Victor, for the novelty of it. Do you think I will be portrayed on the stage?"

"Most certainly."

"Then we must go tonight."

We entered the Alhambra Theatre that same night, as he wished. We took a small box on the side of the stage, on the level of the pit, where we were subject to the usual catcalls and ribaldry of the lower classes. Bysshe was not recognised, of course, but from his appearance and bearing he was obviously a gentleman. If the fellows of the pit had known that he was the subject of the melodrama, there would have been an uproar. The small orchestra had just struck up a plaintive tune, when there was a knock on the door of our box. "Who the devil is it?" Bysshe asked me. "Come!"

"May I?" A face appeared from behind the door, fleshy but not unpleasing. "May I join you?" A young man, dressed in sky-blue breeches and a jacket of gaberdine, entered cautiously. "There were no boxes left. And these gentlemen—" he gestured to the pit—"would not have left me alone."

"By all means, sir," I replied. "There is a seat here."

"So the attendants told me."

"I know that man," Shelley whispered to me. He could say no more. The curtain was parted, to a crescendo from the orchestra, and the stage revealed. An actor, dressed in black, was sitting within what might have been a cave, a secluded chamber or a garden retreat. He was writing on a curled piece of manuscript with an absurdly large quill. "*I act in defiance of all known laws,*" he announced to the audience. "*I say that there is no divinity in the heavens above. There is no God!*" Some of the audience jeered at this sentiment, while others cheered and clapped their hands. "I think," Bysshe whispered, "that this gentleman is supposed to be me." The jeers and applause were succeeded by whistles when a young woman appeared on the stage. She walked in a very stately manner to the supposed atheist, and gently caressed him. "*Ah, my beloved,*" she said. "*You are the light of the world to me.*"

"She does not resemble Harriet in the slightest," Bysshe said.

There was some stage business of no consequence, after which the young woman stepped forward and addressed the audience. "*If only I could persuade him,*" she said, "*of the existence of a just and merciful God. Then with good conscience I could marry him! I would give my life for him to see the truth!*"

"To see your tits!" one of the pit called out.

"She can marry him," Bysshe said, "or give her life. She cannot do both."

There then followed a scene in which the devil—or, at least, an actor dressed in red—began to leap around the young woman to her evident distress. The atheist on stage proved incapable of seeing this demon, on the evident presumption that he who knows no god knows no devil. It was all very ludicrous, and the gentleman sharing our box began to show signs of restlessness. "It is my belief," he said, "that men create more damage on each other than the devil ever did."

"I agree with you, sir," Bysshe replied.

"This is sad stuff."

"Execrable."

"I would not have missed it for anything." The gentleman was quite at ease in this narrow and grimy box, and I believed that he would have been at ease anywhere. He was in his early manhood, and had the most beguiling smile; it was as if he understood all the tricks of the world, and saw the comedy of them.

"Forgive me, sir," Shelley said. "But I think I know your name."

"Oh, indeed?"

"You are Byron."

"I was when I last looked."

I expressed my surprise. "Lord Byron?"

He glanced at me with amusement. "Is there another one?"

The intelligence interested me greatly. I had heard of Lord Byron, of course, but had not read any of his verses. Bysshe had the advantage of me in that respect, and had already spoken to me warmly of the early cantos of *Childe Harold's Pilgrimage*. "I am delighted to meet you, sir," he said. "I am an admirer."

"I would repay the compliment, I am sure, if I knew your name."

"You have just seen me on the stage, I believe."

"You are the one?"

"The atheist."

"Shelley? I wondered why a gentleman would come to such a place! So you are Shelley! I have heard a great deal about you from Hogg."

"You know Tom?"

"He has become a neighbour of mine in Nottinghamshire. He has read me all of your poetry. It delights me. It is pure music." Then he turned to me with a flattering expression of interest.

"And this," Shelley said, "is a very dear friend of mine. Victor Frankenstein."

"Are you also a poet, sir?"

"Oh, no. I am nothing at all."

"Delighted to hear it. There are too many poets in the world. One is enough. Is that not right, Shelley?"

"Victor is too modest, my lord."

"Just Byron. I come to my name. Like a dog."

"Victor is a great inventor."

"And what do you find?" He had a quick, high-spirited manner of talking. "If it is not too great a secret."

"I have no secrets, sir. Like Newton I am picking up seashells on the shore."

"Admirable. That is all any of us do. We are dazzled by shape and colour, are we not?" The orchestra had begun to play, as an interval between the acts, and Byron turned back to Bysshe. "Are you tired of yourself yet, Shelley?"

"I could not endure another minute of me."

"Splendid. So you will both dine with me at Jacob's. We will raise a glass to atheism, and alarm the waiters."

We left the theatre and made our way towards the Strand, Byron talking all the way and gesticulating with a finely carved ebony cane. "I have never understood," he said, "the positive rage for bad drama in London. The cockney public loves nothing more than a thoroughly disgraceful performance by ill-favoured actors. There are so many finer melodramas on the streets of the city. Nothing on the stage bears the slightest comparison with the characters one sees every day in the ordinary business of living. Do you not agree, Mr. Frankenstein, that the events of real life are infinitely more surprising and unusual than anything written down by a scribbler?"

"I have that impression, my lord."

"Merely Byron."

"There are incidents in life which would be deemed improbable or even impossible by the ordinary observer."

"Precisely my point. Why, I could tell you a thousand coincidences and accidents that would be laughed off the boards. Polidori. Are you here? This is a surprise." He stopped to greet a small sallow-looking young man.

"I had expected to find you drinking in Jacob's," the man said.

"You find us going to Jacob's instead." He introduced us to Polidori—"Dr. Polidori," as he named him—and together we walked the few yards to an ancient and dimly lit chop-house where Byron was obviously a frequent and honoured guest. We were installed in a private room on the first floor, where Byron ordered steak *barbare*. "It is my homage to the French people," he said. "Napoleon has led them to disaster. We can at least support their cuisine." It transpired, in the course of conversation, that Polidori was personal physician and attendant to Lord Byron; he had been enrolled at the university of Prague, of which city he was a native, before making his way to the university at Edinburgh. I could not help remarking on the parallel with my own journey from Ingolstadt to Oxford, and he evinced much interest in my studies.

"Victor wishes to create new life," Bysshe said from the other end of the table.

"Really? I am a student of medicine, too, Mr. Frankenstein. I enrolled at the medical school in Edinburgh. Now I am reading the hermetic philosophers." There was an element of condescension in his manner that I found disagreeable.

"Polidori," Byron said, "is a great occultist. He whispers to my liver and makes it well. Now I can drink as deep as I wish."

The food was then brought in by two elderly waiters, who removed the covers and laid down the sauces in perfect unison. It was evident that they still took pleasure in the performance, rehearsed over many years. Over the meal Byron and Bysshe began to talk of poets and of poetry, while Polidori and I resumed our conversation. "Do you find much among the ancients, Dr. Polidori?"

"Ancient wisdom. What else is there to find? You will not be surprised to learn that Galen is still taught in some of our universities. But I discount him. I am more interested in Paracelsus and in Reuchlin. Do you know his *De Arte Cabalistica?*" I shook my head. "But you are interested in creating life? Is that not so?"

"By means of the electrical fluid, sir."

"And have you had success?"

"Of the slightest kind."

"Precisely. There are other means. In the *Corpus Hermeticum*, collected by Turnebus, there is the figure of the golem. You are aware of it?"

"Of course. It is the creature of the Kabbalah, made out of dust and red clay. It is awarded life by the invocation of ritual words. I have not given that method any serious attention, Dr. Polidori. The electrical charge is more powerful than words."

"Have you been to Prague, Mr. Frankenstein?"

"Alas not."

"In the public records kept in the library, there are many reports of the creature. Reports over the centuries." He leaned forward, and I could smell wine on his breath. "There is supposed to be one in existence even now."

"Truly?"

"It is said that a local rabbi created him, and keeps him in confinement."

I must say that Polidori had engaged my attention with his story. "Of what dimensions is this creature?"

"A little larger than human height, but proportionately much stronger and swifter."

"And why is this prodigy not known to the world? Surely it would overturn all existing concepts of life and creation?"

"The Jews keep it hidden. I am myself of that faith, so I speak of what I know. They do not wish to be derided as sorcerers or diabolists."

"And how is this being, this golem, concealed?"

"He lives in awe of the rabbi, his master. The rabbi could destroy him as easily as he created him."

"That is interesting, Dr. Polidori. Can you explain it to me?"

"He has kept back a residue of the materials that created the golem." He looked at me intently, as if to ascertain my motive in asking such a question. "He would merely have to return them to the creature, by overt or by hidden means, and then pronounce some ritual words. When they are uttered the golem collapses into dust."

"Do you know the words?"

"Alas not."

"Can you discover them for me?"

"You have become agitated, sir. Are you unwell?"

"Not at all. I am excited at the advent of new knowledge. I seek it for its own sake."

"A true philosopher."

"I venerate wisdom in any form it is offered, sir. Will you be able—will you be permitted—to ascertain these words?"

"It is possible. I maintain a correspondence with scholars in Prague."

"That would be a great boon to me."

"Why so?"

"As I said, I seek for knowledge."

At this moment Byron proposed a toast—not to atheism, as he had suggested in the theatre, but to the Luddite frame-breakers who had "made their protest against the society of the machine." Bysshe joined the toast enthusiastically, and hailed the spirit of revolution that had manifested itself in the North.

"It is a damn tiresome exercise to quote a man's words back to him," Byron said. "But as soon as Tom Hogg read them to me, Shelley, I wanted to embrace you." He remained standing, and in a loud clear voice recited:

"From the dust of creeds outworn,
From the tyrant's banner torn,
Gathering round me, onward borne,
There was mingled many a cry—
Freedom! Hope! Death! Victory!"

Bysshe joined in the last line, and raised his glass again with an "hoorah!" that brought one of the waiters back into the room.

"Is everything satisfactory?" he asked Polidori.

"They are saluting the future, Edmund."

"Then they have better sight than I have, sir."

"They are poets."

"I wish them luck then, sir." The waiter retreated with a bow, having decided that his services were not at that moment required.

"And now, gentlemen," Byron announced, "let us drink to cunt."

Bysshe seemed startled by the proposal; he was of a more delicate temperament than Lord Byron, and had always shrunk from any coarseness of expression. But he raised his glass, and drank the wine with evident relish.

"You are employed by Lord Byron?" I asked Polidori.

"His lordship feeds me. In return I prepare compounds for his general health. At the moment I am urging him to lose some of his fatness."

"He seems fleshy. But no more."

"Have you seen his mother? He has inherited a tendency. It is better to thwart it now."

"What methods do you employ?"

"Purgatives. I hasten the passage of food through the body. And purgatives burn off the fatty tissue."

It seemed a novel form of medicine to me, but I was more intrigued than ever by Polidori himself. "How do you find the English people?" I asked him.

"My Lord Byron being the exception?"

"If you say so."

"I like them well enough to live among them. And you?"

"They are great experimenters. They take nothing for granted."

I was about to expand upon this theme, when he put his hand upon my arm. "I have noticed, Mr. Frankenstein, that you have a slight nervous tremor below your left cheekbone. What is troubling you?"

"Nothing in particular troubles me."

"You are not being frank with me. You have become an Englishman." He laughed. "No matter. I will question you no further. Perhaps it is an affair of the heart. Perhaps it is *tremor cordis.*"

"My heart is intact, sir."

"Yet I can help the uneasiness in that nerve. I suppose you have tried tincture of opium?"

"I have been given it. When I was in a fever."

"I have something better. I have my own especial preparation of powder, to be mixed with the opiate."

"Do you dispense it to *him*?" I looked at Byron, who was deep in talk with Bysshe. I heard him utter the phrase, "a modern Prometheus."

"Of course. He calls it his Muse."

"And this tremor, as you call it, will cease?"

"Without a doubt. On the instant."

"I will be indebted to you, Dr. Polidori."

"I will be helping the cause of experimental philosophy. You will return to your work with renewed vigour and fresh perception."

"It is as powerful as that?"

"It works marvels."

It seemed likely that Bysshe and Byron would talk into the night, but I was already weary and needed rest. I took my leave of them after a few minutes but, before departing, I noted down my address for Polidori who thereupon promised to visit me on the following day.

Stepping into the Strand I recalled Byron's words concerning the true dramas of urban life—how many of these huddled men and women, shrouded now in a fog, would be affected by the events I had unleashed into the world? Since the creature had the power to hurt, and to kill, how many would be directly or indirectly touched by his evil? In a great city many are at risk.

"It is diabolical," someone said to a companion. "I can't see a yard ahead of me."

I took some comfort from Polidori's description of the golem. I did not put much trust in the existence of this being, but I was nevertheless gratified by the story of its possible destruction. If he obtained a copy of the ritual words, then I would be tempted to employ them upon the creature. I was meditating this when, inadvertently, I knocked against a tall man who had loomed suddenly out of the fog.

"I beg your pardon, sir," he said. "Good lord, it is Mr. Frankenstein."

I recognised Selwyn Armitage, the oculist. "I apologise, Mr. Armitage. I was not looking where I was going."

"No one can look very far in this, Mr. Frankenstein. Even my eyes cannot pierce the gloom. May I walk this way with you?"

"I would be grateful. How is your father? I have the most pleasant memories of his conversation."

"Pa has passed away, alas."

"I am very sorry to hear it."

"It was sudden. An imposthume in his throat. In his dying moments he called for Dr. Hunter to cut it out. He was in a delirium."

"Your mother bears up?"

"Yes. She is strong. She insists that we continue the business. Now I am behind the counter. But you know, Mr. Frankenstein, you have inspired me."

"How so?"

"Your discourse to me on the electrical fluid led me to thinking. And thinking led me to tinkering. And tinkering led me to a galvanic machine."

"You constructed it?"

"I went back to first principles. It is a very simple contrivance of wires and batteries."

"For what purpose?"

"Did you know that Pa had a collection of eyes?"

"No, sir. I did not."

"Many of them are perfectly preserved in spirits. The eyes of dogs. The eyes of lizards. The eyes of human beings."

"You need not tell me the rest, Mr. Armitage."

"I have caused the pupils to contract. And the irises to tremble."

"I am obliged to you, Mr. Armitage, but I must be on my way. Good evening to you, sir." Before he could return my farewell, I had walked across the road and lost myself in fog. I could not endure the recital of his experiments. I was now so thoroughly ashamed of my own labours and ambitions that I could not bear to see them shared by anybody else. What if this electrical mania were widespread? What would be the end of it? Slowly I made my way home through the fog.

→ Eighteen ←

"THERE IS A STRANGER at the door," Fred said.

"What stranger?"

"He is small. He looks like a bruised pippin."

"That will be the doctor. Bring him in."

"Doctor? Whatever is wrong with you?"

"He is going to take off my leg." He looked at me in horror. "There is nothing the matter with me, Fred. The doctor is a friend."

"If you say so, sir. I have never heard of a doctor being a friend before." So, with a certain amount of suspicion, he brought Polidori into the room.

"Ah, Frankenstein, I trust you are well."

"He is very well, sir," Fred said. "Tip-top."

"That will be all, Fred."

"Call me if you need me, sir." Fred reluctantly left the room, watched intently by Polidori.

"I notice that these London boys," he said, "have a tendency to rickets. It makes them somewhat bow-legged."

"I have not seen it in him. I think in the city that the walk is known as a swagger."

"Really? It is social, then, not physical?"

"They imitate each other. Or so I believe."

"You are a keen observer, Mr. Frankenstein. Now, I have

brought it with me." He opened the small case that he carried with him, and took out a glass-stopped phial. "I have already mixed the powder with the laudanum. Five or six drops will be sufficient for you in the beginning."

"In the beginning was the word." I do not know why I said it. I simply said it.

"There will be no words, I hope. Only peacefulness."

"At what time of day is it recommended?"

"I favour the early evening. You will feel its benefits on the following day, after a profound slumber. But if the tremor causes you anxiety—or if there is any other great anxiety—then you should take it at once."

"What is the cost, Dr. Polidori?"

"It will have no adverse effect upon your constitution."

"No, I mean the price of this liquid?"

"It is a gift to you, sir. I will accept nothing for it. If in the future you wish to procure more, then we will arrive at some sensible settlement."

We left the matter there. I was grateful for the cordial, but I could not shake off the disagreeable sensations Polidori aroused in me. He was too watchful. He told me that Bysshe and Byron had spent the entire evening carousing in Jacob's while he slept with his head upon the table. When eventually they walked out into the Strand, they spent an hour or more looking for a hackney carriage. "I have left his lordship," he said, "nursing a swollen head. I must return to my charge." I thanked him again for his ministrations, and he urged me to call upon him and Lord Byron at their house in Piccadilly.

I left the phial on the table where Polidori had placed it. "What is this?" Fred asked me when he came into the room.

"It is a cordial," I said. "To help me sleep."

"Like porter?"

"Not exactly. But it has a similar effect."

"You will be careful then, sir. My poor father—"

"You have told me of Mr. Shoeberry's early death."

"His toes was just twitching." He paused, and picked up the phial. "His face was cold as any stone."

"Be so good as to leave the bottle where it is, Fred. It is precious fluid."

"Precious?" He put down the phial very gently.

"As gold."

In truth, ever since the onset of my accursed ambition, I had been labouring under a weight of nervous excitement and irritability that no human constitution could properly bear; my animal spirits rose and fell disproportionately, so that I was in a continual battle with fear and doubt. There were many occasions when I suffered a peculiar sensation within my stomach of harbouring rats that were attempting to gnaw their way *out*.

Yet I did not touch the opiate all that day. From my chair I contemplated the glass phial, gleaming in the rays of the weak and fitful sun that penetrated into Jermyn Street. In the early evening a particular form of melancholy, not at all pleasing, customarily fell upon me. It was then that I measured out six drops of the opiate and swallowed them.

The effect was not immediate. But gradually, over a space of approximately half an hour, I became aware of a sensation of mild warmth spreading through my limbs; it was as if I were stretched out in the sun. This was succeeded by feelings of calmness and equipoise, so that I seemed to glide rather than walk across the room. I felt utterly self-possessed, with an elevation of spirits that I had never before experienced. Fred came into the room, with my evening dish of tea, and at first did not seem to recognise my enhanced state.

"Ah, Fred, immortal Fred."

"Beg pardon, sir?"

"You bring the fragrance of the Indian plains."

"I have just been in Piccadilly, sir." Then he noticed the silver spoon with which I had measured out the drops. "It is the liquor, sir, is it? Perhaps you might sit down."

I had not been aware that I was pacing the room. "No, Fred. I must savour the moments of ease."

I walked over to the window. The pedestrians and porters and carriages in the street below me seemed to be united in one continuous melody, as if they had become a line of light. Instinctively I realised that this was not a compound that would stupefy my faculties but, on the contrary, one that would awaken them to fresh and vigorous life. I went into my bedroom, and lay down upon the bed in a delicious reverie. Fred hovered by the door, but he had become part of my sensation of bliss. I may not have slept, but I dreamed. I was lying in a warm boat, moving across the calm surface of a lake or sea, while all around me the light dappled the water. Above me were no clouds but the deep blue empyrean reaching into infinity.

It was one continuous dream, and I rose from my bed on the following morning utterly relaxed and refreshed. I believed, too, that my intellectual powers had been awakened, and with great ardour I took from my shelf a copy of Tourneur's *Tables of Electrical Fluxions*. I found that I was able to calculate with ease, and from the very shape and fitness of the numbers I gathered an enormous intellectual pleasure. I could even visualise the stream of the electrical charge. With the phial of laudanum in my pocket I travelled down to Limehouse where once more I began to experiment with my electrical machines. I believe that the sensation of equipoise lasted for a further eight hours, by which time I had grown weary enough to settle into a chair.

I had taken no more of the opiate, but I had the sensation of being conveyed across a broad sheet of water with the light playing all around me. The sky had become a deeper blue than before, and I realised that the nature of the water had changed. I was moving upon a river. I knew it to be the river Thames. I could see the reflections of overhanging trees on its surface, and I was at once aware of another world within our own where the trees grew downward and the sky was below me; there I wandered, amazed, and through the veiled atmosphere I saw an image of myself looking down upon me. And in my face I saw wonder.

The craft was travelling faster than in my first dream, and the notion of a destination provoked in me some discontent. Yet I settled back into a reverie, where the banks and fields beside me were bathed in light and where the grass seemed gilded. And I murmured to myself, "I have found the word golden." The boat now had lost its momentum, and was drifting slowly with the current of the Thames. I felt a gentle wind upon me, and the rustling of leaves was like the whispering of many voices. For some reason I felt the first vague symptoms of unease. I came within reach of the bank, and felt the softness of the earth and grass: the colours of the blossom were so bright and fiery that for a moment I closed my eyes. The boat of its own will then turned and found the current once again. Never had the sky seemed so clear to me, and there below me was its reflection even more bright. I was surrounded by skies. I let my fingers trail in the warm and slowly moving water, sensing the freshness of its flow. Then something grasped my hand. It grabbed hold upon me firmly, and tried to pull me down. I awoke with a start, my opiate dream dissolved in a moment of terror.

It was night. I had slept for several hours, and quickly I lit the oil-lamps so that I would not be utterly cast into darkness. I sat trembling upon the chair, fearful that I was still in a dream.

Then with an enormous effort of will I resumed my calculations. I realised, too, that to leave Limehouse at this hour would invite the notice of footpads and vagabonds. Yes, my fears had returned. In my opiate condition I fancied that I was no longer part of the tumult of life—that the fever and the strife had been suspended—and that I was capable of repose and rest. The burden had been put down; the anxiety had been lifted. But now all those sorrows had been revived. The enemy, fear, had returned. The battle was renewed. I was no longer master of myself.

I examined the phial for several minutes—how could such a small measure provoke such extraordinary changes in the human frame? There were mysteries here as obscure as galvanism and reanimation. I decided to experiment with two drops only of the tincture. After a short while I found myself walking, as I believed, down an avenue brilliantly lit by naphtha lamps; I was back in Geneva, and I was hurrying to meet my father and sister with news of my success at university. I was filled with such youthful enthusiasm that I leapt high into the air and soared effortlessly over the city and the lake.

Then I found myself sitting in the workshop, as before, my calculations spread about before me on the table. My equations were of the utmost lucidity—I recognised that from the neat formulations I had managed and from the comments of "precise" and "wonderful!" in the margins. But what was this? I heard the sound of oars pulling against the tide, and the creaking of a boat upon the water. Who would be rowing upon the Thames at this hour? I went to the door of the workshop and opened it by a fraction. The familiar smell of mud and brine assailed me. But there was another odour, too. I peered out and saw a shallow vessel making its way slowly to the jetty. "Who is there?" I called out. There came no answer. "For God's sake, tell me who you are!"

The boat had come to a stop beside the wooden platform of the jetty itself. I could hear the water lapping beside it. Then Harriet Westbrook—Harriet Shelley—stepped out. She was not as she had been in life. She was infinitely more bright and splendid. Then I noticed that she was carrying upon her shoulders a coarsely woven sack. "Why are you here, Harriet?" She did not answer, but seemed to turn back to someone else in the boat. There was some murmuring, and I recognised the voice of Martha. Then there was a light note of laughter. Now she turned again to me. "I am not here, Victor. You are here." So I awoke again at the table, the papers strewed about it.

Throughout that night, and for the next morning, the dreams or visions emerged and then disappeared. I was in a position of complete enslavement, helplessly in thrall to whatever hallucination passed before me. I was in the estuary, walking among its sad flats and wild marshes with the gulls crying overhead; the strong savour of salt was in the damp air. I was somehow aware of some great, dark shape brooding in the distance—out of sight—and then I knew that the malevolent presence was that of London. Man had created London. Man had not created the estuary. I was seized with a great fear that this land had just emerged from the sea, and that the incoming water was about to overwhelm me. So I ran inland—or what I believed to be inland—and sought shelter in a small and crudely built hut that stood alone upon a mound in a field of pasture. In contrast to the world outside, it was perfectly dry and warm. There was a crackling sound, as of branches and twigs burning in flame, but I could see no fire.

Then I found myself walking down a street in London. It was a street of black stone, with no doors or windows or openings of any kind. But, as I walked upon it, the stone began to shriek—in agony, in fear, in consternation, I knew not what. I turned the corner and there before me was another street of stone; as soon as I ventured upon it, it gave out a loud cry of pain, which came from the walls as well as the ground. I could not bear the cacophony but as I hurried down the streets, and turned down other alleys, the screaming grew more immense.

⤛⤜

WHEN I AWOKE, it was broad day. I was too troubled by these laudanum dreams to resume the study of my papers, so I left the workshop and walked into Limehouse. There was a carriage stop at the tavern by the church, and I waited there for the next vehicle. I knew the crossing sweeper who stood here and who, for a penny, would hold the horses while the driver refreshed himself in the tavern or relieved himself in the churchyard. He was a black man by the name of Job. "Job," I said. "When did the last one leave?"

"He be gone a good half-hour. It be a good half-hour yet."

"Was it full?"

"Pretty tight, sir. There was a seat on the top."

So I went into the tavern and brought out two mugs of porter. "There we are, Job. Sluice the dust from your throat."

Job had told me in the past that he had been shipped from Barbados as a captain's boy, or slave, and that he had been abandoned by his master on their arrival in England. The ship had docked at Limehouse, and he had lived in the neighbourhood ever since. He survived now on the few coins he obtained from those using his crossing, and from the drivers of the carriages. "Where do you live?" I asked him as we sat on a wooden bench outside the tavern.

"Along the street yonder." He pointed out to me an alley of tenements that led off Limehouse Church Street. "It is a mouse-hole, sir."

"Are you married, Job?"

"I never be married. Who want a poor black man like myself?"

"Your race does seem to be unfortunate."

"We be harried and cursed and beaten. Some of these fine gentlemen will aim a kick at me on the crossing. Some of them swear dreadful."

I do not know whether it was the effect of the powder, but I experienced a sudden and overwhelming feeling of pity for the sweeper. "Come inside," I said. "It is a raw day."

"No permission, sir. Mrs. Jessop will not abide black people."

"Then I will bring another drink to you, Job. I wish to learn more of you." When I returned I questioned Job closely about his life in Limehouse. Much to my surprise, he had stories worse than his own to relate: of newborn babies abandoned on the streets, of small children forced to wade into the stinking cesspits in search of the cheapest items of any value, of the dead buried under the floorboards to save the trifling expense of a pauper's funeral.

At night Job himself would go down to the foreshore, and search for objects that he might use or sell; on one occasion, he told me, he had found an ancient dagger that he had sold for a shilling to a tobacconist in Church Row. It was now on display in the shop window. "But some nights," he said, "there is something happening in the river."

"Happening?"

"Something arriving. From downstream."

"You mean some kind of boat?"

"No boat. No. Something moving fast under the water. All the shore is silent when it passes."

"A whale?"

"No. No fish. A thing."

"I do not understand you, Job."

"Have you been hearing, sir, how the estuary is haunted? Down by Swanscombe Marshes?" I shook my head. "No one goes near. Even the fishermen will not work there."

"What is this apparition? Does it have a name?"

"No name, sir. It is a dead thing living. It is greater than a man."

"How do you know this, Job?"

"It is my supposal. My mother told me the stories she had heard."

"These were the stories of the slaves?"

"Yes, sir. But the stories come from far back. When there were not slaves. My mother told me of the *dogon*. It is a dead man brought to life by magic. Living in the forests and the mountains. A phantom, sir, with eyes of fire."

"Surely you do not believe that such a thing lives on the estuary?"

"I know nothing, sir. I am a poor black sweeper. But I wonder what this thing is that moves under the water."

At this point the carriage arrived, with Holborn as its destination. Job stood up and went over to the horses, which seemed to recognise him. They became still when he spoke to them and stroked them. I called up to the driver. "Do you have a seat?"

"Inside, sir. One of the parties is leaving."

So I mounted the step and, within a short time, the carriage was on its way to the city.

⤜ ⤛

WHEN I CAME BACK to Jermyn Street, I went at once to my study where I had left some of my calculations. I renewed my work with fresh enthusiasm, knowing that I was close to a precise formula for the reversal of the electrical charge in the process of its formation. If I were able to create and to maintain this negative force, it might subvert and utterly undo the power of the original charge.

I was interrupted by the sound of voices, and of laughter; then Bysshe and Mary came into the room, with Fred following. "I could not stop them, sir," he said. "They rushed me from the door."

"I cannot be stopped, Fred." Bysshe was in the highest spirits. "I am Phaethon in his fiery chariot. Have you heard of Phaethon?"

"There is a fly driver in Haymarket, sir."

"Fly? That is a new word, is it not?" Then he turned to me. "May I present to you, Victor, Mary Shelley?"

I rose from my chair, and embraced them both warmly. "When did you do this?"

"This very morning. In St. Mildred's, Bread Street."

"For the sake of any future children," Mary said, "we observed the form."

"It was a lovely ceremony, Victor. Mr. Godwin cried. I cried. The parson cried. God bless us all!"

"I did not cry." Mary was smiling as she spoke. "And I do not think that God will bless us."

"Old Father Nobody had nothing to do with it," Bysshe replied. "We are free. We are not exiles on the earth. Will you join us for tea at the Chapter? I can promise you the finest Marsala in London."

"Do come," Mary urged me.

It was not a place, in truth, I would recommend to the newly married. It was one of those eating houses that have preserved the manners of the last century while manifesting all the inconveniences of the present one. The parlour was dark, even in the early afternoon, since precious little light filtered through the thick and small-paned windows. The beams were large, the roof low, and the space was partitioned into a number of dark wood compartments or "boxes" as the Londoners call them. The word has always reminded me of coffins.

The three of us were shown to a "box," and Bysshe immediately ordered a round of ham sandwiches with a bottle of sherry. An elderly waiter, of gloomy demeanour, proceeded to serve us. He was wearing knee-breeches, in the old style, with black silk hose and none too spotless cravat. I gathered from Mary that his name was William. "Will the foreign gentleman," he asked Bysshe, "be requiring mustard?"

"I will ask the foreign gentleman." He said this in the most grave manner. "Will you be requiring mustard?"

"I think not."

"You have your answer, William."

"Very good, sir."

Mary burst out laughing, after he had walked away with dignified step. "He has never been known to smile," she said. "People have perished in the attempt."

She broke off as William returned with the sandwiches. Bysshe fell upon them as if he were quite famished. "We have good news, Victor," he said. "Byron has invited us to join him on the shores of Lake Geneva. Your old home."

"He has rented a villa there," Mary told me. "In the event of an imminent marriage, as he put it, he has thrown the doors open to us. You are invited."

"Me?"

"Why ever not?" she replied.

"Do you know the name of the villa?"

"Diodati," Bysshe replied for her.

"Diodati? I know it well. I have climbed into its garden at night, and tasted the fruit."

"An omen, my dear Victor," he said. "You must taste the fruit again. We will travel to Switzerland together."

Bysshe was in a state of great exhilaration, and I could not resist the tide of his enthusiasm. So I consented. I believed, too, that a suspension of my labours and calculations might assist me; the mind needs rest as surely as the body, and I trusted that a period of indolence would restore all my faculties. We agreed to set out within the month.

"We will speed across the plains of Holland—" Mary said.

"—And see the castles of the Rhine nestling in their turpitude," Bysshe added.

"And you, Victor, you will see your old familiar places."

"I am afraid," I replied to her, "that I will seem a stranger there."

Bysshe laughed and signalled for another bottle. "You are a stranger everywhere, Victor. That is your charm."

"I wonder that Lord Byron has invited me."

"He must enjoy your company," Bysshe replied. I was not so sure that I would enjoy his, but I said nothing. "Byron is an odd being. He is at once courageous and defensive, deeply proud and deeply uncertain."

"I think," Mary said, "that he feels shame. He feels his deformity."

"I take it," I asked her, "that he has a club foot? That is the phrase, is it not?"

"Yes. That is the phrase. But the pain goes deeper. He is ashamed of life. He wishes to expend it quickly."

"He can be very fierce," Bysshe said, "with the people around him."

"That is because he is fierce with himself," she replied. "He has no mercy."

William, without prompting, had brought over another plate of ham sandwiches. Bysshe attacked them with renewed appetite. "I wonder," he said, "that he has not been wholly spoiled by his success. I have said that he is proud. But he has no vanity."

"You mean," Mary replied, "that he deigns to speak to mortals such as ourselves." Bysshe seemed offended by this. She noticed his reaction and added, very quickly, "Of course he respects you as a poet, Bysshe. He is disparaging of his own verse."

"It comes too easily to him. He sees no merit in that which flows freely. He relishes a struggle."

"I agree with him there," I said. "Out of adversity comes triumph. All great natures aspire."

Bysshe raised his glass. "I commend your spirit, Victor. Death or victory!"

Mary evidently disliked this turn of the conversation. "That is easy for you to say. Men have an appetite for glory."

"And women have not?" he asked her.

"We wish for a different kind of renown. We do not seek conflict. We seek harmony."

"I drink to that," he said. "But sometimes the world will not allow it. That reminds me, Victor. Byron wrote of dreadful storms."

"We are used to storms in the mountains."

"No. These are out of all reckoning. The local people prophesy a season of darkness. From some unknown cause."

"I look forward to it," I said. "I like the aberrations of nature."

⇒ ⇐

AT THE END OF THE MONTH we assembled at Dover—Bysshe and Mary with their young serving maid, Lizzie, myself and Fred. It was Fred's first journey out of England, and he was in a state of high excitement. He had never seen the open sea. "I expect," he said, "that we will see islands and such like."

"There are very few of those, Fred," I replied, "in this stretch of water."

"Just a bare flat plain of sea, then?"

"I am afraid so."

"How deep is it, sir?"

"I have no idea, Fred. You must ask the captain when we board."

"Deep enough for whales?"

"I am not sure."

"I would welcome the opportunity of spying one of them," he said. "I saw a print of one knocking over that boat." He was referring to an incident eleven months before, when the *Finlay Cutter* was broken up by an irate whale. "Beg pardon, Mr. Frankenstein. Not meaning to suggest any danger." He had gathered up our luggage and, whistling to a porter, spoke to him very confidentially and persuaded him to transport it down to the quay where our boat was berthed. The *Lothair* was undecked, and with much pulling and pushing we were eventually lodged in two small and uncomfortable cabins. "This is snug," Fred said.

"We will not be here long."

"That must be the smallest window in the world."

"I do not think that is the word in English. There is a nautical term for it. Porthole."

"It is of glass, sir, and you can barely see through it. So I call it a window."

The captain, a surly fellow named Meadows, scarcely bothered to stop as he walked along the corridor between the several cabins. "We set sail now," he said. "Without delay. The wind is fresh."

Within an hour we had begun our journey and were upon the open sea. Fred could scarcely contain his excitement. "It is very boisterous, sir. My stomach hits the floor and then comes up into my mouth."

"You should sit, Fred. You will be ill."

"Not me, sir. I have ridden in my father's cart. The streets of London are worse than any sea. Look, sir. Over there. There is the whale I mentioned." I looked out of the porthole, but I could see nothing through the spray. "Did you not see that creature following us? It popped its head in and out of the water." I looked again, and for a moment thought that I glimpsed something. But it had gone beneath the waves.

"It was a piece of timber, Fred. A plank."

Bysshe came into our cabin. "Mary is unwell," he said. "She wishes to be left with Lizzie. I have given her a powder, but the sea is very high."

"High and low at the same time," Fred said. "It is a regular seesaw."

"But we are making progress, I think. Come and sit with me, Bysshe."

"Yes. We will discuss old tales of sea adventures. We will relive the journeys to Virginia and the Barbadoes. We will hail the sapphire ocean!" Bysshe had a wonderful ability to rise above circumstances and, as we sat in the tossing cabin, he entertained me and Fred with the tales of sea journeys he had read as a child. He recited with vigour the lines from the *Odyssey* where Odysseus sails up the narrow strait between the islands of Scylla and Charybdis where the sea "*seethed and bubbled in utter turmoil, and high overhead the spray fell on the tops of the cliffs.*" It was Bysshe's own translation, and I am sure that he composed it as he went along.

There was a sudden knock on the door of the cabin, and Lizzie stood before us. She gave a little curtsy. "Please to tell you, Mr. Shelley, that my mistress is a deal better and craves a little bit of your company."

"I shall be there, Lizzie, before you are gone." He gave me a hasty adieu, and retired.

Fred and I sat in silence, Fred whistling as he looked out of the porthole. "Do refrain from that noise, Fred. It is giving me a headache."

"There goes that whale again."

"Are you sure? I am not convinced that whales frequent these waters."

"Where there is water, sir, there is a whale. Look."

I went over to the porthole. "I can see nothing, Fred. You are dreaming. Will you please seek out the captain, and ask him how much longer we will be at sea?"

"He is an old cuffin," Fred said on his return from the

captain's quarters. "A matter of hours, he says. How many hours, I says. Am I God, he says. Far from it, I says. Then he slams his door shut."

It was indeed a matter of hours—hours more than I had anticipated, since for a while we lay becalmed in the wallowing sea. Eventually Bysshe came into the cabin. "We are approaching land," he said. "The seamen are scampering about."

There was in fact some delay, and our ship was becalmed just before we reached the harbour; but a sudden gust was admirably caught by the captain, and we reached our moorings. There was a line of various coaches and carriages along the dockside, some already taken and some waiting to be hired. Mary, with what I soon discovered to be her usual expedition, went up to one of the drivers and engaged in some form of bargain: we had agreed to hire a carriage to take us through Holland and part of Germany, even though Bysshe had expressed a desire to travel through France and Italy. Yet his wish was quite ignored by Mary, and it was agreed with the driver that we would ride through the plains of Holland before going onward to Cologne. "I have heard from others of ruined France," Mary said as we settled in the carriage. "The Cossacks have spared nothing. The villages are burned, and the people beg for bread. The *auberges* are filthy, too. There is disease everywhere. Really, Bysshe, France is not the country of your imagination."

"No country ever can be," he replied. "But I live in infinite hope."

The five of us were comfortably accommodated in the vehicle, and there was a stair to a seat on the roof in case any of us should prefer the air. Lizzie and Fred were engaged in an elaborate charade of unconcern; they did not speak to each other, nor even glance at one another. Fred sat next to me, by the window in one corner of the carriage, looking out at the passing landscape; Lizzie sat beside Mary, in the opposite corner, busily engaged in the same pastime. The landscape was uniform enough in this part of Holland, with the occasional dwelling or village that might have been drawn by the pen of Van Ruysdael except for the fact that they were invariably dirty, ill-kept and unrepaired. I pointed this out to Bysshe, who preferred to dwell with rapture on the view of the Alps that we would find at our destination. "Humankind needs grandeur and solitariness," he said. "Not these placid pastures."

"There is much to be said for quietness," I replied.

"It is the quietness of decay," he said. "The spirit of the age has passed on. Now it belongs to the hero, to the individual soul facing its destiny." Then he began to quote from one of his own poems, declaiming the words out of the carriage window as we passed through one Dutch hamlet:

"I saw not, heard not, moved not, only felt
His presence flow and mingle through my blood
Till it became his life, and his grew mine,
And I was thus absorbed, until it passed."

Our journey continued across Holland, and at last we ascended the road towards Cologne. The air was fresher here, close to the Eifel mountains, and we were entertained by fresh prospects of heath and forest. I knew the juniper and the beech from my childhood days, but I had never known them to grow in such profusion: here, too, were great outcrops of stone that are a sure token of the mountains beyond. We rested in Cologne, in a small lodging house close to the principal square. "I will not visit the cathedral," Bysshe announced. "I detest cathedrals. They are monuments to pain and folly. They are tributes to superstition. Cold and gloomy places."

"You will walk with me through the markets," Mary replied. "The prosperity of the people will not disturb you."

"Not at all. Trade is a great solvent in the eventual union of mankind. It is a general blessing." So we set out, on the following morning, on a tour through the mercantile districts of Cologne close to the river. The old merchants' houses there reminded me of Geneva, and I was seized by a fervent longing to return to the place of my birth. I consented willingly, therefore, when Bysshe proposed that we take a boat upon the Rhine as far as Strasbourg. From there we would hire a coach to Geneva itself.

My native tongue was now of use, and I bargained with the captain of a barge; his main trade was in conveying cloths from the East to the markets of Cologne and elsewhere, and he was about to return to Strasbourg after delivering a large consignment. Our route would take us through Mainz and Mannheim before reaching our destination. We purchased cold provisions, and made ourselves pretty comfortable for a journey that would last several days. Mary was in high spirits as we set off from the jetty at Cologne. "It is believed," she said, "that the Rhine and the Thames were conjoined in some distant age of the earth. They formed one mighty river."

"That is Thomas Burnet's theory," Bysshe replied. "How can it ever be proved?"

"Poets need no proof, Bysshe. You always laud the power of the imagination. Of intuition."

"True, Mary dear. I declare this to be the Thames. We are sailing past Oxford on our way to Richmond and the Tower!"

We made steady progress along the Rhine, and I must say that I marvelled at the landscape; along some stretches of the river were extensive vineyards and gently sloping hills, where the virtues of calm nature were preserved. But these were succeeded by rugged mounts, and crags, and precipices, where castles had been erected among rocks and torrents. "There," said Bysshe, pointing to one of them, "is tyranny visible. Every stone is fashioned out of blood. It is built upon foundations of suffering."

Mary sat at the prow of the boat, looking eagerly ahead as we made our way. "The spirit of this place is more friendly than you suppose, Bysshe," she said. "It is more intimate with humankind. Do you not see? How much more harmonious than those mountain peaks and abysses you praise so highly! This landscape is touched by the human spirit."

"Please, Miss, but your hair is unloosed." Lizzie spoke out from the middle of the boat. "Are you wishing me to fix it?"

"No, Lizzie. In the open boat we are free."

"It will hang down awful," the girl replied.

Bysshe laughed. "By all means see to the appearance of your mistress, Lizzie. She is now a married woman."

I had moved to the stern of the barge, where a small wooden bench had been set up. Fred sat down beside me and whispered, "Lizzie is very bold, sir. Talking to the mistress like that."

"Is she bold in other matters, Fred?"

"I don't talk to her. I don't look at her. I don't consider her."

"You must not be so bashful."

"Ma warned me about London girls. That Lizzie comes from Bethnal Green."

"How do you know that?"

"Mr. Shelley told me so. He said that she had been rescued by the mistress." He needed to say no more.

⇒ ⇐

WE MADE GOOD PROGRESS up the Rhine. By day we passed several populous villages, as well as the fields and vineyards tended by labourers; by night I could hear the soughing of the wind in the trees mixed with the distant bells and the calls of the wolves resounding in the woods. Never had the world seemed so vivid to me. The new poetry of nature, which Bysshe extolled, seemed then to settle in my bosom.

Nevertheless I was overjoyed to reach Strasbourg. It marked the end of our river journey, and the latest milestone on our progress to my home town. The landscape by degrees had now become more rugged and more majestic, filled with intimations of the grandeur of the Alpine region that we would soon be entering. We hired a carriage to Geneva as soon as we reached the market square of Strasbourg, and before long we were upon the highway to Switzerland. I rejoiced in the sight of my native country, where every prospect reminded me of my happy infancy. I remarked to Bysshe with pride that here the inns were clean and wholesome. He concurred, and commented also upon the bracing air of the region. "It sustains the soul," he said. "We are living in the higher realms."

My first sight of Geneva elevated my spirits to the utmost degree: here I could return to what I might call my native innocency. My visits to the hallowed spots where my father and sister lay buried would serve to strengthen me against any calamity, and my walks in the familiar forests would restore my calm. These, at least, were my expectations. I ordered the coachman to drive us directly to the Villa Diodati, where Byron had already installed himself. It was beside the lake, surrounded by a large garden that sloped down to the water; I remembered it well, having as a boy roamed through the neighbourhood. We had come off the principal avenue that skirted the lake, and were with considerable difficulty manoeuvring our way down the narrow road that led to the villa, when suddenly Byron was striding beside us. "I glimpsed you from the balcony," he said. "Only you would arrive in a Strasbourg carriage."

We were soon tumbling out of the vehicle onto the lawn. Byron embraced Mary with the greeting of "*Bonjour*, Madame Shelley!" Then he shook hands with Bysshe and myself. "You are on home ground, Mr. Frankenstein," he said to me. "Do not forget to worship the Penates of this house. You will bring us good fortune."

I was about to reply, when Dr. Polidori emerged from the far side of the lawn. I cannot say that I was pleased to see him. "William is here to minister to me," Byron said. "But he spends his days reading beneath the trees. I have warned him against the study of books, but he will not listen to me." I could see all around me the wild rhododendron and mountain roses I had known as a child; the air was very still, and the surface of the lake unruffled. I knew that in this region the twilight was of short duration, and I could sense the arrival of dusk and the night. "This gentleman," Byron said, looking up at the driver, "is in desperate need of being paid. Pray do so. The servants will take in your bags."

We were soon comfortably ensconced in the villa. My own room overlooked the garden and the lake, and in the gathering darkness I could see the feeble lights of the villages on the further shore. There were sounds of shouting, and of a general commotion, coming from somewhere in the distance; but I paid little regard to them. I was too much in thrall to the spell of this place, and to the force of my own old memories.

⇒ Nineteen ⇐

"THE SERVANTS TELL ME," Byron said as we sat down to breakfast on the following morning, "that a sea monster has been glimpsed in the lake. Surely that is a contradiction?"

"What kind of monster?" Bysshe asked.

"I presume one monster is very like another. I have read of the great serpents that inhabit the deep, but they were never clearly described. But now I have it." Byron put down his fork. "This is what we will do. We will launch an expedition across the lake. We will hunt the monster! It will be an escapade!"

"Is that wise?" Mary was visibly perplexed.

"If I did what was wise, I would do nothing at all. My boat is properly rigged, if that is what you mean."

"No. I meant that to chase a serpent—"

"There is no serpent, Mrs. Shelley. I am quite confident of that. But it will be an adventure. We will stand forth as the Argonauts, braving the waves to hunt down a legendary creature. It will be splendid."

I stayed silent throughout this exchange but, after the meal was over, I agreed to go with them in the two-sailed skiff that Byron had purchased in Geneva. Mary declined the voyage preferring, as she said, to observe the myriad lizards that inhabited the southern wall of the garden. "I prefer my monsters to be diminutive," she said.

So we set forth, stirred by Byron's high spirits, on the bosom of the lake. We made for the further shore, so that we might see the setting of the Villa Diodati against the background of the mountains: the prospect was one I knew well, but Bysshe and Polidori professed themselves enchanted. Beyond the banks were slopes of vines, with a number of other villas and gardens situated amongst them. Behind these were the various ridges of black mountains, and towering behind them all was Mont Blanc itself hiding its summit among clouds. The lake was as blue as the sky, with sundry gleamings and twinklings in the varied light of the morning. I looked down into the water, the clearness of which allowed me to see the pebbles in its depths and the occasional shoals of small fish forming and reforming in a galvanic dance. All was pure and limpid. I let my hand trail in the water for a moment.

Suddenly Byron began to sing—or, rather, to wail one high note which echoed across the water. Then he broke into laughter. "That is my Albanian song," he said. "I learned it from the tribesmen themselves. It is a wild howl, is it not? It may lure the sea-serpent from its lair." We made our way across the lake, moving steadily further from the shore; Shelley and Polidori were debating the relative merits of Alexander and Napoleon, when our attention was arrested by shouts and calls on the northern bank. A group of people had assembled on an outcrop of rock that jutted into the water, and were pointing towards the middle of the lake. Much to my consternation Byron gave out a whoop of joy, or of excitement, and began steering the craft in that direction. "The good citizens," he shouted, "have seen some wonder. We must investigate."

A bank of dark cloud had come down from the mountains,

driven by one of those sudden strong winds that are so common in the region; Byron and Bysshe paid no attention to the change in the weather but looked intently ahead. "There *is* something," Bysshe exclaimed impatiently. "We must reach it. Over there." I saw nothing but the black glint of the increasingly turbulent water. "Do you see it now, Byron?"

"I see a shape," he replied. "It has a peculiar movement. It seems to be writhing in the water."

"It is the unusual light of the lake," I told them. "It casts unfamiliar shadows."

We sailed onward. And then there came upon us a sudden squall, ferocious, that rocked the boat almost to overturning. I had of course heard often of these lacustrine storms, erupting and subsiding in minutes, but I had never before experienced one of them. Then, most strangely, the boat began to turn in increasingly smaller circles; the wind had taken its sails and was spinning it around. More strangely yet, I began to hear a sound of scraping or clawing from beneath the boat. "Did you hear that?" I shouted. "There is something below us!" The others were distracted by the shrieking of the wind and the rapid turning of the boat. We were helpless before the peril of the storm. "Hold fast!" Byron shouted. "It is not over yet!" With brute force and animation he caught hold of the mast and managed to unloosen the sail from it, clinging to the canvas as the boat was still in danger of oversetting. His fingers were pudgy, his nails bitten to the quick. When the sail came down the momentum of the boat was halted. The squall passed, and we drifted back towards the shore. It had been a moment of sudden and intense peril that left us all exhausted. Some workers in an adjacent vineyard ran over to us. I spoke to one of them who described how he and his companions had seen *"une forme"* sporting in the water. He gave an involuntary shudder of horror, as he described to me its unnatural shape. Yet I still persisted in my belief that this "shape" was no more than an accidental effect of light and shadow, misinterpreted by the superstitious peasantry. I assured myself, too, that the sounds I had heard beneath the boat were the scraping of pebbles thrown up by the tempestuous lake.

The sudden squall presaged a greater storm. When we arrived at the villa, some hours later, the sky had already grown very dark. Mary and Lizzie had been seated in the garden, marvelling at the clouds, but now retreated with us indoors. "It was the most extraordinary sensation," Byron was telling Mary as we entered the drawing room. "The boat tossed and turned upon the water as if it had no weight at all. I could sense the savage power of nature. It is capricious, like a woman. How I would enjoy being consumed by her!"

"Nature is an action, not an attitude," Polidori said. "It has no personal intent."

"You do not truly believe that," Byron told him. "You think you are right. But you know that you are wrong."

"On the contrary. My knowledge and belief coincide. Ah. Here is tea." Lizzie had brought in a copper kettle to place on the fire.

"It is remarkable," Bysshe said, "that the heat of our bodies has wholly dried our clothes. I was soaked through to the skin. Each of us must have a furnace within."

"Energy," I said. "Electrical energy. It pulsates in every living thing. It is the life force."

"Is that," Polidori asked me, with the trace of a smile, "the same thing as the human spirit?"

"Oh, no. I think not. That concerns itself with values and with morals. The electrical pulse is purely energy. It is blind force."

"But energy can be joyous," Bysshe said. "An infant laughs, does it not?"

"The infant is experiencing life," I replied. "That is all. It has neither virtue nor vice. It laughs or cries on an instinct. Instinct does not possess qualities."

At that moment there was a peal of thunder. Bysshe laughed. "You have the elements on your side, Victor. They applaud you. The season of darkness begins."

"The thunder is electrical too, is it not?" Mary asked me. She was taking up the kettle with a cloth, and pouring the boiling water into a pot. "How is the energy of nature to be distinguished from the electrical force within the body?"

"It is not. It is not different in essentials. It animates all matter. Even the stones in the garden can be electrified."

"We are surrounded by it, then?"

"I am afraid so. Yes."

"Why be afraid?" Byron asked me. "What is there to fear in the primal nature of the world?"

It had grown quite dark, and Lizzie busied herself with lighting candles. It was a large drawing room, stretching from the front to the back of the house, and some portions of it were still in shadow. "On such a night as this," Bysshe told us, "we must amuse ourselves after dinner by telling stories of elves and demons. If there is a lightning storm, so much the better."

The cook, who came with the house, prepared a meal of veal and boiled cabbage; it was a favourite of the region, but it was not so much relished by our English poets. They complained of too much butter and of pepper in the sauce. We settled down comfortably enough after dinner, however, and Byron brought down from his room a collection of German tales translated into English. He told us that they were all of a wonderfully morbid and eerie nature, coming under the general title of *Fantasmagoriana*. By the light of the candles, placed on either side of his chair, he began reading one of them aloud. But then he threw the book aside. "This is all very well," he said. "But it is not the thing. The genuine article. What I mean is this. We must tell our own stories on these dark nights. We must entertain ourselves—with truths, with inventions, what you wish. They will be a wonderful accompaniment to the storms." He turned to Bysshe. "That is, if you can endure—"

"Oh, yes. I am not of a nervous disposition. I am perfectly happy to take part."

It was agreed between us that, over the next two or three days, each of us would prepare a tale of terror which would then be read aloud. I retired to my room, that night, in a state of some perplexity. I had one tale that would fill them with horror, strike them to the root, but how could I narrate the history of the last months without my heart beating violently as a testament to its truth? I would seem to them an accursed thing, a manic or an outcast—it would not matter which. No, it could not be done. So at breakfast on the following morning I excused myself from the collective task. "I am not a poet," I told Bysshe. "I am not a writer of tales. I am a mere mechanic and experimenter. I cannot divine the secrets of the soul."

"You criticise yourself unjustly," he replied. "The great experimenters are poets in their way. They are travellers in unknown realms. They explore the limits of the world."

"But not in words, Bysshe. That is where I will fail."

Mary had been listening intently. "I have the words," she said. "I have thought of a story. I remained in the drawing room last night, after you had retired, when all at once it came to me as an idea far more powerful than any reverie. A sequence of images rose up before me, unbidden—"

"I know that sensation," Bysshe said.

"In the first of them some pale student of unhallowed arts was kneeling beside a man stretched out, but yet it was not a man at all—"

At this moment Byron entered the room. "Have I missed the cutlets?" he asked Lizzie, who was standing behind Mary's chair. "Be a good girl and rescue one for me from the kitchen." He sat down beside Bysshe. "Where is the good Dr. Polidori?"

"He has not risen," I replied. "Fred tells me that he heard him snoring."

"Only if he put his ear to the door, I suspect. Fred is incorrigible."

At that instant Polidori came into the room. His shirt was crumpled and his waistcoat undone. "You have not washed your face, Polidori," Byron said in greeting. "Good day to you."

"I am late, I'm afraid. I spent half the night in thought."

"Thought of what?" Bysshe asked him.

"Of a horror." He looked at me for a moment.

"This is for our feast of stories, I take it?" Mary was also looking at me strangely.

"I think it may be too dreadful to be told."

"Oh?"

"Have you ever been in the process of thought—or even of a dream—when a face emerges in front of you? A frightful face. Full of terror and malevolence. And at the sight of that face all your most secret and intense fears spring up—the fear of death, the fear of what might happen after death, the fear of fear itself, all those sensations converge upon this malignant face."

"That is all?" Byron asked him.

"No. Not all. I have a story."

"Go on."

"I call it 'The Vampire.'"

"You have a good beginning," Byron said. "But do you have a middle and an end?"

"I have set it along the romantic coastline of Whitby. Does anyone know of it?"

"There was a synod there," Mary said. "The abbess Hilda."

"Precisely so. The abbey church is perched upon steep cliffs. The rocks below are treacherous, the foam of the beating sea striking high up the stone sides of the cliffs. I have seen it. There, one dark night at the end of the last century, a schooner was making its perilous way among the rough waves. There was a tempest raging, and every dwelling in Whitby was bolted with the windows barred and locked. So no one saw the vessel coming closer and closer to the rocks. Then one great wave lifted the boat higher than before; it reared up on the turbulent sea, and then with a sigh of agony it settled on the rocks at the base of the cliff. There it was suspended, shivering like some wounded thing.

"At the break of day, after the tempest had subsided, the cry of shipwreck went up. The inhabitants of Whitby gathered eagerly on the clifftops and looked down upon their prize; some ropes were lowered and the young men of the town clambered down upon the deck of the broken and beleaguered vessel. There was no crew to be found. There was no captain, or purser, or first mate. The ship was deserted. They reported only one remarkable find. Four coffins had been lashed to the main deck with strong ropes and twine. They had been fastened so securely that they had survived the storm and the shipwreck. Truly this was a ship of the dead. The coffins were taken on a pilot boat to the little harbour, where they were laid in a row upon the shore—"

"Enough!" Byron cried out. "You are all substance and no style. It is too wearisome."

I sensed that Polidori was enraged, yet he remained to all outward appearance quite composed. I had laughed, and he gave me a look of such malevolence that I should have been warned. "When one of the coffins was opened," he went on, "there was a voice crying out, 'What more do you want from us?'"

At this moment Bysshe shrieked and ran out of the room. Mary followed him in consternation. She called out to us for assistance, and, on entering the room, we found Bysshe stretched out on the carpet in a dead faint. With much presence of mind Polidori, bringing in a jug from the breakfast table, poured ale over his face. This revived him a little. "I have a restorative," Polidori then said to Mary. "Pray give me your handkerchief." He fetched a small case from his room and, taking out a bottle of green liquid, applied the contents to the handkerchief. He put it against Bysshe's nose; to our great surprise Bysshe then sneezed, and sat upright. "I am sorry to have caused such commotion," he said. "The truth is—I had an

experience very similar to that which Polidori has just told us!"
He raised himself from the carpet, and grasped Mary's hand.
"Shall we go back to the dining room?" he asked us calmly
enough. "I am quite recovered." We resumed our seats and
Bysshe, his composure fully restored, told us his story.

"I was in my last year at Eton, living in Dr. Bethel's house.
The name will mean nothing to you, but I mention it here in a
desire to be accurate. One evening in one of my restless
wanderings I left the school and the town far behind, and
found myself walking by the river in the vicinity of Datchet. I
came upon a small boathouse here, that had an open gallery on
two sides—it was a most curious construction, of which I still
have a vivid recollection. It was quite deserted, and the boat
itself was gone; I assumed therefore that the owner had decided
to embark upon an evening voyage, and I sat down in the
gallery to enjoy the silence and seclusion of this restful spot.
Who knows what dreams took hold of me? I only know that, in
this portion of my life, I delighted in wild fancies and ideas that
were only half-formed. My mind was the sky through which
clouds passed. Then, after some time taken up in this idle but
inexpressibly delightful pursuit, I heard the splash of oars in
the water. I sprang up from the gallery and went down to the
bank; the sound of the craft came nearer, and I put my hand
above my eyes to see it more clearly as it made its way past a
small island in the middle of the river. It was a white boat, as
purely white as any I had ever seen. Its rower had turned away,
looking upstream; he seemed absent-mindedly to move the
oars, as the boat drifted gently towards the bank. And then he
turned to face me. It was my own image, my double, my second
self, staring at me. It opened its mouth, and its words were,

'How long do you intend to remain content?' I swooned upon the bank. When I awoke the boat, and its occupant, had gone. The boathouse had vanished. I was lying beside an utterly unoccupied part of the river. So, you see, I shrieked when I heard the words from the coffin in Whitby. It reminded me so forcibly of that moment in my life."

"You have never told me this before," Mary said.

"I have never told anyone. I do not know why I am telling you all now. It was the surprise of it, I suppose."

"Well now, you see," Byron said, "how our own stories are more interesting than the German tales." He went over to Bysshe. "That is the most interesting case of the doppelganger I have ever heard. Do you recall if, at the moment it was most alert, you felt weak?"

"I was close to fainting. And then I fell."

"Precisely. The double image always saps the strength of its source. No doubt it will appear to you again, Shelley. It may offer you advice or counsel. Do not listen to it. It is sure to deceive you."

"It has no shadow," Mary added. "At least that is what I have read."

"Be sure not to confuse it with your husband." Byron was laughing. "There would be the devil of a row."

"Who is to say what is true and what is false?" she replied.

"Mary was about to describe her story to us," I said. "It was concerned with the unhallowed arts. Am I correct, Mary?"

"No. I will say no more about it. I will brood upon it, Victor. I will nourish it secretly, until it is ready to enter the world." She got up from the table, and walked over to the window. "These storms will never cease."

"You can sit beneath the awning on the balcony," Bysshe replied to her. "Then the rain will be delightful. You will see it nourishing the earth. The garden here will be replenished."

At that moment Polidori leaned over to me and said, in a low voice, "I meant to tell you yesterday. But there was no proper occasion. I have discovered the words for you."

I knew at once his meaning, but I did not know his intent. "The words for the golem?"

"I have been in correspondence with my old master in Prague. He did not wish to write them down but I persuaded him that, in the interest of science, it would be a noble gesture. It is here." From his waistcoat he took out a slip of paper. I placed it in the inside pocket of my jacket. I did not wish to look at it. Not yet.

⇒ Twenty ⇐

A FEW MORNINGS LATER, Mary confessed to an alarming sensation in her stomach; she complained of a great ache accompanied by a tingling pain. Bysshe and Byron had not yet appeared, so Polidori and I sat alone with her in the dining room. She could not eat, and sat on a small sofa by the window. "There is a blockage somewhere," Polidori told her. "The fluids are hindered. Will you allow me to help you?"

"By all means," she replied. "Lord Byron has told me of your magnetising."

"May I sit opposite to you? Here." He moved a chair from the breakfast table, and brought it over to her. "Now, will you allow yourself to become quite inert? Let your arms hang by your sides. Let your head fall. Good. You are now relaxed?"

"Am I allowed to speak?"

"Of course."

"Yes. I am relaxed."

Polidori drew his chair close to Mary, so that their knees touched. Then he leaned over and took her arm. "I am applying a gentle friction," he said. "Do you feel anything as yet?"

"No. Not yet. Yes. Now I do. I sense a warmth in the shape of a circle. A small coin."

"Now, Mary, I am not being indelicate. I wish you to put

your knees between mine so that we are in a manner locked together. Will you do that?"

"As long as my husband does not see us."

"Shelley approves of my work already. Fear nothing. Where exactly is the pain?"

"Here. Just above the abdomen."

"That is the site of the hypochondriac organ. I do not need to put my hands there. I will place them on your temples. They are well named. If you will be so kind as to lower your head. Just so." He put his fingers to the sides of her head, and began a series of stroking movements. "What do you feel now?"

"There is a warmth in my big toe. On my right foot."

"Well now. Visualise that warmth moving upwards through your body. See it as a fire. It will burn away the impurities as it progresses." I was about to speak, but with a look Polidori urged me to keep my silence. "The body," he said to her, "is made up of little magnetic centres comprising the great magnet of the human frame." He looked at me for confirmation.

"So the electrical fluid is beginning to flow freely through me? Is that it?"

"Precisely so. Do you not feel, Mary, the warmth of the current?"

"Oh, yes." She sighed. "The pain is dissolving."

"It will soon pass altogether."

"I must sleep," she said. "I want to sleep." She rose from the chair and, without looking at us, left the room.

Polidori looked at me, almost slyly. "She is drawn to magnetic slumber," he said. "All of them feel the need to sleep."

"I believe, Polidori, that you are on the wrong path. Magnetic slumber is not the cause. It is the effect. The consequence of far larger powers."

"I do not understand you."

"There are forces of which you know nothing."

"Then I will be obliged if you inform me of them."

"It is premature, Polidori."

I believe that, from this time forward, he decided to pursue me with all the subtlety and cunning at his command. He became the hunter, I his quarry.

"At any rate, Frankenstein, will you allow me to indicate the pulses in your own body?"

"If you wish it," I said.

"Oh, yes. Most certainly."

When Byron came down to breakfast he found Polidori leaning over me with his hands upon my thighs. "We used to do that at Harrow," he said, apparently not in the least surprised.

"I am instructing Frankenstein in the mysteries of magnetism."

"Is that so? I thought you were about to bugger him. Where are the kidneys?" Byron surveyed some dishes laid out on a side-table. "And answer came there none." He piled some smoked bacon upon a plate, and carried it over to the table. "Where shall we travel today? Where in this region will we beat a path? Tell us, Frankenstein."

"Well, my lord, we might climb. We have mountains." In the presence of Byron it was impossible for Polidori to continue his instruction, so I moved over to the window.

"I think not." I had forgotten, for a moment, his deformed foot. He had never alluded to it, but I believe that it was a source of embarrassment to him. I knew, too, that deformed persons are often born with strong passions. "Now that we are beside the lake, we must use the lake. Water is my element. Did you know that I once swam across the Hellespont?"

"There is a small castle further along the shore," I told him. "You might care to visit it. It was once a fortress and a prison."

"Like the famous Chateau de Chillon?"

"Not so striking," I said. "But it is picturesque. It is rumoured to be haunted."

"Do you believe in ghosts?" Polidori asked Byron.

"I deny nothing. But I doubt everything. We must encounter these ghosts, gentlemen. Shelley will faint."

"Mary will support him," Polidori said.

"Yes," Byron replied. "She is the stronger of the two, I think. It is a question of the hen fucking the cock." I was shocked by his language, but took care not to show it. "Depend upon it, that girl has steel within her."

"She has the electric force within her," Polidori said. "I have just calmed her with it."

"Did you stroke her thighs?"

"I applied some friction to her skin."

Byron was about to say something else, but broke off as Bysshe entered the room dishevelled and dazed from sleep. "Well, Shelley," Byron said to him, "good morning to you. We are going on an expedition to a prison. What is this place called, Frankenstein?"

"The Chateau de Marmion. It belonged to a family of that name. I do not know who owns it now."

"We will leave our cards, at any rate. Eat up, Shelley, I long to be gone."

I retired to a small alcove, where I was hidden from them by a screen that divided the breakfast table from some scattered chairs and tables on which newspapers and journals were piled. Shelley soon left the table, confessing that he needed a chamber pot, so that Byron and Polidori were alone together. I began to read an essay on the merits of the Clapham sect, and disregarded the murmur of their voices. But then I began to listen to them. "She has two faults unpardonable in a woman," Byron was saying. "She can read and she can write."

I could not hear Polidori's muttered reply.

"Forgive me," Byron said to him. "I am as unsocial as a wolf taken from the troop." It seemed that they were not aware of my presence.

"You seem convivial enough," Polidori replied.

"I do my best to conceal my feelings. I do not want them to be wasted on anyone other than myself."

"You are very magnanimous."

"I have my silent rages, though, when to the world I seem indifferent. You know that."

"Oh, yes. I have witnessed your contortions. You go a very bright red. But some of your rages, my lord, are not so silent. Do you recall that evening in the Haymarket, when you struck that man down?"

"My dear Polidori, I always have screams and insults at my command. Did you know that I can cry at will? Watch. I will show you." There was a silence for a few seconds.

"Bravo," Polidori cried out. "They look like the genuine thing."

"They are the genuine thing. I just need a reason for them."

I did not catch the next few words between them: I think

that Byron had gone over to a side-table and poured more coffee. When he came back he must have been standing, for his voice became more distinct. "You know, when I was a child, I could not bear to read out loud any poetry without disgust. Now I am unaccountably attached to the habit."

"As long as it is your own poetry."

"No. Not necessarily. Tell me who wrote this." Then his voice changed to one richer and more melodious:

"Did I request thee, Maker, from my clay
To mould me man? Did I solicit thee
From darkness to promote me?"

"Milton!" I called out from behind the screen.

"What? Are you here?"

"Yes. *Paradise Lost.*"

⇒ ⇐

LATER THAT MORNING we set sail. Mary had expressed a desire to join us, professing herself quite well; so there were five travellers on board the *Alastor*, as he had named her. The chateau was some three miles distant, along the eastern shore, and as we sailed slowly towards it in a fitful breeze I recalled my childhood wanderings in the same lakeland region. Many times I had walked among the pines, or laid myself down in the scrub, in an ecstasy of communion with the world. Those happy far-off days now came before me again. "There it stands," I said to them, leaning on the prow and pointing towards the shore. It was an old fortress of darkened stone, rising above an escarpment by the lake; there had been some upheaval here, in earlier ages of the earth, for the bank at this point was made up of rocks and boulders long since deposited. "Look at the loneliness of it," Bysshe said.

"It will be a damned hard job to secure our mooring." Byron stood by the prow, with the rope in his hands. "I can get no purchase on these rocks."

"There is a landing bay there," Polidori said. "By that outcrop of stone."

Within a few minutes we were standing on the shore. There was a path leading from the landing stage and climbing upward to the chateau itself: I went on ahead, to introduce the party to the present residents. When I knocked, the door was opened by a young man of no very prepossessing appearance; he had a weak left eye, and the purple stain of a birthmark on his left cheek. Assuredly, one side had let down the other. I introduced myself as one of a party of travellers, among whom was a famous English lord of great family. My lord had expressed an interest in visiting the fortress. Would it be possible for our party to be admitted? He replied in French that he and his wife were caretakers and that the owner, a German businessman, was away from home. I knew at once the language he would most easily understand. I brought out my purse and offered him a French louis, which he most gratefully accepted. By this time the others had reached the door.

The young man led us into the master's quarters, as he called them, a suite of rooms on two floors from which the windows looked out upon the lake and the Jura mountains. "We have not come to see the views," Byron said to me. "Will you ask him to take us to the dungeons?"

The caretaker had recognised the last word and, with a

glance at Byron, he beckoned us to follow him down a stone staircase. There were two floors in the lower part of the fortress. On the higher of them were three cells, side by side, each of them with a narrow window carved out of the rock. They were in such a state of preservation that the leg-irons and manacles were still embedded in the walls. Shelley seemed ready to swoon, and Mary took his hand. "It has passed," she said.

"No. It has not passed," he replied. "The doom is still in the air."

Byron had entered one of the cells and was carefully examining the leg-irons. "They are rusty. What do you think, Polidori? Caused by water or by blood?"

"A witches' brew of both, I should think."

"And here are marks in the floor," I said, "where the chains scraped into the stone. Do you see these grooves?"

"They are the marks of woe." Bysshe had gone over to the last cell, and was holding onto the bars with a keen half-tremulous and half-expectant look. "I am trying to summon them up," he said to me as I walked over. "I am trying to find them."

"They are long gone, Bysshe. Why should they wish to stay here? Of all places?"

"Where suffering is most intense, we will find traces of it."

"I wonder who made up this jolly crew," Byron was exclaiming to Polidori. "Poisoners? Heretics? It is all one now. The prisoners and the gaolers have all gone down to dust. And where are you going, Mary?"

"To the lower depths. There is another staircase here."

I followed her down the narrow stone steps, which led into an enclosed space. There were no cells here, but I experienced an indescribable sense of menace and privation at the first sight of the stone walls and the stone floor. The caretaker came down behind us. "This was the place of execution," he said to me in French. "Do you see that?" There was a blackened wooden beam running beneath the ceiling. "There the rope was suspended." I translated this for Mary.

"And this?" she asked. "What is this?" She pointed to a wooden trapdoor in the middle of the floor.

"The waters of the lake were higher then," the caretaker said to me.

"I think," I told her, "that this was a sluice gate for the bodies of the condemned."

"Alive or dead," he said. "The living were bound with ropes."

"He tells me that they were dropped into the water."

"Then this is the condemned hold." She looked at me steadily. "Abandon hope."

"I think," I replied, "that we should join the others."

We climbed the stone staircase, to find Byron and Bysshe arguing over the proper name for the manacles that fastened the prisoners to the wall. "Gyve is a verb," Bysshe was saying.

"It is a noun," Byron replied. "They are called gyves." He turned to Mary. "You have been in the lower reaches?"

"I feel as if I am sleepwalking," she said. "Sleepwalking among the dead."

"Then we must revive you. Why not retire with Frankenstein to the upper mansion? There will surely be wine for you."

I asked the caretaker if we might rest in the living quarters, for a short while, and he willingly assented: no doubt he was anticipating another louis. He brought us two glasses of the sweet wine of the region, and we sat by a window overlooking the vineyards of the estate. "I cannot say I like this place," Mary said. "In fact I have a distaste for it."

"Byron revels in it."

"Oh, he has a passion for excitement. He would visit Hell itself, just for the sensation of being there."

"He may have no choice in the matter."

"I am surprised at you, Victor."

"I am sorry. To speak of a friend in that way."

"No. Not that. I did not know that you believed in Hell."

"As far as I can see, Mary, Hell is all around us. We live in a fiery world."

Byron and Bysshe came into the room, followed by Polidori. "What was that about fire?" Byron asked me. "We have need of one here. Can one be lit?"

"It would have been cold enough in those dungeons." Bysshe had gone over to the window. "And there is another storm coming. Thank God we are off the lake."

There was a sudden flash, followed by a roll of thunder. Byron called out for wine, and showed every sign of joyful anticipation. The gathering storm clouds darkened the room in which we were sitting and the young caretaker, after kindling a fire, lit several candles in sundry old corners giving an effect of what Mary called "ghastly gleaming."

"I have an idea," Byron said. "We must take advantage of this gloom, as Mary thinks it. We must hold a seance."

"Here?" Polidori asked him.

"It is the best place in the world. Shelley has no doubt concluded that there are ghosts in the dungeon."

"I do not exactly think that."

"Where better to raise the spirits?"

"The Swiss are a practical people," I said to him. "They do not harbour ghosts."

"All lakes are haunted, Frankenstein. Large bodies of water attract lost souls."

"They may not wish to be called," Mary said.

"They will be in fighting form then. Ready for a tussle with the living. Do not be alarmed, Mary. I always have a firearm in my pocket. We will sit at this table in the corner. Bring over the chairs, Polidori."

Byron then pulled the heavy velvet curtains over all the windows, so that the tremulous light of the candles became more intense. The storm was raging outside, as if all the elements were in contention.

"You are acting," Bysshe said, "as if you were the stage-manager of chaos."

"I know it. I was born for my own ruin. We need one more chair, Polidori."

So we sat around the table, our hands spread in a circle with our fingers touching. The table was in a dark corner of the room, but it was favoured by the heat of the fire.

I felt ill at ease from the beginning, not least because of the intensity of my companions. I had expected Byron to be a sceptic in all spiritual matters, but he took part with all the excitement of a fervent devotee. I had long suspected that the English, despite their air of business and practicality, were a wholly credulous and superstitious nation. Why else do they love the tales of horror, as they call them? We all waited in darkness as Byron attempted to address "the spirits." After he had finished his conjuration I thought I heard something move beneath the table. Mary heard it, too, and glanced at me. Byron spoke aloud once more, and then there was a hiss. I felt something crawling upon my feet. I screamed aloud, and then this—thing—leapt upon me. All was confusion. Polidori lit another candle, by the light of which his face was a mask of terror, and then he pointed at my lap. "A cat!" he said. "We have disturbed the cat sleeping beneath the table!"

Bysshe sat through the proceedings with the strangest expression of apprehension upon his face. Mary was looking at him, no doubt recalling his reaction to Polidori's tale. But he did not relapse into the same state. He began to laugh, a quiet convulsive laughter that racked his entire frame. She went over to him and put her arm around him. "I am calm," he said. "Nothing whatever the matter."

Polidori opened the curtains. "I can see," he said, "some faint patches of blue coming over the mountains. The storm is abating."

"Great God, I hope not." Byron rose to his feet. "I live in storms."

I believe that it was at this moment that I decided I would leave my companions. I had warned them already that at some point I would make my way to the family estate at Chamonix. I wished to visit the graves of my father and my sister, unseen by me since the time of their deaths; but in truth I also craved solitude and silence. The endless chatter of this journey had wearied me. When I announced my decision that evening, on our return to the villa, Mary looked at me with something like resentment—I believe that she envied my departure to the Alpine regions of frost and snow. Bysshe urged me to stay, remonstrating with me in the most flattering terms of friendship, but I was not to be moved even by his persuasions. Byron said nothing, obviously considering my decision to be of little or no consequence to him. I had in fact conceived a certain dislike for his lordship. He gave the impression of being a great predator, both spiritually and morally, who would feed on one's substance before casually casting one aside. He was a born actor, also, who at all times took pleasure in his performance. Such men are dangerous.

I retired to my room, where Fred had put out my sleeping clothes, and lay down to rest. I must have slept for an hour or so, when I was awoken by a tapping at my window.

❧ Twenty-one ❧

THE CREATURE WAS STARING at me. With his usual agility and speed he must have climbed up to the balcony before my room, and was now waiting for me to unlock the casement. I hesitated, and he knocked quite violently upon the window. Fearing his discovery, I allowed him to enter. Now he stood before me, looking at me with what seemed to be an expression of infinite pity. "Why are you here?" I asked him.

"Where else am I to come, if I seek for a companion?"

I was overcome at once by a sense of misery and foreboding. "I had not expected to see you. Not after—"

"Marlow?" He put his hand up to his face, in a gesture of self-abasement. "I had rather be a piece of clay than what I am. Anything without sensation."

"You feel sorrow then? And regret?"

"I do not know what I feel. I know only what I do not feel. Yes. Once I felt joy. In the first expression of my new life I felt wonder and gratitude. I was free. I looked upon the world with fresh perception of its glory. I was newborn, and in that state I felt the bliss of all creation. The hope and bliss have fled. This thing has crept into my heart, weighing me down to the dust."

"Guilt for your crimes."

"If you say so."

"You have murdered two young women, for no other reason than that they were in my company."

He turned from me, and walked back towards the window. "I wish that I had joined them."

"Do you mean that you wish to die?"

"Look at me. Do you see me clearly? Why would I wish to live?"

"Let me understand you better."

"I find no rest in the darkest night, or comfort in the brightest day. Is not death easy in comparison? Is it not to be desired?"

"You wish to break this pact we have? This pact of life?"

"So that I might be no more. So that I might abide in darkness and blackness and empty space."

I bowed my head, thinking of what he might have been and what he really had become. And was there also some blame to be attached to me?

"Of all creatures, I should not be saved from death."

"If you wish to end, then surely you could hurl yourself from the summit of a high mountain or envelop yourself in flame?"

"You know better than that. You have told me yourself. He who has died once can never die again. I have lain beneath the surface of the river, and my lungs have filled with water, yet I could not succumb. I have thrown myself from a cliff into the wild sea, but I have emerged unharmed. So I come back to you. The source. The origin of my woe." He turned back to face me. "I know that you have repaired the electrical machines."

"You once tried to destroy them."

"Now they may be my deliverance."

"How so?"

"I have been considering my plight. I do not know the precise means by which you restored me to life, but I have speculated. I have spent days and nights in meditation. I am aware of the galvanic force of the electrical fluid. That must have been your method, in some form or another. Surely you can alter the fluid accordingly and reverse the process of animation? Surely you can counteract the force?"

It astonished me that the creature had arrived at conclusions similar to my own; it was as if there were a connection between us that surpassed the ordinary powers of sympathy. It surprised and delighted me, too, that he seemed now to embrace the prospect of his own destruction. There would be no reason to deceive him with promises of a female partner. "I can work to that end," I replied. "I can study and experiment."

"Do not be long."

"I will work with expedition, when I have returned to England, but you will need to be patient. You still live on the estuary?"

"In my little hut? Yes. No one comes near me."

"Will you go back there, while I persevere in my studies?"

"Where else may I rest my head? I am a pale roamer through the night, but in the night and darkness I will remain."

"I will find you."

"No. I will know when you are ready. I will be there." With these words, he left me. He went over to the window and leapt onto the balcony before vanishing into the quiet night.

⇒ ⇐

I COULD NOT SLEEP. When I guessed that the others had retired I went downstairs and let myself into the garden. I was reflecting upon the creature's words, when someone sat beside me. It was Mary. "I wish you were not leaving us, Victor. I need your company."

"You have the others."

"What? Byron? Polidori? They are too concerned with their own selves to consider me." She was silent for a moment. "I am fearful for Bysshe, Victor. He has become too excitable. Too fanciful. Recall his hysterics at breakfast. When I first knew him, such behaviour would have been unthinkable. Don't you agree? Something is weakening him. You may think that it is his marriage to me." She went on quickly. "I do not think so."

"It never occurred to me at all, Mary."

"And this is also odd. He never mentioned the story of his double before. Something is preying on his mind. He is becoming light-headed with anxiety. With some fear. Or premonition, perhaps."

"Of his fate?"

"Yes. Precisely that."

I knew then that she feared his early death; she believed that Bysshe was acting strangely because he had some sense of his own demise. Why else had he become so interested in seances and ghosts and ghost stories? I tried to reassure her. "Surely he is excited by his travels," I told her. "And, more especially, by the company of Byron. Bysshe has never lived in such proximity to another poet. It will affect him."

"Do you think so? I would wish that to be true."

"He is a delicate organism, Mary. One small touch—"

"Yes. I know. But there is something else. I also fear a

disaster! Over the past month I have experienced the strongest sensations of nervous apprehension. I have believed misfortune to be close to us."

"Do not say so." I put my hand upon her arm. "I have noticed a change in Bysshe, too. But I think you are wrong, Mary. It is not fear. It is frustration. Unsatisfied yearning. He deems himself to be a good poet—"

"A great one."

"I grant that. But his work is known to very few. He has no audience to delight. Not yet. In the company of Byron, whose volumes sell in their thousands, is there any wonder that he should seem ill at ease? That he should have fits of extravagant behaviour? It would be more wonder if he did not."

"I had thought of that. But Bysshe has no worldly temper, Victor. He is all fire and air. There is no earth in him. No jealousy."

"I was not speaking of jealousy. I know that he is not an envious man. But, you see, his words are not being received. He writes of love and liberty, but no one hears him. You can see how that would exasperate him. To be understood by so few."

"Yes, I do see that. Perhaps you are right, Victor. It may be that his friendship with Byron does him no good. His lordship is in many ways quite thoughtless. Have you noticed that? He treats Polidori as if he were a manservant. And Polidori resents it. He resents it bitterly. I would not be at all surprised if they did soon part company."

"And what of you and Bysshe?"

She seemed horrified. "We are not about to part!"

"No. I mean, where will you go next? If you are not happy in the villa."

"There is some talk of Italy. Oh, I am so weary of travelling, Victor. I long for England. I long to set up a household with Bysshe. And my father. A small house in Camden would suit." There was a sudden movement between the trees, and a rustle among the fallen leaves. She stood up and peered into the darkness. "I hate rats," she said. "Do you mind if we return to the house?"

⤳ ⟵

ON THE FOLLOWING MORNING I left them. I travelled with Fred in a hired chaise to Chamonix, high among the mountains. We observed the rocks and glaciers, we climbed the passes. I pointed out to Fred a great waterfall. "Do you see," I said to him, "how the wind carries it away from the rocks? The fine spray of its descent passes before the mountain like a mist."

"I see it, sir. It reminds me of fire-pumps."

We travelled up the valley of the Arve, from Bonneville to Cerveaux, where the cataracts roared down into the river. Fred looked on, unimpressed. The summits of the mountains here were hidden in cloud but there were moments when their peaks were visible in the sky, like monuments carved by a giant race before the Flood. "Imagine standing up there," I said to Fred. "Imagine looking down from the heights into the abyss."

"I think, Mr. Frankenstein, you had better not do it. You would never come down again."

"You have no poetry, Fred."

"If it made me climb them mountains, sir, then I am better without it."

After the journey of two days we arrived at my old family house in Chamonix; it was locked and bolted, under the care of an old custodian, Eugene, but I managed to arouse him after repeated knocking on the doors and windows. He was astonished to see me, arriving unannounced after so long an absence, and began to talk in a distracted fashion about my father's wish that I should one day move back.

"That is for the future," I told him. "For the present, can you make up the beds? My boy will sleep in your quarters."

He seemed to take kindly to Fred, and I watched them that evening in the garden feeding the squirrels. I saw Eugene pointing to the glacier above Chamonix which each year advanced several feet, leaving a trail of split and shattered pines. I had observed that glacier since childhood, and it had become for me a symbol of overwhelming cataclysm. As a student I had read Buffon's prophecy that at some future period the world would be changed into a mass of ice and frost. Who could deny the power of a frozen world? Nature held within itself the seeds of destruction, utterly vast and waste. I had grown up among desolation.

⇝ ⇜

ON THE FOLLOWING MORNING I set off by myself to the small cemetery of Chamonix where my sister and father were buried. They had been placed in the same grave, with *Frankenstein* etched on the marble tomb. I bowed my head in sorrow, but I could not help but consider the peacefulness of death. It was akin to innocence. All around me was the whiteness of the mountains, with Mont Blanc towering among them; the light of the sun struck their pinnacles, and the brightness became intense—almost intolerable. I closed my eyes for a moment. In that moment death, and the light, came together.

I came back from the cemetery with my faith renewed in the power of the sublime. I was filled with a sense of purpose. I would return to London, and test the electrical fluid. I would alleviate the suffering of the creature by returning it to nonentity.

"We are going back," I said to Fred as soon as I entered the house.

"To the villa?" He looked downcast.

"No. To London."

I saw him later doing a little jig in the garden.

※

THE JOURNEY WAS SLOW and laborious. By the end of the first week, we were thoroughly exhausted. Then we faced the rigours of the sea, where we lay becalmed for two days before a friendly wind sent us towards England. I had never been more thankful, when we passed the Nore and began our short voyage up the Thames. The flat lands of the estuary lay around us on both shores, and of course I looked with keen attention towards the region where I believed the creature to live. But all seemed waste and wild. The contrast with the Alpine region from which we had come could not be more marked: there was no grandeur here, no sublimity, only weariness and gloom. Perhaps that is why the creature, immured in the marshes, had tired of life.

We passed Limehouse, and I could see the workshop pale in the twilight.

The tide was coming in, and we floated with it towards London Bridge. On our arrival in Jermyn Street Fred unpacked the baggage and prepared for me a bowl of sassafras which, he said, was a restorative after travelling. I must say that I felt the welcome relief of the hot milk, but my peace was suddenly disturbed by a sharp exclamation from him. "What!" he shouted. "What do you want?" Then he threw one of my boots into a corner. "A mouse!" he said. "It has crept here while we were away!" He went over to the corner and peered down onto the floor. "I have killed it."

"Well, throw it out of the window."

"I do not like to touch it."

"You are happy to murder it. But you are afraid to touch it. What is the matter with you?"

"I do not like the thought of dead things coming alive, sir. It might seem dead, but what if it were to wriggle in my hands?"

I opened the window and looked out into the night. I could smell the coal and charcoal from the domestic fires. Then I went over to the corner, picked up the mouse, and threw it down into the street. "There now. All your terror has gone. Would you prepare my bed?"

⇒ ⇐

ON THE FOLLOWING MORNING I was about to set off for Lime-house, eager to test my new theory concerning the electrical charge, when Fred announced a visitor. Polidori entered the room, visibly excited, and flung himself down in a chair without invitation. "You are surprised to see me, Frankenstein? I hoped to find you here. You did not return to the villa, so I guessed that you had gone back. I could stand it no longer. Byron has become insufferable, and the poor Shelleys seem to follow his bidding in everything. I got back last night." He was speaking in a disjointed manner. "You know that Byron is a danger?"

"I have my doubts about him."

"Doubts? Certainties. He has seduced one of the girls in the neighbourhood of the villa, and the people there are ready to lynch him. His temper has become unbearable. He screams at the servants, and has abused Shelley to his face."

"In what way?"

"He called him a doodler and an unknown scribbler."

"And how did Shelley respond?"

"He went pale. Then he turned away and walked out of the room. I could take no more of it, Frankenstein. I left without warning, in case Byron should try and prevent me. When I last saw him he was on one of his drunken sprees, wandering in the garden and slashing at the trees with his cane."

"Your laudanum would have calmed him."

"You cannot give an opiate to a madman. It fuels his madness."

"You think him insane?"

"Deranged. Degraded. Whatever word you wish."

"No, Polidori. Madness is silent and secret. Don't you think so? This ebullition of temper is the sign of an oversensitive constitution. Nothing more."

"Whatever the cause of his lordship's frenzy, I do not wish to witness it. So I have come back."

"Do you have lodgings?"

"No." He looked at me almost defiantly.

"Where are you going to stay?"

"I was hoping, Frankenstein, that I might stay with you."

I could think of no convenient excuse for the moment. "Here?"

"This is where you live, is it not? I know that you have room to spare."

In the course of that day, then, the bold and resourceful Polidori moved into Jermyn Street. There was a small room at the back that, he said, fitted him admirably. When I broke the news to Fred, he merely rolled his eyes.

"The doctor will be welcome, will he not?" I asked him.

"Oh yes, sir. Ever so welcome. I hope he eats cutlets."

⇒ ⇐

WHEN POLIDORI WAS SETTLED, I told him that I was obliged to return to my work. He nodded. He seemed to require no further explanation. So at twilight I travelled east to Limehouse. I had locked and bolted the workshop, to prevent the intrusion of neighbours, and I had barred the windows to forestall inquisitive eyes. So everything had remained untouched. I began at once to charge the electrical columns, and I was pleased to see them glow with new life. Within a few hours I was able to begin my experiments in altering the direction of the electrical fluid; I observed, for example, that by changing the position of the metallic plates and circuits that surrounded the columns, there was some momentary deflection in the fluid. I continued this work late into the night, but I could achieve nothing further. I needed greater force than any I could yet summon. I surmised, too, that I needed to discover another source of electrical attraction that would bend the fluid to its will. All this lay ahead of me.

I decided to walk back to Jermyn Street, hoping to clear my head in the quiet hour before dawn. Yet a strong wind had risen. As I walked through the streets, every falling leaf seemed to cast its shadow as it was dashed to the ground by the wind. I could see my own shadow, too, against the brickwork. It was bent forward, hastening onwards as if it had an existence of its own. And then once more he was walking beside me. He said nothing to me, but matched me pace for pace. "I have kept my promise," he said at last in that clear sweet voice I had come to know so well. "You see. I will always be closer to you than you can imagine." He stood still, and waited until I had taken a few steps further down the street. When I turned around, he had gone.

⋙ ⋘

WHEN I ARRIVED in Jermyn Street, I was surprised to find Polidori in my study.

"My apologies, Victor. I wandered to your room quite by chance. I am in a wandering vein." He seemed uneasy.

"You may wander where you will. I have no secrets."

"Truly?" He looked at me warily, and not without a trace of malice.

"Why should I lie to you?"

"You are deep, Victor. Very deep. I do not think I will ever reach your depths."

"There will be no reason ever to try."

"I do know that you suffer from nervous fear."

"Oh, I suffer from many things." I cleared my throat. "I admit that there are times when I experience fear."

"Are you afraid now?"

"Of what?"

"Of me."

"Whatever is your reason for saying that?"

"You suspect me of something."

"Suspect?"

"You tell me that you have no secrets. But you are afraid that I will find them out." He laughed, but he was looking at me intently. "Have you ever done a wicked thing, Victor? Just to prove that you *could* do it?"

"Byron has asked me the very same question."

"He is obsessed with the idea. He told me the story of one Monro, a clerk in holy orders. Did he tell you?"

"No."

"It was some years ago now. Before you and I arrived here. This clerk had quite lost his faith. In his heart he said, there is no God. Yet still he took part in the services, gave out the wine and bread to his parishioners, preached from the pulpit on the Last Judgement and salvation."

"A most arrant hypocrite."

"He knew this. He reproached himself with bitter laments. He wept. He cut himself with knives. All this he confessed later. He had a great desire to free himself from his torments. But how was he to break free? By degrees he conceived a scheme— no, it must have happened all at once. He hit upon an act of the utmost unreason."

"Go on."

"If he were to commit a crime of malignant evil, without motive, he would be able to redeem himself. Say that he were to kill a child, for example. He would take no pleasure in it— he would choose a child at random, and then stifle it. Then he would be free of God. And what if he did take pleasure in the act? He would, as he put it to himself, become a god. There was no force in the universe higher than himself. There were no consequences to his action—no punishment, no shame, no guilt, no hell. He would have gone beyond the gates of good and evil. He would prove that all is allowable. That is what he said to himself."

"And did he commit the crime he longed for?"

"He murdered an old woman. According to his testimony he picked her out of the crowd, one evening at twilight, and followed her home. He had taken off his clerical garb, and wore a simple coat and breeches. She lived alone in a cottage just beyond Hammersmith. It was there that he killed her. He stabbed her repeatedly with a knife taken from her own kitchen, and then made his escape under cover of darkness. The crime was widely reported but the murderer could not be discovered. The clerk, meanwhile, continued his ordinary life at the church. But he exulted. He led the divine service with greater fervour, and preached more eloquently than ever. He had found his salvation in one unreasonable act."

"But then how was he apprehended?"

"This is the curious thing. He felt no remorse. He felt no guilt. Not even shame. On the contrary, he felt proud. So then, as the weeks passed, he experienced an overwhelming desire to tell his crime. He wished to announce his part. He wished to put it into words. He tried to restrain himself. But the desire to speak—to utter the final chapter, as it were—proved overwhelming. One Sunday morning, in his church, he mounted the pulpit and divulged his deed to his parishioners. He produced the knife from the folds of his cassock."

"And then?"

"He was arrested and questioned. He was taken before the Lunacy Commission. He is now in St. Luke's Hospital for the Insane."

The story made a strange impression upon me. I excused

myself and retired to my bed, but I could not sleep. I had been seized by a sudden fear that banished all thought of repose—what if I felt an overwhelming need to speak and to confess? In that very thought I planted the seed. Yes. Of course I wished to divulge all the horrors for which I was responsible. To unburden myself of the fact that I had brought life to this creature. But did I sense within myself triumph rather than guilt? Of this I was not sure. I believe that I burned with a sudden fever and, when eventually I slept, my dreams were frightful.

⟩ ⟨

I AWOKE LATE on the following morning. I could hear Polidori talking to Fred in the kitchen, and I listened more eagerly. Polidori was questioning him about the customary routine of my day—my meals, my hours, and so forth—and I sensed that Fred was reluctant to answer him.

I rang my bell and waited.

"Yes, sir?" Fred put his head around the door.

"The usual," I said.

He brought in the tea, and began preparing the soap and razor. "You are entertaining our guest, Fred. What were you discussing?"

"Nothing, sir."

"Nothing can come of nothing."

"Sir?"

"Speak your mind."

"He says he is concerned for you. Doctors, he says, are always concerned for others. Then he says something about equations. I don't know what equals what, sir, and I told him so."

"And what else did you tell him?"

"I told him nothing that was a lie, sir. But nothing that was a truth neither."

"You have done well, Fred. Now watch Dr. Polidori when I have left the house."

⇒ ⇐

I DRESSED MYSELF and walked towards Covent Garden. It was the day that Londoners call Sweep Fair and, much to my disquiet, I saw a gaggle of climbing boys at the other end of the Piazza. They were a queer sight. Their clothes were in rags, so sooty and black that they betrayed their profession at once: they might just have been dragged out of a chimney, except that they were trailing white ribbons, tied to their arms and legs. There was silver foil on their hair, and their cheeks were painted. As I walked closer to them, I could see patches of gold and silver foil plastered to their dirty clothes and faces; it was altogether a most forlorn spectacle. Then, to the sound of drums, the boys began their march. They waved their climbing tools, their rods and brushes, in the air above their heads; they sang some frightful song, full of oaths and execrations, at which the spectators laughed. Then I saw Polidori, just by the portico of the church there. He was looking around with great eagerness, and I knew at once that he was searching for me. He had been following me. I turned the nearest corner, and hailed a cab for Limehouse.

⇒ ⇐

IT WAS LONG PAST MIDNIGHT when I returned to Jermyn Street. I called for Fred, but there was no reply. I went over to the

335

window and looked down at the dark street; for a moment I thought there was a movement among the shadows, but then the moment passed. So I retired to bed.

On waking the next morning, I noticed that my clothes had not been laid out. I arose quickly, and left my room: the kitchen door was open, but there was no sign of Fred. He had never absented himself before, and I could think of nothing that would have detained him for the whole night. I dressed myself and went out into the street, with no definite course of action, and wandered into Piccadilly. There was a coffee-stall there, by the corner of Swallow Street, that I knew to be patronised by Fred. "Have you seen my manservant? Fred Shoeberry?" I asked the young girl pouring the coffee into tin mugs.

"Fred? The one with the crinkly hair and the tooth missing?"

"Him."

"I have not seen him since yesterday morning, sir, when he commented on the state of the weather. Foul it was."

I moved on, carried as much by the crowd as by my own volition. Of course I had no chance of finding him. London can be a wilderness, for those who seek out a particular face. And although I knew that Fred was experienced in all the ways of the city, I also knew how easy it was for a boy to vanish altogether as if snatched from the streets into oblivion. I believe that many were forcibly impressed as seamen; as for the fate of others, I had no notion. Of course I feared that the creature might have seized him; but in my last interview with him he had exhibited such shame and repentance, had so eagerly forsworn any further violence, that I dismissed the speculation.

What possible motive could he now have in perpetrating such a deed, when he was anxiously anticipating the end of his earthly life?

I came back into Jermyn Street despondent. Many would have treated the sudden departure of a servant with no great emotion, but I had not realised how attached I had become to Fred. And then I remembered Mrs. Shoeberry. It was possible that she was sick, or ailing, and that Fred had been obliged to stay with her. I knew from him that she lived in one of the courts off Drury Lane, at the upper end of that street, and I made my way there on foot. Everyone knew Mrs. Shoeberry in that quarter, and I was directed to the tenements in Short's Rents where I was assured she would be "rinsing." There was another laundress by the pump in that court, with soap and pumice stone, and I supposed that the water ran more freely here: I asked her for Mrs. Shoeberry's lodging, and she pointed to an open window on the second floor. "*She*," she said, emphasising the word, "is in there." I made my way up the staircase, not so clean as it might have been, and found Mrs. Shoeberry's apartment. The door was ajar, and I could already smell the familiar sour odour of London laundry. I knocked, and pushed open the door, but I could see no sign of the laundress herself. Sheets and linen were hanging in profusion all about the room.

"Whoever is it?" Mrs. Shoeberry's voice came from behind a sheet.

"Victor Frankenstein."

"Why, Mr. Frankenstein. Beg your pardon." She stepped out, clutching a brace of wooden pins and a roller. "What has Fred done now?"

"He has done nothing, Mrs. Shoeberry. I was hoping to find him here."

"He ain't been here, Mr. Frankenstein. He only comes on a Sunday, when I need him for the lifting." I had no idea what she meant. "Has he gone, then?"

"I have not seen him since yesterday evening."

She considered the matter for a moment. "That is not like Fred."

"I know."

She looked at me steadily. "Has he been in any trouble, sir?"

"Not that I am aware of."

"There will be something on his mind. I know that boy. When the late Mr. Shoeberry passed off, Fred hid himself away for two days. Said he had been sleeping on the boats. He never mentioned it again. He is deep, that boy." She went behind the sheets, from which came the sound of an enormous sneeze. After a few moments, she recovered. "Never you mind it, Mr. Frankenstein. He will be back by Sunday. He would not leave me to the lifting."

I departed a few minutes later, having given her a florin for her "trouble," and walked back to Jermyn Street. I had been to some degree reassured by her confidence that Fred would return by Sunday, and so once more I devoted myself to experiment. I went to the workshop each day, where I refined the galvanic mechanism in the light of my further researches: the problem of reversal was still one that exercised me, and led me to a thousand different variations in the batteries and machines. I was confident of a solution, however, and did not weary in my efforts.

FRED DID NOT RETURN by Sunday. Mrs. Shoeberry came to Jermyn Street in a state of consternation, and asked me whether we should alert the officers of the parish. I did not put much faith in the constables, or in the watch, but I agreed to go with her to the compter in St. James's Street. There had of course been no reports of a missing boy, but she felt that she had somehow discharged her duty. However, she was not in a comfortable state of mind. She feared something. She asked me if I wanted one of her other sons to take the place of Fred, but I declined the offer.

As the days passed, I was so intent upon my work that I paid very little attention to my outward circumstances. Polidori continued to lodge in my chambers, and often questioned me about the state of my researches. I could not, as a gentleman, ask him to leave. I never referred to his sudden appearance at Sweep Fair, but I took care to reveal nothing to him. We were, as a result, uneasy companions.

Two weeks after Fred's disappearance I received a letter from Mary Shelley, informing me that the household (in which she included Lord Byron) had left Switzerland and made their way south to Pisa where they had procured lodgings on the Lung'Arno:

It is sufficiently commodious, and we pay only thirteen sequins a month. We have an excellent mezzanino, and three rooms on the fourth floor. From here we have a view of the sunsets, which Shelley deems incomparable. Lord Byron has taken up residence in a

much grander house, but he deigns to dine with us each evening.
He is at this moment reading to Shelley some passage out of a
poem he has recently composed. I cannot make out the words. He
wishes to remove us all to the Gulf of Spezia, but the prospect of
yet another journey appals me.

When I read this out to Polidori, he grimaced. "The man is
demented," he said. "He would drive a saint to madness. He has
a demon inside him that will not let him, or anyone, rest."

"But wait. You have not heard Mary's postscript. She must
have written it some days later." I read out to him the forlorn
message with which she ended the letter:

We have now moved on to a dwelling built on the shore at Lerici.
It is known as Casa Magni and, although it is indeed large, it
hardly qualifies as a house. It is more like a fortress buffeted by
the sea and the sea-wind. There is a rough path to take us to the
little village of San Terenzo, where we can purchase only the
most rudimentary provisions. And there is only one chimney
for cooking! There is no garden, and the rear of the house faces
a thick wood. It is the most gloomy spot imaginable, and only
the prospect of the sea lifts my spirits. Oh, how I long to be in
London now!"

I put down the letter. "She is tired of travelling."
"She is tired of Byron, too, I imagine," Polidori said.

⤜⟨

THEN, TWO WEEKS LATER, I received another letter. I recognised
the handwriting on the envelope to be Mary's, but it was so

scrawled and strained that I knew that it contained fearful news:

There is something I cannot say. And I can barely express it in words. Shelley is dead. He was drowned at sea. He died with a companion, in a boat that has not yet been found. They had set sail from Livorno into the Gulf of Spezia, when by all accounts they were overwhelmed by a sudden summer storm.

Her letter broke off at this juncture, but then at some later time she resumed it on a separate sheet.

Yesterday he was recovered. He had been washed onto the shore, near the mouth of the Serchio river, two miles from here. Lord Byron formally recognised the body. I could not do it. Bysshe was wearing the double-breasted jacket and nankeen trousers he purchased in Geneva. Do you remember them? The officials here demanded that he should be buried where he was found, with his grave filled with quicklime, but Byron and I revolted at such a coarse procedure. For once I felt grateful to Byron for assuming the manner and authority of lordship. We were given permission to cremate poor Bysshe on the sea-shore. Two servants of the house, together with Byron, built up a funeral pyre on the beach. It was a day of bright sun. How I wish you had been with me, Victor, during these last rites. We placed Bysshe on the flames, and Byron poured wine, salt and frankincense on the conflagration. I could not look, but Byron plunged his hand into the fire and took out Bysshe's heart still intact. He means to bury the ashes in the Protestant cemetery at Rome, but I could not endure any further time in this country. I must leave. And there is an end of all but despair.

THE DEATH OF MY COMPANION had so thoroughly unnerved me that for two days I lost all sensation of living. I do not know how I conducted myself, or where I travelled; I awoke in soiled linen and, as far as I am aware, I did not eat. I believe that Polidori avoided me, in consideration of my grief, but on the third morning he knocked upon the door of my study.

"Mary is returning next week," he said. "Here is a note from Byron."

The imminent return of Mary roused me from my stupor. For some reason inexplicable to myself, I wished to destroy the creature before she arrived in England: I did not allow myself to suppose that there was any real threat to her, as there had been to Harriet and Martha, but I wanted to be free of that foul burden before I saw Mary again. I wished to protect her in her grief—and, perhaps, to console her. How could I perform such a task with the creature still alive? I had in any case reached the pitch of my experiments, when success now seemed to me to be assured. By the use of conducting wires, and a series of metal plates placed at variable levels and degrees of inclination, I had at last been able to alter the direction and strength of the electrical fluid. I had tried the experiment on a stray dog, tranquillised by ether, and it had immediately expired under the charge.

For an extravagant sum I now purchased a Barbary ape from a sailor in Wapping: I could not test my theory upon my fellow beings, and I believed that the ape was the closest to our species for the purposes of experiment. I tranquillised it with ether, as before, and after securing it upon the table with leather straps I subjected it to the electrical charge. It was thrown into severe convulsions, with many spasms and contortions, and expired after sixteen seconds. Then I applied the charge again: even as I watched the body began to decay, the skin shrivelling and the flesh dissolving. The stench was terrible, but I was determined to see the experiment to the end. I administered a further shock, and very soon the body was reduced to a skeleton; then the bones themselves began to fragment until they crumbled into dust. I had succeeded.

➤ Twenty-two ⬅

I LEFT LIMEHOUSE in a state of exaltation. I was sure that my long bondage to the creature was now at an end. I walked down the highway, past the small streets where those in search of strange sights and sensations were always to be found. I walked in perfect safety. I turned a corner and, glancing quickly to my right, I saw Polidori. He was standing in the shadows, but he was perfectly recognisable to me. In my mood of triumph I decided to make a chase of it. I stood in the street and gave him ample time to notice me. Then I walked with rapid step towards Ratcliff and Whitechapel, and threaded my way through the narrow streets that comprise the neighbourhood. I believed that I could hear footsteps somewhere behind me; so I turned into an alley, and waited. When Polidori passed me I stepped out and took him by the arm. "Good evening," I said. "I see that we frequent the same neighbourhood."

He turned towards me, and became quite still. "Perhaps I am in search of adventure?"

"No. You are in search of me."

He was silent for a moment. "You interest me, Victor, I admit it. You have an understanding altogether more vast than mere—"

"So you have gone through my papers, as I suspected. Is it

not so?" I no longer cared to conceal anything. "What have you seen?"

"Wonderful things. But I cannot find the key."

"And I hold the key. That is why you follow me."

He had recovered his self-possession. "I told you that I wish to know your secrets. I believe that you are conducting, performing, how shall I put it, something unusual?"

He had found the proper opportunity. My exhilaration and sense of achievement were such that I might have cried them aloud in the streets. "Mine is a strange case," I said.

"I knew it."

"You will not believe me."

"There is conviction on your face. That is enough for me."

"Not conviction. But triumph. We cannot speak here." I must have been perspiring very freely, for my clothes were quite wet.

I hailed a cab and we made our way to Jermyn Street. We sat in my study. I could hardly wait to tell the story of my success.

"Mine is a strange case. I don't think there has ever been a stranger. I believe it to be unique."

"Are you being serious, Frankenstein?"

"I dare say you will be ready to laugh at me."

"Not at all. I want to understand you."

"Oh, then you would have to go a long way back." I told him then the whole story of my experiments. Throughout the long discourse, he said nothing. He was observing me in the most unusual way. "I can assure you, Polidori, that what I have told you is true and exact. Every stage of the proceedings is as I have outlined."

When I paused, having told him of the first awakening of the creature, he leaned forward and whispered: "So this thing lived? Is that what you are telling me?" He put his hand to his forehead, in a gesture of extreme astonishment. His eyes were very wide.

I nodded. Then I added, in a low voice, "It still lives." Polidori looked around the room in terror. "No. Not here. It lives on the estuary of the river. Away from human habitation."

"You have seen it again?"

"Wait until I have reached the end of my story." Then I told him the tale of Harriet Westbrook, and of the unlawful condemnation of her brother for her killing. I wept throughout the narrative, for in truth up to this time I had done my utmost to suppress it from my thoughts. Then I related to him the abduction and murder of the servant, Martha, beside the river at Marlow. I began to tell him the history of the creature's subsequent visits to me. "It threatened me," I said, "with such dreadful—" I stopped, and found myself to be shaking.

Polidori rose from the chair in an involuntary movement. "Is this possible, Frankenstein?" Again he looked around the room. "Why has this not been screamed out in the public prints? How can it live amongst us? Why has it not been hunted down?"

"It desires to live occluded and unknown. It does not wish to be hunted down, as you put it. It has ways of hiding itself from public view."

"You must take some more wine," Polidori said. He was as thoroughly frightened as I was, but he poured me another glass which I drained at once. "Are you calmer now?"

"Yes, very calm. And you?"

"Calm enough."

"After a period the creature ceased to threaten, and began to plead with me. He wanted to be released from his miseries. I think he felt shame—regret—horror. All of those. I have sometimes thought that he may have committed some further act of foulness, and that it preyed upon his mind. Of this I cannot be sure. But he came to me asking for oblivion."

"Thank God."

"And I can grant him that wish." I described to him the experiment upon the Barbary ape, omitting nothing of interest, and then I shared with him my plan for the destruction of the creature. "He will come to me now," I told him. "I know it. He has a strange susceptibility to me. He will understand that the moment has come for his deliverance. Tomorrow I will see him for the last time."

"May I suggest to you, Frankenstein, that you invite me also?"

"I doubt that he will wish for any other witness."

"Yet in the case of failure or only partial success—"

"There will be no failure."

"Do you remember the secret words for the golem? I have not told you this. They must be addressed to the golem by a Jew. Otherwise they will not prevail." He paused for a moment. "I am of that faith."

"Oh, I understand you now. You wish to deliver the words of anathema. You will pronounce the Jewish curse over him. It will not be necessary."

"Allow me the possibility, at the very least."

"If you wish. But he would be disturbed by your presence. I know it."

"Then I will wait somewhere, in secrecy, for a message."

"And how will I find a messenger? No. I believe that the creature will come to me at twilight. Twilight is his time. Leave me alone with him for a few hours. He may wish to make a final confession to me, or speak to me of other things. Come at midnight."

⇒ ⇐

I COULD NOT SLEEP. I was exhausted, but I was in such a fever of expectation that I could find no rest. I started up each moment, with a fresh image of the creature. Only towards dawn did I fall into a doze, broken by the sound of Polidori going down the stairs and opening the door into the street. I rose at once, washed myself, and prepared for what I believed to be a conclusive day in my fearful life.

As soon as I arrived at Limehouse I opened the door that led out to the river.

I waited for three or four hours, looking expectantly onto the water; in the late afternoon I walked to the little landing stage, and inhaled the scent of mud and tar that lingered on the bank. I was not impatient: I had known, even as I hurried from Jermyn Street, that he would not come until twilight. Slowly the air grew darker. A light breeze ruffled the water which was flowing steadily on an incoming tide, and I could see a flock of starlings heading for the marshes on the other side of the river. There was a faint light on the horizon, as the sun dipped lower through clouds. And then I saw him moving through the water; he reared himself upright as he approached me, and then ducked back into the river. I turned and walked into the workshop. I was quite calm when he stood in the doorway. "I have been waiting for you," I said. "I knew that you would come."

"How could I stay away, when my deliverance is near?"

"You are aware that my experiments have been successful? That my ambition has been accomplished?" He nodded. "So. What do you wish me to do?"

"You know what I wish for. Death. Forgetting. Oblivion and darkness."

"I can promise you these things. Come forward." He stepped into the light of an oil-lamp. He was wearing a pair of canvas breeches, such as shipmen wear, and a brown jacket; he had a shirt, but no stock, and I could see the yellow hairs upon his chest. He was barefoot, too. I surmised that he had led a harsh existence on the estuary.

"Do you have anything you wish to say before—anything you want to tell me?"

"Only that I suffer for my crimes. And I wish that suffering to end."

"You repent?"

"Surely, sir, it is you who should repent? I did not ask to come into this world. I did not wish to rise again in such a form. Am I monstrous? Or are you monstrous? Is the world monstrous?" He stood in the flickering light, as woeful as I had ever seen him, and seemed to be studying the electrical equipment. "Am I to lie down here? This is where I was born, is it not?"

"If you could remove your clothes."

"Otherwise they might burn?"

"It is possible. Yes. And then take your place upon the table. Your head facing this way." He undressed and lay down in the position I suggested. I secured his wrists and ankles with the leather straps. There came from him the stench of mud and slime.

"The smell of the marshes," he said as if he had guessed my thought. "I will stay quite still. You need not bind the straps too tightly."

When he was prepared, I placed the electrical charges on his temples and at the very base of his spine. I looked at him, to assure him that all was ready. He closed his eyes, and sighed. When I released the electrical fluid his whole body shook violently, and then arched upwards breaking one of the straps upon his wrists; he seemed about to scream but the noise that came from him was a rasping cough. Dust came from his open mouth. Then his body subsided.

To my horror he opened his eyes. He could not speak but with his free hand he touched me. I started back with the knowledge that he had not been destroyed. "All is not lost," I said to him. I realised that he could understand me. He nodded. "I will augment the level of the fluid. You are prepared for this?" He closed his eyes in assent. The second attempt was fearful. Again his body trembled and convulsed; there was some scorching of his left leg, and the smell of burning flesh filled the room. He seemed to fall into unconsciousness, with heavy and stertorous breathing. But still he was not dead. Without seeking his permission I tried a third time; again his flesh was charred, but all the signs of vital life remained. I could do no more. I released the straps by which he had been bound and, without seeing if he would rise, I sat down on a chair facing the window onto the river. I was utterly wearied and defeated. I had failed to destroy him: this thing, this burden, still weighed upon my life. After a while he joined me, sitting on the chair beside me; I could smell his burned flesh, but I felt no disgust or disdain. It was I, after all, who had been responsible. He tried to speak. His was no longer the melodious voice of the past, but a low murmur.

"I cannot die," he said. "I will be in the world until the end of time. Is that so?"

"I do not know."

"You know."

"I have not the courage to look forward."

"Yet what shall we do? My flesh will soon heal. That is nothing. Yet my mind and spirit will never heal."

"We will share that fate then."

He sat there, bent over, rocking backwards and forwards. "Make it stop," he said. "Make it stop."

I bowed my head, too. I do not know how long we sat there, side by side, but eventually we were roused by the sound of footsteps. It was Polidori. He had come down to the river bank, and was making his way across the landing stage. He came to the door of the workshop, and paused on the threshold. There was a look of bewilderment upon his face.

"Now you see my handiwork," I said.

He came in, holding up a lamp, and stood before us.

"Behold the creature. This is what I have made."

"Where?"

"Here. Before you."

"There is no one here," he said.

"Have you lost your wits? See here. Beside me. Here he sits."

"There is nothing beside you, except an empty chair."

"Nothing? I do not believe you. I know you lie."

"Why should I lie, Victor?"

"To deceive me. To betray me. To enrage me."

"There is nothing here. No one is with you. There is no creature." He walked over to my electrical engines. "This is sad stuff, Victor."

"What are you saying? Tell me this then. Tell me who killed Harriet and Martha?"

He looked intently at me. "I do not know who killed them."

"There now. You have no answer."

"You have lived in your imagination, Victor. You have dreamed all this. Invented it."

"How so?"

"Perhaps you wished to rival Bysshe. Or Byron. You had longings for sublimity and power."

"*Enough*. You are filling me with despair."

"And what evil you may have done!" He paused for a moment. "What has happened to Fred?"

"Who is Fred?" the creature asked me in a whisper.

I did not know how to respond. How could I explain the disappearance of the child who had loved me? How could I say that his body was to be found in the limepit by the fore-shore?

Polidori looked at me and then he asked: "Did you destroy Fred also?"

"I said *enough!*"

I sprang at him. I lunged forward and destroyed him. No, not I. The creature tore him to pieces with his bare hands.

Then we wandered out, the creature and I, into the world where we were taken up by the watchmen.

Given to me by the patient, Victor Frankenstein, on Wednesday November 15, 1822.

Signed by Fredrick Newman, Superintendent of the Hoxton Mental Asylum for Incurables.

PETER ACKROYD is a master of the historical novel: *The Last Testament of Oscar Wilde* won the Somerset Maugham Award; *Hawksmoor* was awarded both the Whitbread Novel of the Year and the Guardian Fiction Prize; and *Chatterton* was short-listed for the Booker Prize. His most recent historical novel is *The Fall of Troy*. He is also the author of *London: The Biography*, *Shakespeare: The Biography*, *Thames: The Biography*, and Ackroyd's Brief Lives series.

A NOTE ABOUT THE TYPE

The text of this book is set in Legacy Serif, a typeface created by Ronald Arnholm and released in 1993 by ITC (International Typeface Corporation). ITC Legacy is a revival design inspired by the Venetian Old Style types by the fifteenth-century printer and publisher Nicolas Jensen. Named after the first roman typefaces that appeared in Venice in 1470, Venetian typefaces were initially designed to emulate the handwriting of Italian Renaissance scholars. Characterized by their clarity and legibility, these typefaces were created as book type and still serve that function well today.